Praise for *Alien Influences* . . .

"A well-conceived, well-executed novel."
—*The New York Times Book Review*

. . . and for Kristine Kathryn Rusch

"[Rusch] is already far better than should be allowed."
—*Nexus*

"Whether [Rusch] writes high fantasy, horror, sf, or contemporary fantasy, I've always been fascinated by her ability to tell a story with that enviable gift of invisible prose. She's one of those very few writers whose style takes me right into the story; the words and pages disappear as the characters and their story swallow me whole." —Charles de Lint

"Accomplished . . . exceptional." —Edward Bryant

"Kristine Kathryn Rusch never stray[s] from the path of good storytelling as she dissects her characters and their situations for the reader's benefit. She integrates the fantastic elements so rigorously into her story that it is often hard to remember she is not merely recording the here and now." —*Science Fiction Weekly*

"[Rusch's] writing style is simple but elegant, and her characterizations excellent." —*Beyond*

"Kristine Kathryn Rusch's . . . stories are exceptional, both in plot and in style."
—Ed Gorman, *Mystery Scene*

THE
DISAPPEARED

A RETRIEVAL ARTIST NOVEL

Kristine Kathryn Rusch

A ROC BOOK

ROC
Published by New American Library, a division of
Penguin Group (USA) Inc., 375 Hudson Street,
New York, New York 10014, USA
Penguin Group (Canada), 90 Eglinton Avenue East, Suite 700, Toronto,
Ontario M4P 2Y3, Canada (a division of Pearson Penguin Canada Inc.)
Penguin Books Ltd., 80 Strand, London WC2R 0RL, England
Penguin Ireland, 25 St. Stephen's Green, Dublin 2,
Ireland (a division of Penguin Books Ltd.)
Penguin Group (Australia), 250 Camberwell Road, Camberwell, Victoria 3124,
Australia (a division of Pearson Australia Group Pty. Ltd.)
Penguin Books India Pvt. Ltd., 11 Community Centre, Panchsheel Park,
New Delhi - 110 017, India
Penguin Group (NZ), cnr Airborne and Rosedale Roads, Albany,
Auckland 1310, New Zealand (a division of Pearson New Zealand Ltd.)
Penguin Books (South Africa) (Pty.) Ltd., 24 Sturdee Avenue,
Rosebank, Johannesburg 2196, South Africa

Penguin Books Ltd., Registered Offices:
80 Strand, London WC2R 0RL, England

Published by Roc, an imprint of New American Library,
a division of Penguin Group (USA) Inc.

First Roc Printing, July 2002
10 9 8 7 6 5 4 3

Printed in the United States of America

For Spike,
with love always

ACKNOWLEDGMENTS

I owe a lot of gratitude to Stan Schmidt for his comments on *The Retrieval Artist,* the novella that got this series started; to Laura Anne Gilman for believing in the series and for her insightful suggestions; to Merrilee Heifetz for all her help on everything; and to my husband, Dean Wesley Smith, who always seems to know which stories are going to capture my heart.

1

She had to leave everything behind.

Ekaterina Maakestad stood in the bedroom of her Queen Anne home, the vintage Victorian houses of San Francisco's oldest section visible through her windows, and clutched her hands together. She had made the bed that morning as if nothing were wrong. The quilt, folded at the bottom, waiting for someone to pull it up for warmth, had been made by her great-great-grandmother, a woman she dimly remembered. The rocking chair in the corner had rocked generations of Maakestads. Her mother had called it the nursing chair because so many women had sat in it, nursing their babies.

Ekaterina would never get the chance to do that. She had no idea what would happen to it, or to all the heirloom jewelry in the downstairs safe, or to the photographs, taken so long ago they were collector's items to most people but to her represented family, people she was connected to through blood, common features, and passionate dreams.

She was the last of the Maakestad line. No siblings or cousins to take all of this. Her parents were long gone, and so were her grandparents. When she set up this house, after she had gotten back from Revnata, the human colony in Rev territory, she had planned to raise her own children here.

Downstairs, a door opened and she froze, waiting for House to announce the presence of a guest. But House wouldn't. She had shut off the security system, just as she had been instructed to do.

She twisted the engagement ring on her left hand, the antique diamond winking in the artificial light. She was supposed to take the ring off, but she couldn't bring herself to do so. She would wait until the very last minute, then hand the ring over. If she left it behind, everyone would know she had left voluntarily.

"Kat?" Simon. He wasn't supposed to be here.

She swallowed hard, feeling a lump in her throat.

"Kat, you okay? The system's off."

"I know." Her voice sounded normal. Amazing she could do that, given the way her heart pounded and her breath came in shallow gasps.

She had to get him out of here and quickly. He couldn't be here when they arrived, or he would lose everything too.

The stairs creaked. He was coming up to see her.

"I'll be right down!" she called. She didn't want him to come upstairs, didn't want to see him here one last time.

With her right hand, she smoothed her blond hair. Then she squared her shoulders and put on her courtroom face. She'd been distracted and busy in front of Simon before. He might think that was what was happening now.

She left the bedroom and started down the stairs, making herself breathe evenly. For the last week, she hadn't seen him—pleading work, then making up travel and a difficult court case. She had been trying to avoid this moment all along.

As she reached the first landing, the stairs curved, and she could see him, standing in the entry. Simon wasn't a handsome man. He didn't use enhancements—didn't like them on himself or anyone. As a result, his hair was thinning on top, and he was pudgy despite the exercise he got.

But his face had laugh lines. Instead of cosmetic good looks, Simon had an appealing rumpled quality, like a favorite old shirt or a quilt that had rested on the edge of the bed for more than a hundred years.

He smiled at her, his dark eyes twinkling. "I've missed you."

Her breath caught, but she made herself smile back. "I've missed you too."

He was holding flowers, a large bouquet of purple lilacs, their scent rising up to greet her.

"I was just going to leave this," he said. "I figured as busy as you were, you might appreciate something pretty to come home to."

He had House's security combination, just as she had his. They had exchanged the codes three months ago, the same night they got engaged. She could still remember the feelings she had that night. The hope, the possibility. The sense that she actually had a future.

"They're wonderful," she said.

He waited for her to get to the bottom of the stairs, then handed her the bouquet. Beneath the greenery, her hands found a cool vase, a bubble chip embedded in the glass keeping the water's temperature constant.

She buried her face in the flowers, glad for the momentary camouflage. She had no idea when she would see flowers again.

"Thank you," she said, her voice trembling. She turned away, made herself put the flowers on the table she kept beneath the gilt-edged mirror in her entry.

Simon slipped his hands around her waist. "You all right?"

She wanted to lean against him, to tell him the truth, to let him share all of this—the fears, the uncertainty. But she didn't dare. He couldn't know anything.

"I'm tired," she said, and she wasn't lying. She hadn't slept in the past eight days.

"Big case?"

She nodded. "Difficult one."

"Let me know when you're able to talk about it."

She could see his familiar face in the mirror beside her strained one. Even when she tried to look normal, she couldn't. The bags beneath her eyes hadn't been there a month ago. Neither had the worry lines beside her mouth.

He watched her watch herself, and she could tell from the set of his jaw, the slight crease on his forehead, that he was seeing more than he should have been.

"This case is tearing you apart," he said softly.

"Some cases do that."

"I don't like it."

She nodded and turned in his arms, trying to memorize the feel of him, the comfort he gave her, comfort that would soon be gone. "I have to meet a client," she said.

"I'll take you."

"No." She made herself smile again, wondering if the expression looked as fake as it felt. "I need a little time alone before I go, to regroup."

He caressed her cheek with the back of his hand, then kissed her. She lingered a moment too long, caught between the urge to cling and the necessity of pushing him away.

"I love you," she said as she ended the kiss.

"I love you too." He smiled. "There's a spa down in the L.A. basin. It's supposed to be the absolute best. I'll take you there when this is all over."

"Sounds good," she said, making no promises. She couldn't bear to make another false promise.

He still didn't move away. She resisted the urge to look at the two-hundred-year-old clock that sat on the living room mantel.

"Kat," he said. "You need time away. Maybe we could meet after you see your client and—"

"No," she said. "Early court date."

He stepped back from her, and she realized she sounded abrupt. But he had to leave. She had to get him out and quickly.

"I'm sorry, Simon," she said. "But I really need the time—"

"I know." His smile was small. She had stung him, and she hadn't meant to. "Call me?"

"As soon as I can."

He nodded, then headed for the door. "Turn your system back on."

"I will," she said as he pulled the door open. Fog had rolled in from the Bay, leaving the air chill. "Thank you for the flowers."

"They were supposed to brighten the day," he said, raising his hands toward the grayness.

"They have." She watched as he walked down the sidewalk toward his aircar, hovering the regulation half foot above the pavement. No flying vehicles were allowed in Nob Hill because they would destroy the view, the impression that the past was here, so close that it would take very little effort to touch it.

She closed the door before he got into his car, so that she wouldn't have to watch him drive away. Her hand lingered over the security system. One command, and it would be on again. She would be safe within her own home.

If only it were that simple.

The scent of the lilacs overpowered her. She stepped away from the door and stopped in front of the mirror again. Just her reflected there now. Her and a bouquet of flowers she wouldn't get to enjoy, a bouquet she would never forget.

She twisted her engagement ring. It had always been loose. Even though she had meant to have it fitted, she never had. Perhaps she had known, deep down, that this day would come. Perhaps she'd felt, ever since she'd come to Earth, that she'd been living on borrowed time.

The ring slipped off easily. She stared at it for a moment, at the promises it held, promises it would never keep, and then she dropped it into the vase. Someone would find it. Not right away, but soon enough that it wouldn't get lost.

Maybe Simon would be able to sell it, get his money back. Or maybe he would keep it as a tangible memory of what had been, the way she kept her family heirlooms.

She winced.

Something scuffled outside the door—the sound of a foot against the stone stoop, a familiar sound, one she would never hear again.

Her heart leaped, hoping it was Simon, even though she knew it wasn't. As the brass doorknob turned, she reached into the bouquet and pulled some petals off the nearest lilac plume. She shoved them in her pocket, hoping they would dry the way petals did when pressed into a book.

Then the door opened and a man she had never seen before stepped inside. He was over six feet tall, broad-shouldered and muscular. His skin was a chocolate brown, his eyes slightly flat, the way eyes got when they'd been enhanced too many times.

"Is it true," he said, just as he was supposed to, "that this house survived the 1906 earthquake?"

"No." She paused, wishing she could stop there, wishing she could say no to all of this. But she continued, using the coded phrase she had invented for just this moment. "The house was built the year after."

He nodded. "You're awfully close to the door."

"A friend stopped by."

Somehow, the expression in his eyes grew flatter. "Is the friend gone?"

"Yes," she said, hoping it was true.

The man studied her, as if he could tell if she were lying just by staring at her. Then he touched the back of his hand. Until that moment, she hadn't seen the chips dotting his skin like freckles—they matched so perfectly.

"Back door," he said, and she knew he was using his link to speak to someone outside.

He took her hand. His fingers were rough, callused. Simon's hands had no calluses at all.

"Is everything in its place?" the man asked.

She nodded.

"Anyone expecting you tonight?"

"No," she said.

"Good." He tugged her through her own kitchen,

past the fresh groceries she had purchased just that morning, past the half-empty coffee cup she'd left on the table.

The back door was open. She shook her hand free and stepped out. The fog was thicker than it had been when Simon left, and colder too. She couldn't see the vehicle waiting in the alley. She couldn't even see the alley. She was taking her first steps on a journey that would make her one of the Disappeared, and she could not see where she was going.

How appropriate. Because she had no idea how or where she was going to end up.

Jamal sampled the spaghetti sauce. The reconstituted beef gave it a chemical taste. He added some crushed red pepper, then tried another spoonful, and sighed. The beef was still the dominant flavor.

He set the spoon on the spoon rest and wiped his hands on a towel. The tiny kitchen smelled of garlic and tomato sauce. He'd set the table with the china Dylani had brought from Earth and their two precious wineglasses.

Not that they had anything to celebrate tonight. They hadn't had anything to celebrate for a long time. No real highs, no real lows.

Jamal liked it that way—the consistency of everyday routine. Sometimes he broke the routine by setting the table with wineglasses, and sometimes he let the routine govern them. He didn't want any more change.

There had been enough change in his life.

Dylani came out of their bedroom, her bare feet leaving tiny prints on the baked mud floor. The house was Moon adobe, made from Moon dust plastered over a permaplastic frame. Cheap, but all they could afford.

Dylani's hair was pulled away from her narrow face, her pale gray eyes red-rimmed, as they always were when she got off work. Her fingertips were stained black from her work on the dome. No matter how much she scrubbed, they no longer came clean.

"He's sleeping," she said, and she sounded disappointed. Their son, Ennis, was usually asleep when she got home from work. Jamal planned it that way—he liked a bit of time alone with his wife. Besides, she needed time to decompress before she settled into her evening ritual.

She was one of the dome engineers. Although the position sounded important, it wasn't. She was still entry level, coping with clogs in the filtration systems and damage outsiders did near the high-speed train station.

If she wanted to advance, she would have to wait years. Engineers didn't retire in Gagarin Dome, nor did they move to other Moon colonies. In other colonies, the domes were treated like streets or government buildings—something to be maintained, not something to be enhanced. But Gagarin's governing board believed the dome was a priority, so engineers were always working on the cutting edge of dome technology, rather than rebuilding an outdated system.

"How was he?" Dylani walked to the stove and sniffed the sauce. Spaghetti was one of her favorite meals. One day, Jamal would cook it for her properly, with fresh ingredients. One day, when they could afford it.

"The usual," Jamal said, placing the bread he'd bought in the center of the table. The glasses would hold bottled water, but it was dear enough to be wine—they would enjoy the water no less.

Dylani gave him a fond smile. "The usual isn't a good enough answer. I want to hear everything he did today. Every smile, every frown. If I can't stay home with him, I at least want to hear about him."

Ever since they found out Dylani was pregnant, Ennis had become the center of their world—and the heart of Jamal's nightmares. He was smothering the boy and he knew it. Ennis was ten months now— the age when a child learned to speak and walk—and he was beginning to understand that he was a person in his own right.

Jamal had read the parenting literature. He knew he should encourage the boy's individuality. But he didn't want to. He wanted Ennis beside him always, in his sight, in his care.

Dylani understood Jamal's attitude, but sometimes he could feel her disapproval. She had been tolerant of his paranoia—amazingly tolerant considering she had no idea as to the root cause of it. She thought his paranoia stemmed from first-child jitters instead of a real worry for Ennis's safety.

Jamal wasn't sure what he would do when Ennis had to go to school. In Gagarin, home schooling was not an option. Children had to learn to interact with others—the governing board had made that law almost a hundred years ago, and despite all the challenges to it, the law still stood.

Someday Jamal would have to entrust his boy to others—and he wasn't sure he could do it.

"So?" Dylani asked.

Jamal smiled. "He's trying to teach Mr. Biscuit to fly."

Mr. Biscuit was Ennis's stuffed dog. Dylani's parents had sent the dog as a present from Earth. They also sent some children's vids—flats because Dylani believed Ennis was too young to understand the difference between holographic performers and real people.

Ennis's favorite vid was about a little boy who learned how to fly.

"How's Mr. Biscuit taking this?" Dylani asked.

"I'm not sure," Jamal said. "He's not damaged yet, but a few more encounters with the wall might change that."

Dylani chuckled.

The boiling pot beeped. The noodles were done. Jamal put the pot in the sink, pressed the drain button, and the water poured out of the pot's bottom into the recycler.

"Hungry?" he asked.

She nodded.

"Long day?"

"Two breakdowns in dome security." She grabbed a plate and brought it to the sink. "Every available person worked on repairs."

Jamal felt a shiver run down his back. "I've never heard of that."

"It happens," she said. "Sometimes the jobs are so big—"

"No," he said. "The breakdown in security."

She gave him a tolerant smile. "I usually don't mention it. The dome doors go off-line a lot, particularly near the space port. I think it has something to do with the commands issued by the high-speed trains coming in from the north, but no one will listen to me. I'm too junior. Maybe in my off time . . ."

But Jamal stopped listening. Another shiver ran down his back. It wasn't Dylani's news that was mak-

ing him uneasy. The kitchen was actually cold, and it
shouldn't have been. Cooking in such a small space
usually made the temperature rise, not lower.

He went to the kitchen door. Closed and latched.

". . . would result in a promotion," Dylani was saying. Then she frowned. "Jamal?"

"Keep talking," he said.

But she didn't. Her lips became a thin line. He recognized the look. She hated it when he did this,
thought his paranoia was reaching new heights.

Maybe it was. He always felt stupid after moments
like this, when he realized that Ennis was safe in his
bed and nothing was wrong.

But that didn't stop him from prowling through the
house, searching for the source of the chill. He'd never
forgive himself if something happened and he didn't
check.

"Jamal."

He could near the annoyance in Dylani's voice, but
he ignored it, walking past her into the narrow hallway
between the kitchen and the living room. He turned
right, toward their bedroom.

It was dark, the way Dylani had left it, but there
was a light at the very end of the hall. In Ennis's room.

Jamal never left a light on in Ennis's room. The boy
napped in the dark. Studies had shown that children
who slept with lights on became nearsighted, and
Jamal wanted his son to have perfect vision.

"Jamal?"

He was running down the hallway now. He couldn't
have slowed down if he tried. Dylani might have left
the light on, but he doubted it. She and Jamal had
discussed the nightlight issue just as they had discussed
most things concerning Ennis.

They never left his window open—that was Dylani's

choice. She knew how contaminated the air had become inside the dome, and she felt their environmental filter was better than the government's. No open window, no cooler temperatures.

And no light.

He slid into Ennis's room, the pounding of his feet loud enough to wake the baby. Dylani was running after him.

"Jamal!"

The room looked normal, bathed in the quiet light of the lamp he had placed above the changing table. The crib nestled against one corner, the playpen against another. The changing table under the always closed window—which was closed, even now.

But the air was cooler, just as the air outside the house was cooler. Since Ennis was born, they'd spent extra money on heat just to make sure the baby was comfortable. Protected. Safe.

Jamal stopped in front of the crib. He didn't have to look. He could already feel the difference in the room. Someone else had been here, and not long ago. Someone else had been here, and Ennis was not here, not any longer.

Still, he peered down at the mattress where he had placed his son not an hour ago. Ennis's favorite blanket was thrown back, revealing the imprint of his small body. The scents of baby powder and baby sweat mingled into something familiar, something lost.

Mr. Biscuit perched against the crib's corner, his thread eyes empty. The fur on his paw was matted and wet where Ennis had sucked on it, probably as he had fallen asleep. The pacifier that he had yet to grow out of was on the floor, covered with dirt.

"Jamal?" Dylani's voice was soft.

Jamal couldn't turn to her. He couldn't face her.

All he could see was the gold bracelet that rested on Ennis's blanket. The bracelet Jamal hadn't seen for a decade. The symbol of his so-called brilliance, a reward for a job well done. He had been so proud of it when he received it, that first night on Korsve. And so happy to leave it behind two years later.

"Oh, my God," Dylani said from the door. "Where is he?"

"I don't know." Jamal's voice shook. He was lying. He tried not to lie to Dylani. Did she know that his voice shook when he lied?

As she came into the room, he snatched the bracelet and hid it in his fist.

"Who would do this?" she asked. She was amazingly calm, given what was happening. But Dylani never panicked. Panicking was his job. "Who would take our baby?"

Jamal slipped the bracelet into his pocket, then put his arms around his wife.

"We need help," she said.

"I know." But he already knew it was hopeless. There was nothing anyone could do.

The holovid played at one-tenth normal size in the corner of the space yacht. The actors paced, the sixteenth-century palace looking out of place against the green-and-blue plush chairs beside it. Much as Sara loved this scene—Hamlet's speech to the players—she couldn't concentrate on it. She regretted ordering up Shakespeare. It felt like part of the life she was leaving behind.

Sara wondered if the other two felt as unsettled as she did. But she didn't ask. She didn't really want the answers. The others were in this because of her, and they rarely complained about it. Of course, they didn't have a lot of choice.

She glanced at them. Ruth had flattened her seat into a cot. She was asleep on her back, hands folded on her stomach like a corpse, her curly black hair covering the pillow like a shroud.

Isaac stared at the holovid, but Sara could tell he wasn't really watching it. He bent at his midsection, elbows resting on his thighs, his care-lined features impassive. He'd been like this since they left New Orleans, focused, concentrated, frozen.

The yacht bounced.

Sara stopped the holovid. Space yachts didn't bounce. There was nothing for them to bounce on.

"What the hell was that?" she asked.

Neither Ruth nor Isaac answered. Ruth was still asleep. Isaac hadn't moved.

She got up and pulled up the shade on the nearest portal. Earth mocked her, blue and green viewed through a haze of white. As she stared at her former home, a small oval-shaped ship floated past, so close it nearly brushed against the yacht. Through a tiny portal on the ship's side, she caught a glimpse of a human face. A white circle was stamped beneath the portal. She had seen that symbol before: it was etched lightly on the wall inside the luxurious bathroom off the main cabin.

Her breath caught in her throat. She hit the intercom near the window. "Hey," she said to the cockpit. "What's going on?"

No one answered her. When she took her finger off the intercom, she didn't even hear static.

She shoved Isaac's shoulder. He glared at her.

"I think we're in trouble," she said.

"No kidding."

"I mean it."

She got up and walked through the narrow corridor toward the pilot's quarters and cockpit. The door separating the main area from the crew quarters was large and thick, with a sign that flashed *No Entry without Authorization.*

This time, she hit the emergency button, which should have brought one of the crew into the back. But the intercom didn't come on and no one moved.

She tried the door, but it was sealed on the other side.

The yacht rocked and dipped. Sara slid toward the wall, slammed into it, and sank to the floor. Seatbelt lights went on all over the cabin.

Ruth had fallen as well. She sat on the floor, rubbing her eyes. Isaac was the only one who stayed in his seat.

The yacht had stabilized.

"What's going on?" Ruth asked.

"That's what I'd like to know," Sara said.

She grabbed one of the metal rungs, placed there for zero-g flight, and tried the door again. It didn't open.

"Isaac," she said, "can you override this thing?"

"Names," he cautioned.

She made a rude noise. "As if it matters."

"It matters. They said it mattered from the moment we left Earth—"

The yacht shook, and Sara smelled something sharp, almost like smoke, but more peppery.

"Isaac," she said again.

He grabbed the rungs and walked toward her, his feet slipping on the tilted floor. Ruth pulled herself into her chair, her face pale, eyes huge. Sara had only seen her look like that once before—when they'd seen Ilana's body in the newsvids, sprawled across the floor of their rented apartment in the French Quarter.

Isaac had reached Sara's side. He was tinkering with the control panel beside the door. "Cheap-ass stuff," he said. "You'd think on a luxury cruiser, they'd have up-to-date security."

The door clicked and Isaac pushed it open.

Sweat ran down Sara's back, even though the yacht hadn't changed temperature. The smell had grown worse, and there was a pounding coming from the emergency exit just inside the door.

Isaac bit his lower lip.

"Hello?" Sara called. Her voice didn't echo, but she could feel the emptiness around her. There was no one in the galley, and the security guard who was supposed to be sitting near the cockpit wasn't there.

Isaac stayed by the emergency exit. He was studying that control panel. Ruth had crawled across her cot and was staring out the panel on her side of the ship. Her hands were shaking.

Sara turned her back on them. She went inside the cockpit—and froze.

It was empty. Red lights blinked on the control panels. The ship was on autopilot, and both of its escape pods had been launched. A red line had formed on a diagram of the ship, the line covering the emergency exit where the noise had come from. More red illuminated the back of the ship.

She punched vocal controls. They had been shut off—which explained why silence had greeted her when she tried the intercom, when she hit the emergency switch, even when she had touched the sealed door.

Warning, the ship's computer said. *Engines disabled. Breach in airlock one. Intruder alert.*

Sara sat in the pilot's chair. It had been years since she'd tried to fly a ship and she'd never operated anything this sophisticated. She had to focus.

Warning.

First she had to bring the controls back on-line. Most of them had been shut off from the inside. She didn't want to think about what that meant. Not now.

Intruder alert.

She needed visuals. She opened the ports around her, and then wished she hadn't.

A large white ship hovered just outside her view, its pitted hull and cone-shaped configuration sending a chill through her heart.

The Disty had found her—and they were about to break in.

2

Miles Flint stepped inside the crew tunnel leading to the docks. He thought he had escaped this place. Two months ago, he'd been promoted to detective—a job that would allow him to remain inside Armstrong's dome and solve crimes, rather than arrive in the port at 0600 and launch at 0645, to play traffic cop in the Moon's orbit.

Of course as a space cop he'd seen a few detectives in the Port, but only rarely. Most crimes found by traffic cops had clear perpetrators. Those that didn't were referred to Headquarters and usually the crimes were solved without the detective ever setting foot in the Port.

Just his bad luck that he would get a case that required his presence here. He suspected that he and his partner, Noelle DeRicci, had been chosen specifically for this one, primarily because he knew how the Port worked.

DeRicci walked several meters ahead of him. She was a short, muscular woman who had been a detective for more than twenty years. Her dark hair, shot with gray, remained its natural color because she felt people gave more respect to older detectives than younger. She hadn't paid for other cosmetic enhancements either, for the very same reason.

She scanned the sheet on her hand-held as she walked. Flint wondered how she could see. The old colonial lighting was dim at best, the energy cells nearly tapped out. The light was yellowish-gray, giving the tunnels the look of perpetual twilight.

The crew tunnels were one of the few original underground structures left. They'd been reinforced after a few cave-ins had convinced Armstrong's governor to spend the funds to prevent more lawsuits.

The public tunnels leading from the Port to the dome were newer—if something that had been around for fifty years could be considered new. They were wider and safer, at least, built to the code finally developed for underground structures once Armstrong realized it couldn't expand horizontally any more.

But cops weren't allowed in the public areas, unless they were acting as security. Armstrong made a large chunk of its income off tourists who came to see the Moon's history, wrapped in one place. Armstrong not only boasted a large number of original colonial structures—the first ever built on the Moon—it was also the site of the first lunar landing, made when human beings wore bulky white suits and jettisoned into space in a capsule attached to a bomb.

Flint took several long strides to catch up to De-Ricci. "What've we got?"

She gave him a sideways look. He recognized the contempt. She'd been trying to intimidate him from the moment they became partners. For some reason, she seemed to think intimidation would work.

It was probably his face. He looked younger than he was. His ex-wife used to say that she sometimes thought she had married an overgrown baby. In the early years of their marriage, she'd said that fondly, as if she loved the way he looked. That horrible last year, she'd spat out the words, angry that the grief which had consumed both of them and devoured their marriage hadn't left its mark on his face.

"Well?" he asked, knowing DeRicci wouldn't answer him if he didn't press.

"Won't know what we have until HazMat's done," she said and clicked her hand-held closed.

He already knew why they had come here. A ship with bodies aboard had arrived at the Port sometime that afternoon. But he knew there had to be more information than that. He used to tow disabled ships as part of his space-cop duties. Before ships got towed, the space cops entered, and usually their reports were sent onto the investigative team if one was needed.

He would find out what happened soon enough. They were heading toward Terminal 4, where derelict and abandoned ships were usually towed. If the ship had a living crew member or a recognizable registration, it went to Terminal 16. Ships whose owners were suspected of criminal activity went to Terminal 5, and ships carrying illegal cargo went to Terminal 6.

The tunnel opened into the office ring. Square offices, walled off by clear plastic, clustered against the wall. This section of each terminal looked the same— tiny desks inside tiny rooms, littered with notices, signs, and electronic warnings. A few of the desks had their own built-in system—again on the theory that direct uplinks were untrustworthy—but most of the Command/Control center was on the upper levels.

Signs pointed the various directions the crews went, many to clock in, others to find their uniforms before beginning shift. Also down these corridors were interrogation rooms, holding cells, and the required link to customs. Flint had taken several illegals into that link, never to see them again.

The main corridor went to the terminal proper. Each terminal had its own dome that opened whenever a ship needed to dock. More tunnels led to the docks, only these tunnels were open, made of clear plastic just as the offices were. They had their own environmental controls, which could be shut off at a moment's notice. The tunnel doors could also slam closed with a single command from Terminal 4's tower—a security precaution that Flint had only had to use once in his eight-year stint on Traffic.

Two uniformed space cops were waiting at the edge of the docks. DeRicci touched the chip that made the shield on her collar flash.

"Which way?" she asked them, but Flint didn't wait for their answer. He could see which dock held the ship. The HazMat crew's orange warning lights covered the tunnel, warning Control not to set any ship down in a dock nearby until HazMat had cleared the area.

As Flint walked toward the affected tunnel, he scanned the far end, searching for the ship. He had to squint to see it, small against the tunnel's opening.

A space yacht. Its design—narrow and pointed—made it of Earth construction. It was a fairly new ship, built for speed not luxury, certainly not the kind of vehicle that was usually abandoned or left derelict in the Moon's orbit.

In fact, he couldn't remember the last time he had seen a yacht in Terminal 4. Sometimes yachts were used for contraband, and sometimes they were used to transport illegals, but never did they arrive here, where someone had to trace their registration to see who had abandoned them. Yachts were stolen and often resold, but never abandoned. They were too valuable for that.

Two more space cops stood near the tunnel entrance, hands behind their backs, staring straight ahead. Flint recognized the posture. They were guarding the entrance, a duty given only to the cops who found the vessel. When a space cop was in charge of a vessel, that charge didn't end until HazMat was done and the vessel was released to the appropriate authority.

The cops were both male, and at least ten years younger than Flint. He introduced himself, pressed the chip that illuminated his badge, and said, "I take it you two towed in the vessel."

The cop closest to him, whose hollow cheeks and muscles spoke of deliberate malnourishment in the name of exercise, nodded.

"What've we got?" Flint asked.

"It's in the report," the other cop said. He was older, more experienced. His almond-shaped gray eyes had a flat expression, as if he resented talking to a detective.

Flint peered at the cop's last name, sewn across the pocket of his uniform's jacket. Raifey. "I didn't have a chance to read the report. Why don't you fill me in?"

The cops glanced at each other, then looked away. Neither of them, it seemed, wanted to say anything.

This was going to be harder than Flint thought. "Listen," he said. "I was just transferred from Traffic to Armstrong proper. My partner doesn't like to share and, frankly, I don't think she'll understand this one anyway. Before she gets here, tell me what's different, so that I can—"

"The bodies," said the first cop. The name above his pocket read McMullen. "I've never seen anything like them."

Flint glanced at Raifey. McMullen's words were a cue for the more experienced partner to comment on the younger partner's naivete. But Raifey didn't. He didn't say anything at all.

"What about the bodies?" Flint asked.

"How anyone could do that—" McMullen started, but Raifey held up his hand.

"Regulations," he said, more to his partner than Flint. "Let the detective make his own determination."

Technically, Raifey was right, but often space cops told detectives what to see, what to find.

"Murder?" Flint said.

McMullen made a choking sound and turned away. Raifey's mouth curved in a slight smile. "Why else would they call you?"

There were a thousand reasons. Theft, illegal cargo, damage to the ship, sign of illegals in an abandoned vessel. But Flint chose to ignore the belligerence.

"What else?" He continued to look at Raifey, not McMullen. Flint wanted to prove to the older cop that they could work together if they had to.

Raifey met his gaze for a long moment, as if measuring him. Behind him, Flint heard DeRicci's boot heels clicking on the metal floor.

Raifey's gaze flicked over Flint's shoulder, obviously taking in DeRicci's approach. Then Raifey leaned forward and lowered his voice.

"The bodies weren't that unusual," he said. "You'll recognize it. It was the autopilot. Someone set that yacht on a collision course with the Moon. They should have left the thing to float in space. I would have. But instead, they wanted it here."

Flint nodded. That was unusual. Bodies were found in abandoned vessels all the time, and some of those bodies were murder victims. But usually they were victims of a failed life support system, inoperative engines, or a lack of fuel. In all of those cases, the ship continued on its regular course or floated when the fuel was gone.

He'd never heard of anyone setting autopilot for a collision course with the Moon itself. Such a course was guaranteed to draw Traffic's attention.

Flint said, "Were they—?"

"HazMat is nearly done." DeRicci had come up behind him, talking over him deliberately. She glared at both space cops, who looked away, their expressions neutral once more.

Flint suppressed a sigh and peered down the tunnel. Sure enough, the HazMat team was coming off the yacht, carrying their gear as they walked. As they moved through the tunnel walls, the orange warning lights turned yellow.

No hazardous materials on board. No lethal biological agents. Normally that meant that the port crews could process the vessel. But the yellow lights meant that a police investigation was under way. No one could go through that tunnel without the proper authorization.

The space cops stood back as the first members of the HazMat team came out of the tunnel. Their protective gear made them all look like something alien, even though they were all clearly human. It covered them from head to foot like a second skin, obscuring their facial features. The gear provided its own environment. The thick webbing allowed nothing to pass through to the people inside—at least nothing that HazMat had encountered so far.

The team's leader touched a spot on the gear's neck and the facial protection fell away, revealing a middle-aged woman with delicate features. Her gaze met DeRicci's.

"You've got a hell of a mess in there."

"Any ideas?" DeRicci asked.

"I've got plenty of ideas," the HazMat team leader said. "We'll talk when you're done if you want, but I think it's pretty self-explanatory."

DeRicci nodded. "Okay, Miles," she said. "Looks like it's just you and me and three dead—"

"Anything we should watch out for?" Flint asked the team leader, deliberately ignoring DeRicci.

That was the question she should have asked. Sometimes HazMat ruled unidentifiable objects as potentially hazardous, should they be touched in the wrong way or accidentally opened. Technically, HazMat was supposed to warn any team going in of such things, but sometimes—particularly in cases of gruesome death—they focused so strongly on the corpses that they sometimes forgot to warn about the other problems.

The team leader glanced at DeRicci. DeRicci's skin had flushed a deep red. She wasn't used to being overridden by Flint. He'd been courteous to her from the day they'd started working together, suffering her insults and her derision.

But he wasn't about to go on a yacht with three dead bodies on board without asking the proper questions.

"There's nothing suspicious," the team leader said after a moment. "At least as far as we're concerned."

Flint nodded. Then he glanced at DeRicci. She raised her eyebrows at him, both mocking him and telling him to go first. He stepped into the tunnel.

All port tunnels smelled the same: the cool metallic scent of consistently recycled air, the faint stench of sewage from overflowing ship systems, and the industrial deodorizer that attempted to mask all of those smells. He felt his shoulders relax. He was used to this place.

The tunnel was short. Most of it was permanent, but the shipside end could be extended or retracted depending on need. He stepped past the warning lights and took the small door on the side instead of going straight into the ship. He wanted to examine the exterior first.

~As he stepped down, he saw DeRicci sigh heavily. She was only a few meters behind him. She glanced at the ship's closed airlock door, then at him, apparently deciding she didn't want to enter the yacht alone.

She came down the steps backwards, holding the railing as if she were coming down a ladder. That confirmed it for him; DeRicci rarely handled the Port. They had gotten this assignment because of his experience, not hers.

She reached the main level and looked around. He tried to imagine the dock from her perspective. The dome was metallic, without a view of space the way Armstrong had. The artificial lighting was on the lowest regulation setting, so dim that shadows and darkness predominated.

"Lights full," Flint said, adding the command code. The lights rose.

The dock had been built for vessels one hundred times the size of the yacht. The yacht seemed small inside the enclosed area—more like a robotic repair vehicle than a spacefaring one.

Flint walked toward it, noting that the name—normally painted in large letters on the side—had been taken off. The lack of a name was a violation of most interstellar regulations. He suspected they would find more violations before they were done.

"You recording this?" DeRicci asked.

Flint started. He hadn't even thought to make a video record. "I figured HazMat did."

"We need our own." DeRicci approached the hull as Flint pressed one of the chips on his uniform sleeve. He would record everything from now on.

She was looking at a scorch mark that ran along the side, but she didn't touch it.

"Weapons fire?" she asked, and she was checking with him. She hadn't done that before either.

He nodded. He moved closer. The yacht had an expensive blast coating, but not enough to protect it from whatever had shot at it.

"Looks like only a few shots," he said. "Powerful, but I'd guess they were meant as warning shots."

"How old are they?"

"Fresh enough." Flint touched the hull. It was smooth against his fingers. "It looks like the blast coating got reapplied regularly. This hull should be pitted from space debris—happens to all ships over time, no matter how well shielded they are—and this one isn't."

"No name either," DeRicci said.

Flint nodded. He'd worked his way to the back of the ship. "And no registration All the required parts codes have been removed as well."

Parts codes were placed on all pieces of material for ships made on earth or to be used at human-run ports. There were a thousand ways to identify a ship aside from its own registration, and judging by the cursory examination, this ship had gotten rid of all of them.

"Someone spent a lot of money to keep this ship in working order and its identity secret," DeRicci said.

"Looks like it didn't work," Flint said.

"You can't be sure that whoever killed the people inside this ship knew who they were," DeRicci said.

As he rounded the side of the ship, he stopped. "Noelle," he said, calling her over. He usually didn't use her first name. She came quickly, just as he expected her to.

She frowned at the ship. "What is it?"

"The escape pods are gone. The hatches are still open."

"So someone escaped," DeRicci said.

Flint nodded. "And no one inside the ship closed the hatch doors. If I were under attack, I'd make sure those hatches closed quickly. One good shot in them could do serious damage to the ship."

"Why wouldn't they close automatically?" DeRicci asked.

"Redundant technology," Flint said. "This ship is a medium-level yacht, not high end. The logic is that if you have to abandon ship, the ship is lost. No need to protect it or its cargo any longer."

"Two pods for a ship this size?"

"Regulation. If you had the suggested-size crew and passengers, everyone should be able to fit into the pods. It would be a tight squeeze, and you'd better pray someone would find you pretty fast, but you'd be all right for a few days."

"So we should be looking for some pods."

"We'll put Traffic on it. We also should ask anyone

who comes into the docks in the next two days if they've seen or picked up pods."

DeRicci nodded. "That's a break then."

"Maybe." Flint glanced at her. "If our killers used the pods, they might have had another ship waiting nearby."

"If they had another ship, why would they use the pods?" DeRicci asked.

"Good point." Flint scanned the rest of the hull and found nothing except a few more blast marks.

"You ready to go in?" DeRicci asked.

"You coming with me?" Flint asked.

DeRicci nodded. "I worry when HazMat says we have a mess. They usually concentrate on their job, not ours."

That had been Flint's sense of it too. He took the stairs two at a time and stepped back into the tunnel. The tunnel's mouth attached to the yacht's main entrance. Before he pressed open the outer door, he paused.

"What?" DeRicci asked. She had stopped right beside him.

She was actually letting him take the lead instead of trying to intimidate him or browbeat him. She really had to feel out of her depth here.

"This ship was attached to something else, and just recently." He pointed to the scrape marks beside the door. "Something which isn't regulation and couldn't latch onto the ship properly."

"Are you saying they were at a different port?"

He shook his head. "If I had to guess, I'd say they were boarded."

DeRicci's mouth formed a thin line. "In that case, jurisdiction—"

"Is ours. The bodies ended up here."

She nodded. "Make sure you get that on the recording."

He already had. He palmed open the outside door. The HazMat team had left the interior door closed, just the way the airlock would have been in space.

"Damn HazMat," DeRicci said, looking down. "God knows how much evidence they trampled here."

He hadn't even thought of that. He still had a lot to learn as a detective. As a former space cop, he saw HazMat as a godsend, not a potential problem. "We should have bagged their boots."

"We'll get them if we need them."

Flint moved his arm, making sure he got everything in the tiny airlock recorded. There was so much about investigation that he didn't know.

"What're you waiting for?" DeRicci asked, and he realized she expected him to open the door.

He didn't answer. Instead, he pushed the main door open.

The smell hit him first. Urine, blood, feces, and the beginnings of decomposition. In all his years, he hadn't smelt anything that foul.

"They turned off the environmental systems," he said, through the hand he'd put over his face.

"HazMat?"

"No, whoever was here last. Maybe the folks who left on the escape pods." He got a small swatch of Protectocloth from his pocket and stretched the cloth to fit over his nose and mouth. The cloth was just like HazMat gear, only smaller and for emergencies. He considered this stench an emergency.

"Not all of the systems are off," DeRicci said. "I recognize that smell. That's decomposing flesh, which can only happen in an oxygen-rich environment."

"But the system should have scrubbed this smell out of everything," he said, "and it's still here."

"Even if the bodies are here?"

"On a yacht like this, bad smells get engineered away. Even if the bodies are still here."

DeRicci had put a Protectocloth over her face too. "Let's stick together."

They stepped into the crew work area. A control panel flashed to Flint's left. Just beyond it, the door to the cockpit stood open. A small galley faced him, and beyond it, a corridor. To his right was another door, and it was closed. It probably led to the passenger section.

The cockpit would hold the answers, but DeRicci had opened the passenger door.

"Flint," she said.

He stepped beside her. Blood bathed this compartment, rising up along the walls, spattering the ceiling and the floor. The gravity had been on when the killings occurred and it stayed on throughout the entire flight.

The bodies were staked side by side, the yacht seats moved to accommodate the sprawl. One of the bodies was female, the other male, both on their backs, both spread-eagled. They had been eviscerated—probably while they were alive, judging by the blood—and their intestines looped into a familiar oval pattern.

"A Disty vengeance killing," DeRicci said.

Even Flint recognized that, although he'd never seen such bodies in person before. Only in class, as one of the many things he had to learn about alien killings.

"Only I've never seen one done in space before." She frowned, crouched. "Everything else is textbook."

"Doesn't that make it suspicious?" he asked.

She shook her head. "The Disty are precise about this sort of thing. They have to be."

He shuddered. Disty vengeance killings were rare on the Moon. They happened most often on Mars, which the Disty more or less ran. If this was a Disty vengeance killing, there would be nothing he could do. Under hundreds of interstellar laws, under even more multicultural agreements between the member species, cultural practices like vengeance killings were allowed.

Although Flint was a new detective, he knew how this case would run. He and DeRicci would check the victims' DNA to see if they had outstanding Disty warrants against them, and if they did, then the case would be closed. According to the various agreements, no crime would have been committed.

Even sending the yacht to the Moon made sense in this instance. The bodies had to be accounted for. The Disty used vengeance killings as a deterrent. They would want everyone to know that these people, who-ever they had been, had died because they had done something wrong.

The problem would come if the Disty hadn't tar-geted these victims. If this was, in fact, a real crime made to look like a Disty killing.

But if that were the case, why send the yacht toward the Moon?

"The third body has to be somewhere else," De-Ricci said.

"I vote for the cockpit," Flint said. "We have to go there anyway. I want to find out when those pods were ejected."

DeRicci glanced at him. "The pods don't fit, do they?"

"Not with a Disty vengeance killing. Unless we find

the pods later, with the occupants either gone or dead in just this way." Flint stepped over blood spatter and through the main doors back into the crew area. No blood here. But if a Disty ship had boarded the yacht in flight, and the Disty had committed the killings, it would be logical to find some trace in this room.

The control panel still blinked as he went past. He paused to look at it. Someone had bypassed the controls to open this door, and the system was still complaining about it—weakly. There should have been a vocal component to the complaint, which should have continued no matter how long ago the breach had occurred.

He made a mental note of the override, then headed into the cockpit—and stopped. The third body faced him. It was not spread-eagled like the others. It had been strapped to the command chair. The evisceration was the same, but the rest of it—the rest of it was much worse.

Flint turned away and found DeRicci watching him.

"She was the one they wanted." DeRicci's voice was flat. "The others, they were merely warnings, something that happened to the helpers. She was the one they blamed the most."

"If this was the Disty."

She nodded. "If."

But she sounded convinced. Maybe he was too. He wasn't certain.

"I was going to check the logs, the databases. I was going to—"

"You can't," DeRicci said, stating the obvious. No one could get into that room without disturbing the body—or what the body had become. "We have to wait for the forensics team. The bodies have to be removed now. Then you can check the logs."

Flint took a deep breath. He had been thinking like

a space cop again. Check the logs, find out what happened, let the team on the ground worry about the next step.

Only now he was the team on the ground—and with a mess like this, he doubted that the two space cops who'd found this ship had even tried to download the logs.

"If we're lucky," DeRicci said, "the DNA will come back positive and you won't have to go in there at all."

"Oh, but I will," he said.

She looked at him as if she didn't understand him.

He gave her a cool smile. "We have to know who released the pods and why. There might be more people out there, more people the Disty are after."

"It's not our problem," DeRicci said. "If the Disty are doing vengeance killings, then they have every right to hunt those people down."

"And if these people are only peripherally involved?" he asked.

"You know the law, Miles," she said. "We stay out of it."

He knew the law. He'd just never faced it before. So far, his cases had involved humans committing crimes against humans. He always knew he would deal with the various alien cultures that existed in this part of the universe, but he hadn't expected to so soon.

"I'd read about these things," he said, "but I had no idea how gruesome they really are."

Something in her face caught him, softening, a look behind the tough woman she always pretended to be. "You'll have to get used to it. The Disty are one of our nearest neighbors and closest allies. We never complain about them, no matter how hideous their sense of justice is."

Then she walked away, heading back toward the passenger cabin, effectively ending the conversation.

Flint stared at the body scattered around the cockpit. That desecrated corpse had been a human being not too long ago. He shook his head, willing the thought away. He had learned, after his daughter died, how to keep his emotions and his intellect separate from each other. That was one of the reasons he'd been promoted to detective.

He didn't dare lose that detachment at his first gruesome crime scene. He studied the carnage until it became a puzzle, needing to be solved, and then, like DeRicci, he left.

3

Ekaterina leaned back on the plush seat of the space yacht. The man who had brought her here, the man who said his name wasn't Russell even though that was what she should call him, had told her to get some rest.

But she couldn't rest, anymore than she could eat. She kept playing that last encounter with Simon over and over again in her mind. That would be the last time they would ever see each other. The last time they dared see each other, and it hadn't gone the way she wanted it to. If she had had the chance to do it her way, she would have told him everything, sworn him to secrecy, and apologized for getting involved with him in the first place.

But she hadn't done that. She couldn't do that. Even if he promised never to reveal a thing she had told him, he might not be able to live up to that promise.

One small sentence would be enough for a slip to get a Tracker following her. And a Tracker would report to the Revs.

The passenger section of the yacht was big. It seated ten in the front where she sat now, and the seats folded out into single-bed-sized cots. The back boasted four suites: bedroom, living quarters, and bathroom designed, she supposed, for the Disappeared who paid some sort of premium.

Or perhaps the suites were standard on a yacht of this type. She had no idea and no one to ask. She had expected to be one of many on this yacht, all of them going to new lives in new places. New identities, new jobs, new ways of approaching the world. She had imagined conversations—not about what they'd done or why they believed they needed to be Disappeared, but about their fears, their hopes, their dreams.

She still had dreams. There was only one she stifled, and that was the one about returning to her old life, to San Francisco and to Simon.

She had to be someone else now. It was the only way she, and the people she loved, would survive.

Ekaterina stood and paced, as she had been doing ever since the yacht left Earth orbit. It felt odd to be sitting in the passenger section of a ship this small. When she was in college, she'd made money running orbital ferries during the summer. She took tourists around Earth, and showed them the sites from orbit. The job got old after a while, but handling the controls didn't.

Maybe the folks at Disappearance Incorporated would use her piloting experience and give her a similar job on another world. Maybe she would have a chance to try something she had dreamed of doing. She knew she wouldn't be practicing law anymore— that would be too obvious—but perhaps she would work in a related field.

She touched the petals in her pocket. She was surprised they were still there. She had expected to be searched when she got to the space port, but she hadn't been.

The man who wasn't Russell had walked her inside as if nothing were unusual. They had gone through side doors that led to a series of private yachts. She had never taken a private space flight before. All of her previous trips had been on commercial flights, and the regulations there were strict. Everyone was searched. Only so much extra weight could go on board, and everything was examined for its potential harm to the flight.

Days before she left home, she had put a laser pistol in her purse. She had thought she might have to use it before she Disappeared, but no one had approached her. Even as she was finishing her final preparations for her Disappearance, she had left the pistol in her purse. The people at Disappearance Inc had told her to trust no one—not even the people who were to take her from place to place.

The laser pistol, miraculously, made it out of Earth's orbit, something that never would have happened on any other flight.

If she had known that those regulations would be so lax, she would have brought a few other things. Her engagement ring, maybe, or a tiny silver pin that had been made by a Maakestad ancestor in the seventeenth century.

One or two tiny things to remind her of home.

Of course, that was precisely what she wasn't supposed to do. Precisely what, the administrator at Disappearance Inc had told her, most people who got caught did wrong. They couldn't let go of their past. They couldn't let go of their own identities.

They got caught because they didn't understand how important it was to be reborn as someone else. No baggage, no past life, nothing except the person Disappearance Inc told them to be.

You have to forget who you were, the administrator said. *And you have to become someone new.*

Ekaterina could do that. She had known it from

that first conversation with Disappearance Inc three weeks ago. She might have known it even before she approached them.

But it still felt odd to be stripped down to her core self. Nothing would remain the same, not her job, not her name, and maybe, if the company felt it necessary, not her face. The only thing she would have would be her memories, and she wouldn't be able to share them with anyone. Ever.

The door to the crew section slid open. The woman who told Ekaterina to call her Jenny entered. She was slender, her features as flat as Russell's. Everyone she had met at Disappearance Inc had been so enhanced that they no longer looked like the person they had once been.

It made Ekaterina uneasy.

The door slid closed. Jenny handed Ekaterina a hand-held. Ekaterina hadn't been linked for nearly a week. She usually wore security chips that linked her to her house's system, her office, and the net. She had never gone for the full package—total linkage all the time—because she had valued her privacy.

But not being linked now reminded her how alone she was. She couldn't tap a chip and record a conversation, and she couldn't—with a silent command—have House call emergency services. If Ekaterina were attacked now, she'd have to fend off the attacker on her own—no police, no instant 911 recording, no way of getting immediate help.

The hand-held felt hard against her fingers. She hadn't used one since she had gone to college on a scholarship, long before she could afford security chips and total linkage.

"What's this?" she asked without looking at the screen.

"Your new identity," Jenny said. "Read it, understand it, and prepare for it. We'll give you links and chips before you leave the yacht. Some of this information will be downloaded to you for easy access, but the rest has to come naturally. You have to make this fit."

Ekaterina nodded. She'd heard the speech before. It seemed to be standard at Disappearance Inc.

"We used all the forms you filled out and your psych profile." Jenny's voice was soft. She had clearly given this speech a lot. "Remember, we can't change anything. That's not our job here. This is the best DI could do. It's up to you to make it work."

She gave Ekaterina a false smile and stood up.

"Have you read this?" Ekaterina asked.

"It's coded," Jenny said. "You should have gotten the password before you left."

Ekaterina had, but she wanted to double-check Jenny's answer.

"So we're nearly there," Ekaterina said.

Jenny shrugged. "I was instructed to give you the hand-held at this point in the journey. Where we are and where we're going is not something I know much about."

She left the passenger area. Ekaterina watched the door close behind her. What would it be like to ferry people from place to place, not knowing where you were going or why? Did people like Jenny take the job for the excitement, the possibility that something might go wrong, and she might have to use her expensive security training? Or did she take it for the opportunity to travel? Or were her reasons more altruistic than that? Was she one of the political ones, the ones who believed that alien laws should not be able to target humans, no matter what the humans had done?

Once, Ekaterina would have said that she had no opinion on that matter. She did now that it was too late.

She settled into the yacht's lounge chair and tapped the hand-held, twisting so that her body protected the screen as she punched in the code.

Her new name was Greta Palmer. She stared at it for a long time, trying mentally to make it work. All her life, her name had had a lot of syllables, had been almost a language in itself. Greta Palmer seemed too simple, too plain to be her name. To be anyone's name. It sounded made up to her.

Ekaterina supposed any name would sound like that. If it were too fancy, she would worry that it sounded contrived. Too simple obviously bothered her as well.

But she couldn't hide with any variation on her name. She had to accept the new one.

Only she wished they had let her pick it out herself.

She read her new bio with interest. Greta was the same age Ekaterina was, born on the Moon just as she had been and moved to Earth at age three just as she had, and had gone to high school in San Francisco. After that, their bios diverged. Greta had stayed on Earth, not even taking an orbital until she accepted her new job. Ekaterina had traveled to the outer reaches of explored space. Her early training had included guaranteed jobs on three different alien-owned colonies, including Revnata, where she had gotten in trouble.

Once she had planned on being a lawyer who was certified to argue in front of the multicultural tribunals. Instead, she was running from one of their rulings.

She hated the irony.

With a sigh, Ekaterina shifted position, and continued to read. Her new job was recycling textiles. She froze. Textile recycling meant taking ruined fabrics, like torn blankets and ripped upholstery, and remaking them into something cheap and functional. The job was menial and labor intensive. It was about as far from lawyering as a person could get. Intelligence was not an asset at a job like this. It was a liability.

Surely there was a mistake. Maybe when she got to her destination, she would be reassigned. Or maybe they thought she could hide at a textile plant for a few years, since it would be the very last place the Rev would look.

But would it really be a good hiding place? She was an educated woman, whose accent, whose simple sentence structure, made it clear that she had spent years studying with some of the galaxy's greatest minds. Hiding that would be difficult, and might even be impossible.

Surely Disappearance Inc would have thought of that.

Maybe they had. Maybe it was buried deeper in the information they had just given her. Or maybe she had the wrong idea about plant workers. Maybe her objections had more to do with her own prejudices than with her abilities or lack of them.

The idea of working in a textile recycling plant, with fibers floating in the air, not to mention the filth that had to be cleaned off other people's possessions, made her queasy. She hadn't had a job like that ever.

Her palms were damp. She rubbed them on her pants and looked at the rest of the profile.

The textile plant was in Von, a town she'd never heard of. She would have her own apartment—a one-bedroom, company-provided by the plant—and if she managed to save enough money, she might be able to buy a place of her own.

She ran a hand over her face. Money would be a problem. She had been short on funds before, but she'd always had the family money in a trust. This time, she would have no backup. When she got the company-owned apartment, they would own her. She would need the job and the terrible pay, and she would have to begin all over again.

For the very first time, the reality of the change she was undertaking was sinking in. Before she had understood the loss, but not the future. She hadn't thought about where she was going because she had no idea. She had decided not to fantasize about her new life because she hadn't wanted to be disappointed.

But she was disappointed anyway.

An impoverished thirty-five-year-old woman whose skills only let her do manual labor, who lived in an unknown town.

She frowned, wondering where the town was. There was nothing about her upcoming destination in the bio. It had to be somewhere else in the material Jenny had given her.

Or perhaps it was in the hand-held's database. Most computers carried the same basic information—dictionaries of over a thousand main languages, food compatibility charts for human/alien physiologies, and, of course, maps. She searched the hand-held for a moment, wondering if its memory had been purged of non-relevant information, and finally found what she was searching for.

The map function. She typed in Von and added that it had to be in territory that could be occupied by humans. She got only one hit.

It was on Mars.

She stared at the map for the longest time. The blinking feature showed that Von was in Mars' northernmost region, above the Arctic Circle. Obviously the town was big enough to have its own dome, but not really large enough to be well known.

And that bothered her, because she'd been to Mars and she knew what this place would look like.

Mars was run by the Disty, small creatures with large heads, large eyes, and narrow bodies. They hated the feel of wide open spaces and built their own colonies like rats' warrens. When they took over human colonies, the way they had on Mars, they added corridors and false ceilings and narrow little passageways, so the entire place felt claustrophobic.

She could get used to that. She knew there was a possibility she would go somewhere that wasn't controlled by humans but where humans were tolerated. Initially, she'd even thought she'd go to Mars because the Disty and the Rev did not get along. They avoided each other's colonies and were barred from each other's home worlds.

Then she had done some research. Both the Disty and the Rev had ventured into each other's colonies in the past few years searching for Disappeareds. Because the Disty and Rev had similar missions, they respected each other's warrants and often helped each other find Disappeareds on each other's land.

Both alien species had caught onto the game that the Disappearance services were playing and were foiling them on the ground. Instead of hiding Rev fugitives in Disty territory and vice versa, the good disappearance services were now going for less obvious hiding places.

Her stomach twisted. She thought she had done the

right research. According to everything she'd looked for, all the people she'd talked with, Disappearance Inc was the best disappearance service in the known universe.

Why then would it hide her in a place the Rev surely would look?

She put the hand-held on her lap. Maybe the administrators at DI had misunderstood. After all, she hadn't written down who she was running from. She'd told as few people as required by DI's business practices, but she never told them what she had done because, they said, it wasn't relevant, and she told only a few of them who she was hiding from since they had to know to keep her out of certain places.

Like Mars.

Unless things had changed even more than she realized. Maybe their research was more up to date than hers.

But, judging by the personality profile they pulled, the job they gave her, and the place they had chosen to hide her, their research was shoddy. Either that, or they had confused her with another client.

She picked up the hand-held again and scanned the rest of the information. Her name wasn't in it, of course, but that bio suggested that this was hers.

Ekaterina stood, her restlessness growing. Damn them for not allowing her to bring anything along. She couldn't even carry a hard copy of her agreement with DI because that was like carrying a piece of identification. She wasn't linked, so she couldn't use the password they had given her to access the information.

Had they planned it this way? If so, why? So that she wouldn't complain? Were the reports of satisfied customers made up?

She had no idea.

Her stomach turned again, that queasy feeling remaining. The Rev never gave up searching for fugitives from their justice system. If she got caught, she'd spend the rest of her natural life in a Rev penal colony.

She'd seen Rev penal colonies. Working in a textile recycling plant in a Disty-run Mars town would seem like heaven in comparison.

She would do it if she had to. The problem was that she didn't feel this identity would hide her.

But she had no idea what her options were. She tried to remember the text of the agreement she'd signed. Essentially, she was putting her life into DI's hands. It was, she knew, the only way to survive.

She hadn't even asked the lawyerly question: what if they were wrong? She had done what all naïve clients did. Once she had completed her research, she had trusted blindly.

Of course, she had been panicked at the time. Her case had been denied by the Eighth Multicultural Tribunal. The Rev warrant, issued so many years ago, stood, and the Rev would come for her immediately.

An old friend who clerked at the Tribunal had sent her a warning before the Tribunal made their announcement. She had no idea how long she had until the Tribunal spoke, but she knew it wouldn't be long.

So she had done what she could, researching and finding a disappearance service. But she hadn't been as thorough as she should have been.

That was incredibly clear to her now.

She'd allowed her panic over being discovered to override her natural caution. She still had funds. Accessing them would be tricky, but it could be done. She could hire a different disappearance service if she had to.

And she just might have to.

At least there was one clause in her agreement with
DI that she had memorized. She had done that on
purpose, worried that if she hadn't, she would be stuck
in just this situation.

She could terminate at any time.

DI wouldn't be liable for her safety, of course, but
they were required to take her to a settlement. They
couldn't just eject her in space and hope that she
survived.

She swallowed hard. Firing DI was as much of a
risk as disappearing in the first place. But she had to
trust her own instincts. Maybe she could browbeat the
crew into taking her to DI's nearest headquarters and
they could rerun her profile. Maybe they could see
what went wrong in the San Francisco offices and repair it.

She shut off the hand-held and slipped it into her
purse. Then she slung her purse over her shoulder and
walked to the door separating the passenger section
from the crew areas.

The door wasn't locked as it was supposed to be.
Clearly Jenny had forgotten to reseal it when she had
brought out the hand-held. Either that or the crew
hadn't sealed it at all, thinking one slight female passenger wouldn't be a problem, no matter what she
had done.

Ekaterina pushed the door aside and walked
through. She had never been in this part of the crew
area. The airlock was to her left, a small galley to her
right. The carpet was still plush here, although it got
thinner closer to the cockpit.

The theory was that the crew didn't need luxury,
not like the passengers on the space yacht did.

No one sat in the galley. She walked toward the cockpit, her boots making no sound as she moved.

Voices filtered toward her. She couldn't make out the words, but the tone sounded official.

As she peered through the cockpit door, she froze. Through the main portal, she could see the orange and blue stripes of a Rev penal ship.

"We'll be evacuating the yacht in thirty Earth minutes," the pilot was saying through the interlink. He was clearly talking to the Rev. "She won't know we're gone. Give it another thirty minutes and you can board."

Jenny was sitting beside him, her hands behind her head, as if she were watching a vid. The co-pilot was on the other side, tapping something into the ship's system.

The pilot continued. "I'll be picking up the ship from impound in a week or so. If there's permanent damage, I'm coming after you."

Ekaterina's mouth was dry. The pilot was selling her to the Rev. He would make more money from them than he would as a contract employee of DI. Supposedly, services like DI screened out people like him.

But not in this case.

The Rev would take her and imprison her for life. Few humans survived in a Rev penal colony for more than ten years. The work alone was too much for the human frame. That didn't count the xenophobia, the way that Rev inmates treated someone who was completely different.

She eased away from the door. No one in the cockpit had seen her.

She had been given a slight chance to save herself. Now she had to figure out how to use it.

4

As they stepped out of the ship's tunnel, DeRicci's hand-held beeped. She cursed and took it out of her pocket. She punched the screen, information already blinking. "As if we don't have enough to do. We've got another."

"Where?" he asked.

"Terminal Five," she said, more to herself than him. Terminal 5, while technically next door to Terminal 4, was a healthy hike from where they were. "What the hell's that one again?"

"Suspected criminal activity by a ship's owner."

DeRicci glanced at him. "You're useful in the docks."

"I'm useful most of the time," he said.

There was nothing else on the hand-held. Just the order to report to a ship tunnel in Terminal 5. Someone would meet them and explain the situation.

"I hope to hell this isn't something complicated," DeRicci said as she headed back to Terminal 4's main entry. "I want to put this Disty thing to bed."

Flint was feeling uncomfortable. Detectives got one, maybe two cases down here per week total. Now he and DeRicci were getting two in one day.

"We're better off taking the train between terminals," Flint said. "If we walk, we'll lose that time advantage Headquarters wants us to have."

DeRicci frowned. She clearly didn't like his new outspokenness. But he was tired of letting her run things. She was out of her depth in the Port. He was going to take over this partnership whether she liked it or not.

He led her to the interior train system. It had been designed to link the various terminals after the Port had taken over the bulk of space traffic control for the Moon. At that point, the Port had mushroomed into something with unwalkable distances. Fifty interior trains ran at set times. Only one ran all the way around the Port, and it was usually crowded.

Flint took DeRicci to the tracks that worked for the shuttle between Terminals 4 and 5. Because the locals weren't advertised in the Port, they served mostly as crew shuttles. If tourists had to go from one terminal to another, they took the main, crowded train.

The train pulled up, its dark glass sides reflecting the lights in the waiting area. The doors slid open silently and three workers in blue uniforms got off. Then Flint walked on. DeRicci followed.

There were no seats. Passengers held on to bars and metal hand rings. The tougher passengers stood, feet braced, in the center of the car. It took skill and talent to ride the trains that way without getting hurt.

Flint had learned how to do it, but hadn't enjoyed it. He gripped the rail now, and DeRicci did the same. They had the car to themselves.

The moment the door closed, the train sped backwards in the direction it had just come. After a moment, it reached its top speed, moving at a velocity faster than the high-speed trains that ran between the various domes littering the Moon.

DeRicci looked startled and reached her other hand around the metal bar. The train slowed and then, smoothly, stopped. Even though the movement was even, Flint watched DeRicci's body yank forward, then back. She glared at him as if the effect of the train were all his fault.

He supposed, in an odd way, it was. He should have warned her about the speed. These trains had been designed for efficiency, not for comfort. Back in the days when the interior train system was first built, Armstrong Dome had been known for its efficiency.

A lot had changed since then.

The doors opened. DeRicci touched a hand to her short hair, as if the swift ride had created a wind that ruffled her.

"You okay?" he asked.

"You did that to torture me."

"Maybe that was a secondary reason," he said with a smile. To his surprise, she smiled back. The expression surprised him.

He had been blaming her for her unwillingness to give him a chance, when he had once treated his new partners in Traffic the same way. DeRicci had gone through five new partners in five years, all of them beginning detectives. Perhaps it wasn't so odd that she expected him to prove himself before she started to give him the benefit of the doubt.

They emerged from the train station into Terminal 5. It was set up the same as Terminal 4. If a person ignored the signage, the only way to tell the difference between the two terminals was to look at the ships docked nearby. Terminal 5 was nearly full, and none of its tunnels had yellow warning lights.

A slender man, his dark skin shiny with sweat, stopped in front of them. He had his arms wrapped around a stack of warning signs, hugging them to his chest as if they were more important than he was.

"Officers?" he asked.

"Detectives," DeRicci corrected. She always did that. To her, being called an "officer" was the same as a demotion.

"Detectives." He bobbed his head and bit his lower lip. "I'm Stefan Newell. I'm in charge of this terminal. I take it you've been briefed?"

"We'd only been told to report," DeRicci said. "We've just come off another assignment in Terminal 4."

"Oh, dear." Newell glanced at Flint. "I was hoping you would have brought more people with you."

That caught Flint's attention. "Why?"

"Because we have an unfolding situation. I told your dispatch that. We need as much help as we can get—"

"We were already at the Port." DeRicci spoke slowly, as if she were talking to a child. "I'm sure others are on their way."

"I hope so. I'll send the distress call again."

"First," Flint said, "tell us what we're dealing with."

Newell bit his lower lip again, so hard this time that the skin below it turned an odd shade of white. "The border patrol caught a ship leaving Moon orbit. They're bringing it in."

"The border police are equipped to handle their own problems," DeRicci said. "I'm sure—"

"What's the problem?" Flint asked, not letting her finish. She was going to try to leave, and he had a hunch that decision would have been bad for all of them.

Newell hugged the signs tighter. "It's a Wygnin ship."

Flint felt himself grow cold. The Wygnin almost never ventured into human-occupied space. They rarely left Korsve, their homeworld.

"Definitely a border problem," DeRicci said. "Come on, Flint. We have a case to finish—"

"Ma'am. Detective. Please." Despite his words, Newell's tone had grown harsh. "I'm not handling the Wygnin alone."

"You'll have the border patrol."

"They'll have their hands full."

"What's on the ship?" Flint asked.

"Children. Human children," Newell said. "And the Wygnin lack the proper warrants."

DeRicci sent the second call to headquarters herself. She requested backup and a squad of lawyers who specialized in Wygnin law, as well as translators so that nothing would get misunderstood.

The entire settled universe had learned to fear the Wygnin.

Flint had gone to the dock where the ship would land. The dome above it was already opening. The fleet of lawyers and cops and translators wouldn't arrive in time. He and DeRicci would have to handle the first Moon contact and pray that they didn't screw it up.

The Wygnin had a harsher view of law and custom than any other species humans had come into contact with. The Wygnin view became apparent only over time, as humans learned the hard way not to cross them.

Every space cop learned about human-Wygnin history, partly as a cautionary tale, and partly so that they would do precisely what DeRicci did when she found out what they were up against: ask for legal advice and help with translations. Anything else could result in terrible—but legal—consequences.

"I don't like this at all," DeRicci said coming up beside him. "The Wygnin usually don't try to slip the border patrol."

Flint nodded. He watched as a golden ship flanked by three border ships slowly eased its way through the dome. Two of the border ships guarded the dome's top. The other ship came down with the Wygnin ship.

Flint had only seen Wygnin ships in vids, holos or flats. None of them did the vessels justice. The gold winked, even in the thin light, and the ship seemed to float down. There was no obvious propellant, and the entire movement would have been silent if it weren't for the hum of the border ship's engines.

The border ship landed with the usual thud. The Wygnin vessel set down as if it were made of air.

At that moment, the dome closed and the two other border ships flew off, probably to continue their rounds. The problem of the Wygnin belonged to the third ship and Armstrong authorities—as personified now by Flint and DeRicci.

Lucky them. This was turning out to be a hell of a day.

"Should we go down the tunnel?" Flint asked DeRicci.

"I want to stay as far away from those bastards as we can," she said. "The longer we wait, the better our chances of handing them over to the lawyers."

For once, he agreed with her logic. Two traffic cops came over and flanked the tunnel entrance, clearly on request from DeRicci. She tapped her departmental interlink again, trying to find out where the backup was. From her harsh tone, it was clear to Flint that they were nowhere in sight.

The door to the Wygnin ship opened and DeRicci cursed again. She shut off her interlink and sighed.

"Looks like I get the Wygnin," she said.

"I can—"

"No, you can't." She swallowed hard. "I at least have some experience with them. I know a few things to avoid. You have none. I'm just going to baby-sit in holding until backup gets here. You handle the kids, okay?"

He didn't want to go near the children. He hadn't been near children since Emmeline died.

"Flint?" DeRicci said.

He didn't have to answer her because activity started in front of them. A border officer stepped off the Wygnin ship first. From the distance through the tunnel, she looked small. She waited as the Wygnin disembarked.

Flint had never seen Wygnin before. They moved like their ship, lightly, as if a gust of wind would make them float away.

They were more ethereal than they seemed on film—almost like negative images of living creatures. There were five of them, although it took him a moment to realize that. They were so thin, they seemed to have no mass at all. And their bodies were nearly flat.

But he could feel them approach. Something changed in the air around him. Maybe it was a smell, but if it was, it wasn't one he could readily identify. It was as if the Wygnin themselves were changing the quality of the recycled air, making it more buoyant, richer, just for their presence.

As they stepped out of the tunnel, they searched the area. Their gazes fell on him one at a time and he resisted the urge to step backwards. Their eyes

were the most human eyes he had ever seen on an
alien. Maybe they were even more human. They carried expression and emotion so vivid, he could feel it
as if it were his own.

"Look down," DeRicci whispered. "Show respect."

He immediately looked at the floor. Now he was
relieved that DeRicci would be handling the Wygnin.
He had no idea he had nearly screwed up one of
their customs.

She took a step forward and said something that
sounded like a muffled sneeze. So she even spoke a
bit of their language. That was a start then.

"I'm afraid the greeting is all I know," she said. "I
hope you speak English."

English, the language humans had chosen as their
language of trade. She could have tried Chinese or
Spanish, even Japanese, but most aliens learned English first if they learned a human language at all.

"—We—shall—require—translator—" one of the
Wygnin said. Its voice was surprisingly deep, given its
body's flat shape.

"One is on the way," DeRicci said. She turned
toward the border officers. "Can one of you act as
translator until then?"

"We'll stay until your people arrive," the female
border cop said. "Standard procedure is to take the
Wygnin to customs."

"Let's follow it," DeRicci said.

Flint still had his head pointed down. He felt at
a disadvantage.

"Where are the children?" DeRicci asked.

"On the border ship," the cop said. "We thought it
better to separate them."

"My partner will take care of them."

"—No—"

The word echoed the way that Flint was feeling, but he hadn't uttered it. He looked up. The Wygnin were rocking slightly as if there was a breeze in the terminal. If there was, he couldn't feel it.

"—They—belong—with—us—" The Wygnin that spoke stood in the very front. Oddly, the other Wygnin's tiny mouths moved as his did.

"Produce the proper papers and I'll give them to you," DeRicci said.

Flint studied her. He'd never seen her so emotionless and so tough at the same time.

"They don't have the proper documentation," the border cop said. "That's the problem. They don't have any warrants at all."

She added something in the same sneezy language that DeRicci had used. The Wygnin tilted its head sideways, its golden eyes sending a message of such sadness that Flint felt its echo inside of him.

Then the Wygnin spoke in its own language and the deep voice seemed melodic, appropriate. As it spoke this time, the other Wygnin did not move their mouths. It seemed like speaking English required a group effort, but speaking its native tongue did not.

"Tell them that they'll get the children back if they have proper warrants," DeRicci said.

"I have," the border cop said. "They seem to believe that they don't need warrants, that notice has already been served."

"Remind them they are on our turf right now and we require documentation. Notice served is not enough."

The border cop nodded and translated.

"Tell them we will keep the children in holding until this is settled. If it is settled in their favor, then they will get the children back."

The Wygnin's golden gaze had found DeRicci. Flint noted that she kept her gaze averted. He was beginning to believe that she wasn't doing it out of respect, but as self-protection.

"—This—is—wrong—" the Wygnin said.

"We abide by your custom," DeRicci snapped. "You can abide by ours."

The border patrol guard shot her a warning glance, but DeRicci didn't seem to notice. The muscles in Flint's shoulders tensed. He had no idea what the Wygnin would do if crossed.

"—We—speak—to—leaders—" the Wygnin said.

"As you should," DeRicci said. "I don't give orders. I just follow them. I have no choice in this matter either."

The border guard nodded once, and Flint felt his shoulders relax. DeRicci had covered their asses, making the difficult situation someone else's problem.

Then, without saying a word to Flint, DeRicci and the border guard led the Wygnin away from the ship. Flint watched them go. He was amazed that something so beautiful could be so dangerous. He shouldn't have been, he supposed. He had found space beautiful when he patrolled it, but a single mistake out there could kill.

The entire terminal seemed to freeze while the Wygnin walked through. Everyone watched the aliens go by, but no one approached them and no one challenged them. And Flint found that odd in and of itself.

When he'd worked down here, he'd seen aliens subjected to all sorts of treatment, from fan-like adulation to complete and utter contempt. A few humans had even attacked aliens, spitting on them or throwing something at them or, in the case of the peace-loving Peyti, physically assaulting them.

Sometimes Flint wondered if alien reactions to humans were as irrational, but he supposed he would never know—not really. What he saw were codified, legal reactions, in constrained circumstances like this one.

The Wygnin had been gone for more than five minutes before the door to the border patrol ship opened. Flint suspected that had been planned. The border officer who had gone with DeRicci had probably sent some kind of signal to her compatriots, so that they wouldn't bring the children out while the Wygnin were still there.

Four border guards exited, backs straight, and weapons obvious, even from this distance. Border guards usually didn't make a show out of their laser pistols and protective gear, but these guards did.

They were as worried about the Wygnin as everyone else was.

Then a woman came out of the ship. She was heavyset, and her uniform was in disarray. She wasn't wearing her jacket. The shirt that she wore beneath it was too tight, as were her uniform pants. Her hair was down, long enough to reach the middle of her back, which wasn't regulation either. She wasn't carrying a weapon.

She stopped in front of the door, holding out one hand in a gesture of supplication. It took Flint a moment to realize she was trying to coax a child out. That was why she looked so casual. With all the weapons and uniforms about, her appearance was designed to calm the children.

A small hand took hers, and then a boy ran out, slamming into her and clinging so hard that he nearly knocked her over. The boy was heavyset too, with red hair so bright it seemed like the only spot of color in the entire terminal.

Flint couldn't judge the boy's age from this distance, but he knew the child was too old to be that clingy. A normal child would have kept his distance.

At least he wasn't a baby. A half-grown child he could deal with. He wasn't sure he could deal with a baby.

Flint steeled himself, watching the door for more children. Instead, another border guard came out, this one male. He cradled something in his arms.

Flint swallowed and made himself watch the red-haired boy.

The female border guard tried to disentangle the boy. When that failed, she walked with her hand around his back, letting him cling and move with her at the same time.

The male border guard followed closely behind. Flint could see human skin now, a tiny hand clutching the guard's arm.

A young child, then. An infant.

Flint felt his heart lurch. He took a deep breath and reminded himself that this was his job. He was at work, and he had to remain calm. Detached. Mind and heart separated, just the way they needed to be.

When the female border guard reached the main door, she scanned the area until she saw Flint. He tapped his badge, illuminating it, and she nodded, coming forward.

"Fala Valey," she said. She hadn't stated her rank, and Flint suspected that was on purpose. The boy, still clutching her, looked frightened enough.

"Miles Flint."

"My orders are to give you custody of these children until the Wygnin claims are verified." She sounded official, but her hand, still on the boy's back, rubbed it softly, as if she were comforting him while she spoke.

"Yes," Flint said.

The male guard came out of the tunnel. Flint's attention remained on the boy.

He had to be about eight. His skin was so white as to seem chalk-like, a color that had become extremely rare. Right now, his features were blotchy and his eyes swollen. His nose was so chapped, it was peeling. This child had been crying for a long time.

"This is Jasper," Valey said. "He isn't ready to tell us his last name yet, are you, Jasper?"

The boy responded by hiding his face against her arm.

"We don't know how long he's been with them," she said, speaking more softly this time. "It's got to be fairly recent. His clothing was manufactured here. But that's all we got."

Flint nodded. "It's a start."

"Who's taking this child?" the male border guard asked.

There was no way around it. Flint would have to deal with the baby.

He stepped forward. "I am," he said, and looked at the baby for the first time.

The baby was younger than Emmeline had been when she died. She'd been eighteen months old, a toddler with a gap-toothed smile, a child whose first and most favorite word had been "Daddy."

The old ache twisted his heart. She'd been dead more than ten years, and he still couldn't bear to think about her—even though he couldn't stop.

Her hair had been golden, like his. Not at all like

this baby. This baby had a crest of black hair that curled against his dark skin. His eyes were closed, long lashes against his full cheeks. He didn't look distressed at all. Either he was too young to know what happened to him, or he hadn't been with the Wygnin long.

"Here then," the guard said and handed the boy to Flint.

He had forgotten how much babies weighed, how compact and muscular their small bodies were. This child was warm and smelled of talcum. Someone had changed him on the ship if, indeed, he was still wearing diapers.

Flint ran a cautious hand over the boy's head and closed his eyes, remembering the feel of a sleeping child in his arms. His daughter used to bring out the same feeling of tenderness, the same protectiveness. He had thought it died with her. He had thought—

He shook the memory off. If he kept thinking about Emmeline, he wouldn't be able to do this. He had to think of this boy in his arms as something separate, a problem to be solved.

Not a baby. He couldn't deal with a baby that had been taken by the Wygnin. The Wygnin took children to pay for their parents' crimes, and the children never returned.

There was silence around him. Flint looked away from the child in his arms. If he didn't look at the baby, he could almost imagine it was Emmeline.

He willed the thought away. Everyone was watching him. He cleared his throat. "Do we know this child's name?"

"We know nothing about this one," the male border guard said.

"How many more are there?"

"Just these two," Valey said.

Good. Flint wasn't sure he could take any more than that. He wasn't sure he could take these.

If the Wygnin had valid warrants, these children would go to Korsve. The infant in Flint's arms would become something other than human. But Jasper—even though they'd try to turn him into a Wygnin, he was too old. He would be broken, something not human, not Wygnin.

Flint would have to let it happen. In fact, he would have to make it happen. It was his job, one he had lobbied for, one he had looked forward to.

He'd known he might face moments like this.

But knowing and experiencing were two different things.

He had to keep this a puzzle, a job, something for his brain. His emotions would only get in the way.

But the child in his arms—warm, alive and so very human—wasn't touching his brain. The boy was cradled against his heart.

5

Ekaterina waited until the pilot severed his link with the Rev before taking the two steps into the cockpit. She put her laser pistol against the pilot's head.

Jenny's arms dropped, and the co-pilot reached under his seat.

"Try anything and your pilot dies," Ekaterina said. "Now, you may not care about him, so let me tell you my plan. After I finish killing him, I'll shoot up the controls so none of us can leave. Then I'll lie to the Rev, telling them that you all were my partners, and you'd double-crossed me, which was why you were trying to sell me to them. That way, if they get me, they'll get you too."

Her heart was pounding hard, but her hand was steady and so was her voice. She probably seemed calm on the outside. Her courtroom training was paying off in all sorts of ways. She hadn't expected that her ability to bluff other lawyers would come out now.

Jenny eased back into her seat. The co-pilot hadn't changed positions.

"Hands on your heads where I can see them," Ekaterina said.

Jenny put her hands on her head.

"Do it," Ekaterina said to the co-pilot. "Or do you want me to shoot you first?"

His hands went to the top of his head.

"How'd you get the gun in here?" Jenny asked. "We told you not to bring any personal items."

"I look at guns as impersonal," Ekaterina said.

The Rev ship hovered outside the portal. She knew they couldn't see inside the ship, but she felt their presence all the same.

She didn't have much time.

"Here's what we're going to do," she said. "You're going to contact the Rev and tell them there's been a change of plan."

"Lady," the pilot said. "I'm not crossing the Rev."

"Then you'll die." Ekaterina made her voice flat and matter-of-fact. Her negotiation voice, the kind she used when she was plea-bargaining with prosecutors.

"Maybe you don't understand," the pilot staid. "If I cross the Rev—"

"Maybe *you* don't understand," Ekaterina said. "You're planning to sell me to the Rev. There's nothing worse than that as far as I'm concerned. You'll do as I say and maybe you'll have a chance to get out of this. That's more than you were willing to give me."

Her hand shook with the force of her anger. She managed to steady herself, but Jenny saw the movement. The other woman's eyes got large. Ekaterina's momentary unsteadiness seemed to have frightened Jenny even more.

The co-pilot was watching all of them, his entire body tense. So far so good.

"Now," Ekaterina said, speaking slowly as if she were talking to a young child. "Here's what you're going to do. You are going to contact the Rev. You're going to tell them that you've gotten new orders. You need the yacht for another mission."

"Lady, we've never done it this way. They'll know—"

"You will tell them that you are going to eject me in one of the escape pods. All they have to do is pick it up, but they have to wait until the yacht has been gone for an hour before they do so."

"This won't work," the pilot said. "Even with an hour's lead, the yacht can't stay ahead of the Rev ships. Not on autopilot. They'll be monitoring you. They'll know exactly where you are and they'll catch you. You'll be doing this for nothing."

She was afraid of that. But she wasn't going to let him see that he had tapped into one of her main fears.

"You three will be in the pod when it's ejected," Ekaterina said. "Maybe you'll be able to find a way to get the pod out of the area before the Rev pick you up."

"That won't work." Jenny's voice was shaking. "We'll be crossing them. You know what they'll do."

"Actually," Ekaterina said, "I do. The Rev pride themselves on their fairness. Blame me for your failure. It'll be true enough. You'll be victims, according to the Rev, and they probably won't touch you."

"Probably?" The co-pilot spoke for the first time. His voice squeaked. What Ekaterina had taken for calm was extreme panic.

"Probably," Ekaterina said. "When you take a calculated gamble with the Rev, you have to realize it is, after all, a gamble. Now, contact them. Remember. If you screw with me, I'm shooting you and declaring war on the Rev. None of us get out of here alive."

"Oh, Jesus," the co-pilot said.

"Just do what she wants," Jenny said.

The pilot tapped the communications array and used the ship's call letters to contact the Rev. Ekaterina made certain his fingers touched the audio-only buttons. Most ships didn't use video imagery when communicating with alien vessels, but she wanted to make sure that the pilot wasn't trying anything sneaky.

"This had better be important." The Rev didn't even bother with a greeting.

"It is," the pilot said. "I just got a coded message from my headquarters. I need to keep the yacht."

"We have an agreement—"

"Which I'm living up to. All I wanted to do was let you know that I'm dumping her into a pod. You can pick it up an hour after we've left the area. Is that clear?"

"We'll pick it up now," the Rev said.

Ekaterina felt a chill run down her back.

"No!" The pilot sounded panicked. "There are other ships in the area. If they witness the exchange, then we'll never be able to do this again."

The Rev didn't respond immediately. Jenny shot the pilot a frightened look. The co-pilot whimpered.

"We shall do so this one time," the Rev said. "But this will not become policy, or our business is done."

"It's not policy," the pilot said. "It's just a—"

Ekaterina shoved the muzzle of the pistol against his skull.

"—blip. Something went wrong at headquarters that they want the yacht for. I don't have as much flexibility as usual."

"All right then," the Rev said. "We shall follow your terms this time. But should you try this again, you will feel our wrath."

"Yeah," the pilot said. "I know."

He signed off. Ekaterina let out a silent sigh of relief. The first part down. Now she had to get them to the pod.

"Put your hands on your head," she said to the pilot.

"Look, you heard them," he said. "They're already suspicious. I lied to them. The Rev hate it when you lie to them. When they find us, I'll make sure they know it was your fault. When they realize what happened, they're going to come after you. You might not survive the day."

She didn't answer him. She had a hunch dying was preferable to going to a Rev penal colony. At least she was going to try to get out of this. At least she had a chance.

"Put your hands on your head," she said. "I'm not telling you again."

He did. She caught a whiff of sweat mixed with fear. He was frightened too. Probably not of her, but of what would happen when the Rev opened that pod.

Even though she knew Rev law pretty well, she wasn't sure what they'd do. She'd lied about that. She might be costing these people their lives.

But that was the trade-off. Theirs for hers. They were selling her, when they were supposed to be saving her. She couldn't worry about them. Not right now.

"Get up," she said.

They did. This was going to be the difficult part. She would have to keep them under her control and make sure none of them attacked her while getting them to the pod.

She had no idea where the nearest pod was.

The pilot was taller than she was. She took a step back and pointed the pistol at all three of them.

"You've read my profile," she said, hoping that they hadn't. "You all know that I'm known for my marksmanship."

The co-pilot swallowed so hard she could see his neck move.

"You," she said to the pilot. "Open the pod."

It was a calculated gamble. If this yacht had standard features, there would be a pod near the cockpit. But this was a private yacht and, she knew, private yachts could be modified to fit the owners' needs.

The pilot glanced at his friends, as if he were asking them for help. Ekaterina waved the pistol as if she were urging him forward, but also to make herself seem just a bit more dangerous than she was.

She had no idea if it worked, but the pilot did step forward. He walked around the main console and went to a nearby wall. He pressed a hidden panel and the wall opened.

Ekaterina's hand tightened around the pistol. An escape pod should have been clearly marked.

The opening revealed the sleek black sides of an escape pod. The pod even had markings on it, showing the yacht's name and manufacturer.

"Get in," she said.

"It's built for two," the pilot said.

"I don't care if it's built for a single Disty, you're going to get in," Ekaterina said.

The pilot glanced at the others, then pushed open the sliding door on the pod. There was enough room for two people to sit comfortably. The third would have to sit on the floor or crouch. Obviously this pod was designed only for the pilot and co-pilot. Theoretically, the pods in the back—if there were pods in the back—would have more room for passengers.

"I'm not going to tell you again," Ekaterina said.

The pilot bent at the waist and extended a leg inside. He was a bit too tall for the pod's specs.

"Get on the floor," Jenny said, as if she were tired of all this drama. "I'm taking the main seat."

Then she moved in front of him and climbed onto the seat, managing the movement while keeping her hands on her head.

The pilot sat on the floor behind her, and the co-pilot took the remaining seat.

With her left hand, Ekaterina punched the pod's door closed. She kept the pistol trained on them, even after it would do no good. She wouldn't be able to shoot through the pod's hull.

She closed the panel that hid the pod and, after studying the controls for just a moment, found the nearly hidden eject button.

The yacht dipped, and she tumbled backwards, terrified for a moment that the pilot had found a way to disarm her. She slid along the floor and banged her head against the console, but somehow managed to keep hold of the pistol.

No one got out of the emergency panel. No one else moved.

Then she realized that the yacht was poorly designed. The force of the ejection caused the yacht to dip. She stood. Through the side portal, she saw the pod fall away.

She was alone on the ship.

Her head throbbed. She only had an hour to get to safety, maybe less if the Rev didn't listen to the instructions the pilot gave them.

She slid into the pilot's chair, still warm from his body, and studied the controls for a moment. Newer than she was used to. Fancier. But the basics were the same.

Before she did anything else, she found her purse, also crammed against the console, and slid the pistol back inside. Then she put her purse over her shoulder. The gun had to stay beside her at all times.

She leaned forward and took a deep breath. She had less than an hour now, and she couldn't do this on autopilot.

It was up to her.

The panel told her one thing: they weren't anywhere near Mars yet. They were about halfway between the Earth and the Moon—no man's land. No one's jurisdiction, no one's actual control. Laws did apply here, but only laws of the Earth Alliance and its allies. Not laws of a region, a nation, or a planet.

Bastards. They tried to sell her the first chance they got.

Well, she couldn't go to Earth. The Rev would expect her to do that, maybe even to go home. And the pilot would tell them she was supposed to go to Mars.

Which gave her only one viable choice—and it was a choice the Rev would figure out quickly enough. All she was doing was buying hours, maybe even seconds.

But as she had learned a few moments ago, seconds might be enough.

With the help of the yacht's computer, she plotted the shortest course to the Moon.

6

The Wygnin gave Noelle DeRicci the creeps. They stood against the walls, not quite leaning on them, and watched her. Even though she had offered them chairs—and she knew they sat in chairs; she'd been at conferences where Wygnin used chairs just the way humans did—the Wygnin refused.

They were refusing everything.

They wanted to have control of those children again. But she didn't want to give them the children. Humans did not belong with the Wygnin, no matter what the law said.

The room was small, but it was the only one available in interstellar holding. There were no windows, of course. Nothing this deep in the Port had windows and that made the institutionally gray walls seem even duller.

The table was old, made of some cheap material that had grooves etched into it, and the chairs looked as though they could collapse at any moment.

This was not the most impressive place to bring an angry group of aliens.

Five other police officers waited outside the door. An interpreter sat beside her, seemingly unconcerned with the Wygnin's insistence on standing. Two lawyers who specialized in interstellar law, with an emphasis on Wygnin, also sat at the table.

DeRicci didn't sit. She paced. She wanted out of there as badly as the Wygnin did.

The room would have been tiny with just two people inside. With this crowd, half of them Wygnin, De-Ricci felt claustrophobic. It didn't help that the lawyers had made this her game.

They had explained it to her outside: Even though they were legal advisors for Armstrong Dome, they had no authority here. All they could do was advise her. According to the law, the police had to handle this, and she was the representative of the police.

The moment the lawyers told her that, she contacted the chief and asked for someone higher up to take this case off her hands. But the chief had laughed—it sounded like a phony laugh to DeRicci—and had told her she was doing just fine.

She was qualified for this.

Qualified her ass. No one else wanted to deal with the Wygnin. Her only problem was that she didn't have enough rank to order her way out of this.

And she was too nice to dump Flint in here. He was going to be a good detective, but he was still green. He didn't even know how to speak to the Wygnin, let alone how to deal with them.

But protecting Flint from the Wygnin was only half of it. The other half was personal, something she wouldn't admit to anyone.

She didn't want to see those children. If she had to send them to Korsve, she didn't want their faces, their voices—*them*—on her conscience.

The last hour had been a grind. The interpreter was reviewing everything that had been said, to make certain both sides understood each other.

Already DeRicci was at a disadvantage. She had to take Traffic's side, and they'd already left. Their report said they'd stopped the Wygnin ship based on a tip from the ground. The immigration computer at Gagarin Dome had finally run the Wygnin identification cards and realized there were no matches for any of the human children on board the ship. The computer sent the information to Traffic, which stopped the ship, double-checked, and agreed.

In fact, one of the children claimed he was being kidnapped, and the Wygnin couldn't produce a warrant to prove otherwise. So Traffic had to bring the entire ship back to the Moon. And since Gagarin Dome wasn't equipped to handle Wygnin, they came to Armstrong—and DeRicci.

The main Wygnin, the one who had a smidgen of English, was talking animatedly to the interpreter. Korsven was a musical language. Each word had its own tone, but the tone varied depending on where the word was in a sentence. The sentences themselves had an interior musical structure, and that structure expanded depending on how many sentences were spoken in a row.

Korsven was extremely difficult to learn and it had taken DeRicci nearly a year to learn the greeting she hd spoken in the terminal. Even though she had two years of Korsven as part of her police training, she still couldn't follow this conversation.

"They say they have a warrant," the interpreter said.

The interpreter was a woman. She had had a lot of enhancements, most of which DeRicci found creepier than the Wygnin. Her hair and skin were a matching gold, and her eyes were gold-lined. She didn't look like a Wygnin—no human could—but she looked like some of the humans who had been recovered from the Wygnin. Damaged humans, many of whom spent the rest of their lives institutionalized.

DeRicci had no idea why anyone would emulate that. To her knowledge, the interpreter had never been to Korsve let alone been held prisoner by the Wygnin. It was all part of a cultural trend DeRicci didn't pretend to understand.

"They didn't produce that warrant for the border guards," DeRicci said.

The lawyers were watching and recording everything. They looked more nervous than she felt.

The Wygnin stared at all of them. DeRicci could feel the personalities behind the gaze, the constructed emotion, the purposeful sadness. She had built a barrier around herself so that she wouldn't allow it to touch her.

She knew that much at least.

The Wygnin spoke softly. The interpreter didn't look at them either. She was watching DeRicci. "They say they don't need a warrant."

"They said that in the terminal, and they're wrong. As I told them there, they're on human soil now and on our turf, we require warrants. We consider that proof."

The Wygnin leaned forward slightly, as if its upper body were pushed by a strong breeze. It continued to speak.

"They say all you have to do is look at your records. You will see that the children belong to them."

DeRicci cursed silently. That was probably true. And if it was true, then it would only be a matter of time before the children left the Moon for Korsve.

"It's not my job to look up records," DeRicci said. "You have to provide the information. That's how our rules work."

"Technically—" one of the lawyers started, and De-Ricci kicked him under the table. She knew what he was going to say. Technically, warrants were on file, and she could look them up if she wanted to.

But she wasn't going to. If these bastards wanted to take children as punishment for some crime their parents did, then let them work for it. She wasn't going to help any more than she had to.

"Technically?" the interpreter asked.

The lawyer cleared his throat. He had obviously re-thought what he was going to say. "Technically, the detective has a point. If we took the word of every person who claimed the right to someone else's child, we would be losing children off the Moon all the time. And not just to the Wygnin. Humans often claim each other's children in custody battles, and then there are the Fuertrer. . . ."

DeRicci tuned him out, resisting the urge to kick him again just to shut him up. She thought lawyers were supposed to be good liars, not dry idiots like this guy. No wonder he was working for the government instead of branching out on his own.

The Wygnin spoke again, and the interpreter nod-ded. "Both children belong to the Wygnin per rulings from the Eighth Multicultural Tribunal. They can cite the reference numbers if you would like. The rulings in both cases happened more than a decade ago."

"Again," DeRicci said, threading her hands to-gether. "It's not my job to look this crap up. They're supposed to do it and provide me with the informa-tion. If they need local legal counsel, I'm sure we can find some for them. But losing two children is not something we take lightly, and—"

"Careful, detective," one of the lawyers said quietly. Fortunately the interpreter didn't translate that, even though at least one of the Wygnin probably understood it.

DeRicci chose to ignore the advice.

"It can't be something we take lightly," DeRicci said, more to the lawyer than to the Wygnin. "For the very reasons your friend there cited. We need every detail to be exact. If we fail in this, we could hurt ourselves with our own people. Surely the Wygnin understand that."

The interpreter did relay that to the Wygnin. The lead Wygnin moved its head down and up, in an attempt at a nod.

"Would you like outside counsel?" DeRicci asked. "I'm afraid we don't have Wygnin here, but we have people who specialize in representing aliens on the Moon. I'm sure one of them would be willing to help you."

Again, the Wygnin moved its head up and down.

"I'm going to take that for a yes," DeRicci said to the interpreter.

"It is," she said.

"All right. Then I'm afraid we've got to do things by the book." DeRicci hated this part. This was what everyone else had been avoiding, this moment of confrontation.

She faced the Wygnin. The force of their magnificent eyes met her head-on. In addition to the sadness—which she was convinced was mostly manufactured—there was a deep anger. It threaded through her own. She imagined that emotional shield around her growing even thicker. She couldn't lose her temper now.

"The border guards brought you here under suspicion of kidnapping, which is a crime in Earth Alliance. Do you understand that?"

The Wygnin raised its flat hands and spoke. DeRicci

resisted the urge to look away. When the Wygnin used gestures, it was a sign of agitation.

"He's insisting that they have the proper warrants," the interpreter said.

"I know what he's insisting." DeRicci had to struggle to keep her own voice calm. Why the hell did she have to do this? Why couldn't someone else handle this mess? She was a detective, not a diplomat.

A detective with such a spotted record that no one cared if she were forced to leave the force. No one would care if she crossed the Wygnin either. She was someone no one cared about, period, and the entire department knew it.

"I'm explaining to him the things I'm required to do because of the circumstances." DeRicci folded her hands over her stomach. She didn't want to show the Wygnin any agitation at all. "Can you make that clear?"

"I don't know." The interpreter sounded uncertain. "There are some things that are hard to explain."

DeRicci narrowed her eyes. "Try."

The interpreter licked her lips and began speaking. DeRicci watched her, wondering what the interpreter thought of all of this. Her appearance marked her as one of those strange humans whose sympathies lay with the Wygnin on most things. Did she envy the children their chance at going to Korsve? Or did she understand that if the children left the Moon, their chances for a normal human life would end forever?

The Wygnin spoke in response, and then the interpreter sighed. "He says it is his belief that their warrant takes precedent over our procedures."

"But not over our laws," DeRicci said. "Remind him that according to our laws, he has no warrant. Not yet anyway."

One of the attorneys shifted in his chair. DeRicci ignored him. She knew she was on thin ground. She was going to stay there until it fell away beneath her.

The Wygnin spoke again, this time without waiting for the interpreter. DeRicci almost nodded. She'd known that the bastard understood more than he was letting on.

"He will go to the Armstrong government. He will protest to the Multicultural Tribunals," the interpreter said.

"He will need his warrants for that," DeRicci said. "I am cooperating to the fullest extent I can."

Not technically a lie. She didn't say to the fullest extent of the law.

"I have offered counsel for them," DeRicci continued, trying to sound reasonable. "But until this matter is settled, the children remain here and the Wygnin must be held under guard. I cannot bring either side together until I'm sure that all the legal requirements are met. I'm sure the Wygnin can understand that. After all, their laws have strict requirements as well."

"Detective," one of the lawyers said, his voice filled with caution.

If she had known they were gong to interfere with her bluffs, she would not have allowed them in the room. Next time, the lawyers waited outside.

She didn't even acknowledge him. Instead, she went to the door, signaling the end of the meeting. "If this matter is settled in the Wygnin's favor, the Earth Alliance as represented by Armstrong Dome will be happy to turn the children over to the Wygnin."

The interpreter was repeating everything she said, but her gaze was now on the floor. No one was looking at the Wygnin. No one except DeRicci.

"Until then, I will make sure you're comfortable

and your needs are met. If you need anything, let us know." She paused, staring into all those golden eyes. It took all of her strength to do so. "And remember, if you decide to leave the children here, you're free to go at any time."

DeRicci let herself out of the room. The lawyers followed. One of them caught up with her. The nervous one. The one she'd kicked.

"Dangerous game you're playing," he said.

"How would you feel if it was your kid the Wygnin had?"

He shrugged. "I wouldn't've crossed the Wygnin in the first place."

"What guarantee do we have that these parents did?"

"The Wygnin are careful. They usually don't make mistakes."

"Usually?" She increased her pace slightly. "You want someone to lose a child because the Wygnin are *usually* careful?"

"If the Wygnin see you as an impediment, you could get in trouble."

"With them or with Earth Alliance?"

"Try all of the above," he said. "And throw in Armstrong Dome and your department for good measure. Do you really want to risk your career on this? Or worse?"

Then he walked past her. The other lawyer passed her too, shooting her a look over his shoulder that seemed like sympathy.

DeRicci was shaking. The lawyers were right. She knew they were right. But she couldn't stand this part of her job. The laws weren't right either.

No child should be forced to pay for his parents' crimes. No matter what Wygnin law said. No matter what the agreements were between cultures. No matter how the damn courts ruled.

The courts didn't have to handle these things. Neither did the lawmakers or the diplomats who made the agreements. Even the heads of government, the chiefs of police and departmental supervisors stayed away.

Leaving people in the field to handle it, and to suffer if things went wrong. People in the field who had no clout, no authority, nothing except a law they didn't believe in.

She was glad she hadn't seen those kids. At least their faces wouldn't haunt her when she failed.

The children had to stay in holding. It was a depressing gray suite in the basement of the Armstrong City Complex. The suite had no windows, a single door that led into a narrow hallway, and a black reflecting wall that hid a viewing booth beyond.

The furnishings in the living area were sparse: a dilapidated couch, a thin rug, and some pillows thrown into corners. A toy box sat beneath the reflecting wall, but most of the toys were broken.

Jasper didn't seem interested in them anyway. He was more concerned about the fact that his border guard had left. A couple from Social Services had arrived. Flint had met them before on human cases here on the Moon.

Opal and John Harken. They specialized in taking care of children in crisis, particularly children who had to remain in police custody while battles shook out. Many children got to go into foster homes, but it seemed like an increasing number didn't. They had to remain in this dismal suite or one just like it while parents fought over jurisdiction or until claims from people in outlying colonies were answered.

When Flint arrived, Opal Harken had taken the infant from him and put him into the crib kept in the nearest bedroom. Flint had watched her—had watched the boy, actually—as if he could protect the child by staring at him.

The boy was gone, but Flint could still smell him, talcum and that sweet smell that all human children under the age of three had. Flint had been holding him for so long that the child's scent had gotten on his uniform.

Opal left the back door open and took a seat beside the crib, so that she would be there when the boy woke up. John Harken sat cross-legged on a pillow in the corner of the living room and watched Flint interact with Jasper—or try to.

Jasper was having a hard time controlling his tears.

The Harkens had already sent for a doctor, just to make sure both boys were well treated by the Wygnin. But John Harken had told Flint outside that Jasper's reaction wasn't that unusual. Children his age who were abducted seemed to lose all their moorings and didn't know how to cope.

Flint was sitting on the arm of the ruined couch, Jasper beside him. The boy had sores on the backs of his hands and arms from enhancements that the Wygnin had removed. Obviously Jasper's parents had some money; they had hooked their son up to various links and to a security system that the Wygnin had somehow circumvented.

Flint held out little hope that the Wygnin had left Jasper's identity chip. All children born into the Earth Alliance got one, but not all parents kept the information updated. Still, it would give Flint a place to start.

He'd activated one of the readers on the palm of his own hand, and he kept his fingers curled over it until Jasper gave him permission to try.

"I don't want to hurt you," Flint said again. "I just want to see if you have an identity chip."

"I'm Jasper," the boy said. He kept his face averted whenever he spoke to Flint, just as Flint had seen DeRicci do with the Wygnin. He didn't know if the boy did that because he was nervous or because the Wygnin had already gotten to him on a deep level.

"I know," Flint said. "I want to find out who your parents are. I want to let them know you're all right."

Jasper kept his head bent. A tear fell off his cheek onto the back of his hand.

"I'm sure they'll want to hear."

Jasper shook his head.

He frowned. Was he wrong? Had this boy been picked up for a reason other than familial crime against the Wygnin?

He decided to try a different tack. "How did the Wygnin find you?"

"I don't know." The words came out small, choked, as if Jasper had been wondering that himself.

"What happened when they found you?" Flint asked.

Jasper bit his lower lip. Blood oozed between his teeth. Flint wasn't even sure the boy noticed.

Had the Wygnin killed his parents? Or had he been on his own before that?

It wasn't like the Wygnin to kill adults. The Wygnin didn't kill anyone for anything. It wasn't part of their code. They did what they believed just. They took something of value when something of value was taken from them. But they did not take a life for a life.

"Jasper," Flint said. "Sometimes it helps to talk about these things."

"I just woke up," he said. "I woke up and they were there. I thought it was a dream and then they grabbed me and I didn't even have time to scream. Maybe if I screamed. . . ."

He stopped himself and shook his head.

"Maybe if you screamed," Flint prompted.

"I'd still be home." Jasper said that last in a whisper.

"We might be able to get you home now," Flint said.

"No!" Jasper turned so fast that Flint wasn't prepared for it. The boy grabbed his arm. Small fingers dug into his skin, pressing some of his police enhancements against bone. "Don't. Please. Don't take me home."

"Why not?" Flint asked. "What's wrong with home?"

"Nothing." Jasper's eyelashes stuck together like little spikes. His eyes were red. "Home's perfect."

"Then why not go?"

"Because." His grip remained tight.

"Because why?"

"Because then they'll realize they got the wrong guy."

John Harken made a slight movement across the room. It was surprise. Flint recognized it. He felt the same thing himself. But he didn't dare move. It was the first time anyone had gotten the boy to speak.

"Who's the right guy?" Flint asked.

Jasper shook his head.

"Jasper, I can't help you if I don't know."

The boy's eyes narrowed and then filled, but this time the tears didn't fall. "They said it wasn't my fault."

"Who said?"

"Those creatures."

"What wasn't your fault?"

"Why they came. They came because someone else was bad."

"Who?"

"I don't know." His voice rose into a wail. "I don't know, but what if they make another mistake? June, she's only three, and Jocelyn, she's just a baby, and if they get taken, they're not going to understand. At least I understand, Mister."

"I don't," Flint said, and that was partly true. He wasn't sure he understood what the boy was getting at.

"Those Wygnin. They steal children, Mister. And they don't like it when people don't do what they want. They got really mad when I talked to those cops. I shouldn't have said nothing."

"If you hadn't said anything," Flint said gently, "you'd still be with the Wygnin."

"But they told me I'd still have to go with them. They said the cops were wrong. And I'm scared." Although his voice had stopped shaking. It seemed as if, now that he had started to speak, he was getting a bit calmer.

Flint nodded.

"What if they don't want me anymore?" Jasper asked. "What if they think I'm bad? They might take my sisters, just to show me. You know?"

Flint understood the fear. He also knew the only way to combat it would be through logic. He had to find out who Jasper was, and in order to do that, he had to get past the boy's terror.

"The Wygnin won't take your sisters," Flint said.

Jasper's grip tightened. It felt like he was cutting off the circulation in Flint's arm. "How do you know?"

"Because," he said, "if they wanted your sisters, they would have already taken them. The Wygnin were in your house that night, weren't they?"

Jasper nodded.

"Before you woke up, right?"

Jasper nodded again.

"So they'd probably looked at everyone before they decided on you."

"But what if Mom and Dad come, and they leave the girls home, and the Wygnin get them? It'll be all my fault."

This wasn't his fault, but Flint didn't know how to explain that. He didn't want to scare the boy any more. If Jasper was who the Wygnin wanted, then one of his parents had done something wrong. And if he wasn't, then all Flint would be doing in telling the boy that was setting a fear in deep, a fear that any time his parents made a mistake, the Wygnin would come.

"We'll make sure someone protects the girls while your parents are gone." Flint could guarantee that if Jasper was from anywhere in the Earth Alliance. While the negotiations with the Wygnin went on, all the children could get protection, even though it was usually the first-born that the Wygnin wanted.

"Promise?" Jasper whispered.

"I promise." Flint had a small window. He could feel it. He had to take advantage of it now. "May I see if you have a chip now?"

Jasper took a shaky breath and let go of Flint's arm. Flint put his hand on the boy's shoulder. He felt a slight click, then saw the information float across his eye. Jasper Wilder, followed by an address in Tycho

Crater. The information had been updated recently. It was current.

"Thank you," Flint said.

Jasper seemed calm now. It was an eerie calm, as if he had no emotions left. "The Wygnin said I belonged to them. Is that true?"

Flint had learned early in his space cop days that lying about such things did no good. Telling only part of the truth was all right, but lying was the worst thing he could do.

John Harken watched intently.

"I don't know if it's true," Flint said.

"So I might have to go back with them?" Jasper asked.

"That's what we're trying to find out."

Jasper's lower lip trembled. "How could I belong to them? I don't even know them."

"I know," Flint said.

"You're gonna save me, right?"

Flint let out a small sigh. That was a sentence he knew he'd never forget, no matter how this went.

"Right?" There was desperation in Jasper's voice.

"I don't know." Flint lightly touched the boy's bruised hands. "But I'm gonna try."

7

The First Rank Detective Unit had been locked down for the night. Flint pressed his palm against the door. The lock registered his print, along with his body temperature and the movement of blood within his veins, verifying that it not only had the correct hand, but that the owner of that hand was alive. There were a thousand ways to circumvent such a lock, but thwarting all of them took so much technological advancement that the Dome couldn't afford the upgrades.

The Unit was on the fifth floor of the First Detective Division. The law enforcement buildings encircled the Armstrong City Complex. In the Moon's early days, when Armstrong was still an Earth colony, manpower was scarce. The Dome's police force found itself not just monitoring inside the dome, but activity outside—and activity in orbit around the Moon itself. Those duties got grandfathered into the force, and now law enforcement had become one of the most important professions in Armstrong.

This part of the Unit, where lower ranking detectives—first year like himself, and those who couldn't move higher, like DeRicci—worked, was the largest section. Still, each detective had his own office, small as they were. Assistants, most of whom were hired outside the police force, sat in the grouped desks in the center.

Flint walked past the assistants' desks. They were clean, surface computers off, lights turned down. The assistants were supposed to field tips and leads, and do basic legal research into the various laws that the detectives were supposed to uphold, but more often, they did a lot of the legwork and didn't get paid for it.

Flint had examined that job years ago, when he first thought of entering the force. In those days, he was more suited to the assistant job. He had been designing computer systems, and one of his specialties had been creating hacker-proof security programs. Not that any system could ever be completely hacker-proof, but most could be upgraded.

In order to make something hacker-proof, he had had to learn how to hack, and he had been good at it. When he first applied with the force, they wanted to use those skills.

He had been the one who had insisted on Traffic. Something different. Something far away from the City Complex, and the memories it held.

Flint pushed open the door to the small office he had just off DeRicci's slightly larger one. Inside, he kept a handful of mementos: his crystal graduation certificates—the first from the police academy and the second from his successful detective's training—and tokens from important cases he'd had as a space cop, from a tiny necklace an Ebe child had given him when he saved its parents to a seashell he'd confiscated from a smuggler carrying Earth artifacts.

But he kept his most important memento in the upper left-hand drawer. A small stuffed dog, its fur rubbed smooth, its hind leg thin from the grip of a tiny hand. He hardly ever looked at it and almost never touched it. But knowing it was there kept him honest and reminded him of all the reasons he'd chosen this crazy profession, all the reasons he stayed.

He sat down and rubbed his eyes with the thumb and forefinger of his right hand. As soon as he left the holding suite, he had contacted Jasper's parents, Jonathon and Justine Wilder. They had been ecstatic, planning to get the first available shuttle out of Tycho Crater. Before he called them, he had contacted the Tycho authorities and explained his problem; they promised to send someone to the Wilder house to make certain that the younger children were protected.

That was all Flint could do in that case.

It was the baby that worried him—and not just because of the reminders of Emmeline. The boy had had a chip in his left shoulder, just as Jasper had, identifying him as Ennis Kanawa of Gagarin Dome. Young Ennis's mother had answered Flint's call and had expressed her profound gratitude that the authorities in Armstrong had found her son.

She had not asked why the boy had been with the Wygnin.

That disturbed him. He hoped it was an oversight, that she was so joyful to know her son was alive that she had forgotten to ask the next question. But his instincts told him more was going on than that, and he worried that he had just given a family some false hope.

Flint glanced through the adjoining door. DeRicci was not in her office. She hadn't answered his pages, so he'd hoped he would find her here. He wasn't surprised that he didn't, just disappointed. He wanted to know how her afternoon with the Wygnin had gone.

But her lights were still on, which meant she had

been there recently. So was her surface computer, the one the department insisted all the detectives use for major information searches and for record-keeping. Any work done on the surface computers automatically got recorded in the department's database, which made things easier for the prosecutors come court time.

Flint hated the surface system, with its slower access rate and its inconvenient screen, but he understood the necessity for it. He'd seen more than a few cases shot down because the investigating officer had done the work on his own time and with his own systems instead of the department's.

The theory was that personal links could be modified. The department's couldn't. It wasn't true, any more than taking a palm print to unlock a door prevented a criminal from finding a way around the system, but it sounded nice to a jury.

Flint punched on his surface computer. As he had hoped, a message waited for him on the office system. It was from forensics. They had identified the victims of the Disty vengeance killings. Files were attached.

Flint opened the files and saw faces that had no longer existed when he found the bodies. Two men and a woman, former college friends from Stanford who were on their first trip off Earth. All of them were midlevel managers with no family who lived in various parts of the world.

As he flipped through the bits of information that the system gathered from the identification chips in the bodies, the records that supposedly said who a person was without giving a sense of him at all, he noted something odd. None of the three had space piloting certificates.

In fact, none of them had any piloting certifications

at all, whether in-atmosphere flight or orbital flight. Their jobs were not mechanical in any way. They were supervisors, people who had no idea how things ran.

Flint leaned forward. This information intrigued him. It meant that these three hadn't flown the yacht. They were passengers.

The crew was missing.

He opened a new window on his screen, searching through the day's databases. He found no trace of an escape pod rescue anywhere near the Moon. In fact, the day's databases showed no recent escape pod rescues at all.

Had these three been prisoners, not passengers? That wasn't the Disty style. A Disty vengeance killing didn't happen in space unless it couldn't be avoided. The Disty liked the vengeance killings to be public, as a deterrent. That was probably why the ship had been on a collision course with the Moon, so that someone would find it and then find the bodies.

He shook his head and stood, the restlessness remaining. If the Disty found the three passengers along with the crew, no matter who had committed the crime, the Disty would have killed everyone. The crew would have deserved death for helping the criminals avoid the Disty.

If the Disty had killed the crew, then those bodies would have been on the yacht. But the evidence suggested there had been a battle and during it—or before—the crew, and possibly other passengers, had left the ship.

The Disty would have gone after the pods, and if they found the pods, they would have brought the crew and passengers back to the yacht, killing them all there and then launching it toward the Moon.

Flint cursed silently. He wondered if forensics was

done cleaning the ship. He wanted to hack into the ship's systems. He was sure he would be able to use the ship's records—both official and unofficial—to let him know where the yacht had been when the Disty found it. Then he could have that area checked for pods, pod pickups, and space debris.

The thought of the Disty made him glance at the files again. Mid-level managers, one from New Orleans, another from Nice, and the third from Teheran. None of them had been off-Earth before. No one in their families had been off-Earth. Their companies—three separate Earth-based and Earth-bound companies—had no ties to the Disty.

The three did not work in areas that dealt with international, let alone interstellar, business.

The Disty had no reason to target these people. The Disty had a strong personal code. They did not commit random killings and did not tolerate unnecessary violence among their own in any way. There had not been a Disty-upon-Disty murder in nearly a thousand years.

One of those three had to have some tie to the Disty, something Flint could find. It wasn't in the records—and it should have been.

The Disty wouldn't stop a space yacht and brutally murder three people, leaving them in vengeance killing positions, for no reason at all. The Disty always had a reason.

Always.

Flint ran a hand through his blond curls. The three dead people's records were pretty straightforward. They were in order, as if someone had tidied them to make an application of some sort. Usually when files got opened, pieces carried information tags from various other sources—loan applications, messy divorces, legal actions.

All three files were clean, and that just wasn't normal.

He sat back down and went through the files again. No information tags. Not a one. No hint of anyone looking up these files before the coroner's office did that afternoon.

The hair rose on the back of his neck. He searched for ghosts in the files, to see if someone had been tampering with them, or overlaying these files on older ones. Nothing.

These files looked new.

He started to look for origin dates on the files, then took his hands off the screen as if he'd been burned. To do that work properly, he'd need permission from the creator of each bit of information—the hospitals where these three had been born, Stanford University, even the Division of Motor Vehicles in their various hometowns to verify their aircar permits. That would be the only way for anything he discovered to hold up in court.

But he was beginning to suspect he wouldn't need court.

Still, he didn't dare risk blowing an investigation on a hunch. He'd have to use a different system to hack through the protective walls, and then, if he found something he needed, he'd have to recreate his research—legally—on his own system.

DeRicci wouldn't approve, but she wasn't there. For the first time, he got to investigate something on his own, using his methods. And he had a hunch about what he was going to find.

•

8

Ekaterina had strapped herself into the pilot's chair, and she was glad she had. She was having trouble with attitude control. It took all of her training just to keep the yacht from spinning. It kept wobbling, which the computer—on audio now that she had finally found the controls—kept telling her would be resolved if she traveled at a slower speed.

The computer also told her that the fastest the ship could go on autopilot was two-thirds of maximum, and she needed maximum right now.

At least the pilot hadn't lied to her about that.

She kept checking the ship's flight plan. She had plugged it into the computer and set the course on automatic, hoping that the ship would steer itself in that direction—and it seemed to be doing so. But with as many controls as she was pushing, she was afraid she would knock it off-line and not notice.

The worst thing she could do would be to overshoot the Moon and head out into the bright nowhere. She hadn't checked the fuel beyond a cursory request to the computer, asking if there was enough to take her at maximum speed to the Moon. There was.

But how much would there be if she missed? She had no idea.

She had forgotten how complicated piloting was, even with computerized help. And the computer on this yacht wasn't nearly as sophisticated as the computer she had used decades ago, when she'd been an orbital pilot.

Granted, those ships had to fall under government regulations, and any mistakes she made could be corrected by the computer, so that no tourists would be lost. No one wanted a scandal. But she would have thought that a newer yacht would have a more sophisticated system.

All she could figure was that this one had been stripped down, either so that no one would know what the hell the pilot did, or so that the ship cost less.

She kept looking at the portals, although the blackness outside told her nothing. She expected to see the orange and blue stripes of the Rev ship, knowing that it had found her after all.

The yacht had no weapons. All she had to defend herself was a silly little laser pistol and a lot of moxie. She couldn't even risk getting out of the pilot's chair to search the cabins, to see if the crew had brought their own weaponry.

Not that it mattered. The moment the Rev boarded the yacht, they won. She had to keep them away from her, and that meant speeding to the Moon.

Maybe she could throw herself on the mercy of one of the Moon's governments and hope that it would protect her. But she knew the chances of that were slim.

The chances of survival were slim.

But there was a chance. And that was all that mattered.

The neighborhood had always seemed run-down to Jamal. Run-down for Gagarin Dome standards, which meant the houses were small and the Moon clay adobe was flaking. Some of the yards had the typical desert plants found throughout this part of the Moon, but most of those plants were dying. Only a few seemed to survive, in houses that looked a little less decrepit than the others, and those were the houses that he felt most comfortable approaching.

The others made him nervous.

Such a come-down from those heady days before he went to Korsve. He'd owned two houses of his own and a vacation condo, all in different outlying colonies. He even had use of the company's various space yachts so that he could go back and forth between his homes.

His stomach twisted. He'd been through the neighborhood three times, searching, asking questions. A handful of friends were helping him, as were some of the local cops. They all had different theories on what had happened to Ennis.

Some of his friends believed that Ennis, who was just learning to walk, had gotten out on his own. Dylani fiercely denied that as if, somehow, it reflected badly on them as parents. She had no idea that Jamal's own decision to become a parent was worse.

Why had he thought he was safe?

Denial. He had been warned about it in that short psych session he'd had before his Disappearance, and he had figured he would never experience it. He was a smart man. He knew the risks.

But he also remembered the service telling him that if no one found him in ten years, they probably wouldn't find him. At that point, he could risk starting a life again. Not returning to his old life—he could never do that. But he could start over, as if the past had never happened.

And he had.

Ennis was proof that he had.

And proof that the service had been wrong.

The cops, on the other hand, believed him when he said he thought someone took the child. The problem was, that placed some of the suspicion squarely on him. A lot of parents said children were kidnapped, only to have the kid's body turn up under some cactus plant years later.

He didn't dare tell them the truth, that under multicultural law, he had no right to Ennis, to his own child. His first-born.

Jamal trudged past the last house on the makeshift block. The thin light of day, bolstered by additional lights built into the Dome, had long since faded into the darkness of night. Soon the Earth would rise, and he would see the place his people came from, the place he had never visited and had always meant to back in the days when he had money and believed he could travel.

Before Ennis. Before Dylani. Before the Moon and all of this.

The worst part would be telling her. She would never forgive him, not entirely. Even if she stayed with him. She loved him, he knew that. But her love for Ennis was something else entirely, something fierce and protective. Something he'd always slightly feared.

And this was why.

There were still some police-issue aircars in front of his home. It looked strange to see vehicles parked on the narrow street. In this part of Gagarin, people didn't own vehicles. They used public transport.

The cars were empty, though, the police out searching, as they had been since they'd been called. The only person in the house would be Dylani. A policewoman had offered to stay with her, as had a few of their friends, but Dylani would have none of it.

She wanted to face this alone, without sympathy or pity.

The only reason she stayed home was the slim chance that Ennis would come back on his own. Or someone would call the house system instead of contacting her or Jamal directly. Jamal knew she was expecting a ransom demand—not that they could do anything about that. They barely had enough money to buy groceries every week. He had no idea how they would raise money to ransom their son.

But, of course, the Wygnin would never demand ransom. It was a non-issue, something else he would have to tell her.

The small patch of dirt that passed for their yard bore the marks of dozens of footprints. He hadn't planted anything there, not because he felt he couldn't maintain a desert garden—he could—but because most of the plants in such a garden were sharp, and not recommended for children.

Jamal walked up the single step and pushed open the front door. It hadn't been latched.

The house still smelled of reconstituted meat, garlic, and tomato sauce. The table was still set, the wineglasses looking sad now, the reminder of a quiet night that had never happened, a normal life that might never be normal again.

He heard a choking sound, faint and indistinct. Hope rose inside him—Ennis?—and then he realized that the sound was adult.

Jamal ran through the living room until he reached his bedroom. Dylani sat on the bed. She was sobbing and trying to suppress the sound by keeping her mouth closed, her hands over her entire face.

He stopped in the door, afraid to go farther. Afraid of what she knew, of what might have been discovered.

Maybe the police had found Ennis and Dylani knew and she had shooed them all out of there so she could be alone.

"Dylani?" he asked.

She looked up at him, her face swollen and red, her skin streaked with tears. "Jamal."

She stood and nearly collapsed. He went to her, caught her halfway, and had to hold her up.

"They found him."

His breath caught in his throat. They found Ennis and she was crying. It was worse than he thought. Worse than he had imagined it could be. At least if the Wygnin took him, Ennis would have been alive somewhere. He wouldn't be entirely human anymore, but he would have been alive.

"Where?" He was amazed the word came out.

"Armstrong Dome," she said. "They called."

He hadn't expected that. He had been so braced for the worst that it took a moment for her words to register. "Armstrong Dome. How'd he get there?"

"Border patrol pulled over a Wygnin ship." Her body trembled. "What would the Wygnin want with Ennis?"

He was glad he wasn't looking at her, that he had her in his arms so that she couldn't see his face. "They took Ennis away from the Wygnin?"

"For now. But we have to hurry. We have to get there soon because there's some kind of mix-up." She stepped back, wiped her hand over her face. "Sorry. Sorry about the tears. The relief—"

"What kind of mix-up?" Jamal's voice sounded harsher than it ever had. He couldn't control that. He could barely control himself.

She wiped her hand on the side of her pants, an absentminded gesture. She was studying him, clearly astonished at his reaction. "I don't understand all of it. They wouldn't explain much. Not over a link. We have to go, Jamal. Now."

He nodded, still feeling cold. It wasn't over. All they'd had was a reprieve.

And even that might be a curse in disguise.

9

Flint walked around the floor, seeing who else was working in-house. Normally detectives did very little of their work in the Unit. They left memos for the assistants to track things down, and then passed on the assistants' work as their own.

Six detectives were filing reports and using the system to work on something. Flint nodded to them as he passed. Six detectives was a large percentage of the evening shift, something he hadn't expected.

Still, most of them were working far enough away from him. They wouldn't notice anything he did, and if they did, they probably wouldn't think anything of it.

He went to an assistant's desk not far from his office. He'd learned as a space cop that if he was going to misuse a system, the best way to do it was with someone else's password in a third person's station. That way, if someone felt the need to double-check the work (and not too many people did), he'd find the password of someone who was not in the building on the station of someone else who was not in the building—at least according to the palm records at the Unit's door.

Flint wouldn't be getting them in trouble, and he'd

be protecting his own ass while getting information he needed for his investigation.

He tapped the screen, then added the password of one of the junior assistants, a woman who was dumb enough to use her initials—all five of them. He liked her password the best because it was easy to remember, but most of the assistants had simple passwords. They used birthdates or middle names or the names of children. Those assistants who did follow departmental regulations and used a randomly generated number often kept that number hidden inside their desk. Neither system protected the assistants well, but Flint had used it to his advantage more than once—and had never told DeRicci.

He knew what the forensic file said on those three bodies, so he didn't even call it up again. One of the many things the forensic report had deemed classified was the DNA of the victims.

Law enforcement couldn't use DNA as a source of identification if other sources of identification were present. Even if there weren't other sources of identification, the series of legal twists and turns it took to get DNA I.D. were tremendous. It would take Flint nearly a week to get permission to use DNA I.D. on these three victims if forensics hadn't been able to get a file on them.

But forensics had a file, so he was blocked from using the DNA I.D.—at least, legally.

However, that I.D. would probably tell him a lot more than the identity chips. The Disty didn't have such rules against DNA I.D. It probably hadn't even occurred to them that such rules existed on the Moon.

Flint was going to ignore the legal part of it for the moment.

He opened the HazMat report, which had also been

filed that afternoon. HazMat had to report on all substances found inside a potentially contaminated environment—including DNA. In this case, they had used the blood from all three victims, searching for contaminants, viruses, bacteriological agents, microorganisms, and other things that could spread rapidly throughout domed cities like those on the Moon.

Flint skipped most of the bloodwork information, going instead to that most important information, the DNA I.D. He copied all three of those I.D.s and put them into the Earth Alliance DNA database.

Theoretically, all humans kept their DNA on file with Earth Alliance. Some people could opt to use DNA as a permanent I.D. Others chose identity numbers and some chose to use their names and addresses only. But no matter what people chose, their DNA was on file with the Earth Alliance database.

It only took a moment for the DNA database to kick out these I.D.s—and they were different than the hard-copy I.D.s found with the bodies.

Flint was not surprised.

All three of the victims had been outside the solar system, and all of them had been in Disty-occupied space. He took the names the system had kicked back—Ruth Stern, Sara Zaetl, and Isaac Rothman—and plugged them into the law enforcement database.

He was surprised to get an immediate hit. He had expected it to take some time.

Apparently there were outstanding warrants for Stern, Zaetl, and Rothman, warrants issued by the Disty fifteen years before. Flint frowned at the dates. Fifteen years was a long time to be on the run. Usually victims of vengeance killings died shortly after the warrants were issued, before they could become Disappeareds.

The hit came from Amoma, the fourth planet in the Disty home solar system. Amoma had had human colonies for more than a hundred years. Those humans had managed, for the most part, to co-exist peacefully with the Disty, the way humans and Disty did on Mars.

But the court documents were very clear. Sara Zaetl had murdered a Disty security guard. She had claimed that she did so because he had attacked her and she was acting in self-defense. But anyone who saw a full-grown human woman next to a full-grown Disty male knew who was physically in charge of that encounter.

The Disty were tiny and weak compared with humans. Whenever the Disty exacted punishments against the humans, like vengeance killings, the Disty overwhelmed the humans with large numbers and superior weapons.

There had been only one Disty attacking Sara Zaetl, who was, at the time, eighteen yeas old. She had killed him, leaving behind his family of seven, his employer (which to the Disty was like leaving family), and a network of friends larger than the population of Armstrong Dome.

The Disty had been killed outside his place of employment—an entertainment center often frequented by human teenagers. Zaetl had a history of petty larceny and breaking and entering. She might indeed have felt threatened by the Disty security guard, who was carrying a weapon, but somehow she managed to disarm him and use the weapon on him.

If she had killed him in self-defense, which, given the circumstances as he read them, Flint doubted, Sara Zaetl handled the aftermath wrong. She should have contacted the authorities herself and waited for them, explaining the situation.

Instead, she fled the scene. She asked for and got

the help of her three cousins, who then hid her until they found a Disappearance service for her. The service insisted on Disappearing all of them, and they vanished.

The trials, first on Amoma, and then before the Third Multicultural Tribunal, which issued the warrants, were held in absentia. Sara Zaetl's self-defense claim came from a court-appointed attorney who may or may not have been telling her story. She was no longer around to defend herself.

Flint leaned back and rubbed his eyes with his thumb and forefinger. He could guess who two of the cousins were—Ruth Stern and Isaac Rothman—but he didn't know who the third was. He sighed. He hadn't liked what he found so far. He couldn't imagine that he would like the next part either.

There was nothing else in the record under those names—because the four had Disappeared, successfully, it seemed. He did search the indictments that landed before the Third Multicultural Tribunal at that time, and found the third cousin: Ilana Rothman. He also noted that someone had marked that case closed.

It took a bit more searching to learn why. A few weeks ago, Ilana Rothman had been killed in New Orleans, Louisiana. She had been living in an apartment building in the French Quarter along with three friends who weren't home at the time of her death. The friends, two women and a man, weren't seen again.

But Ilana Rothman's death had also been a Disty vengeance killing. Apparently, the others had avoided the Disty in New Orleans, found a new Disappearance service, and fled Earth—which explained their newly minted identities and the fact that the information all seemed to be in such perfect order.

The case was clear-cut. He wasn't looking at a crime. He was looking at the crime's punishment. The Disty had every right to kill the three of them.

But he had a feeling something was off about this entire scenario. He just hadn't figured out yet what it was.

He stretched his arms above his head, feeling tired for the first time that day. This case had turned out just as DeRicci had predicted it would.

Then he froze, hands still extended mid-stretch. He still hadn't solved the mystery of the missing pods or the crew. He went back to the records, searching through the properly messy individual records of the three bodies he'd found on the ship.

As young people, none of them had flight training. He tried running the DNA scan again, to see if he got other hits from the three of them, to see if he could learn their identities for the fifteen years they were on the run.

Either Sara had gone straight and her cousins had kept her in line or they had managed to avoid DNA scans during their exile. He found nothing.

But those escape pods bothered him. Even though Sara Zaetl's body—the worst of the three—had been discovered in the pilot's chair, he had a hunch she hadn't been flying that yacht. If she had, the Disty would never have boarded. She wouldn't have let them.

Or if she couldn't avoid losing the ship to them, she would probably have taken one of the pods herself and done so in a way that would have made it difficult for the Disty to track her.

But she hadn't. She had stayed. And, at least as a young woman, sacrificing herself for others hadn't been her style.

Flint would keep the space cops and border guards searching for the escape pods just to satisfy his own curiosity. But that would be all it was.

He knew who killed Sara Zaetl, Isaac Rothman, and Ruth Stern. He also knew why they died, and he knew that no legal action was necessary on the part of Armstrong Law Enforcement.

Once he got the official information from the Disty, he would have to close the file. This case was solved.

Dylani huddled against Jamal, her body warm and comforting in sleep. Jamal sat upright in the train seat, staring out the window at the darkness. Sometimes he saw blurred shapes—maybe a rock outcropping or a damaged structure.

The high-speed train between Gagarin and Armstrong Domes took a direct route through a lot of unpopulated territory. There was nothing out there except Moon dust, rocks, and craters. He used to love going through here on cheaper slower-speed trains in the daylight, so that he could view the native scenery.

He enjoyed the Moon's starkness. But not now. He couldn't feel anything right now.

Dylani was exhausted. So was he. But she was able to sleep because she was relieved. She thought they would get Ennis back. Jamal hadn't explained anything to her. He wasn't sure how to do it without putting their relationship in jeopardy. Even if they got Ennis back, through luck maybe or some sort of legal cunning, he wasn't sure Dylani would forgive him.

The very fact of Ennis's birth had put the boy in danger, and Jamal had known that. He hadn't told Dylani of the risks—and she was a woman who wanted to know everything. She was a woman who prepared for everything.

She wouldn't have had a child in this circumstance. He knew it, and he knew she probably wouldn't forgive him for this.

But he didn't know how he'd make it through the next few days without her wise counsel and advice. In many ways, she was the smarter of the two of them, certainly the most logical. She saw holes in arguments he hadn't even imagined. She had an incisive mind, one he wanted to consult now.

He wasn't sure how much he could tell her. She had been raised on the Moon. Her contact with aliens was limited and she thought his was too. How could he tell her even generally about the Wygnin? How could he tell her that this might be a slight reprieve while the Wygnin found a way to prove they had a right to his son?

The only hope he had was that the Wygnin had been brought to Armstrong Dome. Maybe they had the wrong warrant. Or maybe there was some kind of legal snafu, the kind that would give Ennis back to him permanently. Some kind of technicality that would give him his son back for good.

The police wouldn't have called him otherwise, right? They would have checked the warrants, seen that they were in order, and sent the Wygnin on their way.

It was a small hope but it was hope. Jamal kept going over and over the possibilities in his mind, reviewing them the way that fingers played with a stone found in a pocket.

He needed the hope right now. Without it, he would drive himself crazy with what-ifs and what-could-have-beens.

He wasn't sure that he would have been able to go to Armstrong Dome without that sliver of hope. He wasn't sure he would be able to see Ennis, knowing that this time he would never see his son again. Knowing that this time he would have to say good-bye.

The space yacht hurled itself toward the Moon. The computer informed Ekaterina that the yacht would be inside the Moon's territory in a matter of minutes.

The ache in her head grew at the thought. She had spent so much time trying to control the damn ship that she hadn't considered her next step.

She couldn't very well go in there and say she was Ekaterina Maakestad and in need of asylum. No Earth Alliance affiliate would grant that. They didn't dare, no matter what her circumstance.

The I.D. chip in her shoulder hadn't been reprogrammed yet—that was something which was supposed to happen just before she left the comforts of the yacht, and the only identification she had listed her as Greta Palmer, a textile worker on her way to Mars.

What would a textile worker be doing on a yacht and how did she get so far astray? If she were heading to Mars, how did she end up on the Moon?

The ship tilted dangerously, about to go into a spin she wasn't sure she could pull out of. She pushed controls, praying she was doing the right thing. She was dizzy and slightly spacesick and scared.

She hadn't seen any evidence that the Rev were behind her, but they had to be. They wouldn't let her go this easily.

Had the pilot given the Rev the Greta Palmer name? Did the Rev know who she was supposed to be as well as who she was? Was the pilot that organized?

She didn't know. But she would have to take that gamble and she would have to take it soon.

The computer beeped at her. "Entering Moon Occupied Space," the androgynous voice said. "Ship and personal identification required. Official Channel has been opened."

She hadn't programmed the yacht's computer to automatically open communications with anyone. That had to already be in the system.

It probably was in most spacefaring vehicles' systems—a fail-safe, to protect a pilot from herself.

"Identification is legally required." It sounded as if there were annoyance in the computer's voice, although she knew there couldn't be. "The proper communication channel is open."

If she waited, would the computer's instructions get simpler and simpler? Would the computer finally do the introducing for her or automatically turn her and the ship over to the authorities?

She had no idea, but now was the time to take action.

One step at a time. One problem at a time. If she took this moment by moment, she might have a chance to survive.

That was the lesson she had learned on this yacht. That was the lesson she had to take with her.

"Warning." The computer's tone had become more strident. "You must—"

She hit the communications button, cutting off the computer.

"Mayday!" she cried, as loud as she could. "Help me! Someone please. I need permission for an emergency landing on the Moon. Someone. Please. Help me."

The computer was silent. There was no other response. For a moment, she worried that she hadn't sent her message through.

"This is Armstrong Dome Port Authority," a tinny male voice said. "State the nature of your emergency."

The nature of her emergency. The best thing she could do was remain close to the truth.

"My crew is gone," she said. "I haven't piloted any craft in twenty years. I managed to get here, and I think I can land, but I'm in big trouble and I need to land."

"Send us your ship's identification," the tinny voice said.

"I can't find it," she said. "I can give you mine."

"Without ship identification, you will be taken to a restricted area of the Port."

Which might actually be safer. "I don't care," she said. "I have to get out of here. I need help."

She must have put the right amount of panic in her voice, because the Armstrong Dome employee responded, "Calm down, ma'am. We'll get you landed, and then we'll see what we can do about your situation. Just relax. We'll help."

Somehow those words did calm her. Even though she knew the authorities couldn't really help. Even though she knew she had more hurdles to jump through.

She had made it another step. And each step that kept her out of Rev hands was good.

10

The holding section in the basement of the Armstrong City Complex seemed even more depressing in the morning. Flint stifled a yawn as he walked down the steps, then combed his hair with his fingers, knowing he had to look awake and alert when he saw the infant's parents.

He'd slept shallowly all night, remembering what it was like to meet the authorities—the look on the officer's face when she had said, *There's a situation with your daughter, Mr. Flint.* A situation. That was a phrase he made sure he never, ever used.

At least this child was alive, which in some ways made things worse for the family. These parents would take a delicate hand. They would be happy that their child was all right, but they needed to know that they could still lose him.

The desk sergeant who had greeted the parents at six a.m. had already checked their identification. When he called Flint to let him know that the parents had arrived, Flint asked the sergeant to do a triple-check. Which meant not just paper identification, but shoulder I.D. and background checks. He wanted to be as certain as possible that this couple was who they said they were.

When he reached the basement, he resisted the urge to glance at the door of the suite. Instead, he walked to the meeting area. Two officers stood outside the door, and he nodded at them. He didn't ask for a report. He'd get a sense of these parents himself.

The meeting area was a large room with a table down the center and chairs pushed against it. There were no windows, but someone had placed a changing holographic scene on the far wall, programmed at this moment to look like the Alps mountain range on Earth.

Somehow the vista of snow-capped peaks made the room seem even colder. Flint shuddered as he stepped inside.

A dark-haired woman sat at the head of the table, her fingers drumming on its surface. She looked up when he entered. Her face was drawn with worry, her gray eyes shadowed. She looked as if she had only recently stopped crying.

Behind her, a man paced. He was powerfully built— large shoulders and a muscular torso that suggested an athletic past. There was a hint of fat around his middle. Flint wondered if these people eschewed enhancements or couldn't afford them.

"Are you going to take us to our son?" the woman asked. There was an edge to her voice, as if she had asked the question a number of times.

Flint knew what she was feeling and he deliberately blocked it. He had to remain detached, as detached as he could be.

"Yes, I'll be taking you to Ennis." Flint took a step closer. "I'm Miles Flint. I'm one of the two detectives in charge of this case."

The man peered at him. "Jamal and Dylani Kanawa."

"I suppose you have questions too." Mrs. Kanawa sat, her shoulders rigid, as if she were bracing herself for more delays.

"No," Flint said. "You answered the department's questions. I do have to explain a few things first."

"What's there to explain?" Mrs. Kanawa asked. Her husband put a hand on her shoulder, and her mouth thinned. But she didn't say anything else.

Flint thought the gesture interesting. He wouldn't have expected such calm control from a man who had been pacing a moment before. His gaze met Mr. Kanawa's.

Mr. Kanawa looked away.

Flint found that interesting too. He cleared his throat. "Your son was found on a Wygnin ship. I understand he was taken from your home just recently?"

"Yes," Mr. Kanawa said, his hand still on his wife's shoulder. He offered no extra information the way that a couple trying to help the authorities would.

"The Wygnin claim they have a valid warrant, but we haven't seen evidence of any warrant yet."

"They can't," Mrs. Kanawa said. "Neither my husband nor I has had any contact with the Wygnin. You can check our records."

"We have." Flint's voice was gentle. He didn't want to let her know that records could be tampered with. "Wygnin law is somewhat byzantine when it comes to retaliatory rights. The Wygnin prefer to take children as punishment for extremely serious crimes, the younger the child the better. Perhaps another member of your family had trouble with the Wygnin, and now they're claiming the youngest blood relative."

"No," Mrs. Kanawa said. "My family has never been off the Moon. Jamal's family is gone."

"These warrants stay in effect for a long time," Flint said.

"No," she said again.

Mr. Kanawa's hand visibly tightened on her shoulder. This time, Flint watched the man from the corner of his eye. He would swear that Mr. Kanawa knew something.

"I'm telling you this," Flint said, trying to mentally distance himself from the words he was about to speak, "because there is a chance that the Wygnin do have a valid warrant. You'll be able to keep Ennis while the legal aspects of this case get settled, but there is a chance—I have no idea how great a chance—that you might lose him again. You might have to relinquish him into their custody."

"That's not possible," Mrs. Kanawa said.

Flint decided to ignore her and concentrate on Mr. Kanawa. Mr. Kanawa, at least, seemed able to listen. "It might be easier to leave him here. The warrant check should take a few days at most. It'll be hard on all of you, but not as hard as giving him up to the Wygnin."

Mr. Kanawa shook his head. Mrs. Kanawa stood. "Can't you prevent this?"

"We can work to the fullest extent of the law, ma'am," Flint said. "But if they have a valid claim, we must enforce it."

"Even if that means we lose our child because of something someone else did?" She didn't know anything about the Wygnin. He could hear the outrage in her voice and knew that no one was that good an actress.

"Yes," he said. "Even if."

"That's as good as killing Ennis." She crossed her arms.

"No, ma'am. The boy would still live on Korsve. He just would be raised as a Wygnin."

"We'd still lose him." Mr. Kanawa said.

Flint nodded, his heart pounding. He wasn't as detached as he wanted to be.

"What are our chances, officer?" Mr. Kanawa asked.

Flint shrugged. "I haven't seen any warrant, and that's unusual. But the Wygnin are usually pretty precise. They don't venture outside of the Korsve system often, and when they do, they have valid reasons. There was another child on that ship, and the Wygnin may have been planning to pick up more children as they returned to Korsve. I don't know."

"What does that mean for Ennis?" Mrs. Kanawa asked.

"It's all guesswork at this point. They didn't come just for Ennis, which is something in your favor. So is the lack of warrant. But they are certain that he belongs with them, which is a point against you. I'd say there is a good chance that you might lose him to the Wygnin."

"No." Mrs. Kanawa looked fierce. "We will not lose our child because some alien society has a whim. We will fight this."

"Then I suggest you hire counsel, ma'am," Flint said, wishing he could offer her more than that. "You'll need legal representation if the Wygnin provide a valid warrant."

"Has anyone ever successfully fought a Wygnin warrant?" Mr. Kanawa asked.

Flint wasn't going to answer that question. He knew from his studies that no Wygnin warrant had been successfully challenged in the last fifty years.

"I'm not a legal expert," he said. "You'd do better to ask a lawyer."

Mr. Kanawa's gaze met his. The man's expression was as guarded as his wife's was open. "Let me have a moment with my wife."

"Certainly," Flint said, and went outside. They didn't speak as he made his way out. Even after the door closed, he heard nothing.

He had no idea what was happening in that room. He had never had the opportunity to make this choice. One day, he'd sent his daughter to day care, and she had ended up dead.

He wasn't sure if he would have wanted the opportunity to see her alive one last time—and he wasn't sure he would have turned it down, either.

"Problems?" one of the cops outside the door asked. He was slender, younger than Flint, and had a general air of worry about him that some cops just seemed to acquire.

Flint gave him a small smile. "Nothing unexpected."

He crossed the hallway and leaned against the wall, resisting the urge to go into the suite with the children, pick up Ennis, imagine he was Emmeline.

Flint let out a small sigh. Emmeline's death could have been prevented. If there had been a proper investigation into the previous death at her day care, Emmeline would be alive. Instead, the detectives had thought the first child died from some bizarre accident. It wasn't until Emmeline died that they realized some impatient care worker had been shaking crying children so hard that she killed them. She had killed two of them. Another baby girl, and Emmeline.

The door to the meeting room opened. Mr. Kanawa faced him. "We'd like to see him now."

Flint nodded. The choice didn't surprise him.

He pushed off the wall and motioned for Mr. Kanawa to join him. Mrs. Kanawa followed. Flint escorted them down the hall to the suite.

He knocked—four sharp, short raps—the code for the Harkens to make certain Jasper stayed in his room.

A single rap sounded in response. Flint took a deep breath. He still had more business to do.

"I'm assuming you're taking custody of Ennis," he said.

Mr. Kanawa nodded.

"In that case, then, I have to remind you that removing Ennis from Armstrong Dome is a violation of law. If you and your family chose to run, the Wygnin, Armstrong Dome's government, and the government of Earth Alliance will all issue warrants for your arrests. You'd be breaking a large variety of laws, and you'd be putting yourselves, as well as your child in jeopardy."

"We understand that," Mrs. Kanawa snapped. "We're hiring an attorney."

As if that were going to make things better. "I simply had to inform you now, so that you don't do anything rash."

"We won't," Mr. Kanawa said.

Flint nodded, wishing he could believe them. Then he opened the door to the holding suite.

A strange woman was holding Ennis. Her skin was so white that it seemed to glow in the dim light of the room. Ennis squirmed and fussed.

Jamal felt a mixture of emotions run through him, from joy that his son was alive and fine, to terror that he'd lose the boy all over again. For all his bravado with the cop, he knew that his chances of winning this battle were slim.

Dylani let out a small cry and ran across the room. The air smelled faintly of dirty diapers and pizza. Jamal glanced toward the kitchen, hoping that they hadn't fed Ennis anything inappropriate.

Then he smiled at himself. Right now, that was the least of his worries.

Ennis squealed when he saw his mother and leaned out of the strange woman's arms, reaching for Dylani. Jamal's eyes burned. He'd have to have a private talk with the lawyer, see if there was something he could do, something that would leave his family alone.

There had to be an out. He couldn't be the only person in this situation desperate enough to consider anything.

The detective, Flint, had come up beside him. "Good-looking son you have there."

"Yes," Jamal said. He felt rooted to the spot. The moment belonged to Dylani. She squeezed Ennis so hard that he grunted in protest, but he was clinging to her too, his chubby fist clutching the back of her shirt.

"You and your wife had very different reactions to your son's loss." Flint was speaking so softly that Jamal could barely hear him.

"We're different people."

Dylani turned. Tears were running down her face. Ennis was staring at them in a kind of wonder. "Jamal. Jamal, he's here. He's okay."

Jamal went to her, not wanting the detective to ask any more questions. He put his arm around her, cradling Ennis in the process, and tried to memorize this moment.

He leaned his forehead against Ennis's tight curls and inhaled the familiar scent of talcum and baby that was his son. Part of Jamal already had believed Ennis lost to him. That the boy was here, now, seemed a kind of gift. Maybe a cruel gift, but a gift nonetheless.

Ennis put his arms around his father's shoulders, leaning into Jamal so hard that Jamal had no choice but to take him from Dylani. The boy was shaking. He had known something was wrong. Maybe he had even been frightened.

Jamal put his hand on his boy's back, patting it, murmuring words of comfort. He turned, as he often did when he was taking care of his son, and saw the detective watching them.

Flint's gaze was too sharp. He clearly knew that Jamal was lying. But Jamal couldn't trust him, couldn't tell him the truth in any way.

Flint was required by law to support the Wygnin— and right now, Jamal couldn't give them any advantage.

They already had all the advantage they needed.

DeRicci drank the last of her coffee, tipping her cup so that the last drop tumbled into her mouth. She wished she could afford the high-voltage stuff; the Port, like the Unit, only served the cheap low-grade, low-caffeine kind. She needed something to jump-start her system.

She certainly hadn't had enough sleep.

She lingered over the tray of baked goods inside the office, then took a crumb cake, poured herself another cup of coffee, and drank. Everyone could wait for her. She wanted to be alert when she faced the Wygnin again.

Alert would be difficult. She had only gotten four hours of sleep. Instead, she had spent most of her time after she had gotten home talking with the chief of detectives and one of the low-level assistants to Armstrong Dome's government, begging them to take over this case.

She got stonewalled, just the way she had before. They wanted her to handle it and she knew why. Deniability. If she made a mistake, they'd sell her to the Wygnin in a heartbeat. If she did everything right, they'd take all the credit.

If she could do something else, she'd quit this job now and let them handle the fallout. But five years ago, she'd looked at other employment options and didn't like any of them. None of them paid as well as detective, and very few of them used her skills.

She was stuck here. She had to make the best of it.

She finished the crumb cake—which had some sort of synthetic sugar in it instead of the real thing—and sucked down the second cup of coffee as if it were a lifeline.

If nothing else, she could legitimately claim bathroom breaks when handling the Wygnin got too intense.

She should have called Flint this morning and had him beside her. He needed to learn how to do these bogus diplomatic non-detective jobs as well. It was time she stopped protecting him and started to let him do work on his own.

Or maybe she just didn't want to face the Wygnin alone.

She poured a third cup of coffee and carried it to holding. The legal team sat at the table, the Wygnin lined up behind them. The team was one of the toughest in Armstrong, known for its arguments before several Multicultural Tribunal cases.

Nadia Solar was seventy-something, at the top of her form. Beside her sat Xival, a Peyti whose translucent skin looked gray against the walls of the holding room. Xival wore a breathing mask that made her alien features even less recognizable. Her long fingers spread over the table like three tails coming out of her wrists.

Wonderful. DeRicci suppressed a grimace. Now she was dealing with two different types of aliens and their customs. The Peyti weren't fond of the Wygnin, thinking them too harsh, but the Peyti had a finely honed sense of honor which made them perfect for multicultural law. Xival's presence was a bad sign for those children.

DeRicci closed the door behind her, set the coffee on the table, and sat down. She felt very isolated. Seven against one. Suddenly it seemed unfair.

She had called the lawyers who'd been there yesterday, and they had told her to report to them. Cowards. They were all cowards. So was she, if she were honest. She was just the one stuck here.

"What did you get me up so early for?" she asked.

Solar smiled. Her face was softly textured. She'd had some subtle enhancements that blunted the effects of aging while leaving the dignity that age could afford. Sometimes DeRicci wished she had money. She'd love to look like that in thirty years.

"You requested that my clients bring you not just the warrant reference number, but the warrants. I have them for you."

Solar slid a hand-held across the table.

"You could have sent it to my system," DeRicci said, not wanting to go over a warrant with the Wygnin present.

"In the interest of haste," Solar said, "we felt it better to show the warrants to you here. Then you can reunite my clients with their children and let them go on their way."

"The children aren't theirs," DeRicci said.

"By law, they are." This from Xival. Her voice grated through the mask.

"That's the issue we haven't settled yet." DeRicci wasn't gong to give any ground. She trusted lawyers less than she trusted the Wygnin. If she said the wrong thing, she was afraid the lawyers would use it against her—or the children—later.

She pulled the hand-held toward her. The screen gave her a choice: audio or text; English, Basic, or Modified Korsven. She could read some Korsven, even unmodified, which looked to the unpracticed eye like a series of equal-length sticks, but she chose the English text option.

The warrants were old, both more than ten years. They had been issued by the same court, the Eighth Multicultural Tribunal, whose district included Korsve.

Both warrants were short. They listed the name of the offender, followed by the sentence, and then the order of the court allowing the Wygnin to carry out that sentence.

DeRicci didn't recognize the name of the offender on either warrant. The sentences differed, which surprised DeRicci. One warrant—the newest one—demanded the traditional firstborn child of the above-named offender.

The second warrant asked for a family member of choice from the offender's family. DeRicci stared at that for a moment. The second warrant seemed to be less stringent until she thought about it.

The second warrant forced someone to choose among the people they loved, to pick and protect fa-

vorites while sacrificing the least loved in the group—
or the most hated. But what happened if the offender
loved his family, loved that family to distraction?
What if there were no obvious or good choices?

DeRicci shuddered. She studied the warrants for a
moment, then slid the hand-held back to Solar, who
waved it at her.

"Keep it," Solar said.

DeRicci took her hand off it, leaving the hand-held
in the center of the table. "These names are unfamiliar.
The identity chips in the children do not match the
family names in these warrants. There are no pictures,
no histories, nothing for me to go by except the Wygnin's word that they have chosen the correct victims."

"—Children—" one of the Wygnin, probably the
same one that had spoken to her the day before, said.
It was at that moment that DeRicci realized no one
had called the translator, and the Wygnin had not
objected.

Had the Wygnin understood everything she said
yesterday? Or would the attorneys translate for
them later?

"Victims," DeRicci said. "No matter how you cut
it, those children will be innocent victims of the
legal system."

"—Opinion—" the Wygnin said.

"Fact," DeRicci said.

"Detective," Solar said, a tone of condescension in
her voice. "You know that the Wygnin never make
mistakes."

"I know that's what the Wygnin want us to believe,"
DeRicci said. "What I see before me are two warrants.
I see nothing linking them to those children."

"Then you're not looking hard enough," Xival said.

DeRicci gave her a cold smile. "As I told your clients yesterday, it is not my job to look. It's theirs to show me that they haven't abducted the wrong children by mistake. So far they haven't done that."

"The Wygnin are a cautious people. They do not venture from their solar system without just cause. They would not come for these children if they did not know they were right," Solar said.

DeRicci shrugged. "That's not my problem, and you all know it. I'm not letting human children out of here without the proper documentation."

"You're being unnecessarily difficult," Xival said.

DeRicci put her hands flat on the table and leaned toward the lawyers. "I'll be honest with you ladies. I think the Wygnin have the wrong children and they don't want anyone to know it. I think they're playing you, like they've been trying to play me. And I'm not letting them out of here with children they have no right to."

"—Have—right—" the Wygnin said.

"I'll take this to your superiors," Solar said.

"I'll bet you already have," DeRicci said. "I'll bet they said to you what they've said to me, that I'm the one responsible for this case, and all dealings go through me."

Solar's eyes narrowed. Xival's long fingers bent upwards, a tiny gesture of discomfort.

"Which means," DeRicci said, "that I'm holding on to those children until I'm so positive that your clients are incapable of making a mistake that I'm willing to send those children to hell."

"—Korsve—not—hell—"

"Probably not when you're Wygnin," DeRicci said. "But you're planning to destroy everything they are. Doesn't that bother you?"

"Detective," Solar said. "Speak to us."

But DeRicci was looking at the Wygnin, the one who had spoken to her. The golden eyes held her, and she felt the contempt as if it were her own.

The Wygnin spoke rapidly in Korsven. Xival sighed, then translated, "Taking the children punishes the family. But the children will receive a great honor. They will become Wygnin."

"I know," DeRicci said. "Whether they want to or not."

She walked to the door. Then turned.

"Contact me when you have real proof of your claims. Otherwise, I have more important work to do."

She slammed her way out, then paused in the hallway to catch her breath.

The warrants were here, which meant that the proof—if there was any—wasn't far behind. She hoped that the parents got here soon and that the parents could afford good lawyers.

Because there wasn't much more she could do and keep her job.

11

The spacedock dome closed over the yacht. Ekaterina felt a jolt as the yacht landed inexpertly on the flooring. The yacht skidded a bit—she had come in too fast—and then stopped moving.

She rested her face in her hands. For a moment there, she hadn't been sure she would survive the landing. Even with someone from the Space Traffic Control talking her through as best he could, and the ship's automatic systems taking over most of the landing procedure, she had still felt the shakiness of it all. The way the yacht had spun when she tried to slow it down; the tilt when she'd shifted to the automatic controls; the groans coming from the metal as the stresses of the atmosphere change inside the Port's main dome hit the yacht too quickly.

Well. She wasn't dead yet.

The thought spurred her. She sat up and unbuckled her safety harness. She had no idea how long she'd been at the helm of this damn yacht, and she wasn't sure she wanted to know.

However long it had been, it had been twice that long since she'd eaten, and she couldn't remember the last time she'd slept. If she didn't take care of herself, her body would do that for her. She could already feel the effect of fear, space flight, and stress on her overtaxed frame.

In all her wildest imaginings, she hadn't expected to be here, alone, without help. She had expected a new life—something easy and comfortable, unfamiliar but possible. Not this. Never this.

She stood, clutching the console for support. Before she went any farther, she picked up the hand-held that Jenny had given her. On it was her fake name, and the credits that were supposedly in her account.

That might get her somewhere—if she could get off this ship and out of the Port. The Rev would be here any moment, and they would be able to take her from the Port. But most aliens didn't have visas that allowed them outside the Port, especially if they hadn't planned on landing here.

It had been a long time since she'd been to Armstrong Dome, but she was familiar with it. And she was lucky to have landed here. She knew the laws; she probably even knew a few inhabitants, most of them people she defended, people who wouldn't mind bending the law. If she had gone somewhere else on the Moon, she might not have been so lucky. She'd only been out of Armstrong once, for a client in Glenn Station—and then she hadn't seen much outside of the high-speed train, the expensive hotel, and the courtrooms.

She had to concentrate. She opened her purse one last time, unsealed the lining, and slipped the laser pistol into the pouch especially designed for weapons. Now her purse wouldn't bulge, and a cursory search wouldn't reveal much.

It was a risk, but it was one she had to take. She didn't want to go anywhere without that gun. It had saved her life once. She was hoping it would do so again.

Voices sounded through the communication system, asking her for things she didn't have—registrations, identification, passes. She ignored them.

She would have to play this right. She would only get one opportunity to escape this Port.

Her exhaustion and hunger would serve her well.

She put a hand to her head and staggered to the main exit. If someone had gotten in, they would see her movements as consistent.

Ekaterina punched the button that deactivated the airlock door, and heard a hiss as whatever lurked between the airlock and the main door was exhaled out of the ship.

Then the airlock doors opened. Her breath caught. One more step forward. She stepped inside, reached for the main door and released it.

Instantly she was facing police-issue multishot rifles. Five people, all wearing environmental coverings, held the guns on her. She held up her hands to show she meant no harm and stepped backwards.

"Please," she said. "I have to get out of here."

"Not yet," someone said. The voice was muffled by the environmental protections. "You haven't been able to give us registration or anything approximating a ship's log. We don't even know if you have cargo. You have to go through decontamination, and the ship can't be touched until HazMat goes through it."

"I don't care about the ship," she said. "It's not mine. Please, I told someone my story. The Rev took the crew. I'm afraid they'll come for me. All I want is to be away from the dock, away from the ship."

She hadn't really told anyone her story, just different parts of it to different authorities who had contacted her. But she tried to stay as consistent as she could. She had been fortunate in one thing: the Rev generally did not believe in guilt by association. If her story were true, if the crew had truly been targeted by the Rev, the Rev would have left the passengers on board—maybe with a warning.

The Rev would then tow the ship until they checked all the identification, to make certain no one was lying, then they would have let the passengers go. Saying she had gotten the ship out of there quickly added a convincing aspect to her story. If the Rev hadn't had time to check her I.D., they might have come after her.

But if someone who knew the Rev really took the time to think about her story, they would know that she was lying about something. The Rev would have checked her identity before continuing pursuit.

"I'm sorry, ma'am," said the person before her. "Rules are rules."

"Isn't there a place to decontaminate away from this dock? Please. Just get me out of here."

One of the HazMat crew held up a small device that Ekaterina didn't recognize. It crackled as it ran over her.

"Preliminary decontamination findings show no problems," said the person with the device. "Take her to interstellar holding. There's a decontam unit there that isn't used often. It'll get her out of the dock area."

"Thank you," Ekaterina said.

One of the HazMat crew handed her an environmental suit. "Put this on. You're not going to contaminate the entire Terminal because you got yourself in trouble with the Rev."

"I didn't—" Ekaterina started, and then stopped. She had. No matter which story she told, the end was the same. The Rev were after her.

She unfolded the thin material that made up the full body suit. She would let them take her to decontamination. Sometimes HazMat teams let people alone in decontamination chambers. That would be her first chance to escape. She'd wait until the decon unit ran its cycle, and then she'd make a run for it. They wouldn't go after her as a biohazard, maybe only as a fugitive, and maybe not even that. She had a hunch a lot of people got cleared and then bolted from the Port.

If she played this correctly, she might even be able to find her way to one of the high-speed trains between domes. She could cash out a credit somewhere in the Port, and then no one would know where she had gone.

She would vanish, just as she was supposed to do. Maybe she would be able to disappear—all on her own.

Flint was sitting at his desk, finishing the file on the three bodies from the yacht when DeRicci walked in the door. She looked as tired as he felt.

"You're here early," he said.

"So are you." She pulled back the chair on the other side of his desk, sat down, and rubbed her eyes. "Problems?"

"Depends on which case you're talking about."

She stopped rubbing her eyes and peered at him. "Okay. Which one doesn't have problems?"

"The three dead from yesterday. They were legit Disty targets."

"You got the report?"

"Finishing it now." After he had done some fancy legitimate research to find the warrants. He had asked for the DNA scan, but he knew permission for it wouldn't come in for weeks. When it did, he would use it to officially close the file. Until then, he made reference to the holes in the chip files, and how that had led him to the real names. Since this file probably wouldn't see court, he really didn't need an explanation of how he had gotten from A to K, but he provided an approximation of one, just in case.

"What did they do?" she asked.

"One of them killed a Disty security guard and the others helped her escape."

"Idiots." DeRicci shook her head. "They had to know."

"It was fifteen years ago."

DeRicci stood, put her hands on her hips, and sighed. "People seem to get complacent after a while. They must let down their guard or something."

Flint frowned. He had no idea. He hadn't been working on this type of case long enough to know. "Originally there were four of them. These three got out after the fourth got killed."

"So they had some resources."

He nodded. He didn't tell her he still had a search going for the pilot and co-pilot. She would consider it a waste of time, since the case was officially closed.

"Okay." DeRicci rubbed her eyes. "This case is the good news, which means the bad news is with the kids, right? The baby's parents are here. What about the eight-year-old's?"

"Jasper," Flint said.

"Don't get attached."

Too late. Although Jasper wasn't the one he was

attached to. Flint folded his hands on top of his desk. "His folks are coming from Tycho Crater. They should be here later today."

"Tycho Crater." DeRicci shook her head. "That kid's been traveling some."

"Yeah," Flint said.

"So what's the problem?"

"I don't know yet," Flint said.

"You don't know?" She let her hand drop and faced him.

"I have a hunch."

She shook her head. "No proof, nothing concrete?"

"No," he said.

"Then I don't want to hear it. Hunches are worthless, especially when I'm going toe-to-balls with the Wygnin."

Flint grinned. "They have balls? I thought that was part of the problem of gender-typing them."

"Don't get goofy on me, Miles." But DeRicci smiled too. She sat back down. "It's tough right now. They seem to think we should just hand those kids over because they say so."

"No warrants yet?"

"No warrants with the right information. The names don't match and the things are old."

"Old seems to be the theme of the week, doesn't it?" Flint said.

"Yeah," DeRicci said. "Things run in groups sometimes. You've been with me—how long?—and we've been dealing with normal stuff, thefts, murders, that kind of thing. Now we have two alien cases in a row, straight from the docks. Usually they aren't even from the docks."

"That doesn't concern you?"

"It concerns me only when the pattern is a little clearer. If this were all Disty or all Wygnin, I'd be wondering what's going on. But it's not."

Flint nodded.

Then the door to his office opened. Andrea Gumiela, the chief of the First Detective Unit, leaned in. She was a tall woman, heavyset but muscular, with a long, sad face and thin reddish hair.

"Your locators said you were here." Her voice was flat, businesslike. Flint had never heard her sound upset or excited. He wasn't sure she could. "Surprised me. Isn't it a little early?"

"I'm still dealing with the Wygnin." DeRicci sounded bitter.

"I had the first set of parents arrive this morning," Flint said.

"Bad business that," Gumiela said as if she didn't care. "I got your file, Flint. Closed the Disty vengeance killing already."

He nodded.

"Good work."

"Thanks." He didn't smile. Gumiela rarely gave compliments without trying to get something in return.

"Since you two have had all the dock business in the last day or so, I figure you could handle one more, especially since you did such a quick and thorough job on the vengeance killing."

"The Wygnin are going to take a lot of time," DeRicci said.

"Naw." Gumiela grinned. "They're lawyered up. They tried to contact me before they called you. Why do you think I'm here this early?"

"Sorry about that, sir," DeRicci said.

Gumiela waved her hand. "Not your problem, detective. Just get it resolved as best you can, when you can. I need you at the docks right now."

"What's happening?" Flint asked.

"Some tourist says she had a run-in with the Rev outside of Moon Space. She's afraid they'll come after her. I want to know if this is fantasy or reality."

"What kind of run-in?" DeRicci asked.

"Unclear," Gumiela said. "But it's the kind of thing we need to put to bed fast. We don't need any panic from tourists, thinking the Rev or any other alien group are targeting innocents. I want you to get to her before the media does. Is that clear?"

"Yes." DeRicci sighed.

"Where is she now?"

"Decon One in interstellar holding. The HazMat crew locked the area down, afraid she'd bolt. They want someone fast."

"All right," Flint said. "Fast is our business."

"I just came from the Port," DeRicci said.

"Looks like it's your week for this kind of work," Gumiela said. "If anything else comes in, I'll make sure it goes to you."

She didn't smile as she said that, and she closed the door sharply behind her.

"You know," Flint said, "if you didn't complain so much, you wouldn't get assignments you hate."

"Yes, I would," DeRicci said. "Think about it, Flint. I'm not real popular around here."

"Did you ever ask why?"

"I know why," she said as she stood.

"Care to share?"

She shook her head. "You'll learn soon enough."

They locked it down. Damn. Ekaterina paced around the waiting area outside of the decontamination chamber. She had gone through the whole procedure, including having her purse scanned and her clothing chemically purified.

Her clothes itched now, but there was nothing she could do about that. She had to wait until someone let her out.

At least the Rev wouldn't come in here. At least she was protected in that way. But if they arrived and asked for her, the Port was required by law to investigate their request. She would be stuck here for good.

She had to get out before they arrived—and in a way that didn't cause suspicion.

She couldn't claim claustrophobia. She'd arrived in a space yacht. But she could claim starvation. All she had to do was find the communications link inside here. There had to be one, and it probably wasn't obvious. They didn't want unauthorized use of it and besides, most people had their own communication devices.

Hers were on Earth, in her wonderful house, by the lilacs that Simon had given her. By her ring.

She blinked hard. She wasn't going to think about that. She'd promised herself she wasn't going to think about what she'd left behind until she built something new, and she was very far away from that.

Her stomach rumbled, proving that she wouldn't be lying when she said she needed food. She scanned the plain walls, looking for a line that didn't belong, a misplaced bump or a speck of dirt. It had to be somewhere logical, maybe even by the door.

But she didn't see anything obvious. And she knew she was being monitored. If she looked too crafty, they wouldn't trust her with anything. She sat on one of the benches and continued to scan. She'd find it.

If she didn't, she'd try the old-fashioned method. She'd pound on the door. That would get someone's attention eventually. All she needed was the door to open once. Just once, and she had a good chance of getting free.

They were summoned to the main decontamination area in the interstellar holding section, but Flint insisted on stopping in the Port's Administrative Center first.

"Come on, Miles," DeRicci said. "Let's get this over with. We've got more important things to do than protect some tourist from the media."

He shook his head. "I think there's more here. If it were that simple, Traffic could have handled it."

"You think Gumiela sent us on this to test us?"

"No," he said. "I think Gumiela got the call and didn't understand why Traffic was asking for detectives."

DeRicci raised her eyebrows. "You think Gumiela's dumb?"

Flint gave her a sideways look. "I think she doesn't pay attention sometimes."

DeRicci suppressed a smile.

The Port's Adminstrative Center was a large area off the main entrance. Flint led DeRicci through the familiar hallways until he got to Traffic's Port Headquarters. It was a large room, with windows that opened into the hallway. A check-in desk was right up front. The desk sergeant, an elderly man named Murray, grinned at Flint.

"The prodigal son returns."

Flint grinned back. "I don't think the prodigal son was promoted."

Murray snorted. "Yeah, like more work, shit hours, and no overtime is promotion. Should've stayed here, kid, where life is good and cases don't last forever."

DeRicci was looking at all the murals on the wall. Long before Flint arrived, someone had painted the history of spaceships that had traveled to the Moon. If he tried, he could name the type of ship, the year it was commissioned, and in many cases the year it was retired.

It was a great skill to have when he was in Traffic, although it was mostly useless now.

"I'm actually here on business," Flint said.

"And I thought it was because you missed me." Murray leaned forward, his beefy arms resting on the desktop.

"We got called in on that tourist who thinks she's being chased by Revs."

Murray rolled his eyes. "The stolen space yacht. Yeah."

DeRicci turned away from the mural. "No. Nothing was said about a stolen yacht. It was a woman who had arrived alone, in a panic about the Rev. We understand she was in Decontamination."

"Yeah," Murray said, assessing her and, it seemed to Flint, not liking what he saw. "The stolen space yacht. That's why you got called in."

"We were told it was to hear her story before the media got to her," DeRicci said.

"And who's the idiot who said that?" Murray asked.

"Our Unit Chief." Flint smiled. "I take it you made the call?"

"Always do. Told her there was a problem. Said the woman was in decon and didn't know her ship's registration. Said she claimed to have lost her crew to the Rev, and said the ship was in Terminal Five."

Which to any space cop would have been enough to know they were talking about theft. "My colleagues in the First Unit have no idea how the terminals are broken down," Flint said. "I'm afraid you're going to have to walk them through things next time."

"Is that what you came here to tell me?" Murray's smile was gone.

Flint shook his head. "I wanted to find out what you really said before I saw the woman. Figured I didn't want to duplicate your work."

"Take a look at that yacht," Murray said, "and tell me it's not stolen."

"You've seen it?"

Murray shook his head. "No registration. No computerized I.D. When we accessed the communications system in orbit, we got nothing but a straight signal. Someone tampered with something. We should have gotten standard I.D. at minimum. She claims she don't know it either."

"You don't believe her."

"I didn't see her. The cops who caught her think she's scared. Something's going on. We've had three messages from Decon One that she's been banging on the door asking when she's getting out. Most folks take longer to go through the system. We warn them that they might be carrying something microscopic and lethal, and they make sure every crevice is cleaned out. She scurried through it like a five-year-old who's been told to wash his face."

Flint nodded. "So we need to get down there."

"I'd say. She's annoying everyone."

"Why was she put in interstellar?" DeRicci asked. "Wasn't there a closer decontamination center?"

"Precaution," Murray said. "If she is telling the truth, the Rev would ask to inspect all the areas of

Terminal Five and they'd be within their rights if they have the proper documentation—or even something approximating it. This way she's protected in the short term and we're not open to lawsuits."

"Lawsuits." DeRicci shook her head. "Ain't life grand in Armstrong law enforcement."

"Tell me," Murray said. "Half the shit I do is to avoid lawsuits."

Flint had heard this speech before. "Is there any way we can view the ship from here?"

"Sure, but you're gonna want to see it in person."

"Probably," Flint said. "But it sounds like we need to get that woman into our custody before she calls too much attention to herself."

"Worried about the media, Miles?" DeRicci asked.

"One of our jobs is to see if her story is true. If it is, then we need to protect her when she faces the Rev."

DeRicci nodded.

"Come here," Murray said, and beckoned them behind the desk. He tapped the screen before him and a tiny hologram of Terminal 5 appeared on top of his desk. He moved the hologram, tweaking it until he found the dock he was looking for, then blew up the image to a meter.

Flint stared at it for a moment. "Can you put this on the floor? Make it about five times that big?"

"Sure," Murray said.

DeRicci was biting her lower lip. The hologram winked out and then reappeared just behind Flint. He walked around it. The yacht was black and scarred. He couldn't tell from this distance if the scarring was new or old.

It looked like escape pods were missing.

"Is it intact?"

"Pilot escape pod is gone," Murray said. "We don't

know when. That's for you to figure out if you have to."

"The registration's gone?" DeRicci asked, all business now. "What about serial numbers?"

"Nothing we could find. HazMat was instructed to look inside, and they didn't see anything either. But again, that's all stuff for you guys. We did a cursory examination. Our job was to get her out of there, clear the area, and bring you guys in."

Flint nodded.

"I'm not making this up, am I?" DeRicci asked Flint.

"What?" Murray frowned.

"This looks like something we got yesterday," Flint said.

"Tell me what and I'll call it up," Murray said.

"The Disty vengeance killing."

Murray grimaced. He studied the screen before him for a moment, then another ship appeared on the desk top. "Hold on. I'll make it the same size."

It disappeared, then reappeared next to that day's ship. Flint would have thought they were the same ship except the Disty vengeance killing yacht had recent weapons burns, obvious ones.

Murray whistled. He got up from the desk and walked around the holos of both ships.

"This isn't some kind of system echo is it?" DeRicci asked.

Murray didn't seem offended. Instead he shook his head somewhat absently.

"Looks like the same make, model, and year to me," Flint said.

"Me, too." Murray rubbed his chin with his right hand. "If I had some time, I might be able to find the specs for you."

"I'd appreciate it," Flint said.

"Let me try something." Murray went back to the desk. The Disty yacht rose, then floated toward the new yacht. Slowly the yachts merged until the only way it became obvious that there were two ships were the different scars on the hulls and the different positions of the docks.

"Wow," DeRicci said, crouching in front of them. "What're the odds of two space yachts of the same make and model arriving on Armstrong with no identification and possible criminal involvement?"

"Impossible to one," Murray said, and Flint agreed. He wasn't sure what that meant yet, but it had to mean something. And he was determined to find out what that something was.

12

The decontamination unit in interstellar holding was off a mazelike hallway that went through some of the older sections of the Port. This was the original Port. The rest had been built around it, some to modern specifications. But in this older section, pieces had been cobbled together as the need arose and remodeled dozens, maybe hundreds, of times over the years.

It had been years since Flint was back here. He'd come as a rookie on Traffic, escorting a Rev who'd been caught smuggling weapons to a humans-only group on Earth. Flint hadn't even tried to explain the irony to the Rev, who didn't seem too clear on the idea that these humans believed aliens to be inferior, and hadn't realized that the weapons he sold to the group would probably be used against his own people.

The decontamination unit was quite large. Everyone who entered had to check in. That occurred in a boxy room, made to accommodate big groups from the large luxury liners. A woman worked behind the desk, but she was mostly there to provide a friendly face and pretend to answer questions. In reality, most of check-in was done with computers set in isolation booths in case the need for decontamination was real.

It usually wasn't, but the folks working the Port had

learned to be careful. Illness could spread quickly in a dome. Viruses alien to the human population were probably the thing a domed community feared the most, and struggled the hardest to prevent.

As Flint and DeRicci walked toward the main desk, Flint could hear banging to his left. DeRicci flashed her badge. The woman behind the desk looked attentive.

"Is that our guest?" DeRicci asked.

"The woman claiming the Rev are after her?" the woman behind the desk asked. It seemed no one really believed the story. Flint found that interesting.

"Yes," Flint said.

The woman nodded. "She claims she hasn't eaten for at least two days. We have food and she's cleared. You want to bring her something?"

"Good cop, bad cop?" DeRicci asked.

Flint nodded. "Which do you want?"

"I've been dealing with the Wygnin. Give me bad cop."

Flint grinned. "What kind of food do we have?" he asked the woman.

"Sandwiches and some juice. She wants better than that, she has to buy it herself."

"That'll do." He went to the small kitchen off one of the isolation booths and opened the refrigerator. Most places in the Port used the microization units, but a standard refrigerator worked fine here. No one knew how many mouths this place would feed day to day. Get too much food and it would spoil. Too little, and the person at the desk simply ordered something delivered from one of the many restaurants in the Port.

He took out a ham sandwich and something marked vegetables, which looked like fake tomatoes, asparagus, and some sort of lettuce on bread made from Moon flour. Unappetizing to him, but to someone who hadn't eaten for two days, it might look appealing.

He also took one of the recyclable juice cartons and set everything on a tray.

DeRicci waited in the main area for him, her hands clasped behind her back. "Took you long enough."

He smiled. "If that's bad cop, you'll have to work harder."

Her eyes twinkled but she didn't smile. The pounding continued.

"For a woman who doesn't want to call attention to herself, she's pretty noisy," DeRicci said to the woman behind the counter.

"And fidgety. She was really nervous, but she knew how the decon units worked. Most nervous people are just afraid of what's going to happen in the unit. But she's got something else on her mind."

DeRicci glanced at Flint. He shrugged. He liked to make up his own mind about people. DeRicci pulled open the door leading to the first suite of decontamination units. There were a series of doors in the wide hallway. Usually the suite functioned as a series of smaller rooms. But, if the authorities desired, the doors could be opened, and the entire area would become one decontamination unit.

The pounding continued, erratically, as if the woman were getting tired.

Two guards stood off to the side at the end of the corridor. They weren't visible from the door they appeared to be guarding, so the woman would have no idea that she was being watched.

"You think the guards are necessary?" DeRicci asked.

"Yeah," Flint said. "I do."

"She could be the victim here."

"Traffic doesn't think so."

"Traffic aren't trained investigators."

He stopped. "What do you think is going on?"

"I don't know," DeRicci said. "Something that doesn't seem immediately obvious."

"You're warning me, aren't you?"

"You're going in thinking she's done something wrong. We have to play all angles here. As Gumiela said, there's the possibility she's telling the truth."

"You want to switch roles?" Flint asked.

DeRicci shook her head. "You'll do fine. You've come to your own in this Port. In fact, you're coming along faster and better than I expected."

She had never complimented him before. Flint wasn't sure how to react. "Thanks."

"You don't need to sound so surprised. I can't scare you off, so I may as well train you."

Flint switched the tray of sandwiches and juice to the other hand. They had reached the door.

"You're sure she's through decon?" he asked one of the guards.

"She didn't seem worried," he said, shaking his head. "It was like she knew something we didn't."

"HazMat had given her an on-site check," the other guard said. "They should have stayed with her."

"Traffic called us," DeRicci said. "Stay back when we open the door. I don't want her to know you're here."

"Gotcha," the guard said and touched a point on the wall.

Flint heard the door's locking mechanism beep twice, then click. The pounding stopped.

DeRicci nodded at Flint, giving him the silent instruction to go first.

He pulled the door open. "I hear you wanted food,"

he said in his most cheerful voice. He held the tray out as he stepped inside, uncertain how the woman would react.

She was standing to the side of the door, clutching her purse. He had the sense that she had been about to do something and changed her mind.

"Thank you." Her voice had a trace of an American accent.

DeRicci came in behind him, pushing the door closed. The lights came up, and Flint felt his heart lurch.

The woman was one of the most beautiful he'd ever seen. She had delicate features, long blond hair pulled back into a loose bun, and intelligent blue eyes. She wore no makeup and she didn't seem to have enhancements. The high cheekbones, small nose, and dark lips that offset her light brown skin seemed to be all natural.

He made himself hand her the tray.

"When can I leave?" she asked.

"Soon," he said.

"If you tell us what all that noise was about," DeRicci's voice had grown gruff, almost belligerent. She was starting the routine already.

"I was hungry," the woman said. "I haven't eaten in nearly two days. I had no idea how long I was supposed to be in here, and I was getting woozy. You don't mind if I eat?"

"No, go ahead," Flint said. "That's why we brought it."

"You don't look like people who usually serve food," the woman said.

"Because we aren't," DeRicci said. "We're Armstrong Dome detectives. Traffic thinks you have something to hide."

"What?" The woman had been about to take a bite from her sandwich. She lowered it and stared at De-Ricci in disbelief. "I barely escaped with my life. Didn't they tell you what happened?"

"Yeah, they told us," DeRicci said. "Seems odd. The Rev usually don't let—"

Flint held up a hand. "Why don't you tell us what's going on. I used to work for Traffic. Sometimes they get it wrong."

"I don't think so," DeRicci said.

Flint pushed his hand out farther, as if she hadn't noticed it. "Let her eat, Noelle. We can talk while she gets comfortable. She already said she was woozy."

Besides, he wanted to see if she were really hungry or if that had been a ruse. The woman smiled gratefully at him and then picked up her sandwich again. She ate it in three bites, then wiped her mouth with her fingers.

"Sorry," she said. "It's been a long time."

Flint nodded. "Mind if I sit?"

"Sure," she said and moved the tray so that he could sit on the bench next to her. Interesting thing to do. He would have expected her to nod toward the bench across the room.

This was a woman who knew how to use her looks to get what she wanted. He would let her think she was succeeding.

DeRicci continued to stand before the door, her arms crossed. The woman glanced once in DeRicci's direction, but whether she was looking at the door or at DeRicci, Flint couldn't tell.

"You didn't tell us your name," Flint said.

"You didn't get that from—Traffic, was it?" She picked up the other sandwich, picked off the top piece of bread, and inspected it. After a moment, she removed some real olives—waste of good food, Flint thought, proving she didn't come from a colony or an outpost—and then put the top piece of bread back on. "I'm Greta Palmer."

"A textile worker from Mars," DeRicci said.

"See?" Palmer said around her first bite. "They did tell you."

"I want to hear it from you," Flint said.

"Yeah," DeRicci said. "Tell us what a woman with an American accent and enough education to fly a yacht is doing in a textile recycling plant on Mars."

Palmer swallowed the bread hard. Every movement she made was delicate.

"I'm rebuilding my life," she said, and Flint heard truth in that statement.

"Away from Mars?"

"On Mars." Palmer ate the second sandwich slower, but she still went through it pretty fast. Then she put a hand over her stomach, as if the food bothered her.

Flint slid the juice at her. "This should help. Sometimes the stomach rebels when it gets food it's not used to."

"It all looked pretty normal to me," Palmer said.

Except that it wasn't. Bread made from Moon flour didn't always sit well with folks who were used to the real thing. And she probably hadn't had reconstituted vegetables before. Flint could feel DeRicci's gaze on him, but he refused to meet it. If they were playing good cop/bad cop, they couldn't seem like a team.

"Tell us what happened," Flint said after Palmer finished her juice.

She didn't meet his gaze at first, which he didn't like. "We were on our way to the Moon—"

"From?" DeRicci asked.

"Earth." This time Palmer did look up.

"And what was a textile worker doing on Earth?"

"Taking a vacation," Palmer said, with a bit of an edge in her voice.

"Spendy vacation," DeRicci said. "I can't afford a vacation like that on my salary."

"Noelle," Flint said, playing his part.

DeRicci grunted and shook her head.

Palmer sipped at the juice carton even though she knew it was empty. Then she set it down. "We were headed here when the Rev intercepted us. They took the crew."

"You were the only passenger?" DeRicci asked.

Palmer paused. It seemed to Flint that she hadn't expected the question and was thinking about it. "No," she said after a moment.

"Where are the others?"

"Some of them got in the way," she said. "Others took an escape pod."

Well, that explained that, although Flint didn't like it. He made sure he sounded as sympathetic as possible when he asked, "Why didn't you take an escape pod?"

"It all happened so fast. I was asleep in one of the suites. I came out in time to see the crew get dragged off and the other passengers crowding into the pod—"

"How many others?" DeRicci asked.

"Three," she said.

Interesting. Flint didn't know how to signal DeRicci on this one. Those pods in that ship were built comfortably for one, could accommodate two, and were a tight squeeze on three.

"Why didn't they take separate pods?" DeRicci asked.

"I don't know." Palmer's voice rose, suggesting

panic, although her eyes didn't show it. Flint got the sense that there was panic beneath her words, but not the kind she was playing at.

"You walked out and then what happened?"

"No one saw me. The Rev were getting the crew off the ship, and the others were going away. I didn't know where the other escape pod was. I went into the cockpit to find it, and the computer asked me if I wanted to close the outside exit door because I was alone on the ship. That's when I decided to take my chance."

"And run from the Rev?" DeRicci asked, making it sound like a stupid choice.

"I figured it was the same either way, and I'd get out of there faster in the yacht than I would in the escape pods."

Again, it sounded logical even though it rang false. Flint suddenly wished he was playing bad cop. There were a whole lot of technical questions he wanted to ask her.

"Where did you learn how to pilot yachts?" De-Ricci asked.

"I didn't," Palmer said. "I flew orbitals when I was a kid."

"Your record didn't show that you have a pilot's license," DeRicci said.

"Does your record show everything about your life?" Palmer snapped.

Flint raised his eyebrows, surprised she had sounded so cross. He wouldn't. Not when he was facing two detectives, one of whom didn't seem to trust him.

"Yes, actually," DeRicci said. "That's exactly the sort of thing that shows up no matter what."

"Perhaps when you live an isolated little life on the Moon," Palmer said.

"Seems to me your life on Mars should be isolated. Yours isn't the kind of job that allows you to judge other people." DeRicci had her arms crossed.

Palmer's face paled. Flint had seen interview subjects flush or turn a rather sickly yellowish, but he'd never seen them grow pale.

All of these reactions of hers didn't add up. "He said, "Did the Rev chase you?"

She looked at him, startled, as if she had forgotten he was there. Or perhaps the question surprised her. "I don't know. I flew manually—as fast as I could make that thing go. It was scary. I was out of control most of the time."

That jibed with the report Gumiela had given them. Palmer's landing hadn't exactly been controlled.

"The Rev don't come after someone without a warrant. They're not like the Disty," DeRicci said. "They don't kill everyone around the person they're after."

Palmer raised her head. "What are you saying?"

"I'm saying that the Rev should have checked with their new prisoners about your identity. If they come here, they think you've done something."

Palmer's body froze. Her face lost expression.

"You know that's not true," Flint said to DeRicci, hoping that his position as good cop might draw Palmer out. "The Rev take prisoners that they don't want."

"And set them free if the identities don't match any in their database."

"I didn't know that." Palmer's voice was soft. Flint had the feeling that she had taken the few moments of that interchange to come up with her story. "I thought they'd take me like they took everyone else."

"Except the passengers who climbed into the pods," DeRicci said.

"I don't know what happened to them after I left." Palmer's voice shook. It sounded like a controlled response. She picked up the juice carton from the tray and started to play with the straw. Flint watched her left hand. The skin on the third finger had a thin indentation. She had worn a ring there, and recently.

"You didn't think to go back for them?" DeRicci asked. She sounded offended. Maybe she was.

"I was running for my life," Palmer said.

"The Rev don't kill their prisoners," DeRicci said.

"I didn't know that," Palmer said.

DeRicci's eyebrows went up, her look of triumph. "Yet you accuse me of being unsophisticated. Which is it, Ms. Palmer? Are you sophisticated or not? You piloted orbitals. You handled a yacht. You mean to tell me you've never encountered aliens before?"

Palmer's mouth was closed. Her eyes seemed bigger than they had a moment before.

"I find it hard to believe, given that you're from Mars."

"The Disty—"

"Aren't the Rev. In fact, the Disty and the Rev avoid each other, don't they? What better place to hide from the Rev than on Mars?" DeRicci's words hung in the room. "You want to try this conversation again, Ms. Palmer, and tell us the truth this time?"

Palmer looked at Flint, as if waiting for him to bail her out. But he didn't say anything. He wanted to hear her explanation.

"Why is she doing this?" Palmer asked. "I issued a Mayday as I came into Moon space. I asked for help."

"And we'd give it to you," Flint said, "except for one thing."

Palmer froze again. She had this way of not moving that suggested a lot was going on behind her eyes. "What's that?"

He met her gaze and dropped the good-cop mask. He said, "We have reason to believe that yacht was stolen."

She knew she had lost then, that there were no allies here. When the detectives had come in, she had thought the man would be willing to help her. She knew he found her attractive. He got that look that men got around her sometimes, the one that indicated that he would have trouble looking past her features to the personality behind.

At first, she had even attributed the hostility of the female detective, DeRicci, to those same features. And to her partner's reaction to those features.

But Ekaterina hadn't been thinking clearly. She had forgotten that law enforcement was never trustworthy, especially when it had someone in custody. It was a rookie mistake, something she would have chided one of her clients about.

She shut up after the comment about the yacht, not that it mattered. The detectives gave each other a knowing look that communicated a lot without words. Then DeRicci said to Ekaterina, "You're coming with me."

Ekaterina's heart pounded. She felt that same anticipatory nervousness she had felt earlier. DeRicci thought she was tough. If she took Ekaterina somewhere alone, Ekaterina could get away. She knew it. The woman's arrogance would make it easy.

Flint stood and looked down at Ekaterina. She wondered how she could ever have thought him sympathetic. Those blue eyes that had seemed so warm were cool now. She thought she saw contempt in them.

He wasn't a bad-looking man. He had once had a cherubic face, and she would wager he looked younger than he was. But he was almost too thin, and there were lines forming in the center of his cheeks, accenting that thinness. It made him look harsh.

There was no evidence of the attraction now. Had she imagined it?

"Come on," he said in that same gentle voice.

She stood, a little more certain on her feet this time than she had been earlier. The food had helped, and she did appreciate it. It would keep her going for a while.

She picked up the tray and her purse at the same time, making the movement with the purse seem like an unconscious gesture. The last thing she wanted to do was call attention to it. She didn't want anyone to find that pistol.

"I'll worry about the tray," Flint said, taking it from her.

DeRicci hadn't moved away from the door. "Believe it or not," she said, "I have other cases that I'd like to get to. So let's move."

Ekaterina nodded. She had played this entire interview wrong. She had forgotten her new self, forgotten that she was supposed to be a textile worker, not a lawyer. She should have paid attention to the questions they didn't ask, the way they were evaluating her, to see if her comments jibed with her personal history. Of course they didn't. The discussion of the orbitals proved that. If she didn't get away, she was going to have to come up with a way to unify everything she said.

Flint set the tray back on the bench. He came up behind her, not allowing her to go anywhere but with DeRicci. As long as he stayed with them, her plan to use the pistol wouldn't work. He was too observant. She saw him look at her hand.

She knew he couldn't see the areas where the security enhancements had been removed—she'd used a cream that promoted healing—but he stared at her left hand. He saw that thin line where Simon's ring had been.

DeRicci opened the door. Ekaterina felt herself tense. She couldn't make a break for it in here; there would be space cops and officials everywhere. She had to wait until they were outside the Port.

Two guards stepped forward. They had been standing to the side of the door. Ekaterina bit back a curse.

"You're coming with us," DeRicci said to them.

They nodded, and flanked Ekaterina, leading her through the same corridor she had come through. It felt as if she had been in that decontamination chamber forever, but the hallway was a reminder that she hadn't, that she had passed through just a short time ago.

She wondered if the Rev had arrived yet. They wouldn't let her go, no matter what was happening. They would find her if she was still in police custody. And if she was still in police custody, she would be forced to go.

She had to get away somehow. She just wasn't sure how.

Flint still walked behind her. She could feel him. He was too close, probably on purpose. She hated that. She wanted to turn and tell him to get back, but she had called too much attention to her difficult personality already. If she seemed meeker, resigned, they all might relax their guard, and she might have a chance to get away.

What she needed was a plan. But there was no way to have a plan when she didn't know what was going to happen next.

She had to be flexible.

She had to be creative.

And she had to be *fast*.

13

Because the police required him and Dylani to stay in Armstrong Dome, they had offered to pay for a hotel nearby. The hotel was old, near the City Complex, and had some of the poorest security Jamal had ever seen. It was almost as if they wanted the Wygnin to come for Ennis again, as if they would do nothing to stop it.

Fortunately, the Wygnin were still in custody.

The room was tiny, as all of the old hotel rooms were. When this place had been built, Armstrong had been a small colony with a modest dome—one they didn't think they could expand. Technology changed that, but these tiny hotels stayed as a part of the historic preservation movement that had been sweeping the Moon for the last fifty years.

No police officers followed him here. They made it clear that he and his family were on their own recognizance. But Detective Flint hadn't been the only one to warn them that they would be in trouble if they ran. Jamal had heard that from every single officer he'd spoken to.

Even the social workers who had taken care of Ennis had warned him. It was almost as if they knew what Jamal had done in the past and they expected him to do it again.

If he fled again, he would have to take his family. Or split them up. Or send Ennis into exile alone, which was precisely the situation he wanted to avoid.

He had a small break, as Flint had said. The Wygnin did not have the proper warrants, and Jamal might be able to fight that on some kind of technicality. He didn't know enough about multicultural law to know whether or not he would have a chance.

Dylani sat near the window, its plastic surface pitted from years of poor filtration in the old dome. She held Ennis tightly, rocking him back and forth and crooning to him. To Jamal's surprise, the boy didn't seem to mind.

Jamal used the cheap system built into the wall by the only other chair to search for attorneys. He knew this wasn't the best way to go about such a search, but he felt he had no other choice. His own links were minimal—he and Dylani had conserved money by refusing to buy services—and he didn't have access to the most basic information, like directories of other communities. The hotel system also had records of a variety of professionals—doctors, financial consultants, and of course, lawyers. Apparently people who stayed here often needed consultation.

The records contained complaints and citations of merit, recognition in any way, and a history of each professional's mention in various media.

It would take him weeks to sort through all the information on the attorneys in Armstrong alone.

But he needed someone and, worst of all, he had to hire someone he could afford. Even if he and Dylani sold the house and he went back to work full-time, he wouldn't be able to afford most of these multicultural attorneys.

If Jamal wanted to go that big, he needed to ask someone to take him on as a charity case. There had to be someone who was willing to take a risk, someone who was willing to see if the law would bend.

Jamal just had to find him.

When they reached the entrance to interstellar holding, Flint left them. DeRicci seemed to have the matter well in hand, and the guards kept a close eye on Palmer. Flint still wasn't sure what to make of her. She seemed too educated for her work, but a lot of people chose jobs that didn't use their education.

She also seemed skittish, in a way that didn't entirely make sense. Usually, criminals were cocky or terrified. Rarely did they display this combination of controlled panic and instinctual combativeness.

Somehow he felt that was the key to her; that and the missing ring on her left hand. Had she been married or was she simply one of those women who wore rings on that finger? And why had she stopped?

When he caught up with Palmer again, he would ask her those questions. But first he had to inspect the yacht.

It took him a while to get to Terminal 5 and even longer to reach the yacht. Space Traffic Control had docked it at the farthest reaches of the terminal, probably because Palmer's piloting had been wild. It would have been better to keep her as far from other ships as possible, to minimize any potential disaster.

As Flint approached the ship, he touched the chip on his sleeve that allowed him to record. Palmer's inexpert landing was obvious just from the way the yacht was parked. It was facing the wrong direction and the tunnel that usually allowed easy access had been turned almost sideways so that it could come close to the main entrance.

It bothered him that this yacht was so similar to the one used in the Disty vengeance killings. He wasn't sure what the connection was, but he had a hunch that Palmer was involved in something more than simple theft.

As he had the last time, he decided to explore the outside of the ship first. The ship's identification had been removed, as had its name and it secondary identification, just like on the previous yacht.

The difference here was that this yacht had no recent scorching and scarring. All of the damage to its exterior was several months old.

Still, he recorded it, getting the imagery exactly. It didn't look like similar weaponry had been used on this ship. So if it had been in a battle, it had been of a different type.

He would have thought, given the story that Palmer told, that the Rev would have attacked the ship, then boarded it, but no matter how hard he looked, he saw no evidence of attack.

He didn't even find evidence of boarding, such as he had found on the other yacht. No scrapes outside the entrance, nothing to show that another ship's grappling equipment had attempted to pull the door open.

One escape pod was missing, just as Palmer said it would be and, he judged from the placement, it was the pod from the cockpit. The other escape pods were in place.

The exterior was telling him a lot, but not in any fashion he could use, at least not yet. He finished pacing around it and finally decided to go inside.

He had to use a sliding staircase that was stowed in

each dock to climb to the main door. The dock's tunnel hadn't gone that far. The staircase worked like a bridge between them.

He pulled open the door and stepped into the airlock. No signs of violence, nothing out of place. Not even handprints from panicked people being dragged away from the safety of their ship.

If he hadn't heard Palmer's story, he would have no suspicion whatsoever of Rev involvement, of a crisis on the ship, of people dragged away against their will.

A shiver ran through him. The sense he had had from the beginning that she was lying came back. Something had happened, but what?

He stepped through the airlock into the crew area of the yacht. It was amazingly neat. The people who were dragged through here hadn't pulled on emergency switches or reached for makeshift weapons. The computer panels didn't even flash *Warning* or announce an illegal entry.

The disquiet he felt in the airlock grew. The door to the passenger section stood open, the only thing that seemed out of order. He stepped inside.

The seats were neat, as if they had been vacuumed clean. None of them looked as if they'd been sat in, and there was no evidence of a hasty evacuation. Nothing had been left on the seats or in the seat pockets. None of the reclining seats had been left down, and the seats that turned into cots were in their upright positions.

He stepped toward the back and peered into the suites. The beds were made with military precision. No clothing hung in the closets and no personal belongings sat on the dressing tables.

In fact this yacht, like the previous one, was incredibly impersonal. It seemed to follow factory specs. The rugs were the same; the seats were the same; even the linens on the bed were the same.

He liked that less than he liked Palmer's story.

Carefully, he made his way back to the crew area. If this yacht had carried four passengers, as Palmer had said, there was no evidence of it. There wasn't even lint on the floor of the passenger cabin.

He stepped through the crew area into the cockpit. The cockpit was the only new area to him. He hadn't been able to inspect the Disty vengeance killing cockpit because of the way the body had been draped. Maybe he should go back now that forensics was done and see what he could find.

It might provide the link between the two ships.

This cockpit looked lived-in. There were jackets hung in the closet behind the door, and equipment that did not look like regulation. The door to the escape pod was still open—something any good pilot would not let happen. That probably caused some of the problems that Palmer had handling the ship. If the yacht was like others of its class, it was designed to be flown with the pod's exterior and interior doors closed.

He recorded the entire cockpit, noting that three of the chairs looked as if they'd been used. There was even a covered drinking cup stashed in its secure holder near the co-pilot's station. He might have to get forensics in here after all.

According to the computer, the ship's logs were intact. He hadn't expected that. It made this case even more bizarre. Anyone involved in criminal activity would have wiped the logs clean.

Flint scanned them in text first, noting that the encounter with the Rev was logged in, just as it was supposed to be. That surprised him even more. When had the pilot time to log in his encounter with the Rev? According to Palmer, they had boarded and then taken the crew away, while the passengers were in a state of panic.

"Computer," Flint said. "I'm Armstrong Dome Law Enforcement investigating a possible crime. My identification is being pressed to the screen at the pilot's station."

He put his finger on the screen.

"You are required by law to answer my questions. I want audio answers, although I may download information later."

"Understood." The androgynous computer voice signaled that the yacht was of Earth Alliance make.

"What's your ship log default?" he asked.

"I am to record destinations, changes in course, and any incoming or outgoing messages."

"Do you usually operate in default mode or does your pilot control the log?"

"My pilot has added to the log in the past. It has not been touched on this trip."

"So you were in default mode on this trip."

"Yes," the computer said.

"Where did this flight originate?" Flint asked.

"San Francisco."

"Where was it supposed to terminate."

"San Francisco."

"Not Mars?"

"San Francisco."

He felt frustration build. Questioning a computer was not like questioning a person. He wasn't going to get answers this way.

Instead, he hacked into the system.

There wasn't a lot of useful information about the ship's registry. Either it hadn't been entered into the computer or it had been deleted. He did find evidence that the ship's computer system was not original to the design. It had been added shortly after the ship became operational.

The computer was a sophisticated self-contained unit that did not link to any outside nets. It did not answer any more than the most rudimentary questions and, it seemed, it either purged previous missions or had not recorded them.

"Hmm," he said, resting an elbow on the hard plastic console beside the computer screen. The computer's memory seemed remarkably clean, given the condition of the ship's exterior. Search as he might, he couldn't even find ghosts of past information. This system had been thoroughly purged.

Which made him even more suspicious. It was not logical for Palmer to bring a ship here and abandon it so easily when the ship itself so clearly cried out criminal activity. Flint searched the specs for some hidden cargo area, but unless the ship was carrying micro-cargo, he didn't find anything.

Still, he wasn't going to rule out smuggling. He wasn't going to rule out anything.

He scanned the text version of the logs. They confirmed a San Francisco departure, with a turn-around point midway between the Earth and the Moon. Short trip, then. The mission of the trip was not outlined. Neither was the name of the pilot or any member of the crew. And of course he didn't find a passenger list.

Flint hit audio for communications playback. He leaned back in the pilot's chair and listened to routine space traffic commands for a private ship. Nothing out of the ordinary there. The ship had a designation, given to it by San Francisco Space Traffic, and he made certain that he got that information in two separate places.

Whether that designation was legitimate or not wouldn't be hard to check.

From the moment the yacht left Earth orbit, there was communications silence. Until:

"D.I.E.M., this is *Brocene*." The speech had no inflection at all. A computerized voice, although not one from Earth Alliance. This one didn't sound human at all.

"*Brocene*, go ahead." The responding voice was male, and Flint identified it as the pilot's voice. So far he had heard nothing from Palmer at all.

"Rendezvous at the usual coordinates?"

"Roger that, *Brocene*."

Then there was silence. Flint checked the time. The yacht was nearly to its destination coordinates. Then he checked for the initials D.I.E.M. He did not see what they referred to. That was not the designation that had been used for the ship in San Francisco, yet it seemed to be used as a name here.

When the yacht reached the destination coordinates, communications began again.

"*Brocene*, this is D.I.E.M. We have you on visual."

Flint leaned forward and checked for a visual file. There was one. He turned it on and it appeared as a small image on the screen before him, and he was startled to see the blue and orange markings of a Rev prison ship.

It was a small ship, as Rev vessels went, but it was still imposing. And it was large enough to destroy this yacht with a single blast of its weapons.

"Roger that, D.I.E.M." said the computerized voice. Flint now recognized its toneless qualities. It was designed to mimic Rev vocal inflections. "Have you our cargo?"

"Primed and ready. As soon as we receive payment, we are a go."

Flint sat up, a chill running down his back.

"Payment sent, D.I.E.M."

"Checking now, *Brocene*."

There was silence on both ends. Flint wondered how the pilot confirmed the payment being sent. Flint had found no record of credits in the computer system, and the computer was an internal unit. Had there been another computer on board?

He would have to search for it, and for the information on the ship's computer. His work here might take longer than he had planned.

"Okay, *Brocene*. We have a record of payment."

"The agreement is that we get the cargo immediately."

"Nice try." It sounded as if the pilot were smiling. "We do this without direct contact."

"It would be easier—"

"Ease is not the issue and you know it. Caution is. I even hate these communications. If we could find a way around them, I'd sure as hell appreciate it."

Flint let out a small whistle. This was something that had happened before and the pilot thought it would happen again.

"Communication is necessary. In the past there have been problems. Unexpected guests." Somewhere along the way the Rev voice had changed. Flint couldn't pinpoint the moment the computer stopped speaking for the Rev and one of its crew had started speaking directly.

"I remember," the pilot said.

"So if you feel this is not cautious enough, then changing the plan should not be a problem for you."

"We'll be evacuating the ship in thirty Earth minutes." The pilot sounded firm. Evacuation? Palmer had said nothing about evacuation.

He listened as the pilot continued. "She won't know we're gone."

She? Could the pilot be referring to Palmer or someone else? Was the cargo they were discussing human?

Odd that the pilot hadn't dumped any of this from the computer system. Unless he needed it for some other purpose. After all, his voice was the only part of him that appeared here. Even though Flint had searched for crew identification in the system, he hadn't found any—and there were no visuals of the crew either.

"Give it another thirty minutes," the pilot was saying, "and you can board. I'll be picking up the ship from impound in a week or so. If there's permanent damage, I'm coming after you."

The plan was to abandon the ship and its cargo—probably its passenger or passengers—to the Rev. Which must have happened, since the crew was gone. They took the escape pods from the cockpit before Palmer even knew what was happening.

But that still didn't explain how she came into possession of the yacht and why she wouldn't tell all of this to the authorities on Armstrong.

Unless the Rev had a warrant. If they did, she was the one in violation of the law, not the crew of this ship.

The Rev agreed to the terms and signed off. There was silence again. Flint glanced at the log before him. It registered a number of communications files after this one. They probably came from Palmer.

Maybe she hadn't lied about her incompetence at flying a sophisticated ship like a yacht. Any competent pilot would have purged all of this, and anything else that contradicted her story, assuming that Armstrong authorities would only do a cursory search of the computer system and send her on her way.

She probably hadn't even realized that the yacht itself was suspicious. No registration, no serial numbers, not even an I.D. program built into the computer.

He let the communications files spin forward.

"*Brocene,* this is D.I.E.M." The pilot's voice again. Only he sounded different. Strained.

"This had better be important." The Rev didn't seem happy to hear from him either.

"It is." There was more than strain in the pilot's voice. He had an urgent tone, the kind humans got when they were trying to impart information different from what their words implied. "I just got a coded message from my headquarters. I need to keep the yacht."

Flint crossed his arms and tilted his head. Interesting. This wasn't playing out the way he would have expected.

"We have an agreement." The Rev sounded angry. Even though the anger wasn't directed at him, the hair on the back of Flint's neck rose. He'd seen an angry Rev only once. It wasn't something he wanted to see again.

"Which I'm living up to." The pilot spoke so fast that he seemed to have interrupted the Rev, which was a cultural no-no. "All I wanted to do was let you know that I'm dumping her into a pod. You can pick it up an hour after we've left the area. Is that clear?"

Flint frowned. So a woman was supposed to be in the pod. The pilot's story sounded logical, but it didn't explain what really happened.

There wasn't enough information here. Was Palmer the only passenger on the ship? Was she really a passenger at all or a member of this crew?

"We'll pick it up now." The Rev was referring to the pod.

"No!" The pilot sounded terrified. Flint's frown grew. He had learned in his early days as a space cop that a person never argued with a Rev using that tone. The Rev could be manipulated or lied to, so long as the lies were convincing, but a direct argument usually made the Rev angrier. And an angry Rev was likely to go berserk.

Flint winced as if this conversation were taking place in front of him. His entire body tensed.

"There are other ships in the area," the pilot said. "If they witness the exchange, then we will never be able to do this again."

That sounded plausible, but even plausible explanations didn't always appease an angry Rev. This one didn't answer immediately. Flint turned over various scenarios in his mind. Had the Rev come after the crew at this moment? If so, why was there no evidence of boarding on the airlock? Rev ships were no more sophisticated in mid-space boarding than human ships were. There should have been grapple marks on the exterior of the ship.

Flint glanced at the communications logs. They were still spinning forward. The silence he heard was the same silence the pilot had listened to.

It did not bode well.

Finally, there was a click in the log. "We shall do so this one time," the Rev said. "But this will not become policy, or our business is done."

"It's not policy. It's just a—" There was a bumping

sound and a slight grunt from the pilot "—blip. Something went wrong at headquarters that they want the yacht for. I don't have as much flexibility as usual."

He sounded terrified. Any human on the other end would not have agreed to this plan. But apparently, the Rev did not know the subtleties of human vocal cues.

The Rev agreed to the terms and then added, "But should you try this again, you will feel our wrath."

"Yeah, I know." The pilot sounded resigned. Then he signed off.

The communications logs continued to spool. The next communication came from Palmer, claiming she didn't know how to fly the ship, that her crew had been taken by the Rev, and she needed help. She sounded panicked too, but her panic, while louder than the pilot's, seemed more controlled.

Flint could not say why he had that impression, although he did. He listened all the way to the end, as the ground crew in Armstrong talked her down. She said nothing about the conversations between the pilot and the Rev, nothing about the missing woman—if indeed there had been one—and nothing about a plan gone awry.

She sounded like an innocent victim, yet somehow he doubted she was.

He bent over the logs and replayed the last communication between the pilot and the Rev. That bump and pause was the clue. If Flint had to guess, he would say that the pilot was more afraid of someone in the cockpit than he was of the Rev, which was saying something.

He thought back to the woman's story. She claimed she had been one among many passengers. She claimed that three of the passengers had taken an escape pod. And she claimed that the Rev had boarded the ship, taking the crew with them.

But nothing on the ship confirmed her story. Yes, a pod was missing, but it was missing from the cockpit. And if the communications logs were accurate, the Rev were expecting a single pod to drop out of that ship. They would let it float for nearly an hour before picking it up, giving the yacht time to escape.

In fact, that hour would be all that a yacht, flown manually, would need to reach the Moon first. The Rev would be delayed even longer, thinking the pilot had somehow played a trick on them.

Combine that with the lack of boarding marks, no sign of forced entry into the cockpit, and no evidence of passengers at all, and Palmer's story completely fell apart.

Not to mention that she claimed she was on vacation from Mars when this ship had no intention of going to Mars. It was flying round-trip to San Francisco. It had arrived at its mid-trip destination when the pilot contacted the Rev.

Then there was the matter of the matching ships. The Rev and the Disty hated each other. They would not work together for any reason. But humans had no qualms about working with both.

The Disty ship had three bodies of people supposedly on a vacation. Palmer was supposedly on a vacation. She didn't seem like someone who lived on Mars. She had skills and an education that wasn't listed in her file.

And then there was a fact that DeRicci had mentioned: What better place to hide from the Rev than on Mars? The Disty had overrun Mars and the Rev hated them.

The group from the Disty vengeance killing had been found by the Disty in a yacht similar to this one. Flint wanted to hear their logs, if he could. He would wager that, if the logs hadn't been purged, they would reveal a conversation similar to the first one he'd heard here.

Someone was selling people who were trying to Disappear to the very groups that wanted them.

Which meant that Greta Palmer wasn't a victim of an in-space ship takeover by the Rev, nor was she a run-of-the-mill yacht thief. She was a criminal wanted by the Rev, a criminal who had managed to force an entire crew into an escape pod and turn them over to the Rev in her place. Then she had come here, pleading for assistance.

She was too smart to tell the truth, and she was good at survival.

She had mentioned that she thought the Rev would be after her too. Neither he nor DeRicci had thought her protests sounded right—the Rev wouldn't behave the way she had said they would. But the Rev would come if Palmer were their quarry.

They would be here soon, and they would want her.

Palmer was desperate. She might be willing to try anything, including attacking police officers, in order to escape the Rev.

Flint opened his link and hoped he would be able to warn DeRicci in time.

14

Ekaterina clutched her purse against her body, playing the terrified tourist. The terror wasn't that hard to feign. She hadn't heard about any Rev arriving yet, but she knew it would only be a matter of time.

She sat in the back seat of an ancient aircar, a model that she hadn't seen since she was a teenager. It had been modified for police use—there was a plastic protective barrier between the back seat and the front, and there were no door handles on the insides of the back doors.

The rest of the aircar hadn't been changed, however, and she wondered if the police department on Armstrong knew how vulnerable their vehicles were. She had learned all about this model when she'd been defending a client in San Francisco. He'd used a laser pistol to disable the secondary systems while a friend had been driving.

The car had crashed.

She was constantly surprised at how much practical information she had acquired, both from her wild teenage years and her years as a defense attorney. She only hoped it would serve her in good stead now.

One of the guards sat beside her in the back seat. He'd been solicitous—helping her strap in before the car started. He'd also been practical as well. His partner had taken his weapon into the front seat, and anything that Elkaterina could use against the guard went also.

They were treating her as a prisoner—sort of. If they were really worried about her, they would have taken her purse as well. But they weren't certain if she was telling the truth, and they had a myriad of regulations to follow.

A tourist could sue Armstrong Dome for maltreatment, especially if the tourist had claimed she needed help. The media always supported the tourist's claim, and the publicity alone often hurt tourism in an area after such an event. As a result, governments like Armstrong, especially those whose economy had a strong reliance on tourism, tried to prevent problems through regulation.

Often those regulations hampered law enforcement techniques, just as they were doing now. Detective DeRicci hadn't arrested Ekaterina yet. They didn't have enough information. So they couldn't take away her personal possessions because of her potential tourist status.

That would all change once Ekaterina got to the station. She had to make her move before then.

DeRicci drove the aircar manually, which Ekaterina initially thought to be an interesting choice. The car rose only a few inches off the roadway, making Ekaterina wonder why the police didn't use a wheeled vehicle. They probably wanted the high speeds and shortcuts that air routes provided.

Armstrong itself looked different. The area near the Port had been rebuilt—the dilapidated buildings and dusty roads were long gone. Ekaterina felt a deep disappointment. She had hoped that the slum area of

Armstrong would provide her with a means for escape.

Instead, the nearby buildings had the shiny newness of the latest synthetic materials. Some of them actually shimmered in a variety of changing colors, and a few seemed to use the dome wall as part of the building structure—obviously another change in Armstrong building codes.

It wasn't so hard, then, to look around as if she were a tourist who had never seen this part of the universe before. She hadn't.

But the road was familiar, its twists and turns the same as they had been a decade before. DeRicci was not a cautious driver. She took corners sharply, and when she floated the car to avoid obstacles, she went up on a steep and often dangerous trajectory. Other aircars had to swerve to avoid her, and a lot of them used their horns.

Aircar drivers weren't used to surprise. Most of them punched in their destination and let the cars take them there, using set routes. All aircars were linked to the street traffic control system, which prevented most collisions by making sure that each car had its own direct route.

A manual driver screwed all of that up. A manual driver, while being tracked by the system, could make sudden and unexpected moves, and the computerized system couldn't compensate. Instead, the other aircars had to.

Perhaps all cops had to learn to drive aircars manually. That way, no one could hijack the system and prevent cops from chasing criminals on the streets.

Ekaterina suppressed a sigh. No matter where she went in the human-settled universe, everything was monitored. Perhaps she was just deluding herself. Perhaps she had no chance of evading the Rev at all.

Still her left hand, the one farthest from the guard, slipped behind her, feeling the warm plastic of the aircar's window. Beneath it, on the body's interior, she knew she would find a circular opening the size of her fist, leading into the car's secondary systems.

The dome filters were shifting from daylight to twilight, in a vain attempt to mimic Earthlight. The result was simply an odd sort of dusk that seemed like badly lit darkness. The automatic street lights hadn't flicked on yet, and visibility was poor.

Ekaterina's fingers finally found the opening. It was smaller than she remembered, and she felt a frisson of fear. Maybe her client had lied about what he'd done after all.

Still, she unlatched the cover over the opening, then brought her hand back to her lap.

The guard hadn't moved.

The dome was taller here, and newer. Perhaps this section of the city hadn't been completed when Ekaterina had visited. The buildings that surrounded her right now were at least ten stories high, and she didn't remember ever seeing any buildings in Armstrong taller than five stories.

DeRicci turned another corner. The buildings here seemed almost monolithic, attached above in a series of interlinking floors. Ekaterina couldn't even see the dome.

Without the automatic street lights, the areas beneath the buildings was very dark. The aircar's lights came on, but Ekaterina still found herself blinking, trying to get her eyes to adjust.

"Nearly there," the guard said to her, and Ekaterina

jumped. She hadn't expected him to speak. She was very glad she didn't have her hand behind her at that moment.

She nodded. She wasn't going to get a chance to escape into a familiar part of town.

Ahead, the street widened into something approximating a boulevard. The area there was extremely well lit, so well lit that some of the light backwashed into this darker section of town, illuminating the faces of the cops in the front seat.

This was her only chance.

She opened the false side of her purse, grabbed the laser pistol, and flicked it on. It grew warm in her hand. She hoped that this aircar was the model she remembered, because she wasn't going to get another chance.

She turned in her seat restraints, shoved the muzzle of the pistol into the opening and fired. The shot blew a hole through the back, but that wasn't where the damage occurred. The tiny circuitry, attached by even smaller filaments, absorbed the laser's energy, sending it throughout the system. The shot illuminated the back half of the car, the circuitry clear through the synthetic paneling.

The car groaned softly, as if it were in pain. The guard lunged for Ekaterina, his hand closing on her arm. She couldn't pull the pistol out of the hole.

It hadn't worked. She was trapped here, and now her captors knew that she was no troubled tourist. She was a criminal, and they would do everything they could to give her back to the Rev.

Flint grabbed the back of the pilot's chair in frustration. The cockpit seemed small and close, but he knew that was just being caused by his mood.

DeRicci wasn't answering her link. She had to be driving. The only time she blocked her personal communications system this completely was when she was driving an aircar. She always said she couldn't concentrate on all the maneuvers if anyone distracted her.

He glanced at the image of the Rev prison ship, which he'd left on the viewscreen after his scan through the logs. It looked sleek and menacing, portending trouble ahead.

He leaned forward and turned off the image. The interior of the cockpit hummed. Some equipment was still on, even though it shouldn't have been—yet another sign of an inexperienced landing. Before he left, he would have the computer run a systems check, shutting down anything that wasn't necessary.

He was a bit surprised HazMat hadn't done that, but then they touched as little as they could when a ship landed in Terminal 5. They didn't want to destroy evidence.

Neither did he. He tried DeRicci's personal link one more time, and discovered that it was still blocked. So he linked with the precinct system, setting it to send an alert to DeRicci's links the moment she entered any government building.

He would continue to try to contact her, but if she forgot to turn off the block (something she did fairly often), the precinct system would override it.

He hoped that would be enough, even though he was worried that it wasn't.

DeRicci had never heard a car moan before. Light flared behind her, and the guard behind her cried out. They were in the darkest part of the Proscenium Arches, the new shopping and entertainment complex that the city's manager had deemed essential for Armstrong's health—the complex that violated half a dozen of Armstrong's city ordinances, including the one about blocking the dome. There were no other cars around.

Light surged toward her. She had blocked her personal links as she always did when she drove, so she couldn't send an instant emergency alert. Instead, she reached beneath the car's guidance system, sending a message to Street Traffic Control, as the light hit.

Energy radiated up through the systems, burning her fingers. She cried out in pain and pulled her hand back when the car froze.

Her own momentum carried her forward, thrusting her against the restraints. She thought for a moment that the restraints wouldn't hold, and then she realized that the car was flipping, turning upside down.

DeRicci felt the restraints twist even as she continued to go forward; then the restraints forced her to move with the car, sideways, upside down, and then all the way down, landing with a thump on the passenger side.

The air smelled of sweat and panic and burned plastic; around her, people were crying out—men were crying out. The only woman's voice she heard was her own.

The car groaned again, only this time the groan came from the synthetic exterior settling in an unusual position. DeRicci remained suspended in the driver's seat, the restraints keeping her in place.

She had never been in an accident before. Aircar accidents happened mostly to police vehicles because the police were the only ones who used manual controls, but all she had ever done was come to the scene much later, examine evidence, look at the Street Traffic records to see if someone was at fault.

Her heart was pounding and her mouth was dry. It must have taken her a full minute to remember that she had someone in custody.

She reached for the dash to set the car rightside up, but the controls had been destroyed. Below her—on the passenger side—the guard moaned and brought a hand to his head. The back seat was hidden by the darkness.

"Everyone all right?" she asked.

No one answered.

Ekaterina was trapped in her restraints. Her hand, laser pistol clutched in her fist, was stuck behind her. The guard had torn her shirt and broken the skin on her other arm. It ached, but fortunately he wasn't touching her any longer.

He was curled in a ball against his door, unconscious or dead. He had taken his restraints off as he lunged for her—bad mistake, since the car upended at the same moment.

Ekaterina struggled in silence. DeRicci seemed to be the only other person awake in the car, and she was just getting her bearings. She wouldn't act if she thought everyone else was unconscious.

But it was hard for Ekaterina to keep her own breathing silent. With her sore and bleeding arm, she reached for the release on the restraints, finding it and opening it.

The restraints hissed as they rolled back, and she nearly tumbled into the unconscious guard.

"Who's that? Ms. Palmer?" The detective didn't wait for an answer. Instead, she started struggling with her own restraints.

There was no handle on the door. Ekaterina had forgotten that. She wasted precious seconds scrambling for the conventional way out before she remembered she had burned a hole through the back of the vehicle.

The hole wasn't person-sized, but she didn't care. She shoved her injured arm through, clearing a path for herself, then followed. Hot, jagged plastic scraped her face, cut into her sides. Behind her, she could hear DeRicci telling her not to move.

DeRicci couldn't have gotten to her own pistol yet, right? And even if she had, it wouldn't matter. The plastic divider was still up, and all of the controls were dead. The only way to get it down would be by force.

Cool air touched Ekaterina's face and she sucked it in, grateful for its freshness. Then she remembered where she was. There was no fresh air in Armstrong Dome, no breeze. If she thought the air was cool and fresh, that was only by comparison to the air inside the car, which was hot and foul. She hoped there was nothing toxic mixed into that stench. Even though she wanted to escape, she really didn't want to hurt anyone.

She braced her hands—one of them still holding the laser pistol—on the outside of the car and pushed herself out, but her hips got stuck. She hadn't quite made the hole wide enough.

"Am I the only one awake here?" DeRicci's voice sounded muffled and far away. She was apparently still trapped in the driver's seat.

Ekaterina was badly jammed. No amount of pushing seemed to get her loose. Sweat ran off her forehead. Or was it blood? She wasn't sure.

All she knew was that she needed more leverage, and she couldn't get it while her fingers were wrapped around the pistol. She kicked, and her feet found the plastic barrier. She wedged them back, and then shoved with all her might.

Her hips squinched forward a centimeter.

She shoved again, and this time she broke free, her torso falling forward and slamming into the back of the car.

The sound echoed in the arch formed by the strange buildings. Even her breathing sounded amplified.

She squeezed the rest of the way out and fell onto the pavement, its smooth synthetic surface amazingly hard. The car was shaking as DeRicci struggled to free herself.

Ekaterina got to her feet. She was dizzy. The smell, the accident—something had affected her sense of balance. But she still had her purse (how had she gotten that out? She didn't recall pulling it with her) and her pistol.

She clung to both as she looked around. Darkness and tall buildings with bridgelike overhangs behind her. Light and a wide street, filled with people, ahead of her. On either side, more darkness, with even deeper shadows. The shadows could be doorways or windows or another street.

Or people.

She didn't know. But she had gotten another chance. All she had to do was pick a direction, and pray that it was the right one.

15

The lawyer's office was on the other side of Armstrong from Jamal's hotel. The lawyer had offered to come to Jamal, but Jamal had refused. He couldn't judge a man by his clothes; he needed to see the man's daily surroundings. Not that they would tell him everything, but they would help.

Even though it was just past dark, the lawyer's offices were bustling. Associates curled over their desks, researching various cases. Wall screens showed real-time video from off-Moon trials. The sound was off on all of them; if someone wanted to listen, he had to use his link.

Still, it made for a sense of chaos, of information being absorbed at lightspeed, and it made the offices of Laskie, Needahl, and Cardiff seem like the most important place in the universe.

A secretary—a real person, a sign of importance and comfort—found a room for Dylani and Ennis to wait in while Jamal met with the attorney. Dylani wanted to join Jamal, believing that she had more experience with the legal system than he did.

But she was wrong. He knew twenty times more about legalities than she ever would.

He wished she hadn't come along, but she wouldn't

wait in the hotel room. She was afraid to be alone, although she wouldn't admit it. Jamal also had the sense that she was worried that someone would come for Ennis while he was gone. By coming with Jamal, she made sure that Ennis was hard to find.

At least Jamal had managed to talk her out of going into the attorney's office. Ennis's fussiness helped, as did her desire to keep her son in her arms ever since he'd been returned.

The secretary led Jamal to an office at the end of a long hallway. The office door looked as though it was made of real wood, and the carpet seemed to be woven from natural Earth fibers. Incense burned nearby—a spicy, unidentifiable scent that made Jamal want to sneeze.

The secretary knocked once, then opened the door, announcing Jamal as if he were a courtier about to visit an ancient king. He went inside, almost expecting trumpets to herald his arrival.

The office was bigger than his entire house. The right and left walls were glassed in, artificial sunlight pouring down on flourishing green plants. Other plants tumbled off tables and hung from the ceiling, giving the air a freshness it didn't deserve, especially after the incense in the hallway.

The greenery was so startling that it took Jamal a moment to find and focus on the desk. It seemed to be growing out of the floor. The carpet, which had come in from the hallway, covered the sides of the desk. Papers sat on top of it, their very presence a ludicrous display of wealth.

Jamal had expected this lawyer, whom he had chosen based on the limited resources available to him at the hotel, to have humble offices, maybe even a cubicle in a bigger firm. Certainly he hadn't expected this.

A man emerged from the greenery, carrying a plant mister. He was tall and slender, his skin a cross between a whitish gold and burnished bronze—the sort of color that would appeal to anyone. His hair was dark, as were his eyes, and his features had a hawklike precision that suggested he was older than he appeared.

"Mr. Kanawa," the man said in a rich baritone. "I'm Hakan Needahl."

He set the mister on a pile of papers—a carelessness that made Jamal wince—and came forward, hand extended.

Jamal shook his hand, then gave Needahl a cautious smile. "I'm afraid I've already wasted your time, Mr. Needahl. I clearly don't have the funds to hire you."

Needahl's almond-shaped eyes narrowed just a little. The piercing intelligence in them seemed heightened by the movement. "I have been practicing law for sixty-five years, Mr. Kanawa. When I was young and hungry, I took any case I could. Then I took only the cases that would enrich my bank account. Now that I have all the money I need and some that I don't, I take cases that challenge my mind."

"That's all well and good, sir, but I can barely afford to be in Armstrong." Which was, in its way, yet another lie. He couldn't afford to be in Armstrong at all.

"The consultation is free, Mr. Kanawa." Needahl extended his hand toward the amazing desk. "Have a seat. Let's see if I can help you."

Jamal didn't see a chair, but he went forward anyway. As he approached, a chair rose out of the carpet. The chair seemed comfortable, even though it too was covered in the same fibers as the carpet. He couldn't see the mechanism that brought the chair up, but he knew the trigger had to be somewhere.

He touched the back of the chair gingerly, surprised at how soft the fibers were, then sat down. Needahl walked around the desk and sat on a more conventional chair, one that appeared to be made of a leatherlike synthetic.

"Tell me your situation," he said, folding his hands over the only bare spot on the desktop.

Jamal's throat constricted. He hadn't talked to anyone about himself or his problems in years. "Do I have to hire you to keep anything I say here confidential?"

"Sharp question." Needahl smiled in appreciation. "No, you don't have to hire me. This consultation follows the same rules of lawyer-client privilege that you would have if you did hire me. Your failure to hire me would not negate that. I will never be able to divulge what you tell me here."

Needahl's record, or at least his public one, stressed that he never betrayed a client. Other lawyers had, and those betrayals were part of their public record. On the Moon, such betrayals, if they were shown to be for the proper reason, did not result in disbarment or even a reprimand from the Moon Base Bar Association.

Jamal had chosen Needahl for this one factor alone. Nothing else mattered quite as much. Jamal couldn't have Needahl place his own personal ethics ahead of Jamal's interests.

"Not even if you decide that my present behavior negatively impacts someone else's future?"

"You mean, what would I do if I discover that you're going to sabotage a military transport?" Needahl was using the famous example, the one MBBA had based its initial rulings on.

"Yes," Jamal said.

"I would not betray you, even then."

"At the cost of hundreds of lives?" Jamal asked.

"Yes," Needahl said. "At the cost of hundreds of lives."

He spoke so calmly, as if those hypothetical lives would never mean anything to him, and as if his decision wouldn't bother him at all.

Jamal's throat tightened further. He had to trust someone. It was his only chance—and he had to do it based on very little information.

"I will sign an agreement to this effect, if that is what you need," Needahl said. "And believe me, the agreement will serve you in good stead. Should I violate, you may come after me for a hefty portion of my assets."

Jamal found himself staring at the paper in front of him.

"Of course," Needahl said, "I will also protect myself by making certain that any leak of the information you give me does not come from you."

"Of course," Jamal murmured. Then he took a deep breath and nodded. "All right. Let's draw up the document—Earth standard should probably do."

Needahl's eyes widened, this time the movement obvious. "You have legal experience."

"I have a lot of experience," Jamal said. "That's why I need your help."

DeRicci had heard the tearing plastic, felt the pressure from Palmer's feet as they pushed on the back of the seat. And then the pressure left. The woman had gotten out.

DeRicci still couldn't unfasten her restraints, and she was getting dizzy from hanging upside down. The windows were closed, and the air felt close. All of the damn aircar's controls were connected to its main and secondary systems. She couldn't do anything with the systems down.

The guard beside her moaned again, but didn't seem to be conscious. Neither did the other guard in the back. DeRicci had to do this alone.

Her fingers found her own laser pistol. She pulled it from its harness, then braced herself between the back of her seat and the dash. Once she was wedged, she had enough leverage. She grabbed the pistol by its muzzle and slammed its grip into the driver's window.

She cracked the plastic. She slammed it again, then again, finally breaking a hole in it. Using the pistol like a trowel, she made the hole wider.

Cool air flowed inside the car. She hadn't realized how hot it was in there, but she was bathed in sweat. She managed to loose the restraints without falling, and she twisted herself through them, popping herself through the hole in the window.

The street was empty. Up ahead, she could see the lights outside the Proscenium Arches. It was full dark in here, and the street lights hadn't turned on yet. She found that odd, but not unusual. Sometimes the city rotated power outages at night to maintain reserves.

She breathed shallowly, hoping she would hear something. She wiggled the rest of the way out and slid down the car's chassis, landing with a thump. Then she slapped one of the chips on her hand, and light poured out over her fingers, illuminating the entire underbelly of the shopping area.

A few scrawny cats ran past, startled by the light. She swept it over the smooth pavement, to the up-raised sidewalks. Nothing.

Then she saw a movement near one of the door-ways. She walked toward it, trying to see more clearly.

A man huddled there, his clothing in rags. He raised his head, the light reflecting off his skin. He was filthy and unshaven.

She scanned past him, saw nothing—no one in any of the doorways or in the windows—and no streets to run down. The doors would be locked at this time of the evening. The Proscenium Arches hadn't yet been cleared for twenty-four-hour access.

The man made no sound. She wasn't even sure he was aware of her presence. She turned toward the other side of the street and scanned it. More empty doorways and windows. Buildings that couldn't be broken into, not this quickly and not by a woman armed with—what? It had sounded like a laser pistol, but DeRicci wasn't sure where Palmer had carried it. The guards had done a cursory search.

Cursory clearly hadn't been enough.

DeRicci trained the light on the pavement and cursed. Of course that wouldn't work. The pavement here was new, synthetic. One of its great innovations, touted by the city planners, was that it wouldn't show wear, react to substance spills or suffer from the effect of accidents.

Palmer wouldn't have run in the direction they had been going. Too many lights and people ahead. Besides, there would have been the risk that she would be seen.

Which left only one direction for her to go. She had doubled back.

DeRicci ran in that direction, out of the Proscenium Arches, but still saw nothing. The street was as empty here as it had been when she drove through it.

She cursed again, then unblocked her links. Time to call for help.

*   *   *

Ekaterina clung to the inside of the doorway, grateful for the stone façade. Her back was pressed against the top, her arms and legs keeping herself braced. Her muscles shook. She wouldn't be able to hold this position much longer.

She hadn't done anything like this since she was a teenager, and she felt it in every inch of her body. She used to be able to hang above doorways like this for hours. It had been a great way to hide from her parents, from truant officers, from anyone she chose. The ultimate urban warrior, a friend had once called her.

She didn't feel like that now. She'd been here less than fifteen minutes, and her limbs were about to give way.

DeRicci had passed just a few moments before, heading, as Ekaterina hoped, the way that they had come. She hadn't heard anyone else get out of the aircar, but that didn't mean anything.

DeRicci had been the one to break out. The others could have climbed through the hole she left.

At that moment, Ekaterina's right arm buckled. She caught herself, but her arm shook so badly that she knew she wouldn't be able to stay up there any longer.

She grabbed the stone edge of the façade and swung herself down, landing as quietly as she could on the synthetic sidewalk. It absorbed her impact, but not the thud she made as she landed. The sound seemed to echo under the overhangs, and she was convinced that DeRicci had heard it.

Ekaterina held her breath.

No sound of footsteps, no soft rustle of clothing. No breathing. Ekaterina peered around the doorway. The indigent man still lingered in his doorway across the street. He seemed oblivious to everything around him.

The aircar lay on its side in the middle of the road, a dark lump, with no movement around it.

DeRicci stood in the mouth of the overhang, light pouring off her hand. She appeared to be talking, probably connecting with someone on her link.

Ekaterina wouldn't get another chance.

But she didn't run. She didn't dare. Running might be too loud. Instead, she walked, pressing herself against the buildings, breathing shallowly. Her heart raced.

When she hit the boulevard, she would have to find a side street.

Then she needed a place to hide.

Port authorities had moved the yacht where the Disty vengeance killing had occurred to Salvage. Since Flint had closed the file the night before, the yacht was no longer considered a crime scene. The Port would try to track down the yacht's owners to see if they were, indeed, someone other than the corpses, but the priority on that assignment would be low.

Salvage was in the oldest section of the terminal, an area with technology so out of date that it wasn't worth replacing. The docking areas—or what had been the docking areas—were smaller than the ones currently used, although their ceilings were higher. The walls were scored with exhaust traces, singe marks from the rocket fuel used by the early colonists, and dents from poorly docked ships. The air here was foul as well, recycled thousands of times through an ancient self-contained system that should have been retired long ago.

Now the docking areas were used to store ships that were going to be resold or disassembled for parts. Most of the ships were towed here by robotic units, taking them through underground passageways specially built for this assignment.

The first docking area housed the most recent arrivals. It was the sorting space, where specialists figured out clear title to the ship and whether it had more value as an intact unit or as the sum of its parts.

Flint used to hate coming here. Often he had to come to reclaim a ship that had been improperly impounded. Finding it could take an entire day. In those cases, however, the ship's owners had already been through a large and lengthy legal proceeding, and the ship—or what was left of it—would be buried in one of the myriad sorting stations in the other old docking areas.

This time, he was coming for a ship that had just been moved here, and it made a huge difference. The yacht he was looking for was two rows back, near some cruisers of similar vintage.

The airlock doors were closed, but unlatched. He let himself inside and instantly wished he hadn't. He had forgotten about the smell. If anything, it was worse than it had been before—rotted flesh and decaying blood mixed with a trace of feces.

He knew that the bodies were gone. Corpses were not allowed in salvage ships, but no one had bothered to clean this thing out. He wondered if he would even be able to touch the cockpit controls. They'd been covered in intestine the last time he'd seen them.

He put a Protectocloth over his mouth and nose, hoping it would filter out the worst of the odor. Then he slipped into the main part of the ship.

The coroner's office hadn't bothered with the usual niceties. Fluids covered the floor where they hadn't before. Dozens of footprints lined the regulation carpet. Because this was no longer a crime scene, the coroner's people could take the bodies out however they wanted to, no longer caring if they destroyed evidence.

Flint didn't care about the main part of the yacht either. All he cared about was the logs.

The interior of the ship was stifling. Someone had shut down the environmental systems. He knew, though, that they hadn't shut down the main computer. They would need it to track the yacht's owners—if they could. No sense in having to reboot everything when a complete shutdown wasn't necessary.

"Computer," he said. "I'm Armstrong Dome Law Enforcement investigating a possible crime. In order to proceed, I'll need light and fresh air in the cockpit."

"Authorization, please." The computer's androgynous voice sounded just like the one in the other yacht.

"You'll get that as soon as I enter the cockpit. I cannot do it from my current location. I am not asking you to compromise classified systems. I am merely asking for basic life support in one area of the ship."

"Understood."

Lights came on ahead of him. He could see them filtering into the corridor that led to the cockpit. Flint steeled himself, then walked to the cockpit and stopped just inside the door.

The controls were covered with dried blood, and probably other things as well. No one had bothered to wipe them off.

He made a face, then continued forward. The pilot's screen was useless because it was so filthy. But the copilot's screen only had mild spatter.

He pressed his finger against it.

"I am sending my identification now," he told the

computer. "I need to hear your communications logs. I want audio only, although I would also like a download into my own link."

He gave the linking information. Then he took his finger off the screen and resisted the urge to wipe his hand against his pants. This was the most disgusting crime scene he'd ever been in. He only hoped that he wouldn't have to be here long.

"Begin with the last communication and work backwards," he said.

"I do not have communication log information," the computer said.

"I thought your default system automatically recorded incoming and outgoing messages."

"Such messages were wiped from my system when initial destination was reached."

"Wiped or erased?" Flint asked.

"Wiped," the computer said.

"Then reconstruct the information and play it for me."

"I do not have proper authorization," the computer said.

"Yes," Flint said. "You do."

"Authorization must come from the ship's owner," the computer said.

"This space yacht has been confiscated by Armstrong Dome. By law, ownership is transferred to the Port of Armstrong. I am a representative of Armstrong authority, which makes me one of the many new owners." Flint had given that speech a number of times, but never as a detective. Only as a space cop.

"Understood." The computer's voice sounded louder in here. "The ship traveled a great distance without using its communications system. Would you like course coordinates and destination information?"

"Not yet," Flint said. He knew better than to give the computer an outright refusal. Some shipboard computers were so linear that a single outright refusal resulted in a complete inability to get the information later.

"Final spoken communications log," the computer said.

"D.I.E.M., this is *Pong*." The voice was nasal and flat, almost hollow, like most Disty voices.

"*Pong*, go ahead," a man's voice answered. He had an accent that Flint recognized as Earth-based, but he couldn't be more specific than that.

"We will reach the rendezvous point in fifteen Earth minutes. Have you the package?"

"Package, complete with accessories. We'll vacate the moment we get the funds transfer."

"Transferring now."

"Along with accessories bonus," the male voice said.

"As per agreement, accessories bonus sent as well." There was a momentary silence, presumably as the man checked the financial records. Then:

"Always a pleasure doing business with you folks."

"The colloquialism is not appropriate to such a serious matter." The Disty sounded even drier than usual.

"Lighten up, *Pong*. All I was doing was signing off. D.I.E.M. out."

The log spooled down. Flint realized he was holding his breath.

"Penultimate log," the computer said.

"Belay that," Flint said. "One was fine. Have the others been downloaded?"

"Yes," the computer said.

"Then that's all the audio I need." He felt a little

light-headed. Some of that might have been from the smell, but he suspected it was more than that.

This yacht had used the same name as the previous one. That was not allowed in any regs that Flint was aware of. The name seemed to be initials, although he supposed it could have been spelled out, in some way. D'Eye ee'm, perhaps. He'd have to run all of those when he returned to the precinct.

He let out a long breath. "Computer," he said. "Give me all the information on D.I.E.M. in your files."

"I am a default system only. I do not record personal information," the computer said.

"Were you ever used for personal information?" Flint asked.

"No," the computer said.

He nodded. He had expected that. "Then give me a brief history of the scarring on your hull. Did it occur—?"

His link beeped.

"Belay that, computer," he said. "Hold until I tell you."

He answered the link by tapping his earlobe for audio only. He didn't want anyone to see where he was standing—mostly because he didn't want to inflict this crime scene on anyone else.

"Flint?" DeRicci's voice sounded tinny and small, as it often did when she unblocked her links.

"Oh, good," he said. "I've been trying to reach you. You shouldn't—"

"I don't give a rat's about what you want," DeRicci said. "We have a major problem here."

He felt cold. "What kind of problem?"

"Our little prisoner," DeRicci said. "She escaped."

"Escaped?" Flint asked. "Where?"

"Near the Proscenium Arches."

"Have you called for backup?"

"Oh, yeah. I've already humbled myself. But I'm staying on the ground to search. You have to go see the chief."

"The chief?" Flint felt a surge of anger. He was glad he hadn't initiated visual. He didn't want DeRicci to see the fury in his face. "I didn't lose the prisoner."

"Technically you did," DeRicci said. "We're partners, Flint."

"And I tried to warn you she wasn't what she seemed, DeRicci, but your links were blocked."

"Listen," DeRicci said. "I'm not the most popular person at headquarters. I go in, we both get reprimanded. I'm covering your ass, Flint. The least you can do is cooperate."

Her words had a ring of truth. "You don't have to cover for me, DeRicci."

"Yes, I do," she said. "You have a future, Flint. You're good. And I'm not going to let my past taint your career. Got that?"

"No," he said, and then he realized the link had been severed. For a moment, he toyed with reattaching, but thought better of it.

DeRicci wasn't going to change her mind, and Flint was better at interpersonal relations than she was. If he played this right, he might be able to salvage DeRicci's career along with his own.

16

Lights illuminated the road under the Proscenium Arches, all of them focused on the ruined aircar. Two medic units floated above it, recording the scene below. The car had been opened like a can, the injured guards still inside.

DeRicci stood near the doorway leading into the main building. The indigent man was in custody, talking with two uniforms, although they were having a time of it. He didn't seem to know where he was, let alone if he had seen anything.

Dozens of squads had arrived, all of them parking and none of them actually participating in the search—at least not yet. Apparently dispatch had decided to send them all here, not realizing that someone would have to coordinate on-site.

DeRicci sighed. She would coordinate. It was the least she could do for her major screw-up. Also, it was a great last duty for a soon-to-be-dismissed detective to perform.

She stepped into the flood of lights, watching as the uniformed officers gathered near the aircar. Dozens of cars and even more people. She hoped someone had been bright enough to fan out.

She also hoped that someone else was giving overall

orders, sealing off Armstrong so that no one could leave. But she didn't have jurisdiction over that. All she had been able to do was inform dispatch of her mistake, and hope that Flint could minimize the damage to his own career.

The uniforms seemed to be searching for someone in charge. She waved a hand.

"Over here!" she shouted.

At first, no one seemed to hear. She repeated the gesture, waving her arm again, and finally some of the closer unis moved in.

They all seemed so young, their faces fresh, their eyes alive. She knew that some of them had to be close to her age, but if felt like they were innocent, incorruptible, even though that wasn't true.

The unis, particularly the foot patrols, had the most contact with the citizens of Armstrong. They also saw some of the worst aspects of the city. But most of these folks had signed up because they were interested in the work, not because of the pay.

Of course, a lot of them quit when they realized just how demanding the job was.

"Gather up!" she yelled, and the cry echoed through the ranks. They surrounded her, blocking her view of the aircar. She would never forgive herself if those terminal guards died because she hadn't treated Greta Palmer like a dangerous criminal.

"We have to move fast, people," she said.

They crowded around her.

"You're going to be searching for a woman named Greta Palmer. She disappeared from here not a half hour ago after she engineered that aircar wreck. She's slight, blond, and has unusually pale skin. She does not have obvious links or enhancements. She also speaks with an Earth accent, and she may or may not be wanted by the Rev. We have to find her before she gets out of the dome."

The silence greeting her was immense. Dozens of unis, all listening to everything she said.

"I've downloaded what information we have on Palmer to Central. Pick it up before you begin the search. She's clever, and she's determined. I don't know what her story is, but if you do find her, assume she's smarter than you are and extremely dangerous. Do everything you can to bring her in. Any questions?"

A uni in the front row, a tall man with bulky muscles and a queue that disappeared into the back of his shirt, said, "Is this a Priority One search?"

How was she supposed to know? She'd been here the entire time. "You didn't get the ranking from dispatch?"

"They seem to know less than you do."

So the chief hadn't issued overall orders yet, or she hadn't thought of it. Of course not. She was probably doing damage control. DeRicci hoped that she remembered to give the orders to shut down the dome.

"Yes," she said, making the decision for the chief. "It's a Piority One search."

A Priority One search meant that the unis could use all the tools at their disposal, including force if need be, to find the fugitive. If anyone got overzealous or if the priority turned out to be lower, the blame for that would fall on the person who initially set the priority.

Her.

If she was wrong, then that was one more thing they could pin on her record. Or actually, several more things. As if it mattered.

"I'm going to divide you into quadrants," she said, "using this as our starting point."

Quickly she separated them into four groups. There was no dissension, for which she was grateful. She hoped this would work. She'd never coordinated an effort like this before.

"All right," she said. "Fan out. Let's find her fast."

They were fortunate this had occurred as night was falling. Few trains departed after twilight, and most of the Exterior workers only worked during the Dome Daylight, to keep their schedules the same as everyone else's. That wouldn't hit for hours yet. Only a handful of people would be inconvenienced because Palmer had escaped—provided the unis found her before False Dawn.

The unis moved out in their various directions, sticking with their partners so that they could begin the Priority One search. DeRicci let out a sigh and rubbed the heel of her hand over her face. The adrenaline was beginning to leave her system, and she was feeling bruises that she hadn't noticed when she first pulled herself out of the window.

She walked over to the aircar. After she found out how the guards were doing, she'd resume her search.

She had a hunch the only way she could save her career was to bring in Palmer herself—and the odds of succeeding at that were getting slimmer all the time.

"So," Jamal said. "I was hoping you would be able to help me. The Wygnin do not have the proper warrants. There might be some kind of technicality—"

Needahl held up a hand to silence Jamal, then stood. He picked up his plant mister and stepped into the same green area he had initially come out of. For several minutes, he misted plants, sending a fine spray throughout the room.

Jamal's heart was beating hard. He found it difficult

to sit and wait, but he knew better than to speak. He had to give Needahl time to consider his case.

Finally, Needahl set the plant mister down. "You are not telling me everything."

"I've told you enough," Jamal said. "You know more than my wife."

"Yes." Needahl slipped his hands in his pockets. "You have traveled on an interstellar basis for your job. You had contact with the Wygnin, but there is more than that, isn't there?"

Jamal had glossed over his history. Even though he had decided to trust Needahl, he didn't want to give the man too much information. If Needahl had the right information, he might accidentally let some of it slip.

"What do you mean?" Jamal asked.

"You used a disappearance service," Needahl said. "This is why you're being vague."

Jamal felt the muscles in his shoulders tighten. He didn't deny this, but he wasn't going to confirm it either.

"And if you used a disappearance service, then you did something wrong. I'm assuming, since your wife does not know of your past, that whatever you have done wrong, you did it to the Wygnin. Am I right?"

Jamal's throat closed up, just as it had before. He couldn't speak even if he wanted to.

"And if you did something to the Wygnin, it was probably at least a decade ago, before we completely understood the nature of their laws and customs." Needahl paused and met Jamal's gaze. "Which means that you probably did something inadvertent and horrendous."

Jamal had to look away.

"Which begs the question, then. Why did you have

a child? If you hadn't had a child, you wouldn't be in this mess."

Jamal cleared his throat. It took him a moment to find his voice. "We did not plan the pregnancy." He could barely hear himself. "Or at least, I didn't."

"You think your wife did?"

Jamal shrugged. "I don't think she was as cautious as I would have been."

"Yet you didn't give the child up, nor did you abort it. You knew the consequences."

"Ten years is a long time," Jamal whispered.

"To a human, yes," Needahl said. "To a Wygnin, no."

Needahl obviously knew a lot. He was successful and strong. He liked challenges. Of all the lawyers Jamal could have chosen, Needahl was clearly the best.

"Will you help us?" Jamal asked.

"No," Needahl said.

All the air left Jamal's body. "Why not?"

Needahl leaned against his desk, resting one leg on it and bracing the other against the floor. It was a casual, comfortable position, one designed to reassure someone.

"If I were a young man with no children, grandchildren, or great-grandchildren, I might consider it," he said. "But if I take this, and the technicality turns out to be a false one, or if I inadvertently offend the Wygnin just like you did, I'll be in the same position you are. I'm sorry, Mr. Kanawa. The risk is too great."

Jamal felt his cheeks heat. "I'm not asking you to break any of their laws."

"No one has ever argued technicalities with the Wygnin," Needahl said. "They might not view them with the same leniency that we do."

"Surely if they make a mistake in their warrant—"

"It doesn't negate your actions," Needahl said.

"But they can't forgive one and not the other," Jamal said.

"By our logic, that's right," Needahl said. "But we don't know what their logic is. You know that they don't always communicate such things clearly. We often don't find out until it's too late."

Jamal clasped his hands together so tightly that he could feel the bones in his fingers. "It seems that the risk I'm asking you to take is a small one, especially in comparison to my son's life."

"Your son is an infant, if I'm understanding you."

"Yes," Jamal said.

"He won't lose his life. He'll become a member of the Wygnin family. He'll remain intact."

"He won't be human."

"Not as we know it, no, he won't," Needahl said. "But they'll treat him with love and compassion, as they would their own child. He'll have a good life."

Jamal shook his head. "You know that's not an argument. You know I can't give up my boy for that. It's not right."

"No," Needahl said. "Having the child in the first place, with this kind of sentence over your head. That's not right."

Jamal stood. The tension in his body had become shaking, the kind of shaking he often felt when he held back fury. "I can't undo it. And it goes against everything we believe to have a child pay for my mistake."

"You're right," Needahl said. "We can't undo it. And you've made two extremely serious mistakes. How can I trust you not to make a third? You think this technicality is minor. Your son's life is already forfeit. But my eldest child is a daughter. She's forty-four years old. If the Wygnin take her, they will destroy her. I cannot gamble her life for your son's. It's not an even trade-off."

In spite of himself, Jamal understood the argument. "You said you liked a challenge."

"I do," Needahl said.

"Maybe there's a young, unattached lawyer in your firm, one who could act as your proxy—"

"No," Needahl said. "I'm not going to ask my people to take a risk I will not take."

"What about another lawyer in Armstrong or on the Moon, someone who'd be willing take this on?"

"I don't know anyone." Needahl hadn't changed his position. He still looked as relaxed as he had when the conversation started. "No one is willing to deal with the Wygnin anymore."

"You wouldn't recommend anyone even if you knew someone, would you?" Jamal asked.

"I'm sorry," Needahl said softly.

"What am I supposed to do?" Jamal asked.

But Needahl did not answer him, and they both knew why. Jamal only had one choice. He was going to lose his son because of an accident, a crime he committed without knowing it many years ago.

And, it seemed, nothing he could do would ever change that.

Ekaterina's lungs burned. She didn't think the air was thinner here than it had been in San Francisco, but it felt thinner. Maybe it just wasn't as pure.

Or maybe she wasn't used to the exertion. She'd been running for blocks now, threading her way around the backs of buildings, hoping that most didn't have the kinds of security systems buildings on Earth had.

The aircar had reminded her that technology was at least a decade behind on the Moon, sometimes more. Technology spread throughout the known universe in odd ways: the newest settlements got the most up-to-date equipment, as did the richer colonies; middle-aged colonies often had the most out-of-date items because no one went there unless they had to; and the oldest colonies, which also happened to be the closest to Earth, had whatever they could buy or someone could import.

That might serve her well. She would avoid the most troublesome facets of richer colonies, like sophisticated security systems, and find technology like the kind she had grown up with, the kind she'd learned to subvert to avoid her overbearing parents in the years before she went to live with her grandmother.

But technology was the least of her problems. The police were searching for her, and the Rev wouldn't be far behind.

She had reached a section of the city that seemed to be residential. The homes were small and mostly dark. A few had on interior lights, but they had shaded the windows so that no one could see in, which also meant that no one could see out.

The air smelled faintly of flowers. Apparently some of the residents had gone to the expense of putting in Earth-quality dirt, cultivating plants, and then using their precious water to keep them alive. Strange that they had chosen to spend that much money on flowering plants instead of a vegetable garden.

When Ekaterina had lived on Revnata, the human colonists were not allowed to grow decorative plants. Everyone was required to have a vegetable patch. If a person lacked a gift for cultivation, then someone else ran the garden. It helped supplement the meager food rations, the tasteless supplements, and the handful of edible Rev vegetation.

Her stomach growled. The sandwiches she'd had hours ago in decontamination had gotten her this far, but she had expended a lot of energy since then, and she wasn't going to be able to stop, at least not here.

At least there was no real weather in the dome. The temperatures cooled down at night just because humans expected that (and it saved energy), but she didn't have to worry about rain or snow or deep cold. The elements wouldn't kill her.

But hunger and exhaustion might.

She crouched behind a rudimentary shed someone had assembled on the back of his property. It was hidden behind a fence, probably because it was some sort of building code violation. The flower smell was stronger here, a rich, sweet perfume that she didn't recognize. Maybe the flowers were a violation as well. If so, that would mean that this area wasn't patrolled very often.

Not that she could stay here. She just needed to rest and figure out what her next move was going to be.

Her clothing was filthy. She probably was too. That accident hadn't helped her appearance, and neither had hanging from that doorway. Her legs had gotten scraped as she ran behind buildings in complete darkness, and her hair was tangled. Her arm ached.

She certainly wasn't presentable enough to find one of Armstrong's indigent shelters. Besides, the police had probably alerted them already.

She needed to leave the city, but that wasn't possible either, not without funds—and she had none. If she used the money that Disappearance Inc had put into the Greta Palmer accounts, then it would be as if she had drawn a map for the police.

If she used any of her family money or tapped any of the Ekaterina Maakestad accounts—even the most obscure ones—then the Rev would find her.

There was no way to leave Armstrong Dome without money. The high-speed trains that crisscrossed the Moon were the only transportation between the domed colonies. The preservationists refused to let roads be built across the airless lunar landscape.

There was no way she could slip underneath the dome and walk away from Armstrong, not without an environmental suit. She was trapped here, in the artificial environment, until she could figure out a way to escape.

Her remaining options, then, were theft or seeing if she could find an ally. Despite what she had just done, she wasn't a criminal. She had no idea how to steal and she would probably be very bad at it. Besides, she wasn't that desperate yet.

What she needed was someone who would be willing to help her out of the dome or maybe even off the Moon. That meant finding someone with resources, someone who had a criminal bent, and someone who would be willing to risk upsetting the Rev for helping her.

Most of the people she knew on the Moon were former clients, so the criminal bent wouldn't be hard to find. She'd gotten almost all of the charges against her clients dropped, so finding someone who would be willing to help her might not be hard either. Most of her former clients—at least the ones who had some sort of moral center—would be predisposed to helping her, even if they had to face Rev justice.

The problem was finding someone with current knowledge and excellent resources. If she found a former client who was willing to help but who also happened to be poor, that person might be willing to sell her to the highest bidder. She'd have to avoid that somehow.

Then she shook her head. Resources didn't matter. Her clients were former criminals. They might sell her out just for the heck of it.

She leaned against the poorly constructed building, the ancient permaplastic cool against her back. Her lungs didn't burn as badly anymore, but her muscles were heavy with exhaustion. She'd sleep here if she knew how long the dome would be in darkness, but she didn't, and as exhausted as she was, she might sleep right through False Dawn.

What she needed was the help of a disappearance service, just as she'd had before. Most of the disappearance services on the Moon were branch offices. She'd already checked out the dozen main Earth-based services and had found them lacking.

All but Disappearance Inc. And that had proven wrong. Just because it was wrong, though, didn't mean that she should trust the other Earth-based services.

Instead, she might be better off using a Moon-based service or one with a non-human clientele. If the new disappearance service could get her out of Armstrong safely, she could even pay them using Maakestad funds.

But she would only get one shot at this. A single mistake and she'd be in Rev hands within the hour.

Maybe she was wrong trusting another disappearance service, but she couldn't think of another option. Maybe she would come up with something else.

But whatever she did, she'd have to come up with it soon. She couldn't say on the streets of Armstrong forever.

17

Flint had never been called before the chief of police before. He had seen her, of course. Everyone in the city had. Next to the dome's mayor and the head of its provisional government, the police chief was Armstrong's most visible official.

Her office reflected that. It was in the City Complex, Armstrong's tallest building. Police operations covered the whole ninth floor, and she had a third of that, which she had subdivided into working areas for some of her more important assistants.

Her desk stood in front of the wall of shatterproof windows, with a view of the entire city. During the day, it must have been spectacular. Now, however, it simply showed streetlights and building lights fading into the complete darkness of a Dome Night.

Gumiela, who had told Flint about this meeting, had not accompanied him here. So nice to know he had the support of his boss. Of course, he knew he wouldn't, not with a fugitive on the loose, a fugitive he and his partner had once had in custody.

Assistants had left him in front of the chief's large desk. They had provided a chair for him to wait in, but he was too restless to sit. He had a feeling that a lot more was going on in Armstrong than the escape.

The arrival of the matching space yachts bothered him, as did the presence of the Wygnin. Never, in all his years working space traffic, had he seen a couple of days quite like these.

Something important had changed, and he wasn't exactly sure what that something important was.

And then there was the matter of the baby.

"Miles Flint," a familiar voice said.

Flint turned. Olympia Hobell stood behind him, her hands on her hips. She was shorter than he had expected, barely coming up to his shoulders, but she had an athletic build. Her hair had gone silver—probably a planned effect rather than a dislike of enhancements—and there were lines around her mouth and eyes. Her skin still looked youthful, however.

She wore a black silk pantsuit with a pair of walkers beneath. Obviously she had been out on the town when the call came in and only had time to change to more practical shoes.

"Yes, sir," he said.

"You're costing the city thousands of credits this evening," she said, hands still on her hips. "The sum will go up as long as this fugitive remains at large."

He wasn't costing the city anything, but he didn't want to contradict her. "I should be out searching, sir."

The lines near her eyes deepened. They looked like laugh lines, and the slight movement made it seem as if she were suppressing a small smile.

"You need to talk with me." She waved a hand, and walls came down behind her, shutting her desk off from the rest of her office suite.

He felt almost as if he were being imprisoned. He said nothing as she walked past him toward her desk.

"You realize that we have had to shut down outgoing train service. Incoming trains were ordered to return to their originating cities, unless they were close to Armstrong. If they arrived within the past hour, they were allowed to stay. No one is flying off-Moon tonight, although space traffic is allowing vehicles to land."

She stopped in front of the windows and stared out them. She seemed mesmerized by the sight of the city, as if she had never been up there before.

Then she sighed and continued. "The dome is closed. There will be no outgoing business until this woman is caught. Fortunately, most of the day workers had returned to the dome by the time the dome closure order went out. The weekly workers have enough rations to get them through this week and the next, although the hikers and the recreationalists might be in trouble."

She turned and faced him. "Armstrong has more dome closures than any other city on the Moon."

"Because of the space port," Flint said, then wished he hadn't. She hadn't given him leave to speak.

But she nodded, apparently not upset that he had spoken out of turn. "Yes, because of the space port. But that has other effects on the city. We are considered a less reliable place to do business than, say, Gagarin Dome, and we lose a lot of industry because of it."

He suppressed a sigh. He didn't want to be talking about business or politics. He knew the history of the colony and its business practices as well as anyone, and he really didn't care about them at the moment. He cared about finding Palmer.

"Your little fugitive is a problem," Hobell said. "Generally, escapees are dumber than Moon rocks, but this woman isn't. If your hastily filed report is accurate, she managed to avoid the Rev or steal a space yacht or both."

He had submitted the report on the way to the Complex. He was stunned that Hobell had already read it.

"In other words, she's smart. And so far, she's managed to stay one step ahead of everyone. This worries me, Flint."

Hobell's eyes were a clear gray. They seemed to match the silver of her hair.

"It worries me too, sir," he said.

"What is this?" she asked without humor. "No begging? No groveling?"

Apparently she was used to officers coming in and giving her excuses. He had none.

"I can explain what I believe happened if you're willing to listen," he said.

"I know what happened," Hobell said. "DeRicci is the primary. You're a new detective. You do as she says. She screwed up again, and you weren't able to stop her. It's admirable of you to try to stick up for her, but there's no need to do that. Her record speaks for itself."

Flint felt the muscles in his back tighten as she spoke. DeRicci had predicted this response. He was a bit surprised at the vehemence of the chief's words.

"In my time working with Noelle DeRicci," Flint said softly, "she's shown herself to be personally difficult, outspoken, and rude."

Hobell nodded.

"But," Flint said, "she has also been extremely competent."

"Are you saying the mistake is yours?" Hobell asked.

"I'm not assigning blame," Flint said. "Nor am I making excuses. I'm just saying that Noelle DeRicci has a bad reputation and I'm not sure why. From my observation, she does her job and she does it well."

"She didn't do it well today." Hobell glanced out the windows at the city beyond. "We're all paying for that."

"Yes, we are." Flint couldn't let DeRicci take the blame for this, no matter what she wanted him to do. "As you said, Greta Palmer is smart. She fooled someone in that yacht, whether it was the Rev or the crew. She fooled the space cops on the ground here. And DeRicci and I underestimated her."

"Underestimated? That's the word you use?"

"Yes, sir," Flint said. "You read my report. You know that we were told to report to the docks to deal with a terrified tourist who may or may not cause publicity problems for Armstrong."

The chief raised her head. For the first time in the conversation, she looked up at him, as if she had forgotten to keep her distance.

"We hadn't been informed that the yacht was in Terminal Five, which meant that Traffic thought it was stolen. We found out that information ourselves, and even then, we didn't know what it meant. Greta Palmer's story fit with the revised scenario. She could have been in the wrong place at the wrong time."

"You still believe she was."

"I don't know." Flint wasn't going to tell the chief his suspicions. He didn't have enough evidence to show that the pilot and his crew might have sold out Greta Palmer. Even if he did mention it, that detail wouldn't ease his problem with the chief. She would see that as proof of the fact that Palmer should have been watched all along.

"When one suspects danger," Hobell said, "there are procedures to follow."

"We interviewed her, sir, and heard some suspicious things. But we had been told that she was probably a tourist. We saw nothing that contradicted that possibility." He clasped his hands behind his back, so that he looked like he was standing at attention. "There are procedures for handling tourists as well, sir. We're supposed to go easy with them."

"Well, you certainly went easy with her."

"No, sir, beg pardon, but we didn't." Flint spoke quietly. He could almost hear DeRicci telling him to shut up, to stop digging himself in deeper. But he couldn't let this go. He had a hunch that DeRicci was on her last legs here, and that she didn't have anywhere else to go. "When I left Noelle, she was going to bring Palmer in. She had two guards accompany them. That's not standard procedure for treating tourists. She also used a department prisoner transport aircar. The only thing we did not do was put restraints on Palmer."

Hobell's eyes narrowed. "Why didn't you think restraints were necessary?"

"I found when I worked Traffic that people don't care if they're transported in prison ships. But they do care if their hands are locked together."

"You think that if she was a tourist, she wouldn't sue over the transportation but she would over the restraints?"

"That's my experience, sir." He was taking the blame for this after all. DeRicci would be furious with him if she ever found out.

The chief placed her hands on her hips and studied him for a moment. It was as if she were trying to figure out if he was lying to her just by staring at him.

"You're saying that Greta Palmer is even smarter than I'm giving her credit for."

Flint nodded.

"Which means that she'll be extremely difficult to catch."

"Especially if she has friends here," he said.

Hobell's mouth thinned. "Do you think that she really is wanted by the Rev?"

"I think at the very least, the Rev want to talk with her," Flint said. "After all, she covered her ass when she tried to land the yacht by saying that the Rev would come after her as the lone survivor of their attack—or whatever you want to call that."

"And at worst, she's the one the Rev are after."

"Yes," Flint said.

The chief shook her head, walked to the desk, and leaned on it. Then she shook her head again, as if she were disagreeing with her own thoughts.

"You realize that I planned on reprimanding you and demoting DeRicci," she said.

"No, sir, I hadn't realized that," Flint said. But he had suspected it. So had DeRicci.

Hobell raised her eyebrows. He had a hunch she was unconvinced about his last statement. "I've been thinking about what you said and your report, and I can't find any flaws in your reasoning. I wish I could because I would much rather blame this crisis on your mishandling of Palmer than on her cleverness."

"Yes, sir," Flint said.

She finally smiled. " 'Yes, sir,' " she mocked. "You are deceptively polite, Flint. I looked at your record before you came in. You're not the most docile man either."

"Either?" he asked.

"DeRicci's misdeeds are flamboyant. Yours often stretch the interpretation of the law, but never in a way that anyone can complain about."

He felt a flush begin to warm his face, and he willed the reaction to stop. He didn't dare appear vulnerable in front of this woman.

"I still believe that Noelle DeRicci is one of the most troublesome detectives that we have, but you have convinced me that I might have misjudged her in this incident. When you have a troublesome employee, you tend to blame everything that goes wrong on that employee's errors and not see the facts for what they are."

He almost yes-sired her again, but refrained from doing so. He didn't want her to mock him again.

"I believe she knows that the entire department is watching her closely, and I'm sure she expects punishment in this instance."

"She told me to blame the entire thing on her, sir," he said, "so that my career would be all right."

Hobell tilted her head back. "You could have done that. I wouldn't have thought less of you."

"I would have," he said quietly.

She smiled. It softened her face. He had been wrong about the smoothness of her skin. Light lines covered her cheeks, all of them laugh lines, all of them making her quite attractive.

"We might think of getting you a job in public relations, Flint. You've managed to turn me around. Imagine what you could do with the press."

"That would frustrate me, sir," he said, not certain if she was serious.

Her eyes twinkled. "You don't like lighthearted moments, do you?"

"Not when there's something else I should be doing, no, sir."

"And you should be chasing your fugitive?"

He nodded.

"Well, I disagree," Hobell said. "That's what street patrols are for. They'll find her."

"I think it might take some detecting, sir."

The twinkle had become pronounced. "I'm sure it will, Flint. And if you think of anything the street patrols should know, send the information directly to me. Until then, I have another job for you."

He suppressed a sigh. He was working on enough cases and, despite the story he had just fed the police chief, he did feel guilty about losing Palmer. He'd been going over it and over it, wondering if it had been his fault in some way.

Apparently he had managed to hide his irritation, because the chief continued. "Just before I came in here, I had word from space traffic control."

The tension in his back grew worse. He'd had too many cases at the Port these last few days. He didn't want another one.

The twinkle had left her eyes. "A Rev prison ship is in orbit," she said. "They want Palmer."

He let out the sigh. "I'd expected that."

"So did we," she said. "In fact, given the stories Palmer told, I would have expected the Rev ship sooner. And I'm surprised that it's a prison ship. I would have thought we'd see one of their military ships or even a diplomatic vessel."

"The Rev aren't going to be happy that she's escaped," Flint said.

"We haven't told them that." Hobell hadn't moved from the desk. Her posture appeared to be relaxed, but he could see tension in her muscles too. "In fact, we've led them to believe that we had no idea they were looking for her, that she had done anything wrong."

"They're buying that?"

"For the moment." Any hint of a smile had long ago left her face. "But we are going to have to deal with them, and we are going to have to do our best to keep them calm."

He'd dealt with the Rev before. They came to this part of the Moon often. "The Rev don't take setbacks well."

"I know," she said. "So you're going to have to do your best with them."

"Me?" he said, his heart beginning to pound hard.

"You and DeRicci. You get to find out the real story from the Rev. The Rev usually don't lie, so we can rely on what they tell us."

"They also have a nasty way of taking matters into their own hands if they don't get what they want," he said.

"I know." She slid off the desk and walked around it, staring at the city one more time. Apparently she took her inspiration from it. Or perhaps she thought she could see Palmer from here if she only stared out there long enough. "You can look at this as a punishment for losing the prisoner, Flint."

"Is that what it is?" he asked.

"Maybe," she said. "Or maybe I'm just using my resources wisely."

"Let's hope so," he said. "Because I don't like being around frustrated Rev."

"No one does," she said.

18

Fortunately, Flint did not have to meet the Rev at the Port. They waited for him in one of the interrogation rooms in the First Detective Division.

The room smelled faintly of ginger, a scent someone had once told him was the Rev equivalent of sweat. It was a bit too hot in there for them, and they probably weren't used to being in such a small area.

He had forgotten how large the Rev were. Four of them filled a room built for ten humans. The Rev were pear-shaped. They had tiny heads and long thin necks, with two arms near their necks, and four above their base. When they walked, the four hands formed fists that were flat on top. The Rev used those arms the way a spider would use her legs, moving so rapidly that people who had never seen it before were often surprised.

Neither set of arms was visible when a Rev was at rest. They seemed to fold into pockets of skin made just for that purpose, leaving the Rev's torso smooth and unlined.

Someone had removed the room's table, leaving only a few chairs. Flint was grateful for that. He'd only been inside a moment, and he was already feeling claustrophobic.

The Rev studied him. He greeted them in their own language. His Rev was passable, but not the best. The nearest Rev, a white robe draped around its wide middle and clasped at the neck with real gold, stepped forward.

He bowed his head. Flint did the same.

"You speak Rev," the Rev said in that language.

"Badly," Flint replied in the same language. "But I've sent for an interpreter. We should be able to muddle along until then."

The Rev leaned the upper part of his head back, opening his mouth. That look was what passed for a smile in Rev culture. "Your use of idiom suggests that you are being disingenuous."

"My use of idiom," Flint said, "is confirmation that I've done preliminary interviews with Rev before."

He didn't offer them chairs since Rev did not sit down. He wanted to sit, but he couldn't. They would see it as bad form. Instead, he leaned against the wall, arms crossed.

He wondered where DeRicci was. He had spoken to her on her link the moment he left the chief's office and told her to join him. She had promised she'd be there as soon as possible.

Flint had stressed that she was supposed to give up the search, but he had a hunch she didn't want to. She'd stretch "as soon as possible" into something much longer, leaving him to deal with the Rev himself.

"We have a warrant for Ekaterina Maakestad," the Rev said, the name sounding strange in his plate-sized mouth.

Flint made himself focus on the task at hand. "Who?"

"The woman who arrived in the space yacht shortly before we did. We do not know what she calls herself, but her name is Ekaterina Maakestad. She has been wanted on Revnata for more than a decade."

Flint wished the interpreter had already arrived. He had some questions that he didn't know how to ask with his limited Rev.

He nodded, knowing better than to hold up a hand in this discussion. The Rev found gestures like that to be rude, in the same way that interrupting them would be.

"The woman gave her name as Greta Palmer."

"A deception." The Rev closed his mouth, and the line of his lips disappeared into his pale skin. "Matters are worse than we thought."

"I want you to tell me all about this," Flint said, "but I would prefer to wait for the interpreter. The more accurate my information, the easier it will be for me to help you."

"You may help us," the Rev said, "by bringing the woman to us."

"She is a *human* woman, not a Rev," Flint said, forced to use the English word for "human" since he didn't know the Rev one. "If she were Rev, I could accommodate you. Since she is one of our people, I must follow our rules."

"We have a warrant for her," the Rev said again.

"You have a warrant for a woman whose name I do not recognize," Flint said. "I believe we are not far apart in this, but you do understand that I must respect our rules."

The Rev's small black eyes bulged even farther. It was the first warning sign of Rev anger. Flint eyed the door, making certain he was close enough to get through it if he needed to.

"The woman who came in the yacht," the Rev said. "Where is she?"

"Last I saw her, she was in *decontamination*." He didn't know the Rev word for that either. Either that or he had forgotten it. He hadn't had to use his Rev for nearly two years.

"*De*-what?" the Rev asked.

"*Decontamination*," Flint said. He tried to explain what that was, but found his Rev was even more lacking. Finally he shrugged. "We'll wait for the interpreter."

"If this woman is nearby in *De*-what, we would like to see her," the Rev said.

"As I said, I can't do that," Flint said. "Not until we're sure we're talking about the same woman."

And he found another way to stall them. He hadn't exactly lied this time—the last time he saw her was in Decontamination—but he hadn't told the truth either. He was hoping he could stall long enough for the street patrols to find Palmer. Then he wouldn't anger the Rev.

The Rev did not appreciate shades of the truth. They were always as honest as possible. Early on, that had made them victims of human business schemes. For a while, the Rev had thought humans completely untrustworthy. Then they learned that humans had a different appreciation for truth than the Rev did.

While the Rev understood the differences, it did often cause them to react with anger to a human much quicker than they would with their own kind.

And while the Rev couldn't always figure out a half-truth, they could often sense a complete lie.

"You are stalling," the Rev said.

"Yes," Flint said, relieved not to have to lie about that. "I want to wait for the interpreter."

"Then you will get our woman," the Rev said.

"If we agree that's who she is," Flint said, hoping he wasn't lying now.

The Rev turned toward his companions. They hadn't moved at all during the discussion. They spoke rapid Rev, and Flint only caught every fourth or fifth word. After a moment, the spokesrev turned back toward him.

"We shall wait for your interpreter. You may return when the interpreter arrives."

They were dismissing him. Flint felt an odd kind of relief. "Is there something I can get you that will make you more comfortable?"

"No," the Rev said. "We will not be here long enough to get comfortable."

Flint made himself smile and nod, hoping that the Rev was right.

The night was strangely quiet. It had been a long time since Ekaterina had been inside a dome. She had forgotten how dome acoustics worked. Loud sounds could echo, but unlike Earth on a quiet night, soft sounds didn't seem to register at all.

She moved slower because of that. She was being more cautious than she would have been at home.

The darkened neighborhood seemed to go on for at least a mile. She had crossed a lot of fences, wound her way through a lot of yards.

Apparently, no pets were allowed in this part of Armstrong. She heard no barking dogs, ran across no cats. At the moment, she was very grateful for that.

She had finally reached a poorly tended block. The gardens had died off, and the plants had either gone to seed or disappeared entirely. Some desert plants had grown up in the artificially rich soil—apparently reclaiming the area or seeding from somewhere else.

Most of the houses appeared to be uninhabited, but
those that were had large, ostentatious locks on the
doors, a kind she hadn't seen anywhere on Earth outside of museums. The locks seemed to be there as a
statement, not for protection.

As she got closer to some of the houses, she realized
they were made of permaplastic, a material that wasn't
used much at all anymore. Early colonists on the
Moon and Mars had used a lot of it—the material was
durable, even in unpredictable environments. But then
scientists had developed other materials, many of
which could be grown once the colonists reached the
habitable planet, and permaplastic fell out of use.

She had to be in one of the oldest areas of Armstrong. Her empty stomach knotted. She hoped this
area was just impoverished and not a crime center the
way many other older areas of cities were. If this was
a high-crime place, she might be walking straight into
the hands of the authorities.

Here there were no street lights at all. The air felt
even thinner, and she hadn't been running this time.
She wondered if the processors in the older sections
of the dome weren't as efficient.

On a corner lot at the very end of the block, a
house stood, its doors open. Her heart was pounding
hard. Either the house was abandoned or someone
had deliberately left it this way, maybe to attract va-
grants—or fugitives.

All she knew was that she would have to stop moving soon. She wasn't sure when she last slept, and
she was beginning to have micronaps as she walked.
Eventually her body would force her to rest whether
she wanted to or not—and it might do so out in the
open, where anyone could find her.

If she found shelter, even for a few hours, she would

be refreshed enough to move on. Or as her grandmother used to say, *The body can do without food or
sleep, but it cannot do without both.* And it could not
do without water either. She was getting dehydrated
and she knew it.

She would need to take care of herself, and soon.

She approached the house, breathing shallowly, her
own heartbeat so loud that she was sure people heard
it blocks away. Nothing moved inside—or at least,
nothing she could hear.

The last thing she wanted to do was go into a place
filled with indigents. They could be crazy, violent, or
both. The last time she had been in Armstrong, almost
a decade ago, the city had a large indigent problem.
She doubted things had gotten any better. After all,
what could the city managers do? Throw the indigents
outside the dome?

One wall had fallen inward. Apparently, it had lost
some of its supports, a common problem with old permaplastic. The permaplastic survived longer than the
materials used to hold it together. She stared at the
wall for a long moment. It was a warning to her that
this building wouldn't be very stable. Maybe that was
why it was so silent, because everyone else knew better than to attempt to go inside.

Still, she had to try. She was nearly collapsing with
exhaustion. She glanced over her shoulder. She still
appeared to be alone on the street—not that she could
completely tell in this darkness.

Then she mounted the back stair and went inside
the open door.

The building smelled of old urine and decay. Someone or something had died in here. She couldn't tell
how long ago because one of the disadvantages of
aging permaplastic was that it tended to absorb odors.

The floor seemed sturdy enough. She walked across it, wishing she had a light. It was even darker in here. She hoped she wouldn't step on anyone—alive or dead.

Her feet hit a pile of something that clattered across the floor. She froze, the sound so loud she was convinced they'd heard it on Earth. Her heart pounded, and her breathing sped up.

There was no answering sound. No one swore and came toward her. No one screamed. No one shouted, *There she is!* and burst into the building.

She was really and truly alone.

She crouched, and felt for what her feet had touched. A pile of empty food cartons, their interiors sticky, and clearly the source of the rotting smell. Someone had been here before her, used the shelter, and left.

It was a good sign if no one had touched the food cartons. She went deeper into the building, far away from the collapsed wall and the smell of urine. Some pieces of furniture remained—also permaplastic and worthless.

She felt the chairs, found dust on them, but nothing that was as disagreeable as the decaying food in the other room. She pulled two chairs together. They were wide enough for her to use as a bed, and their arms were high enough to hide her from prying eyes.

All she needed was a short nap. When she woke up, she'd have ideas on ways to get out of Armstrong. If she was still alone. And safe.

19

The interpreter was a balding, middle-aged man who wore an expensive tailored business suit. His face, while thin, had cascaded into jowls, and his neck had a crepe-papery look to it that Flint had never seen on a modern human.

People who regularly did business with the Rev did not use physical enhancements. The Rev saw enhancements as a form of deception and respected no one who used them.

The interpreter was waiting in the main Division— no one had taken him to the Detective Unit upstairs or the interrogation room in the back. The main Division area was full—people in uniform going about their business, the duty clerk processing visitors, and the usual stream of victims, supplicants, and suspects, each there for a different reason.

The volume in here was always loud—shouts mingled with tears, laughter, and everything in between. The smells were omnipresent too—perfumes, sweat, and occasional overwhelming alien body odor. The place never stayed the same, and that was part of its charm.

Sometimes Flint didn't really see the people who filled the entry. They were part of the scenery, an

ever-flowing, ever-changing group that was as normal
a part of this place as the walls.

But the interpreter noticed. He cringed every time
someone brushed against him.

Not a government employee then. Flint would
wager his entire year's salary that this interpreter did
the bulk of his work for private firms.

"Hello," Flint said, as he approached the interpreter, hand outstretched. "I'm Detective Flint. I'm
sorry you were waiting. The Rev are in the back."

The man looked up at him, his eyes pale and wa-
tery. "Are they angry?"

There was a touch of fear in his voice. He didn't
even seem to notice Flint's hand.

"I was told," the man continued, not letting Flint
answer, "that this is a criminal matter. The Rev hate
criminal matters, especially if it's not going their way."

"Right now, they're being patient," Flint said.
"Which is surprising given they've had to deal with
me and my inadequate Rev. But they'll be happy to
have a person who understands their customs and language in the room."

"I've never done criminal work with the Rev before," the man said, "but the chief called me. How
serious is this?"

The chief, huh? Apparently she called the best interpreter rather than use one of the ones on city pay-
roll. Flint couldn't argue with that. Neither of them
wanted this situation to get any worse.

"Very serious," Flint said. "That's why you're here.
Come with me."

It wasn't until they started walking that Flint realized he had forgotten to ask the man's name. Not that
it really mattered. If he needed the guy again, the
chief's office would know how to find him.

They had just reached the duty clerk's tall sign-in desk when Flint saw a familiar figure enter the corridor.

"DeRicci!" he shouted. Then, realizing his voice didn't really carry over the din, he shouted even louder, "DeRicci!"

She stopped, turned, saw him, and made a face. Then she approached. "I thought you were in interrogation."

"I needed an interpreter." Flint nodded toward the balding man standing beside him.

DeRicci's gaze took in everything about the interpreter, and then gave her opinion: contempt. It was an amazing opinion from a woman whose clothing was torn, whose hair looked like as if had been through a windstorm, and whose face was streaked with the brown dust of Earth's dead Moon.

"You just arrived?" she asked the interpreter.

"I just found out about it, yes," he said, bobbing as he spoke to her. Flint was sure he'd never seen such a timid interpreter. He wasn't sure if it was the Division that scared this little man, the fact that he was about to face potentially angry Rev, or both.

"I thought you said to hurry." Now she was speaking to Flint.

"I did," he said, "and it doesn't seem like you listened."

She shrugged, taking in the room. "Screwed up, Flint."

"We both did." Flint had the sense that she was angry at him, but he didn't care. She still had her job, and so did he. "I promised the Revs we'd go in there as soon as the interpreter arrived."

"What a day this is," DeRicci said. "Starts with the Wygnin, moves on to the Rev."

"You're handling the Wygnin?" This time, the voice came from above them. Both Flint and DeRicci looked up.

The duty clerk was staring down at them, her expression pinched.

"On one case, yes," Flint said.

"The children, right?"

"Right," DeRicci said, sounding wary.

The interpreter moved closer to the desk, as if he were trying to get out of the way of the free flow of people.

"Some people just came in from Tycho Station. I put a uniform with them until I found who was supposed to be responsible for them."

"On the Wygnin case?" Flint asked the duty clerk.

"Parents," DeRicci said, punching his arm. Then she turned to the duty clerk. "Where are they?"

"Witness holding," the duty clerk said. "It seemed the most private."

DeRicci nodded. "Come on, Flint."

Technically, the children were his responsibility. He knew what she was doing: she was taking over the entire Wygnin case so that she wouldn't have to deal with the Rev.

He was tempted to let her do it, but that meant accompanying the interpreter to the interrogation room. The longer Flint stayed away from the Rev, the better. That way he wouldn't be forced to lie.

He turned to the interpreter. "The Rev are in an interrogation room. They're probably going to want some refreshments of some kind. It was warm in there."

"I'm not a waitress," the interpreter said.

Flint shrugged. "Suit yourself. I get very cranky

when my blood sugar's low. I wonder what the Rev are like."

"But I don't know where anything is here," the interpreter said.

"The duty clerk will help you," DeRicci said. "Come on, Flint."

"I'll be back shortly," he said to the interpreter. "Go over their warrant, and then I'll join you."

The interpreter was shaking his head, still making weak protests, as Flint and DeRicci walked away.

"They sent someone like that to go head-to-head with the Rev?" DeRicci asked.

"Hobell picked him out herself."

DeRicci whistled. "So that's what happens when there's too much alien contact."

She didn't even smile after the comment. Flint wasn't sure if she was joking or not.

The corridor was wide through here because so many civilians used it. Many of them were witnesses, but just as many were victims or the victims' families, and the designers of this Division, at least, felt that there should be some measure of comfort in the surroundings.

Originally, the walls had been painted a calming blue, but that had faded to a dirty gray over time. The floor was scuffed, and the once-white ceiling had yellowed. Instead of offering comfort, this place always reminded Flint that anything once touched with bright promise could become old and abused.

"You're quiet," DeRicci said. Except for the occasional uniform going the other way, they were the only two people in the corridor.

"Long day," Flint said.

"How'd you keep Hobell from demoting us?"

He shrugged. "I told her the truth."

"Which was?"

"That we were initially told that Palmer might be a tourist."

DeRicci looked at him sideways, a smile playing on her lips. "You're beginning to fascinate me, Flint."

"Why is that?" he asked as they rounded the last corner to the observation decks.

"Because you look so sweet and innocent, and you're not."

"I was a cop for a long time before I became a detective," he said.

"Yeah," she said, "but that face of yours. Unenhanced and so naïve. Anyone would think you're a pushover."

"Did you?" he asked.

"You seemed like it at first." Her smile eased into a grin. "I'm glad you finally came out of your shell."

They reached the double doors that marked the entrance to witness holding. DeRicci put her hand on the security panel. The locks clicked open. As they did, she asked for the witnesses in the Wygnin case. The computer gave her the site of the holding room.

The first time Flint had entered this part of the building, he had thought of it as a hall of mirrors. Instead of walls, on either side of him were floor-to-ceiling windows of one-way glass. The glass overlooked holding rooms—they were too plush to be called cells—where witnesses were told they were to sit and wait until someone came for them.

More than one witness had confessed to a crime in these rooms, and hundreds of others had divulged secrets that they thought would never be overheard. Flint was always amazed at the stupidity of the average criminal and his accomplices, and now he was glad for it.

If every criminal were as smart as Greta Palmer, his job would be a lot harder.

Jasper's parents were in the third room on Flint's right. As DeRicci headed toward the one-way window, she pulled out her hand-held and called up the warrant the Wygnin had given her. Flint watched it appear on the screen, along with images of the crime scene and the so-called criminals which Flint had not seen before.

DeRicci didn't even look down at her hand-held. She wasn't concerned about it, not yet. Instead, she stopped in front of the one-way glass.

Flint stopped beside her. This particular holding area was one of the smaller ones, but it was plush. The room had been done in warm browns and tans. The carpet was thick, perfect to sit on if need be, and the couch looked inviting.

Mugs sat on the table in the center of the room, along with some cookies that didn't look like department issue. The uniform sat on the only metal chair. She was staring at the window as if willing someone to rescue her.

The man—Jasper's father—was pacing, hands in his pockets, body hunched. He had the same red hair that his son had, and his skin was pale but freckled.

His wife sat on the edge of an overstuffed chair, her back perfectly straight, her legs to one side with her ankles crossed. Her brown hair had been pulled away from her heart-shaped face. Her eyes were downcast, her hands folded in her lap.

She almost seemed like a supplicant, waiting in one of Armstrong's many churches for someone to forgive her.

"Damn," DeRicci said.

"What?" Flint frowned at her. She was staring at her hand-held.

"Look at this." She touched a corner, and the holo-representation of one of the images rose above the screen's surface. It was a woman's head, now rendered in three dimensions. She had brown hair, light skin, and a heart-shaped face.

Flint studied it, then moved slightly so that he could see both the hologram and the woman in the room. The woman sitting on the edge of the upholstered chair was older, had had some enhancements that altered the shape of her mouth and nose, but her eyes were the same. And so was her hairline and that uniquely shaped face.

"It's the same woman, only younger," he said.

DeRicci nodded. "That's my take too."

"That's not from the Wygnin, is it?" He had asked that as a question, but he already knew the answer. He'd seen the images in the hand-held. He just hadn't seen them very clearly.

"It's part of the warrant," DeRicci said.

He stared at the face. The woman's holo looked so innocent, so young. Both the innocence and the youth were gone from the woman below. She hadn't moved the entire time he had stood there, although the father continued pacing.

The uniform still looked at the wall as if she could see through it. No one was talking below. It looked as if they hadn't even tried.

He remembered the little boy, his face streaked with tears, trying valiantly not to name his family, afraid his sisters would have to go in his place. Had the child known his mother had done something wrong? How could he? What parent would tell her child that his life would be forfeit for a crime she had committed long before he was born?

"What can we do?" Flint asked.

"I don't know," DeRicci said. "Challenge the warrant, maybe."

"Based on what? The Wygnin will know when they see that woman that they have the right person. We did, and we hadn't had as much time to study her image as they have."

"There's got to be something," DeRicci said. "An eight-year-old child has a fully developed human personality. The Wygnin will destroy him."

"Why didn't these people think of that before they had children?" Flint murmured. "They knew the risks."

"I guess they think they're immune." DeRicci punched the hand-held and the holo-image went away.

"In some ways, they are," Flint said. "It's their children who pay."

DeRicci's gaze met his. "I'm going to the city attorney."

"You're supposed to help me with the Rev."

She slipped her hand-held in her pocket. "Look, Miles. I'm angry, tired, and discouraged. You want me to handle some delicate negotiations with the most volatile creatures we've ever run across?"

He didn't, but he didn't want her to get into trouble either. Besides, part of him wanted her to deal with the parents, not him. He didn't want to think about losing a child, even if that child wasn't his own.

"What can the city attorney do?" he asked.

"Maybe he's run across this before," DeRicci said.

"Reese? He's so new he makes me seem like I've been detecting for years. He can't help us."

"We don't know until we try." DeRicci pushed past Flint and headed toward the door.

"DeRicci," he said.

She stopped as her hand pushed against the double doors. "What?"

"Before you go, you might want to shower, change into a real uniform. Get the dust off your face."

She brushed her cheek with her forefingers, then held them out, as if checking the veracity of his statement.

"I didn't ask you before," he said quietly, "but did you get hurt in that wreck?"

Her hand went toward her left arm, then stopped as if she had thought better of it. She flashed him a self-deprecating smile. "No," she said as she pushed her way out of the door. "Everything bounces off me."

Then the door closed behind her, leaving him alone in the hall of mirrors, staring at a couple who was about to lose their oldest son.

20

Jamal sat on one of the hard upholstered chairs in his hotel room. He had pushed it next to the window and had raised the privacy screen just enough so that he could see the street below.

A lot of people walked around in Armstrong Dome at night. He was used to Gagarin Dome with its strict ordinances and post-midnight curfews. No one would walk the streets in Gagarin. The police would pick them up and give them a stern lecture if they even tried.

He wished he were in Gagarin Dome now. All the people moving below made him nervous.

Jamal leaned his head on the wall and closed his eyes. As if anything could make him nervous. He was past nervous. His body had been cycling through every emotion it could find, apparently trying to find something other than complete and total loss to settle on.

Hakan Needahl had taken away the last of his hope. The lawyer had convinced Jamal that no one would take this case, no matter what he did. Not even if they looked at Ennis's beautiful, innocent face and realized he had nothing to do with this.

None of them wanted to be in the same position Jamal was.

He opened his eyes and sighed. His wife was asleep on the double bed, her body curled around Ennis's, protective even in sleep. Ennis clutched Mr. Biscuit, as if the loss of the stuffed dog had been worse than the loss of his home.

The boy had snuffled himself to sleep, and nothing Dylani had done could soothe him. Ennis probably sensed how his parents were feeling. Their fears were only enhancing his.

There had to be a solution. Jamal just had to find it.

His brain didn't work the way it used to, searching for all the angles, finding all the hidden loopholes. He'd been a passive, quiet man for the past decade, and it had changed how he thought.

Right now, he needed the man he had been, the man who had gotten him into this trouble.

The man who had placed five huge office buildings on sacred Wygnin land.

Jamal tried to shake that memory away, but it didn't work. If he closed his eyes, he could will himself back to Korsve when the shuttle touched down. He had been newly promoted, one of the fastest rising executives his corporation had ever seen, and he believed he could conquer whatever world he was sent to.

He'd even met the Wygnin before and had gotten along with them, which was why the corporation had sent him to Korsve. They believed he would work well with the Wygnin, that his management would make a success out of the company's branch on Korsve.

Instead, he disgraced them all, got charged with criminal negligence by the Wygnin, and had to Disappear.

And the corporation had been lucky because it hadn't had to take the blame. His name had been on each decision. The trail had led directly back to him because he had wanted credit for his brilliance.

His stupidity, actually.

He looked at Ennis, asleep next to Dylani. Jamal had never really imagined a child, never really imagined what it would mean to lose one.

The counselor at Disappearance Inc had told him he was lucky all those years ago. She had said that his parents were too old to be of interest in that Wygnin warrant, and since he was an only child, the line would die out with him.

All he had to do was remain in hiding, and make certain he had no children.

Perhaps this was why the Wygnin behaved the way they did. Punishing a man by imprisoning him or even by putting him to death seemed simplistic. Taking away something he loved was a lot more sophisticated, creating a void that would never be filled.

Just like Jamal had done on Korsve.

He closed his eyes again, saw the pristine piece of property, just outside the Wygnin's only city. The property had been near a river that had flowed red down a mountainside. Flowers grew along its bank, and out of a granite rock cropping that looked as sturdy as anything Jamal had ever seen.

He had come late to Korsve, so he hadn't heard the warnings. The Wygnin didn't completely understand property rights. They often sold the same piece of property over and over again, commenting on the foolishness of humans who thought land could be altered.

Even then no one had really understood that the only inhabited continent on Korsve was strewn with natural caves and hollowed-out boulders that made great dwellings. The city itself was a naturally occurring boulderfield that had been modified just enough to allow Wygnin to live together in large numbers.

The Wygnin did manufacture things, from glass for windows to a substance that was very rocklike, which they used to seal the boulder homes from the weather. But they did not build homes and office buildings from scratch.

When they first saw humans doing that, they had been appalled, and the humans had misunderstood. They had thought that they had chosen the wrong piece of land—because of the nestlings or because of the land's history.

They had never thought that building and altering the landscape was foreign to the Wygnin in and of itself.

In fact, the way that humans learned about that was through Jamal.

He sighed and stood, feeling restless. His conversation with Needahl had continued long after the man had said no one would work for Jamal. Jamal tried various arguments, hoping to engage Needahl's restless intellect.

Apparently Needahl had had a strategy in mind, because his attitude had changed completely after he had seen the warrant.

"This child is young enough," Needahl had said again. "He will survive the ordeal and not understand what he has lost."

But Jamal would. He had even asked if Needahl would recommend a new Disappearance service.

"I'm an officer of the court," Needahl had said. "Disappearance services break the law. I cannot give you this information. I'd be contributing to a crime."

And he'd ended the conversation shortly after that.

Jamal had no money to hire a Disappearance service. But maybe he could make a deal with one.

He stood and paced, careful to move quietly so that he wouldn't wake his sleeping wife and child.

If he explained everything to Dylani, she would be furious at him. She might want him out of her life. He could convince her to Disappear with Ennis, and he would pay all the fees for their Disappearance by indenturing himself to them if he had to. He'd give them whatever paycheck he had for as long as they wanted, if only they'd guarantee that his son and his wife would be safe.

He now knew that no guarantee was forever. But he had to do something. Anything. So long as the Wygnin didn't take Ennis. He didn't care what happened to him as long as his son had a chance to remain human and survive.

With the addition of the interpreter, the interrogation room seemed even smaller. Or maybe Flint felt that way because two of the Rev—not the two Flint had spoken with—had emotion collars fanned out around their tiny faces.

The emotion collars, like other Rev limbs, seemed invisible when they were at rest. When they appeared, they often startled the unprepared observer.

In some ways, Flint thought the emotion collars the most disturbing Rev feature of all. The collars—which had an entirely different name in the Rev language— had been named by early human colonists on Revnata because the flaps of skin resembled the ruffled collars Elizabethans wore in England in the sixteenth century. The collars changed color as a Rev's emotion deepened—starting at pale white and moving all the way to maroon when the Rev's emotion was at its height.

The problem with emotion collars was that they responded to any strong emotion; Flint couldn't tell if these Rev were angry or were feeling something else. These Rev emotion collars were still pale white, but their eyes had bulged out even further than usual.

The Rev Flint had spoken with initially was standing very close to the interpreter. The interpreter had taken the chair nearest the door. He huddled against it, his feet braced as if he were ready to run at any moment.

When the interpreter realized Flint was there, he said, "I thought you were going to be right back."

There was an edge of panic to his voice that Flint didn't like. "What's been going on here?"

"They're getting upset that no one is working with them. Apparently they thought I had some kind of authority."

Flint nodded, made sure the door was closed tightly, then stepped farther into the room. The smell of ginger was even stronger than it had been before. His eyes watered.

"I'm sorry," Flint said in English. "I was checking on some information for you."

The interpreter repeated Flint's words in Rev, starting to speak almost at the same time Flint did. Flint caught enough of the interpreter's words to realize the man was doing his job correctly. From that moment on, Flint wouldn't worry about the translations.

"Have you brought the woman?" the Rev asked.

"I need to see your warrant," Flint said.

The Rev turned to one of his companions, the other Rev without the obvious emotion collar. His left upper arm moved above his robe, reaching into its side and removing a piece of ridged Revina silk. He handed it to Flint.

Flint had seen Rev warrants like this one before.

The Revina silk acted like a screen on an ancient palm-top. The Rev had thoughtfully set the warrant on its English version. Flint studied it.

The accompanying image was of a thinner, brittle-looking version of the woman he had seen in the de-contamination unit. She looked no older now; she'd obviously had some expensive enhancements.

Flint thought it odd that someone who was on the run from the Rev for—he glanced again at the warrant—seven years hadn't bothered to have her features changed.

"The name here is the one you used earlier," he said to the Rev. "Ekaterina Maakestad."

"Yes," the Rev said. "I thought we had covered this."

"We have no one in Armstrong with that name."

"She has changed it then," the Rev said.

"The warrant is unspecific," Flint said. "It only demands that we release her into your custody for an undetermined period of years. What has she done and what will become of her?"

The second part of his question was unusual and he knew it. But he asked it anyway, hoping that the Rev would answer without hesitating.

"She will be placed in a Rev penal colony," the Rev said. "We have several for non-Rev now. The workload is lighter, more suited to the weaker physique of the human. She will labor for us for ten to twenty years, depending on her health and her abilities to continue her duties. Then, depending on her conduct, she will be exiled from Revnata and all its satellites after five more years of contemplation."

As Rev sentences went, this was a light one. The interpreter knew that as well because he gave Flint a sideways look.

"You've been searching for her for a long time," Flint said. "Yet it sounds like her crime was not a great one."

"It is an important one," the Rev said. "She is an example of what can go wrong in the relationships between our peoples."

Clearly some Rev had made that argument with the Multicultural Tribunal and won.

"So what has she done?" Flint asked.

"Her crime is not the issue here," the Rev said. "You must turn her over into our custody."

The interpreter's voice shook as he said that last. Flint followed his gaze. He was looking at the two emotion collars. They were turning pale yellow.

Even though the spokesrev was remaining calm, his companions were not.

Flint did not look at them again. He didn't want their agitation to affect him. But his eyes were still watering from the ginger smell and his palms were getting damp.

"I agree," he said. "Her crime is not the issue. She's been tried and found guilty under your laws, and that decision was upheld by an interstellar court."

The Rev emotion collars were turning white again.

"However," he said, "the woman who came in on that yacht says her name is Greta Palmer. Her history says she has never been anywhere except Mars and Earth, and so I can't turn her over to you."

"You are required to." The Rev shook the silk at Flint.

"I am required to turn Ekaterina Maakestad over to you," Flint said. "Not Greta Palmer."

"You know they are the same woman," the Rev said.

"I *suspect* they are," Flint said. "Which is why, if

you tell me what she's done, I can talk to her, see if she makes some kind of slip-up."

"That seems like a lot of work for nothing," the Rev said. "Test her DNA. Then we'll have clear proof."

"That'll take even more time," Flint said. "Under our laws, I need probable cause to extract DNA from another human. All I have is the fact that she arrived under rather mysterious circumstances. I'll see what I can do, but I can't promise much on that route. However, if I speak with her, I might be able to expedite this."

He hoped he wouldn't have to keep track of his lies. He was making this up as he went along—and he hoped it was obvious to no one except himself.

The Rev swiveled his head one-hundred-and-eighty degrees so that he could look at his companions. Their emotion collars were still white. Apparently they had bought Flint's story as well.

The Rev swiveled his head back toward Flint. "Ekaterina Maakestad practiced law on Revnata. She used deception to win her client's acquittal."

Flint let his surprise show. He had not expected this. "Her human client?"

"No. It is complicated." For the first time since Flint had entered the room, the Rev looked at the interpreter. They spoke for a moment, and Flint only caught half of the interchange. Something about making sure he got all of the details right.

The interpreter was shaking so badly that he looked as if he might come apart. Flint doubted that the man would ever cross the Rev. He wondered why the Rev suspected it.

"Most interstellar cases are complicated," Flint said, when the consultation had finished.

"Not like this one," the Rev said. "Ekaterina Maakestad defended many clients, most of them human, but in this case, her client was Rev. She represented him before a Rev court. Do you know what that means?"

Flint shook his head. Obviously all of these details were important to the Rev, but he had no idea why.

"When a human represents a human before a Rev court, the rules are different. We know that your people do not always understand our laws, and we are more lenient, particularly with your attorneys."

Flint nodded, wondering how many human lawyers practicing on Rev worlds knew that.

"But when a human attorney has the temerity to take a Rev client, we assume she knows Rev law."

"She must have known something of it," Flint said. "She agreed to the case."

The Rev's emotion collar rose, then settled against his neck. Flint wasn't sure what the gesture meant—perhaps irritation?—but whatever it was, it made the interpreter jump.

"She represented a guilty client," the Rev said, and did not add anything else.

Finally Flint said, "Defense attorneys often do. That's how the advocacy system works."

"The human advocacy system—" The Rev didn't break off mid-sentence. The interpreter did.

Again, he spoke to the Rev. He spoke for a long time, his hands moving as if illustrating a point. The other Revs had crowded closer to listen.

Flint only caught a few words. Law. Court. Misunderstanding. The rest was lost in a flurry of Rev.

Then the Rev's head bobbled—it was the Rev's version of a dismissive gesture.

The interpreter turned toward Flint.

"I asked him," the interpreter said, "if I could explain this to you. He isn't a legal expert and he certainly doesn't understand interstellar law. He's the Rev version of a bounty hunter, and having him explain the delicacies of the Rev legal system probably won't work. You'll both get frustrated, and his companions are upset enough."

"All right," Flint said. Then he repeated that in Rev. When he was finished, he added, "Better make it quick."

"Believe me," the interpreter said, glancing nervously at the Rev. "In some ways, the Rev legal system is similar to ours. It appears to be an advocacy system, where two attorneys meet head-to-head in front of a judge. But there's where the similarities end."

The Rev were watching. The spokesrev appeared to be listening closely. Flint wondered just how much English he understood.

"The Rev have two courts: one for the innocent and one for the guilty."

"What?" Flint asked.

The interpreter raised his two forefingers, so that Flint wouldn't speak any more.

"A Rev defense attorney's first job is to figure out whether the client is innocent or guilty. If the attorney believes the client innocent, the attorney defends that client in the advocacy system. If the attorney believes the client guilty, she takes him to another system where they plea-bargain or find a way to settle the case."

The spokesrev nodded. Flint frowned, wondering why this mattered.

"If a Rev attorney defends a client in the advocacy system, the attorney is, in effect, signaling her belief in the client's innocence. The Rev are sympathetic to an attorney who later learns of her client's guilt, believing anyone can be fooled. Where they are not sympathetic is in the case of the repeat offender."

Flint felt his frown grow deeper. There had been nothing mentioned about attorneys or repeat offenses on that warrant. Maakestad was accused of a crime.

"An attorney who represents a client in advocacy court guarantees by her word and bond that the client is innocent. She also takes responsibility for any similar crimes the client commits in the future."

"Responsibility?" Flint asked.

"She is considered an equal partner in those crimes because, the Rev assume, she knew her client's character. She knew that he would go out and commit a second or third crime."

"How can anyone know that?" Flint asked.

The interpreter glanced at the Rev again. They were watching the interchange closely.

"If you don't know, you don't defend the client," the interpreter said. "You take the client to the other court where you plea-bargain. Defending the client becomes too great a risk otherwise."

"So Maakestad defended a Rev client in this advocacy system?"

"Apparently," the interpreter said.

"And this client was a repeat offender?"

"I'm not sure." The interpreter turned toward the Rev and spoke for another moment in Rev. The spokesrev leaned closer, but as he did, the emotion collar on the Rev in the back turned a faint shade of green.

They would have to end this part of the conversation soon. The Rev were getting too upset. Maybe Flint would be able to convince them to return to their ship until he could deliver Palmer/Maakestad.

"This woman," the Rev said, "defended a known criminal who manufactured drugs. She claimed that it does not matter what he did in the past, only that he was innocent of this particular crime. It was a novel concept in Rev justice and made big news."

Which was why the Rev knew about it, then.

"So her client was found guilty?" Flint asked.

The Rev shook its head. "She was successful. However, her client has since been convicted of the same crime, manufacturing drugs, only this time, two of the Rev who took those drugs died."

The Rev homeworld, Revina, and its satellites had been battling the drug trade for a very long time. Because the Rev's emotions were so volatile, many Rev used artificial means to keep those emotions in check. Unlike so many in the human drug trade, this crime on Revnata was a high-end crime, with wealthy clients who often worked for interstellar corporations.

Flint had dealt a lot with the Rev drug trade because the Rev considered caffeine to be one of the worst drugs on their market. Caffeine worked like cocaine on the Rev nervous system, speeding up the thought processes, making the Rev more efficient, and granting a sense of confidence. Caffeine also killed one out of five Rev who used it regularly. Since caffeine was a legal drug in all human colonies, the Rev had to rely on help from border patrols and space cops to prevent shipments to Rev worlds.

Flint wasn't familiar with the manufactured drugs on any of the Rev worlds, but he suspected they were as lethal to the Rev as caffeine could be.

"So he was a repeat offender, and she should have known that," Flint said. "Which is why she's being charged with a crime on Revnata."

"Not charged," the Rev said. "She is guilty. She

defended a known criminal and her deception resulted in the death of two Rev."

"This is, to the Rev, a slam-dunk," the interpreter added, as an aside. "They don't have to prove anything about her except that she defended this guy."

"What did you say?" the Rev asked the interpreter in Rev. Flint recognized that phrase, having used it a lot himself.

The interpreter answered in Rev. The spokesrev nodded, and then continued, "This woman has escaped our justice too long. You cannot allow that to continue."

And Flint wouldn't if he knew where she was. "One more question, and then I'll see if I can get her to admit any of this."

The third Rev leaned forward, his dark eyes bulging. The room was even hotter than it had been before.

"This happened a long time ago," Flint said. "Has this woman been on the run for years? If so, that would explain the alternate name."

"She has fought us in court, citing her status as a human as an excuse," the Rev said. "It would be a valid excuse with a human client, but she had a Rev client, one no other Rev would touch. She should have known better."

Most criminals should have known better than to repeat the crime in any Rev world, Flint thought, but did not say that. Still, this was the first case that had come to him in the last two days that he had no ethical qualms about. If Palmer had indeed muddled in a legal system she did not understand—or worse, if she had tried to change one she did understand—then she knew what the consequences might be.

"I take it she lost her court case."

"Yes," the Rev said. "She was notified two weeks ago to surrender herself to us. Instead, she Disappeared."

That caught Flint's attention. "She what?"

"Disappeared. We went to her home and she was gone. Everything remained, including her accounts, which hadn't been touched for days."

"Yet you found her," Flint said.

"We were notified of her presence on that space yacht. She was supposed to be turned over to us. Instead, she managed to escape."

"Coming here."

"Yes," the Rev said.

That all jibed with what Flint had heard on the yacht's logs. "What happened to the pilot?"

"She forced him, his co-pilot, and another into an escape pod. We have them in custody now."

"Are you charging them with something?" Flint asked.

"No," the Rev said. "You may have them."

Flint nodded, feeling a little light-headed, hoping it was the heat instead of the ginger stench. "They might be able to verify her identity."

"Best to use your method first," the Rev said.

Flint frowned. "Have they been harmed?"

"They were in an escape pod built for two for more than an hour," the Rev said. "They are spacesick."

This time, Flint was the one who was irritated. "Why didn't you turn them over to us immediately for treatment?"

The Rev bobbled his head from side to side, a gesture of discomfort. "We weren't sure whether or not we would need them."

"As hostages?" Flint asked.

"To bargain with," the Rev said, as if that were different.

"Turn them over to us," Flint said. "You won't need bargaining chips."

"As you wish," the Rev said. "We shall send word to the ship immediately."

Flint suppressed a sigh. Were these Rev never going to leave? "Actually, you don't have to wait here. You'd be more comfortable on your own ship. I'll notify you as soon as I'm convinced the woman who got off that yacht is Maakestad."

Lying to a Rev. Part of his brain was appalled at that, still. The interpreter was watching him closely, probably just as worried.

If, under Rev law, a lawyer could be charged with defending a guilty client, could an interpreter be charged with speaking someone else's lies?

Flint didn't want to know.

"We shall stay here," the Rev said, and rocked back on his base, the Rev equivalent of crossing his arms.

Flint knew better than to argue. "I'll make sure you're moved to a more comfortable surrounding. This room is too small and—"

"This is fine," the Rev said in English, interrupting Flint and the interpreter both. The Rev's emotion collar fluttered upward. Apparently he was beginning to see Flint's efforts to move them as stalling tactics.

"All right," Flint said. "If you change your mind, let me know. I'll do what I can to take care of this."

He reached for the door, but the interpreter caught his arm. "What about me?"

"Stay here," Flint said. "Make sure they get that pilot and crew off their ship, and then see if they want some food or something. It's better if they can speak through you than to let them try to communicate themselves."

The interpreter sank back into his chair. "I would prefer to leave."

"And I'd prefer to be off the case," Flint said, as he let himself out of the room.

The air in the corridor was cooler. It took a few moments for the smell to clear from his nostrils.

The Rev's comments confirmed his suspicions. Palmer was a Disappeared, just like the three who had been killed by the Disty. These two cases were linked by more than the yachts now.

If Flint found out who owned those yachts, he might find which Disappearance service was selling out its own clients. Not that that was illegal. It was, in fact, the legal thing to do—which created even more problems for Flint.

And for the children.

21

Ekaterina started awake, her entire body on alert. Something was different. She sat up, her eyes grimy with sleep and dust, her mind muzzy.

She'd managed to get some sleep, but it felt shallow, filled with Rev and flipping aircars and arguments with detectives. They were yelling at her about contacting her former clients, ticking off names as if they were looking at her case history.

One of the names struck a bell.

She rubbed her eyes and sat up. The walls were so old, they were streaked with brown lines. Everywhere else, the once-white permaplastic had yellowed.

And that was what differed. She could see. False Dawn had come, bringing enough light that she could see inside this house. And she wished she couldn't.

The floor was littered with brown dust, discarded food packets, and animal droppings. They looked like mouse droppings, but she wasn't sure how that was possible. Who would have brought rodents to the Moon?

The stench was still noticeable, even though she had been in it for a while. She wondered if her own clothing had absorbed it. She hoped not. She wanted to be able to blend into Armstrong's day crowds.

Even though it was False Dawn, she knew she hadn't been asleep very long. Her body's clock told her that—the muzziness in her brain, the way she was having difficulty waking up. It showed just how alert she was, even in sleep, that a change in the light woke her.

She got up and stretched. Her muscles ached from that short time on the hard chairs. The accident had had more of an effect on her than she first realized. She would have aches and pains from it for the next few days.

If only she could remember the names that had run through her dreams.

The room she had slept in had no windows. A stairway, with the steps broken in the center as if someone had carried something too heavy up them, was built into the far wall. The wall across from her was the one that had collapsed. More light poured in there, revealing blankets, a pile of food packets, and bottles of water.

Someone was using this place—or had in the recent past.

Her stomach growled as she walked toward the stash. The food packets had expired two years ago, but the water hadn't. She picked up the nearest bottle and drained it, feeling better than she had just a moment before.

She had been very dehydrated. She drank another bottle, slower this time, and then looked for something to use as a knapsack. She wanted to carry some bottles with her.

It seemed odd that someone would just leave all this stuff here without coming back for it.

She wandered through what had once been the kitchen, opening cupboards, finding broken utensils and cracked dishes. Clearly someone had looted this place long ago.

Then she went into a third room, which was mostly empty except for the pile of discarded clothes in the corner.

The smell was the worst here. The food packets that she had kicked had landed in here, and there was something green that had once been food growing on the floor.

She eyed the clothes again and saw a boot sticking out at an odd angle. A boot with Moon dust on its sole and pants attached to its top.

And she knew. She didn't have to walk any farther.

Her mysterious host had been here, all along. Dead.

Her stomach turned. She was glad she hadn't eaten anything that morning or it would have come back up. Fortunately, she hadn't had any light last night. She hadn't explored, so she hadn't found him and as a result, she had gotten a few hours sleep and some much-needed water.

She wondered if he had died of natural causes or if someone had killed him. Then she decided that she didn't want to know. It would be better for her not to know, so that she wouldn't worry about it for the rest of the day.

But she had to get out of there.

She took her two bottles of water, and stuck them in the waistband of her pants. Then she grabbed two more bottles and hurried to the open door.

There she paused.

The light was bright outside, reflecting off yet another piece of permaplastic, this one looking like part of the roof. She blinked, then stepped back inside. People would be able to see everything, every bruise, every speck of dirt. She grabbed one more bottle of water and used it to wash her face and hands, scrubbing hard so that she was as presentable as possible.

She couldn't do anything about her clothes, but she could help her appearance. She had always tried to ingrain that into her clients, but some never learned. She'd had to buy clothes for more than a few to help them through court appearances—

—And one of those clients lived in Armstrong. Or had when Ekaterina had defended him. That was why she had been thinking about clients. Because her subconscious had taken a backwards route to one of the names she needed.

Shamus Shank. She was amazed she could ever forget a name like that, even for a short period of time. She used to tease him about it, since she hadn't been sure then—and still wasn't sure now—whether the name was made up.

Ekaterina shook her head. Shamus Shank was the perfect person to help her. He specialized in "clean" crimes, hacking into systems and stealing money or altering security protocols so that he could make a quick getaway.

He'd been caught half a dozen times, but each time he had gone free. And he'd always laughed about the police, saying that they had no idea how much money he'd stolen and how much of their records he'd tampered with.

Shamus Shank. She had visited him here once, nearly a decade ago. He had owned the building, and used it when he was in Armstrong, which he had listed as his permanent home address.

And if she couldn't find Shamus Shank, she might be able to find the people who had testified toward his good character. They had all had unusual names as well, and they used to gather at the Brownie Bar, a place she hadn't believed existed until Shamus took her there once.

The Brownie Bar and Shamus Shank.

Finally she had a destination—and a little bit of hope.

"I'd like to see the boy," Ira Reese, the city attorney, said.

DeRicci ran a hand through her hair and wondered how long it had been since she'd slept. Her body hummed with exhaustion. She had worked straight through the night, and now it looked as though she'd be working all day as well.

She and Reese were outside a conference room in the city attorney's office. They were in a wide hallway that branched into several corridors. A fake tree leaned against one wall, looking out of place. An assistant stood nearby, as if she wanted someone to tell her what to do.

They were waiting for a meeting to end. After talking with Jasper Wilder's parents for a while, Reese had called in a colleague, Damien Carryth, who specialized in Disappeareds. He was alone with the Wilders now.

"Believe me, sir," she said to Reese, "you don't want to see him."

Reese gave her a cool stare. "I do. I want to know what we're fighting for."

We're fighting to keep human children human, DeRicci thought. *We're fighting to make sure some weird alien race doesn't warp this kid's mind and make him into something that's not Wygnin either.*

Instead, she said, "Sir, I don't know what Mrs. Wilder said to you, but trust me, you don't want to see that kid."

"Why not?" Reese faced her. He was taller than she was, broad-shouldered and muscular. He looked more like a soccer player than a lawyer.

"Because if we lose this, that kid will haunt your dreams at night. You'll never be able to close your eyes again."

"I take it you've seen him," Reese said.

DeRicci shook her head. "I learned that lesson a long time ago, sir."

He sighed. Part of the problem, she would wager, was that he wasn't used to waiting on others. He was used to being the one in charge. But his specialty was local government regulations and Armstrong law. He knew nothing about Disappeareds and had admitted it the moment DeRicci had barged into his office.

Maybe if he had known something about Disappeareds, he wouldn't have sent for the Wilder family and he wouldn't have called in Carryth. He would have told DeRicci to cut her losses and leave.

Then the door to the conference room opened. The father came out. He was even smaller in person, his back hunched, his eyes hollow. If anything his face seemed paler than it had in the holding room.

It took him a moment to focus on DeRicci's face. "I'm supposed to wait out here."

He sounded bewildered.

"Who told you that?" Reese asked.

Wilder looked at him as if seeing him for the first time.

"You have the right to be inside," Reese was saying, apparently not noticing the odd expression on Wilder's face. "It's your child, after all—"

"Sir." DeRicci put a hand on his wool sleeve, silencing him.

"My wife," Wilder said, as if his answer came through a time-delayed Earth–Moon communications hookup. "My wife begged me to leave."

"Sometimes it's better for one spouse to handle a case," DeRicci said. She knew why the wife wanted him out of there. The wife wanted to tell Carryth the truth.

"Nonsense," Reese said. "It's—"

DeRicci squeezed harder on his arm. As much trouble as she had gotten into the past twenty-four hours, manhandling the city attorney shouldn't make matters any worse.

"Sir," DeRicci said. "Why don't you take Mr. Wilder for some breakfast. I'm sure he hasn't eaten—"

"No." Wilder spoke with a firmness that DeRicci didn't think he was capable of. "They want you inside."

"All right," DeRicci said. "Then I'll take you."

"Both of you," Wilder said.

Reese studied him for a moment, the situation suddenly becoming clear to him. DeRicci hadn't mentioned her suspicions to him when she had first talked with him—that the wife hadn't told her husband about her experiences on Korsve. DeRicci had assumed Reese would understand that. More often than not, Disappeareds did not confide anything about their previous lives to their current mates.

"She did something, didn't she?" Wilder asked, his voice cracking. "Something that made the Wygnin angry. And she was afraid to tell me. She should have told me. We could have done something, rather than wait for those creatures to steal one of our children. For God's sake, we have two others."

Then he blinked at DeRicci. "Is that why you people insisted on guards for the other two?"

"It's standard in cases like this," DeRicci lied. And it probably would have been if there were cases like this. But to her knowledge, no one ever caught the Wygnin with questionable warrants before.

"Are we all in danger?" Wilder asked.

Reese came closer. "Mr. Wilder, we're doing what we can—"

"But will it be enough?" Wilder asked. "My son is at stake, my whole family. You don't know what that's like."

"No." Behind Wilder's back, Reese gestured toward the assistant. "I don't. But we'll help you in any way we can."

The assistant approached. Her gaze met Wilder's, and then he looked away.

"Let Haru take you downstairs, get you something to eat, let you rest while we go inside. I promise, we'll do the best thing possible for your family."

DeRicci tensed. Reese was making a foolish promise. They might try to do the best thing possible, but they probably wouldn't be able to. All of them were restricted by interstellar law.

The assistant took Wilder by the arm and spoke to him as if he were a child. Apparently she had done this before. Wilder glanced over his shoulder once, the expression on his face both desperate and resigned. Then he turned a corner, out of view, and DeRicci sighed with relief.

"This doesn't get easier," she said to Reese.

His lips thinned. "Let's go join the meeting."

He pulled open the conference room door. The room was completely sealed, no windows and a lot of artificial lighting. The wall had built-in panels that looked like rotating panoramas, but apparently they had been shut off too.

As elegant as the room was, it felt more like a prison than some of the cells that DeRicci had seen.

Justine Wilder sat at the end of the table as if she were getting ready to run a board meeting, her hands folded on the fake mahogany surface. Carryth sat beside her, hunched forward like a desperate lover.

Carryth looked more like DeRicci's expectations. He was so thin that he was gaunt, and his eyes were too small for his face. He had had a cheap enhancement done on his hair to cover a bald spot, and the hair had grown in thicker and a different color. Since the enhancement was on his crown, he probably didn't even notice.

"Mr. Wilder said you wanted us in here," Reese said.

Carryth nodded. "Since I'm technically working for you here and not for Mrs. Wilder, we need your approval for our plan."

"Then what am I doing here?" DeRicci asked.

Carryth's dark gaze met hers. "You're the only one of us who has talked with the Wygnin about this case. I figure you might have some insights."

DeRicci nodded, doubting he was right, but willing to stay here. She was too tired to be searching for Palmer—if, indeed, Palmer was still on the run—and she really didn't want to face either the Rev or the Wygnin. If she stayed here, she wouldn't be called upon to do any of that.

"However," Carryth said, "whatever we say in this room is privileged and cannot be spoken of outside of here. If you cannot agree to that, then you'll have to leave."

DeRicci sank into the nearest chair. It had a soft, upholstered seat, which she did not expect, and was very comfortable. "I can keep secrets."

"Good." Carryth turned toward Justine Wilder. "Mrs. Wilder, do you want to tell them the history?"

Reese sat beside Justine Wilder and gave her a warm smile. She did not smile in return. If anything, she seemed even more tightly wound than she had in the holding room. DeRicci had the odd sense that if she touched Mrs. Wilder, the woman would shatter.

"My husband," Mrs. Wilder said, her voice husky and low, "knows nothing about any of this. I'll have to tell him, but I prefer to tell him my way. All right?"

DeRicci nodded. Reese opened his mouth as if he were going to point out that the confidentiality agreement covered this, but Carryth stopped him with a slight shake of the head.

"The Wygnin's warrant is valid." Justine Wilder bowed her head. "I lived on Korsve fifteen years ago, before I met my husband. I had a different name then—the name on the warrant."

It was as if she were still afraid to mention that name. Maybe the habit of hiding her identity had gotten so ingrained that she couldn't speak the name any more.

"I was the CEO of a small firm that specialized in bottled water products for outlying colonies. The water on Korsve is particularly pure and the Wygnin have no qualms about selling it. They do it themselves now."

DeRicci hadn't known that.

"It's in one of their caves, of course. Just a big one, with tons of high-grade equipment that they bought from us. But I'm getting ahead of myself."

DeRicci wondered how the woman could sound so calm when her body was so tense. Perhaps it was the skill that had gotten her through the past fifteen years.

"I loved Korsve. You have no idea how beautiful

it is there." Mrs. Wilder smiled slightly with the memory. "But we didn't understand the Wygnin. No one did. I'm not sure we still do."

Then her gaze met DeRicci's and DeRicci felt cold.

"They sold me some land in a nearby forest. I built my dream house there." Mrs. Wilder's voice started to shake. "We felled some trees to expand the view and covered over some moss growing on the forest floor. The Wygnin got really upset. They—"

Her voice broke. She put a hand to her mouth. Carryth gave her an encouraging smile, but she didn't seem to see it.

After a moment, he took up the story. "The Wygnin claimed that Mrs. Wilder had committed mass murder."

DeRicci's mouth went dry, even though she had expected this. "Nestlings?"

Nestlings were native Korsve creatures that looked like plants. At first, humans had thought the Wygnin considered the Nestlings food. Later, it turned out that the Nestlings were sentient and the moss that Mrs. Wilder mentioned was made from a spiderweb-like material that the Nestlings used to build egg sacks.

"Nestlings and tree nymphs," Carryth said. "Over a hundred of each."

Tree nymphs lived inside the hollow trees in that part of Korsve. Like the Wygnin, they did not build their own dwellings but used what they found. Unlike the Wygnin, they never built anything else either. Tree nymphs were hunter-gatherers who trafficked in ideas rather than in anything material.

"Were these charges true?" DeRicci asked.

Mrs. Wilder nodded, her eyes filling with tears. "We offered reparations. Money, whatever they would take."

"And they wanted your children."

"The first-borns," she whispered. "All of them, from everyone in the company."

"But it was your house," Reese said.

"The Wygnin believe in a life for a life," Carryth said. "Either Mrs. Wilder could have agreed to indenture her family to the Wygnin in perpetuity or they would have to find other human lives, preferably from her company."

"The Wygnin thought this was a reasonable offer," she said, brushing at her eyes. "They were only taking about half the lives in payment, and they weren't requiring all of them to be from my family. The problem was that while I was single and childless, most of my employees were not. And we didn't have a big enough staff on Korsve. We would have had to use other employees from other parts of the colonized universe."

DeRicci clasped her hands and then rubbed her thumbs, one on top of the other. She knew better than to speak at the moment.

"Didn't these employees sign the standard interstellar waiver?" Reese asked.

He was such an attorney, thinking about the legal end and not the human one. The interstellar waiver had been developed as it became clear that interstellar trading required a relaxation of human laws. The employees of a company were often asked to sign the waiver, which required them to submit to all laws of the worlds on which the company they worked for did business.

"Of course they signed," Mrs. Wilder said. "But how would you like it if someone you never met told you that you had to give up your oldest child because the CEO of your company built a house on top of a native nesting ground?"

Reese covered his mouth. DeRicci continued to rub her thumbs together. It didn't matter how many stories she heard like this, she never ever got used to them.

"So I went to the Wygnin," Mrs. Wilder said, "and I asked them what else I could do. I said that I was the one at fault, that my company had nothing to do with this, and I'd be willing to sacrifice anything to keep them out of it."

"So they demanded your first-born," DeRicci said.

"No," Mrs. Wilder said. "They were beginning to understand humans by then. They realized that reproduction wasn't an imperative for us, that many of us had no children at all. Instead, they demanded that we close up shop, give them the business, and then teach them how to run it."

"I'd never heard of anything like that from the Wygnin," Reese said, which didn't surprise DeRicci. She doubted he knew much about the Wygnin at all. But she hadn't heard anything like that either.

"Then they issued a warrant that said they had the right to my first-born and should I not have a child within the next twenty years, they could take me." She rubbed her eyes, the first real overt sign of strain.

"Why didn't they take you right then and there?" Reese asked, confirming DeRicci's hunch.

Mrs. Wilder gave him a sad smile. "They prefer children. Infants, really. So that they can mold them, make them Wygnin."

"They can't—"

"They try," DeRicci said. "They come close, too. I've met some of the adults they'd taken as children. These people look human, sort of, but they have no concept of who and what we are."

Reese shook his head. "Human is human."

"We're learning that it isn't." Carryth spoke softly, but firmly. It was clear he wanted to move this meeting forward, and Reese was getting in the way. "Go on, Mrs. Wilder."

She seemed to tense even more. "After that meeting, my lawyers recommended that I go to a Disappearance service so that I could go on living my life without fear. So I did. I spent the last of my money buying a new identity. They promised me that I'd never have to worry about the Wygnin again. That was fifteen years ago. I was cautious at first, but then I figured they were right. The Wygnin had the business. They didn't need me."

DeRicci frowned. She had never heard of a Disappearance service making such a promise. "They guaranteed that you'd be all right?"

"Interesting, isn't it?" Carryth said to her as if they were the only two in the room.

"They said because my case was so unusual, they doubted the Wygnin would try to keep track of me." Mrs. Wilder shook her head. "I believed them."

"You think the Wygnin tracked you from the beginning?" Reese asked.

"I don't know," Mrs. Wilder said.

"I'm sure they didn't," DeRicci said. "Or they would have taken your son when he was an infant. They found you just recently."

"It doesn't matter why they waited so long," Mrs. Wilder said. "The key is that he's too old to go with them. They'll destroy him."

DeRicci made herself sit very still. She didn't want to agree with that statement even though she knew it was true. She didn't even want to think about it. She had protected herself from seeing that child for just this reason: she knew she would be bound by law to give him to the Wygnin.

"You said you had a solution," Reese said to Carryth.

"It's a gamble," he said. "And the city would have to take responsibility for it. If the Wygnin refuse our offer, then we'll have to go along with their original warrant."

Reese shook his head. He was clearly going to say that wasn't possible, so DeRicci spoke instead.

"We'll follow the law," she said.

Reese frowned at her. "You came to me to see if we didn't have to, and I don't think this is just. We can't—"

"We can and we do," DeRicci said. "Usually you don't hear about it because everything is very clear. This one wasn't. And that gives us an edge, doesn't it, Mr. Carryth?"

"Actually, no. The warrant is in order," he said. "I've been studying it and its history. Only if you take them together do they give us a loophole."

DeRicci felt her breath catch. Even though she had wanted this, she hadn't expected it.

"Initially, the Wygnin wanted an infant that they could mold. Jasper Wilder is as unsuitable as an adult is. The warrant allows only for the first-born or Mrs. Wilder to be taken, not any other children."

"You know this for sure?" DeRicci asked.

"It was my first question," Mrs. Wilder said. "My daughter is eighteen months old."

DeRicci nodded.

"On this, the warrant is very clear, and we're lucky for that. Which leaves the Wygnin with an unsatisfactory revenge. They don't get the family member they were expecting to make up for all the loss that Mrs. Wilder inadvertently caused."

"Stop the lawyer-speak," DeRicci said, "and be plain."

"The warrant says they'll settle for me if I have no children." Mrs. Wilder's voice had strength in it for the first time. "Mr. Carryth believes we can successfully argue that my first-born is not a suitable child."

"So?" Reese said.

But DeRicci was already ahead of them. She felt a shiver of horror run through her. "You're going to offer yourself?"

Mrs. Wilder nodded. "I'm the one who made the mistake, committed the crime according to their laws. I'm the one who should be punished, not Jasper."

DeRicci leaned forward. "You know this is worse than dying. You know they'll try to graft a Wygnin personality on you, and it'll probably drive you insane."

Mrs. Wilder's gaze met hers. "They'd do the same thing to Jasper."

DeRicci shook her head. "This isn't acceptable. There has to be another solution."

"The Wygnin have a valid warrant," Carryth said. "Someone has to pay for this crime."

"It was a misunderstanding," Reese said.

"A misunderstanding that cost a lot of lives," Mrs. Wilder folded her hands on the table, somehow managing to remain calm. "It's all right, Detective. I'm willing to go."

"What does your husband say?"

"He doesn't know," she said. "We wanted to see if the city would back us in this negotiation first."

Reese's mouth turned down at the corners as if he had tasted something sour. "You've gone through all the options?" he asked Carryth.

"We're lucky to have this one," Carryth said.

"Lucky," DeRicci repeated, not believing it.

"Lucky," Mrs. Wilder said firmly.

Reese closed his eyes and sighed. "Then we'll back you," he said. "We have no other choice."

22

"Jamal?"

He opened his eyes. His neck hurt, and his right foot tingled because the blood flow had been cut off.

He had fallen asleep sitting up in the chair beside the window, in the Moon's crummiest hotel room.

"Jamal?" Dylani had a hand on Ennis's back. The boy was sprawled on his stomach, his head turned, sucking his thumb. One of his arms was wrapped around Mr. Biscuit.

"I'm sorry, Dylani," Jamal said. "I guess I dozed."

"Do you think the police are going to contact us today?"

He blinked, sat up straight, and moved his foot. Only one side had fallen asleep. The other side was just fine. "I don't know."

"How can they just expect us to stay here? Will the Wygnin come for Ennis again?"

Probably. If he didn't figure out what to do. But he felt that there was nothing left to do, unless he found a Disappearance service. The last time, his company had recommended one. This time, he had no idea who to turn to.

"Jamal?"

"I don't know, Dylani."

She sat up. Ennis made a soft sound of protest, but otherwise didn't move. For an active baby boy, he had been very subdued the last twelve hours. Jamal wondered if the police had a doctor on staff that they would let him use at no charge.

Probably not. Everything had its cost. He kept forgetting that.

"Why did they target us?" she asked. "Do they just do that? Target innocent people? Steal babies for no real reason? Can't they have babies of their own?"

She didn't know. Of course she didn't know. Most people didn't. The changes that had evolved over the years had come gradually, and the protests were small and rarely covered on the news. *This is the price we pay for interstellar commerce,* Jamal's old boss used to say, and Jamal later learned that it was the party line, not just for corporations but for the Earth Alliance as well.

The price they all paid—the price Jamal was facing—was the Alliance's dirty little secret, someone else's problem, something that would go away once humans learned how to interact with the aliens.

Or so the rationale went.

And Dylani had never faced any of this. She was an engineer who knew dome mechanics. She never had to deal with all the subtleties of interstellar law, the vast differences between races and cultures, the way that a wink could be a friendly gesture to one group of people and a hostile one to another.

She was in an unfamiliar world, and he hadn't helped her understand it.

"No, Dylani," Jamal said. "It's like the police said. The Wygnin always believe they have cause."

There were lines on her face that hadn't been there

the week before. Her eyes looked sunken, and some of her prettiness was gone.

Then he realized she had asked the question deliberately. Her sharp mind was manipulating him, using everything she knew of him to pull information from him.

"What cause could they possibly have?" she asked.

He froze. He had known that she would ask this question eventually, had known that he would have to give her some kind of answer, but he didn't know what to say.

"They're not saying," he said after a moment.

Her gaze met his, and he couldn't tell if she believed him or not. She had to suspect something. After all, he was taking the point on this. He had talked to the attorney alone. He had asked questions of the authorities that she hadn't even thought of.

Up until this crisis in their lives together, she had been the one who had been the strongest, who had been in charge and in control. It had to have been hard for her to take the passive role here, but she had done so without complaint.

"What do you know that I don't, Jamal?" she asked quietly.

Ennis gave a soft cry and pulled Mr. Biscuit closer, ending the moment. Jamal sighed and stood, stretching, hoping that Dylani didn't feel his relief.

She rubbed her hand over their son's back, soothing him. "You insisted on meeting with the attorney alone, so you must know something."

Her expression hadn't changed. The even rhythm of her hand on Ennis's back was the same also. Yet something in her voice alerted him to buried anger.

Buried anger and suspicion.

Jamal sighed again. Partial truth was all he had the courage for. "I asked him if he'd help us find a Disappearance service."

Her eyes widened. He'd seen them do that so often, in passion, in anger, but never in this kind of shock— or was it fear? He had only seen fear once before and that was a few days ago, when she thought Ennis was gone for good.

"Leave everything?" she asked.

"If we have to," Jamal said.

"Isn't that like admitting we did something wrong?"

"No," Jamal said.

"But we don't need to Disappear. They have the wrong family. They can't have Ennis because we're not the people they're looking for."

"It's not like human law," Jamal said. "We have to prove we're the wrong people, and no one will take our case."

"I thought that's what the police are doing," she said. "I thought they're making sure the Wygnin have the right children."

"Yes," Jamal said. "Making sure they have the right children."

Dylani's hand finally stopped rubbing Ennis's back. Her long fingers extended around his small ribcage. He was breathing easily, asleep, his thumb falling out of his mouth.

"You make that sound like there's bad in that," she said.

He nodded. "If the Wygnin convince the police that Ennis is the right child, nothing we can say will prove them wrong."

"But—"

"No buts, Dylani. Simple truth."

"The lawyer explained that to you?"

He confirmed it, but Jamal had already known it. "Yes. If that happens, the Wygnin will take Ennis."

"Surely that lawyer is wrong. I think we should go to someone else. I think that he lied to you about no one wanting to take the case. I think—"

"He didn't lie, Dylani. He says no one is willing to face the Wygnin anymore. And why would anyone be willing, when they can lose something so very precious?"

This time she looked down at Ennis. Her hand moved up and down with each of his deep breaths. "Are we going to lose him, Jamal?"

"I don't know," he said.

"But you think so."

"We're out of options, Dylani."

"What about the Disappearance services?" she asked.

"The lawyer wouldn't recommend any. Said he can't as an officer of the court."

"So we find one."

"They're expensive," Jamal said.

"It's Ennis," she said. "We'll do what we can."

Jamal nodded. "We might be able to afford to send only one of us away."

Her mouth opened slightly. "You mean send him by himself?"

"Yes," Jamal said.

"But then we'd lose him."

"Yes."

She blinked, looked down, took a deep breath. All of her maneuvers to prevent herself from bursting into tears.

"I still don't see why you'd have to meet with the attorney alone to talk about Disappearance services," she said after a moment.

"I wanted him to make it possible for you to Disappear with Ennis."

"Me?"

Jamal nodded.

"Then what would you do?"

He met her gaze. No matter what happened, they would never be the same. Their relationship would change; their feelings toward the world, toward each other, toward Ennis, would all change.

"I would stay here and work off the debt," he said.

"You could have told me that plan," she said.

"You would have tried to talk me out of it."

"And you're telling me this now because he wouldn't help us?"

Jamal nodded. "I don't know how to proceed anymore, Dylani. I'm afraid if the Wygnin see us approach a Disappearance service, they'll think we're guilty. And we can't ask anyone else to intercede for us without jeopardizing them too."

"We could hide on our own," Dylani said.

He wished it were that simple. "We don't have the resources."

"We can find the money."

"It's not the money," he said. "Do you know how to get false identification that holds up? Do you know someone who'll do illegal enhancements without approaching the police?"

She blinked again, shook her head. "We're at their mercy, aren't we?"

"Yes," he said. "I think we are."

Flint sat at his office desk, hunched over the computer screen. The Rev had gotten him thinking. He had suspected that the link between the cases had to do with Disappeareds, but he wasn't certain until the

Rev mentioned that Palmer/Maakestad was one. That meant that the yachts probably belonged to a Disappearance service, and the service had probably bought them in bulk.

He had a forensic team trying to recover the serial number from Maakestad's yacht, and the Port would try to recover one from the Disty vengeance killing, but he didn't have that kind of time. He wanted to have answers immediately.

As he reached the First Rank Detective Unit, he had received a message on his link that the Rev had turned over the crew of the Maakestad yacht. They were spacesick, as the Rev had claimed, and there was evidence of mistreatment, probably when the Rev learned that the crew had let Maakestad escape.

But he wasn't going to deal with the Rev yet. He wanted this information first. He plugged images of the yachts into the databases, along with the modifications on both ships, hoping that some port would have the original manifestos of both ships.

He also found the make, model, and year of the yachts and sent that through other databases, trying to find out who had bought more than one, maybe even recently.

As the computer worked, he got up and went to the snack vendor. Someone had left a box of fresh croissants beside it, a morning favor that day shift sometimes did them. He took one, and reminded himself to bring in something soon. He also poured himself some coffee.

The door to the Unit slammed open, and DeRicci came in. Her hair was even messier than before, but her face was clean and she had put on different clothes.

"There you are," she said. "I've been looking for you."

"My link is on," he said.

"I didn't want to go through a link. Are we alone up here?"

"I don't know." He hadn't looked to see who else was working this early in the morning. Obviously someone else had been here because of the croissants.

He grabbed one more for DeRicci, even though she grimaced at him. "Get yourself some coffee," he said, "and join me in my office."

He sounded like the senior partner in the team. He thought that odd. Maybe their power relationship had changed since he had met with the chief, saving them both.

DeRicci didn't question him. She poured herself coffee, her hand shaking so badly that she almost spilled it on herself, then followed him to his office.

He sat behind the desk as she closed the door. He put her croissant on a napkin near the edge of the desk, and she set her coffee down carefully as if she didn't trust herself not to spill.

"What is it?" he asked.

She sank into her chair. "I'm going to quit, Miles. I thought you should be the first to know."

Even after all they'd been through in the last few days, he was surprised. "Why?"

"Because I can't do this any more. They can't expect me to continue doing this."

"Doing what?" he asked.

"Offering up sacrifices to the goddamn aliens!" Her voice rose on that last, and he glanced at the door, wondering if anyone had heard.

"Sacrifices?" he repeated. "Jasper?"

"Oh, no," she said. "It's a little more complicated than that."

He froze. "They want all of the children now?"

DeRicci shook her head. "The mother. The mother did something really stupid, and she's going to go instead of the kid. If—and this is a big if—if the Wygnin agree."

Flint set down his croissant. He understood the mother's impulse. He would have done the same for Emmeline if he'd had the chance.

DeRicci stood up and stalked around the small office. "We have to stand by when the Wygnin take that bright, interesting, intelligent woman and destroy everything that makes her who she is. Why can't we punish her? Our laws are humane."

Flint's stomach churned. The coffee he'd been using to stay awake wasn't sitting well with him anymore.

"You don't think what she did is worth a life," he said.

"No, I don't!" DeRicci stopped near the door, peered out of it, then shook her head.

"But the Wygnin do."

Her shoulders slumped. "I know. That's why we have the interstellar agreements, so that we can prosecute crimes in our own ways. It sounds so good in theory, but I'm the one who gets to practice it. I'm the one who has to send this poor woman to the Wygnin, knowing what they'll do. Even if her husband manages to turn the warrant around, she'll never come back intact."

He knew that. "You think the Wygnin will accept the woman?"

"Yes, I do," DeRicci said.

"So you're angry that you met her."

"Yes!" DeRicci whirled.

"Because you tried so hard not to see the children in case you'd have to give them up."

"I'm already haunted, Miles. I don't need another goddamn face."

"Haunted?" he asked.

She closed her eyes and slumped against the door. She was thinner than she had been when he met her, the bones on her face prominent. Had she been forgetting to eat? Or was the strain of the last few days so much that she was burning up fuel at an alarming rate?

"Sit down," he said.

She sighed, opened her eyes, and returned to her chair. She picked up the croissant, but did not eat it.

"Did you ever look at my file?" she asked.

He shook his head. "It's none of my business."

"Jeez, you show amazing restraint."

He smiled. "You looked at mine, then."

"Of course," she said. "I wanted to know what I was getting into."

"So what would I have found in your file?"

She set the croissant back down, as if she couldn't face eating it. "I refused to give a teenage boy to the Disty."

"The Disty?" Flint hadn't expected that. Maybe something with the Wygnin, but not a different alien group.

She nodded. "He hadn't done anything. Not really. But they decided he'd committed cross-cultural contamination, and the Eighth Multicultural upheld."

"What did he do?"

"He taught a hatchling to speak English."

The Disty had three kinds of offspring: male, female, and hatchling. The hatchling was a genderless being that had no value in Disty society. At a certain age, a hatchling, regardless of intelligence or its parents' social status, left the home and went to a special school where it learned the art of service.

Non-Disty rarely saw hatchlings, who usually returned to the family home as servants. A lot of humans who had casual contact with the Disty didn't even know hatchlings existed.

"How did he meet the hatchling?" Flint asked.

"He grew up next door to it," DeRicci said. "They were friends. He did this before he turned ten."

"Before the hatchling was sent away?"

She nodded. "Then the word got out somehow, or the hatchling screwed up and understood something it wasn't supposed to, and he got caught. In the meantime, his family had left Mars and moved here. We had a general order to arrest and deport. I refused."

"What were the Disty going to do to him?" Flint asked, remembering the vengeance killing and shuddering.

"Exemplary justice, remember? They have to make an example out of someone, and do it publicly so that it's a statement."

Flint nodded and took a sip of his coffee. It made his stomach even queasier. He pushed the cup away.

"So," DeRicci said, "they figured the boy made it impossible for the hatchling to function in their society, so they were going to make it impossible for the boy to function in ours."

Flint frowned. "I don't understand."

"They were going to take his tongue," she said.

Flint winced and set the croissant down. "We could replace it."

"Not if it's Disty vengeance, we can't," she said. "He has to live that way."

She spoke in present tense.

"They did it, didn't they? They took him."

She pulled her croissant apart. "Out of my hands, screaming that I had promised him he'd be able to stay."

"What happened to you?"

"The usual. Counseling, reprimand, some retraining, a demotion. You know."

He didn't, not really. He'd never made a mistake in his professional career. At least not one he'd been caught at.

He wasn't sure he would like being punished for doing the right thing.

"I can't go through that again, Flint. I can't watch them take this woman—"

"She won't be screaming," he said. "It sounds like she's volunteering."

"She has no real choice." DeRicci sighed. "I'm supposed to protect and serve, you know? Not make life more comfortable for the aliens among us."

"We didn't make the laws," Flint said.

"Oh, yeah." She sneered at him. "Like you're going to be able to give that baby back."

He froze. "We lost him too? We have proof about his parents?"

"No proof," she said. "Not yet anyway. But the Wygnin had the right warrant for the Wilder kid. Their warrant for the baby's right too."

Flint knew that. He'd been trying not to think about it, trying not to remember how that child had felt cradled in his arms. He didn't want to be the one to hand that child to the Wygnin.

He couldn't be.

"We'll figure out something," he said, more out of hope than conviction.

"Right," she said. "Of course we can."

The computer beeped. The searches were done. Flint had forgotten all about them.

He touched the darkened screen and saw the information displayed there.

"What's that?" DeRicci asked.

"Did Mrs. Wilder mention a Disappearance service?" he asked, staring at his screen.

"Yes, she hired one."

"Did she say which one?"

"Not to me," DeRicci said. "But she probably told Carryth. Want me to check?"

He nodded.

DeRicci touched her link, and murmured into it, while Flint looked at his files.

Only one Disappearance service had bought this model space yacht. They'd got an entire fleet of them at a discount when the model's flaws had become apparent.

Disappearance Inc. Flint stared at that for a long time. He had heard, over the years, that Disappearance Inc was a reputable company. Not all Disappearance services were, and those that weren't usually went out of business quickly.

But Disappearance Inc was one of the oldest and the best, and one of the most expensive. Everyone in this solar system knew that.

He requested more information, the public kind on Disappearance Inc. The history of the company, the ways it avoided legal entanglements—he skimmed all of that until he found what he was looking for.

Six months ago, Disappearance Inc had been sold. It had new owners who publicly announced they were going to update the service.

"He says she used one of the usual companies," DeRicci said.

"Which one?" Flint asked, although he already knew.

"Disappearance Inc."

He nodded, then explained what he found. "I don't like it. Ekaterina Maakestad makes sense. She's a new Disappeared. And technically, so were the Disty vengeance killings."

"But it's the old customers that bother you," DeRicci said.

"Don't they bother you?" he asked.

She came around the desk, tapped a few more screens, going deeper into the information about Disappearance Inc. "Look. They've divided up the company. They're taking it apart and selling the pieces."

Flint let out a small breath. "Including the files."

"That's probably where they're making back their investment," she said. "Think of how much the Disty alone would pay for any criminal's new identity."

"Not to mention the Rev and the Wygnin—"

"And half a dozen others." DeRicci leaned hard on the desk.

"They're selling one file at a time," Flint said.

"Bigger profit," DeRicci said. "When they get to the less valuable ones, they'll sell them all at once."

Flint felt light-headed. He couldn't remember the last time he had taken a breath. "How many clients do you think they've had over the years?"

DeRicci shrugged. "Hundreds? Thousands? They've been around for a long time, and most of these people are probably still alive."

"People," Flint repeated. "Are they all human?"

"Most of them. We're the ones who invented Disappearance services. The other cultures either don't interact or have different laws." DeRicci stared at the screen.

Flint could see her face reflected in the clear surface. Her eyes did look haunted. He wondered how
he looked. Hundreds, maybe thousands of people.

Many of them with children. Many of whom had
crossed the Wygnin.

"Do you know what this means?" she asked.
"We're going to get inundated with cases, down to
the Port, more people just like these poor parents—
years with their kids, deeply into a new life, and then
sold out by people they trusted."

The queasiness in his stomach had become a lump.
He wasn't sure he would be able to give Ennis to
the Wygnin. He couldn't imagine having to repeat the
scenario, over and over, with dozens of other children,
all of whom had parents who thought they were safe
on the Moon.

Flint made himself take a deep breath. "It's not
illegal." Even though he wished it were.

"It's brilliant," DeRicci said. "Cruel and brilliant."

Flint touched the screen, shutting it down. "We
need more information."

"What kind of information? I bet if you ask that
nice family with the baby what service they used,
they'll say Disappearance Inc."

"I know." Flint couldn't think about the Kanawas
right now. They would distract him too much. He
needed to figure out how to stop Disappearance Inc
while still upholding the law. "But we're making some
leaps of logic. This might be a rogue group of staffers,
illegally searching the files and making some extra
money on the side."

"How're we going to figure that out? And why
would we try?" DeRicci said.

"Because if it is, Disappearance Inc will be grateful," Flint said. "They'll stop the practice and fire the

employees, and we won't have this flood of vengeance killings and Wygnin kidnappings and Rev prison ships."

"We'll still have to give up that baby," DeRicci said.

"We don't know that yet," Flint said, standing up. "Come on."

"Where are we going?" DeRicci asked.

"We're going to get some proof," Flint said.

23

Ekaterina's feet ached. When she had put on these shoes, in her old home in San Francisco days ago, she hadn't planned to walk miles in them. Her feet had swollen inside them, and blisters covered her heels.

She was limping and not even caring.

The dome lights were growing brighter, simulating an Earth day. The quality of the fake sunlight was different than real sunlight—thinner somehow, less real, less rich. She had noticed that when she'd visited the Moon in the past, and used to wonder if her reaction to the fake sunlight was simply a snobbish one: if she hadn't known it was different, would she have noticed it?

Ekaterina had taken a risk shortly after she left the abandoned house and had asked for directions. She had planned it carefully, watching a fast-food mart until a large group of people came by. Then she joined them just outside, lifted her index finger as if she were asking the group to wait, and then went inside.

She asked directions to Dome University's Armstrong campus. She figured if she could find that, she could find the student apartments where Shamus used to spend most of his time.

The campus was about five miles from where she

had slept, and she had no funds to use public transportation. She had thought of flagging down a cab and then getting out before she paid, but then realized that would be too visible.

So she walked, and walked, and walked.

She used main streets because it was daylight, and Armstrong was a walker's city. Most people lived near their work and walked there or took public transportation to somewhere nearby and walked the rest of the way. The number of personal vehicles had always been limited in domed colonies—it took a variety of special permits just to own one. So no one would think it odd to see her walking down the street.

Before she got too far, however, she altered her appearance as best she could. She turned her shirt inside out, revealing its white interior (which still looked clean) and she rolled up her pants so that they ended just below her knees.

Even though she felt that would keep her away from all but the most observant police, she was still cautious. She listened for the hum of aircars, and ducked behind or went into buildings whenever one was around.

One of her stops had been in a bakery, and she had resisted the urge to steal a donut off a stack of them on a table in the center. If she found Shamus, she would beg him for some food, but until then, she had to be as careful as possible.

It was getting harder, though, to resist the urgings of her stomach.

Even though the government kept Armstrong's daily temperature moderate, Ekaterina was sweating when she reached the outskirts of Dome University.

The Armstrong Branch had been the first university built on the Moon, and its buildings had the grandeur of an old school. They were a rich gray brick. The bricks were made from Moon dirt, in a painstaking process that had cost a fortune over one hundred years before.

The process had been worthwhile, however. This campus was one of the prettiest that Ekaterina had seen off-Earth.

She stopped near the main sign, a neon affair that blinked off and on, wasting precious energy—yet another example of the university's ostentatious use of its wealth. If she remembered her Armstrong geography right, the apartments that students rented off-campus were down the road to her left.

Shamus tried to live there whenever he could. But she would try his old apartment first. He had told her more than once that he was a creature of habit. He didn't want to think about his living environment, so that he could concentrate on the informational world instead.

The apartments were even shabbier than she remembered. They'd been built around the same time as the university's earliest buildings, only not with the same care. That had been in the era between permaplastic and the new molded synthetic forms. Whoever had invented this material had designed it to look like a cross between plastic and wood. Only over time, the fake wood veneer had faded and cracked, showing the scratched plastic beneath.

Most of these apartments had only one window, on the street side, and that window was decorated with a variety of signs, posters, and blankets, making each apartment a statement. People in their early twenties sat on stoops, conversed in doorways, and sprawled across the cheap artificial turf, reading their palmtops. No one looked at her as she passed. She felt calmer here. She hadn't seen police since she arrived in this neighborhood. She had a hunch they would seem even more out of place than she was.

The building that Shamus used to live in was taller than the rest, but she wasn't sure that could still be a measure. It also had had a bright red doorway, something he had loved.

She walked two blocks, past apartment complexes that all looked the same, some taller than others, until she finally saw one with a red doorway. She went around the side, walking on a cracked path that led to some stone steps. This all felt familiar.

She knocked, and got no immediate response. The window beside the door was small and had a cheap privacy cover. Shamus used to have a privacy cover so that he could work uninterrupted.

The floor creaked inside, and then something fell. She knocked again, and a voice shouted, "Coming! Can't you blokes give it a rest? You have me trapped in here like a ruddy—"

The door opened and the speaker stopped mid-sentence. It was Shamus. His hair was redder than she remembered, and his skin darker. He was heavier too, as if his sedentary habits had finally caught up with him.

"Oh, crap," he said.

"Shamus," she started, but he put a sticky hand that smelled of marshmallows over her mouth. Then he held a single finger to his lips, indicating silence.

She nodded.

Slowly, he let his hand drop, as if he were ready to cover her mouth again should she try to speak. When he appeared certain that she was going to remain quiet, he pointed first to his ankle and then to the door.

She looked at the door first. Tiny red chips, flashing at irregular intervals. Then she looked down at his ankle. He was wearing a clear ankle bracelet, its red lights flashing in unison with the lights on the door.

Shamus was under house arrest. Her first thought was that some judge had been stupid to order that; most of Shamus's work occurred from his house. Then she realized the nature of her dilemma.

Anyone under house arrest could not leave without the court's permission. Nor could anyone go in without that same permission. And, if this were a standard house arrest, Shamus's voice would trigger monitoring devices, so that his conversations and his visitors would be recorded.

This was a dead end.

She looked back up at his compassionate brown eyes, and realized that her luck had finally changed.

Flint had been to the hospital next to the Port several hundred times, mostly to interview suspects or people who had had trouble on various commuter flights between the Moon and Earth. The routine was familiar to him: enter, show identification, say hello to old friends on duty, and then go to the room.

This time, he didn't say hello to anyone. He and DeRicci took the stairs to the only crew member of Maakestad's space yacht who was well enough to speak.

That crew member was the pilot. He was in a standard single room, monitors displayed on the wall behind him, the biobed taking all the readings. The readings were also displayed on the tiny screen outside the door. The door was locked, and Flint had to use identification to enter.

Apparently the pilot and his crew were under arrest

until someone in the port figured out why they had been on a Rev prison ship.

Flint and DeRicci went inside. The pilot was a large man who made the regulation-sized bed look small. His arms, which were outside the covers, were very muscular. Either Maakestad had been very strong, or she had had another way to subdue the pilot.

Flint suspected Maakestad had used the laser pistol, the same one she had smuggled into the aircar.

The pilot watched them walk to the side of his bed. His skin was a sickly grayish green, his eyes yellow, and his lips cracked. The room had the faint odor of vomit.

DeRicci showed him her identification. "We have a few questions," she said. "Do you work for Disappearance Inc?"

The pilot closed his eyes.

"I suggest you answer," she said. "You're in the prison wing of the portside hospital. You were taken off a Rev prison ship, and right now everyone thinks you're guilty of something. If you're doing what I suspect, you're not guilty of anything and we can move you somewhere more comfortable."

Flint clasped his arms behind his back, his admiration for her growing. He might have been used to talking with people in this facility, but he still wasn't used to the delicate side of talking to people he didn't respect. DeRicci knew how to have those conversations.

The pilot's jaw tightened as if he were clenching his teeth.

"Oh, come on," DeRicci said. "We already know you sold one of Disappearance Inc's clients to the Rev who were looking for her, and that she managed to turn the tables on you guys somehow. What we don't know is if you're being a good citizen by yourself, with friends, or on your boss's orders."

He opened his eyes. The movement was slow because his eyelashes stuck together. There was a gummy mucus between them that Flint hadn't noticed before.

"Does it matter?" the pilot asked.

"It matters," Flint said.

"Do I get better treatment if I tell you I was working alone?"

"You get better treatment if you tell us the truth," DeRicci said. "Remember, we also have your friends in custody and your stories had better match."

"Yeah," Flint said. "And I think you were all too sick to coordinate your stories when you were tossed off that Rev ship."

"Taken off," the pilot said.

"After we bargained for you," DeRicci lied. "Want us to send you back?"

The pilot shivered. The reaction made some of the brightly colored lines on the wall diagnostic rise. Apparently, being held on a Rev prison ship hadn't been a pleasant experience.

"It's a new policy," the pilot said. "We get Disappeareds and we give them to the group they're running from."

"You haven't always done this, have you?" DeRicci asked.

The pilot shook his head. "Most of the staff quit when we got new management, but those of us who stayed got bonuses for each successful transfer. That's a lot of money."

"So you don't mind selling out desperate people," DeRicci said.

"Desperate criminals." The pilot slowly lifted a

hand and rubbed his eyes with his thumb. "I was never really comfortable with the way we were flouting the law."

"Then why'd you work for Disappearance Inc?" DeRicci asked.

"Pay was good," the pilot said, "and I got to fly space yachts all over."

Flint shook his head. "How long have you been turning in clients?"

"About three months," the pilot said.

"Only newly Disappeared?" Flint asked.

The pilot frowned. His hand fell to the side of the bed as if he couldn't hold it up anymore. "What else would I be doing? Finding old ones and giving them up? As if they'd come with me."

"But something is happening to the old Disappeareds?" DeRicci asked.

"What do you guys care?" the pilot said. "They're all criminals. They deserve to be caught. Right?"

"So long as we can prove that the aliens are picking up the right people," Flint said. "Sometimes that's hard after twenty years."

The pilot licked his lips. The cracks on them were deep and in some places had developed into sores. "Why should I care?"

"Because," Flint said, "if you're delivering innocents and lying about their identities, then you're committing the crime."

"Well, I never did. And things went well until that Palmer broad stuck a laser pistol in my ear. The Rev had already transferred the credits to our account. They weren't real happy about losing the woman."

"I know," Flint said. "I've been talking to them."

"Well, she's legit. And a newly Disappeared. I'll vouch for that."

"That's good," DeRicci said. "He'll vouch for something we already know. How about giving us something we don't, like whether you're dealing with old Disappeareds too?"

The pilot looked back and forth between them. His stomach rumbled, and he put a hand over it. His skin got even greener. "The room's spinning."

"We'll leave you alone if you answer," Flint said.

The pilot burped. The stale smell got worse. The levels on the wall remained elevated. "All I know is that I was supposed to tell any group I delivered to that there were back files they could download, for a price."

"What was the price?"

"I didn't know. They were supposed to link up to an address I gave them, and then they'd get the information."

"What's the address?" DeRicci asked.

"I don't know." The pilot had that tight, strained sound to his voice that people often got when they were afraid they were going to lose control of their body. "It's on my link."

"Tell me how to download it," Flint said, "and we'll leave you alone."

The pilot held up his hand. The back was covered in tiny chips. He pointed to one, then turned his head sideways, burying his face in the pillow.

The chip he pointed to was smaller than the others. DeRicci touched it. It glowed.

"Probably safer to use your hand-held," he said to DeRicci. He didn't want their personal links compromised by anything the pilot had picked up.

She nodded and removed her hand-held from her pocket. Then she brushed the pilot's chip, initiating a synch, and transferred the information.

"Have there been any complaints about this change in policy?" she asked the pilot while the synch was going on.

"No," he said, his voice muffled by the pillow.

"Because you never see what the aliens do to the Disappeared," Flint said, unable to stop himself.

The pilot looked at hm as if he had just realized that he and Flint did not hold the same opinions on these matters. "Why should I care? They're the ones who made the mistake, not me."

"But no one on Earth has had word of this?" De-Ricci asked.

"Why would they?" the pilot said.

"He wouldn't know if they did," Flint said to her.

She nodded, pocketed her hand-held, and sighed. "I really hate this job."

"And the people you run across," Flint said as he let them both out of the room.

The door closed behind them, the sound of the heavy metal frame echoing in the hallway.

"We didn't thank him for his information," De-Ricci said.

"He's lucky we didn't hurt him just on general principle." Flint started down the hall. The other doors here were metal as well, and all of them had screens above the identifying lock. "He doesn't realize that there are two innocent children here that his company sold to the Wygnin."

"He would say that the parents are at fault."

"The parents probably are." Only Flint had realized he didn't care. He had always thought he'd be able to deal with this part of his job, but holding Ennis had changed that. Flint hadn't expected enforcing the law to make him so angry.

"It's our job, Miles," DeRicci said.

He nodded and kept walking. "You had it right earlier. They shouldn't expect us to enforce something that's so morally reprehensible. They should find other solutions."

"But they won't." DeRicci had to struggle to keep up with him. "And we're still going to give a baby to the Wygnin."

"Not if I can help it," Flint said.

24

Shamus put a finger to his lips and his eyes twinkled. Ekaterina frowned. He bent down and grabbed the bracelet on his ankle, putting his fingers over the twirling red lights. She could see the lights reflected through his fingernails. It was eerie.

Carefully he raised his foot and pointed the toe to the ground like a ballerina. Then he slid the bracelet from his ankle and slowly lowered the bracelet to the floor.

"I don't want any," he said loudly. "I really hate solicitors. So go away."

Then he pushed the bracelet two feet inside, grabbed the door, and pulled it closed. He took her by the elbow and moved her behind a shabby plastic hedge that someone had once thought decorative.

"I'm not going to ask you how you did that," she said to him, feeling like his lawyer once again.

"Good, because I might be obliged to tell you. It's brilliant, really, and brilliance should be shared."

She had forgotten how words just rolled out of his mouth, rich and warm and melodic. Shamus had always been a charmer. That was one of the things she liked about him.

"But I have this hunch you're not here in an official

capacity," he said. "If you had been here in an official capacity six months ago, I wouldn't have had to learn how to take that thing off."

"Why didn't you call me?" she asked.

He shrugged. "Earth, Moon, expenses. You know. The business isn't paying what it used to."

"In other words, you were covering your own legal fees this time."

He nodded. "And see where it got me?"

She smiled. If she had been feeling like herself, she might have said that. But right now, she didn't have the right to be superior to anyone.

He peered over the hedge, then put his arm around her shoulder and pulled her down even farther. If someone had been watching they might have thought the two of them were lovers.

"You're all over the nets," he said. "There's vid of you everywhere, and I wouldn't be surprised if some of the buildingboards are flashing your image."

Buildingboards were wallspace rented to companies so that an image could be projected—usually an advertising image, but sometimes breaking news covered them too.

"Oh, God," she said. "What am I supposed to do?"

"Be smart," he said, "which it sounds like you've been so far."

She leaned against him, relieved to be able to talk to another human being, even if it was Shamus. If she closed her eyes, she could pretend it was Simon. Dear Simon, who probably had no idea what had happened to her.

"You've got a plan, right?" Shamus asked, and she could tell from the tone in his voice that he hoped finding him wasn't the extent of her ideas.

She swallowed, trying to find the strength that disappeared when she saw his ankle bracelet. She had been thinking this through all day. "Do you know any Retrieval Artists?"

Retrieval Artists were private detectives who worked strictly with the Disappeared. Usually Retrieval Artists worked for lawyers or insurance companies to find a Disappeared who was up for an inheritance or was the beneficiary of a policy. Sometimes, though, Retrieval Artists worked for the families who wanted to notify a Disappeared that the search was off and it was all right to come home.

"Retrieval Artists?" Shamus's voice rose. He clearly hadn't expected the question. "What for?"

"I have to get out of here. I have money, but I can only access it once. So I figured if I paid someone to help me Disappear, then I'd be all right."

"Retrieval Artists don't help you Disappear," Shamus said. "They *find* people who've Disappeared and usually for a hefty price."

"I know." She tried to give him a brave smile. The plan did sound silly when she spoke it out loud. "But they do know who the best Disappearance services are."

"I'm sure they do," Shamus said, "and they'll lie to you. They'll send you to someone who can't hide a dog's bone, and then get paid to retrieve you for whoever's looking for you."

"I know the risks." She ran a hand through her hair. It felt gritty, as if some of the dirt from that house had latched onto her scalp. "But on Earth, at least, there are some Retrieval Artists who pretend to be honest."

"There are some that try," Shamus said, "but give them the right price and they'll lead aliens right to you."

"I'm not asking them to find a Disappeared for me," she said. "I'd just be asking for a good Disappearance service."

"The police had your name wrong at first," Shamus said, "so it seems to me you already went through a service and got screwed. Am I right?"

Ekaterina nodded.

"Then why try it again?"

"Because I'm out of options, Shamus."

He sighed.

"You don't know any good services, do you?"

"It's not my line, sweetie," he said. "Most of them have files that are easily compromised if you know what you're doing. I've even gotten into Disappearance Inc's files, and they're supposed to be the best."

She stiffened.

His eyebrows went up. "They're the ones you hired, aren't they?"

"I thought they weren't supposed to keep records," she said.

"They all keep records," he said. "Most of them are coded, and no one's names—new or old—are ever mentioned. But some of them don't even bother with that."

"Do you know anyone who isn't hackable?"

He gave her the same sweet grin he'd given her years ago when he had first come to her for help, and she had asked him if she could put him on the stand to defend himself. *Only if you want me to lie under oath*, he had said.

"Well," he said, "some of the services are tougher to hack than others. But if they have a network, I can break into it. Whether or not I can read it is another matter. But that's not always an indication of reliability. There are a whole lot of factors that make for a good disappearance service. Some of them might have easily hackable bogus records to throw folks off the trail. I don't know. It's not my area."

"But Retrieval Artists are."

He shook his head.

She leaned forward and rested her head on her knees, her hair catching in the plastic fronds of the shrub. She was so tired. Tired and hungry and lost. On the street, someone started to sing a raucous song she didn't recognize.

"This was your plan?" he asked. "You were going to try to Disappear again?"

"I have no other choice, Shamus," she said. "I can't hide here."

He let out a small breath of air, not quite a sigh, more a sound of exasperation. Then he said, "I used to know an honest Retrieval Artist. Very old school. Ethical, if you can believe it."

"Used to?" Ekaterina asked.

"It's been a long time and we didn't part on the best of terms."

"I'll take whatever you have," Ekaterina said.

"I'll give you what I can remember," he said.

And he did.

DeRicci knew it really wasn't any of her business that Flint had gone off to ruin his career. She hadn't been able to talk him out of it, and she hadn't been able to convince him that what he was about to do was serious.

Her only other choices were to report him or ignore what he was going to do.

She chose to ignore it.

Instead, she went to her office and flicked on her large screen. The Wilders were with the lawyers, negotiating with the Wygnin, so DeRicci was off the hook there. The Wygnin wouldn't want to discuss the baby until they were done with the eight-year-old, and for that she was grateful.

It also gave Flint's little scheme, whatever it was, time to work.

Flint didn't say so, but he probably expected her to calm the Rev. She had nothing to say to them either— negotiating with the Wygnin had been above and beyond; she certainly wasn't going to deal with the Rev in the same week—so she checked on the status of Maakestad.

So far, the woman was still a fugitive. DeRicci wasn't sure, but she thought it was some kind of record. She didn't think anyone had eluded the law for more than ten hours in Armstrong—at least, not in the modern city.

It was hard to remain hidden when the entire street patrol was searching for you. And now that False Dawn was over, and everyone knew the dome was in Lockdown, Maakestad's image was being broadcast on all available screens and public downloads.

Someone would report her soon. It was only a matter of time.

But DeRicci would have thought the street patrol would have found Maakestad long before the city-wide alert had become necessary. Lockdown would look bad on her already awful record, too, although it would show that the fugitive was clever—avoiding not just DeRicci, but the rest of the law as well.

A mixed blessing after all.

DeRicci's desk was filthy. Leftover food from other long nights, a half-full coffee cup with mold on top of the liquid, and the clothes she had worn in the aircar accident sprawled across one corner. She shoved the clothes on the floor, set the coffee in the breakroom sink, and tossed out the leftover food. Then she grabbed a towel and wiped off her screen.

There was only one way she could think of to redeem herself on this case, and to redeem Flint, should he screw up as badly as she thought he was going to.

She had to find Maakestad herself. Now that they had the woman's real name, it might not be as hard as it had been the night before.

DeRicci doubted that anyone had run Maakestad's records, not with the woman's name coming so late and a crisis keeping everyone diverted. The chief was dealing with the public relations nightmare, and the street patrols were searching every square inch of the city. If anyone had the presence of mind in all of that looking to link into the main data systems for records, DeRicci would have been surprised.

She plugged in Maakestad's name and let the system do a search. She asked for all the records pertaining to Armstrong as far back as Maakestad's information went.

That would keep the system busy for a while. She set it to beep loudly and repeatedly when it was through. Then she put her arms down on the desk, buried her head in them, and closed her eyes.

"Detective?"

DeRicci didn't recognize the voice. She sighed and sat up. The duty clerk had opened her office door and was peering inside. The woman looked smaller when she wasn't behind her desk. In fact, DeRicci wasn't sure she had ever seen a duty clerk upstairs before.

"What're you doing here?" she asked.

The duty clerk looked nervous. "I tried your links but they were blocked."

Of course they were. Whenever DeRicci tried to sleep, her links automatically went into privacy mode.

"So?" she said. "You could have pinged my hand-held or used the house system."

The duty clerk nodded. "I thought it might be better to see you in person."

"Because—"

"The Rev, Detective. They're getting restless."

Great. That was all she needed. "I'm sure they are. That idiot translator hasn't told them we lost the prisoner, has he?"

"I don't think so, but he is getting awfully nervous."

"I think he was born nervous," DeRicci said.

The duty clerk smiled. The movement was almost involuntary. The worry in her eyes didn't change. "The Rev are agitated and they're in a really small space. . . ."

"Move them, then," DeRicci said. "And tell them we're almost ready to see them."

"Good," the duty clerk said. "That'll help, but I don't know how much. They really want that woman."

"We all do," DeRicci said.

"You are searching for her, right?" the clerk asked.

"The entire street patrol is searching for her," DeRicci said. "And I'm looking up records. Or rather, I'm letting the system do it. I have a hunch we'll find her within the hour."

"I hope you're right, Detective," the clerk said. "The Rev aren't going to wait much longer."

DeRicci nodded. The Rev wouldn't wait much longer, and Flint was off chasing a fantasy. If he wasn't back in a half an hour, she'd page him. She wasn't going to deal with another group of angry aliens.

The data clerk pulled the door closed. DeRicci

glanced at her screen, filling with information on Ekaterina Maakestad. DeRicci didn't feel that she had lied this time. They were close. They'd get Maakestad back.

And then, at least, the problem with the Rev would be solved. At least this one didn't have the ethical considerations the Wygnin cases did. Maakestad was clearly a fugitive who had injured two officers in her drive to escape.

DeRicci could hand her over to the Rev without feeling any qualms at all.

25

Flint loved the oldest section of Armstrong. It was the only part of the city that seemed to have character. A lot of the buildings dated from the colonization and bore scars from the collapse of the first dome.

Parts of the second dome still covered this section of the city, even though the dome had been rebuilt and expanded dozens of times. The old areas were easy to see because they were made from colonial permaplastic. The permaplastic had been clear when the original colonists put it up, but time and wear had turned this section cloudy.

The filtration systems in this part of town were grafted onto the old dome, so the air was filthy. Sometimes Flint left here with his lungs burning, just because he wasn't getting enough good oxygen.

And yet, for all the problems, this was the only part of Armstrong that even pretended to have a sense of history. The permaplastic buildings, yellowing with age, leaned against each other. The city council had tried to knock them down, but historic preservationists took the fight to Earth, where there was money and time to argue over these kinds of things.

Eventually the council bowed to the pressure and kept the original buildings intact, vowing to maintain them as well as possible. So far, upkeep had mostly been shoring up walls, caulking cracks, and placing tiny bronze plaques beside the doors, stating what the building had originally been back in the good old days when Armstrong was barely one square mile wide.

The office Flint headed toward was in Armstrong's first retail section, in a long building that had been divided into several areas, all of them too small to house a store—at least by current standards.

Most of the offices stood empty now—no one wanted a client to come to a place this seedy—but there was one that was still occupied.

It belonged to Paloma, a retired Retrieval Artist.

Paloma had to be the oldest woman Flint knew. Or perhaps she was just the least enhanced woman he knew. She never upgraded her features, preferring to age naturally. But she was abnormally strong and very healthy, so he suspected she used enhancements that just weren't as visible as most other people's.

He had met her when he was a space cop and she was trying to ferry a Disappeared's family off the Moon to meet their retrieved loved one. Her ship had expired licenses, and he could have busted her for that. He also could have followed her to find the Disappeared and turn that person in, but he hadn't. Paloma had convinced him to turn a blind eye, just that once.

Over the years, they became friends, exchanging information and helping each other out. Even after she decided that the business had changed too much for her, she still kept her hand in so that she knew what was going on.

Flint didn't knock, even though the door looked formidable. Paloma had alarms set several yards away from her office and knew when anyone was approaching. The alarms were obviously tied in to some sort of visual system because she unlocked her door automatically for potential clients or friends.

If the door opened when he tried it, he knew that Paloma was inside. She used to be in her office most of the time, but he wasn't so certain what her schedule was these days. He hadn't seen her in months.

He tried the knob and it turned easily. He walked inside, feeling lighter than he had in days. Things were changing for him. He could sense it.

Paloma was sitting behind her rickety desk. She looked tiny and frail, almost birdlike. Her white hair made her skin seem even darker. She wore a long-sleeved sweater that covered the muscles in her arms, and it had taken Flint nearly a year to realize that the skin on the backs of her hands was laced with links and security chips of various kinds.

"Hey, beautiful," he said.

She smiled at him. The look made her black eyes sparkle. "Hey, beautiful yourself. How come you haven't been to visit?"

"I warned you that we'd have trouble getting together once I made detective."

"Is it everything you wanted it to be?"

His grin faded. He couldn't hide much from her.

She sighed. "You're having to make the tough choices already, aren't you, Miles?"

He wished she had a chair for guests inside the office. She liked to keep the clients standing. It kept them off guard. But he could have used the momentary rest.

"I like putting puzzles together, Paloma."

"I know," she said.

"And I like helping people."

"That's why you joined the force in the first place,

you said." She kept her tone neutral. The first time he had told her that, she had laughed at him. Then she had realized he was serious. She had not apologized, but she had been careful of his feelings over that issue from that point on.

He nodded.

"They don't want you to help people anymore, do they?" she asked.

"It's all right when I'm dealing with real criminals."

"Ah," she said softly. "You have to turn someone over. Who is it? The Rev? The Ebe? The Disty?"

"The Wygnin."

She closed her eyes. Her face looked skeletal for a moment. Then she opened them, as if that brief moment of darkness had given her strength.

"You came here on business then," she said.

He nodded.

"Should I charge the city?"

"No," he said. "This is personal. Give me your account and I'll transfer the credits."

"Tell me what you want first, and I'll tell you if I can help you."

"Oddly enough, I need the name of the best and most reliable Disappearance service on the Moon."

She gave him a sharp look. "Did you cross the Wygnin?"

"It's not for me," he said.

She braced her hands on her desk and stood. The gesture made her only a few inches taller than she had been before, but somehow the force and power of it made her seem stronger.

"Did you cross the Wygnin, Miles?"

"Not yet," he said.

"You can't cross them. If they have a target, you

have to give it to them. They'll go after you if you
don't, and you have a beautiful mind. They'll destroy
it and think they did you a favor."

"They won't come after me," he said.

She came around the desk, grabbed his arms, and
shook him as if he were a child. "They go after everyone who crosses them. No one is immune. You cannot
do this. I won't let you."

"Paloma," he said. "I have a window."

"There is no such thing." Her grip hurt. "Go away.
Forget this. I cannot help you."

"I'll find someone who will then," he said.

She looked up at hm, her eyes searching his as if
she could read his every thought. "Is it a woman?"

He shook his head. "A baby."

"A baby," she said. "Like Emmeline."

He yanked himself out of her grip.

"You cannot see everything through the prism of
your own pain, Miles. Emmeline is dead. Children die.
Babies who get taken by the Wygnin have a great life.
They just don't have a human one. Whoever she is—"

"He," Flint said.

"—Whoever he is, then," Paloma said, "his fate was
determined long ago by some careless relative who
never thought actions had consequences."

"The law is wrong, Paloma," Flint said.

"You're telling me that? I've seen more than you
can imagine." She let him go and leaned on the desk.
He had the sense that she was working him the way
she would work a client she didn't know.

"His parents thought they were safe," Flint said.
"And they're not the only ones."

Then he told her about Disappearance Inc, about
all that he and DeRicci had discovered.

Paloma cursed. "I wondered how long it would take one of those services to realize they could profit like that. It would have to be the biggest."

"And what was once the best."

She made a rude noise and shook her head. "Never the best. Only the one with the most publicity which, if you think about it, is exactly what a Disappearance service shouldn't have. If they're good, they're assisting people in breaking these unjust laws of yours."

"They're not my laws," he said.

"They shouldn't be anyone's," Paloma said. "But we have them and we are stuck with them so long as we want trade. Or so the Idiots in Charge tell us."

She went back behind her desk and sat down. It seemed that she had gone back to her role as Retrieval Artist deciding whether or not to take on a new client.

"You realize that the fact these people were betrayed changes nothing. They still, foolishly, broke laws that put them at odds with the Wygnin. If you help them, you will cross the Wygnin too."

"Not if the Wygnin don't know what I've done."

"They'll know," Paloma said.

"Give me some credit," Flint said. "I have a window."

"A window," she snapped. "A window means nothing. Opportunities do not exist with the Wygnin."

"Their warrant is old," he said, "and it's not accurate. If I can stall long enough, I might be able to give these people time to escape."

Paloma stared at him. "You have a plan."

"Of course I do."

"A plan in which they will not track you, blame you?"

"Yes," he said, although his heart was pounding. He was risking his entire being for a child he did not know, for people he did not care about.

But this wasn't about Ennis Kanawa. This was about Emmeline. Flint was risking his being for her as if she were still alive, as he would have done if he had known her life was in danger.

Because he should have known her life was in danger. He should have seen the signs. In his own way, he was as much at fault for his daughter's death as Jamal Kanawa was for his son's kidnapping.

Paloma studied Flint for a moment. She crossed her arms and frowned. "You're asking me to trust you, to believe that you're smart enough to protect your own life when so many others in similar circumstances can't do the same thing."

"Yes," he said.

She sighed and grabbed part of her desk, pulling it forward. It was a keyboard. Flint used to think it odd that she used such ancient technology until she explained it to him once.

The keyboard was silent. Voice commands were not, and she did not use modern screen technology that operated at the touch of a finger because it was easily traceable. The keyboard allowed her to work inside the system, using code, going deep, and if she was smart about it, her movements were impossible to trace.

"You want the best Disappearance service on the Moon," she said. "Not Mars, not Earth. Just the Moon."

He nodded. "We have to be able to get to it quickly."

"You realize that best is relative."

He walked toward the door, feeling restless, wishing this tiny cubicle of an office had a window. "I want someone who can beat you, Paloma."

She snorted. "No one beats me."

He wasn't sure he believed that. But he said nothing.

She worked in silence for several long minutes while he learned the shape of the office, the corners, the uneven lay of the flooring. He avoided the keyboard and computer system altogether.

"All right," she said. "I double-checked what I suspected. There is only one Disappearance service on the Moon worth your time and fortunately, it's here in Armstrong. You've probably never heard of it."

A dig at his comment about Disappearance Inc. Was she implying that he wasn't as smart as he thought?

"Try me," he said.

She inclined her head toward him, but didn't tell him, not yet. Instead, something else caught her attention. She was looking at a screen that had appeared on her desktop.

Flint knew better than to try to look over her shoulder. He'd done that once, and she had barred him from the office for a year—even though all her systems were encoded, and she had managed to make whatever had been on the screen disappear before he ever got a chance to look at it.

"Problem?" he asked.

Her gaze met his. The screen went dark. "As I was saying, this is the only reliable company on the Moon. All their clients successfully disappear, and none of the warrants on them get fulfilled. But they won't work with a cop. I doubt they'll work with me."

He let out a small sigh. Part of him wasn't sure such

a company existed. "That's all right. They don't need to work with either of us. Who are they?"

"Data Systems," she said. "They have offices not far from here. They're as discreet as my offices."

Ugly and without flash. The opposite of many other Disappearance services he'd seen. Somehow he found that reassuring.

A knock resounded through the small space. Flint turned, hand on his laser pistol. The quickness of his reaction showed just how on edge he was.

"I didn't know you were expecting someone," he whispered.

"I wasn't expecting anyone," she said softly, "but someone has come."

The image on the screen. That was the warning she had had, and she wasn't alarmed by whoever was outside.

"Move out of sight for a moment," Paloma whispered. "This could be intriguing."

He frowned. He knew she had a back exit, although he didn't know where it was. He was surprised that she didn't ask him to use it.

Flint moved behind the door, keeping his hand on his laser pistol.

The knock sounded again.

"It's open," Paloma said.

Ekaterina hadn't seen a door without security systems built in since she was a child. The knock felt unnatural, the second one insistent.

This area of Armstrong seemed too impoverished to house the office of a successful Retrieval Artist. Even the roads were coming apart, the material the original colonists had used to pave them crumbling into Moon dust.

If she had felt dirty before, she felt filthy now.

She was about to knock for a third time, when she realized she had heard a voice telling her to come in. The voice sounded as if it had come from inside, yet it was awfully clear.

Maybe Ekaterina was wrong. Maybe the door did have security, only the security was so sophisticated she couldn't see it.

She grabbed the doorknob and it turned easily. She pushed the door open and stepped inside.

The interior was tiny and dark. It took a moment for Ekaterina's eyes to adjust. She saw a tiny, unenhanced elderly woman sitting behind a large desk.

"You're Paloma?" Ekaterina asked.

"Close the door," the woman said.

Ekaterina did. The lights came up just slightly. She stepped deeper into the office. "I got your name from a friend. He says you're a reliable Retrieval Artist."

"I'm retired," the old woman said.

Somehow Ekaterina had been afraid of that, afraid that anyone who looked so frail wouldn't be able to do the work required of a Retrieval Artist.

"All I want is information," Ekaterina said.

"That's all anyone wants," the old woman said.

"It's something you could probably tell me off the top of your head."

"And why would I?" The old woman's eyes were sharp. Ekaterina realized that the woman's appearance might be deliberate, to put people off their guard.

"I'll pay you for it."

"Of course you will," the old woman said, "if I choose to give you information. I don't help just anyone. In fact, I help almost no one, especially now that I'm retired."

"It's just one question. Please," Ekaterina said and

she was surprised to hear her voice quiver. "I'm running out of options."

"That's supposed to make me sympathetic?" the old woman asked. "Why should it when your face is all over the vids, and the dome is locked down because you left police custody?"

Ekaterina's mouth opened slightly. She hadn't seen her own image once she entered this oldest part of Armstrong. She had managed to avoid patrols the rest of the way, and she had kept her head down. So far, no one had noticed her.

"Please," she said. "Just listen to me. I don't know where else to turn."

The old woman sighed. "Just tell me what you want. I don't care what you've done or who you've hurt."

Ekaterina felt her breath catch. The old woman assumed she was guilty without letting her speak. Of course. Most everyone in Armstrong probably did.

"You'll help me, then?"

The old woman shrugged. "I'm intrigued by you. I wonder why someone like you would seek a Retrieval Artist. By rights, I should give you to the police. It's a Retrieval Artist's job to find people, and I found you without any effort at all."

Ekaterina's heart pounded. She had known this risk existed. She had thought she would be able to talk her way out of it.

"I was told you were honest," she said, "that you would help me."

"I don't do what's expected of me," the old woman said. "I do what interests me."

Ekaterina nodded. She had nothing to lose by telling this woman anything. She was already here. If the old woman wanted to turn her into the authorities, she would.

"It's my understanding that Retrieval Artists know who runs the most efficient Disappearance services. I'll pay you for that information. I need it quickly so that I can get off the Moon."

"The most efficient Disappearance service," the old woman repeated. "You mean some service that can defeat a Retrieval Artist? You want to know who has caused my greatest failures?"

"I'm not asking for failures. I'm asking for someone reliable. I trusted Disappearance Inc, and they gave me to the very group that was searching for me. I just don't want that to happen again."

"And they made a tidy profit, I'll bet." The old woman made it sound as though she approved. Then she smiled at Ekaterina. "You know, I've been getting a lot of requests about reliable Disappearance services lately. It seems to be the question du jour."

"Someone else asked you?" Ekaterina said, not sure why she was getting that information.

"Yes," a man said from behind her. "I asked her, not five minutes ago."

Ekaterina jumped, her hand on her heart. The detective with the cherubic face and the cold eyes— Flint?—had been standing behind the door. She hadn't even seen him when she came in.

They had known. The authorities had known she was coming here. Shamus had betrayed her.

It was all over. Her sense outside Shamus's apartment had been right. Her luck had run out, and the Rev were going to take her.

She had no options left—except one.

She slipped her hand in her purse and gripped the laser pistol. She had never shot a person before, let alone two. She wasn't sure she could pull this off.

But there was only one way to find out.

26

DeRicci had just finished making the list of Maake-stad's former friends, colleagues, and clients who lived in the Armstrong area. Maakestad had been an attorney who was licensed to practice in several interstellar courts, but she hadn't come to Armstrong often. The list was shorter than DeRicci expected.

Still, it was unusual for a fugitive to remain at large for so long without help. DeRicci had a hunch one of these people was harboring Maakestad.

She had just sent the list through the public links when she got paged by the duty clerk, requesting her presence in interrogation. The Rev, apparently, were getting unreasonable.

DeRicci made it down to the main area as quickly as she could. She avoided the duty clerk and all of the people waiting in the main Division area. Instead, she skirted down a side hallway toward the interrogation room Flint had used to talk with the Rev.

Through the one-way window, it looked like there were ten Rev in that room. The only human was a balding man who cringed in the corner, hands over his head as if he expected to be hit at any moment.

Not that DeRicci blamed him. Most of the Rev had their emotion collars ruffled, and their weird skin had turned a deep shade of red. There was a lot of anger in that room, and the poor interpreter was alone with all of it.

DeRicci sent word to Flint through his personal link—*Where are you? Situation getting grim here*—and then squared her shoulders. She pulled the door open and nearly gagged on the stench of ginger.

"Hello, everyone!" she said, hoping the interpreter was still coherent enough to do his job. She knew about five words in Rev, since they rarely made it to the Division. Rev problems usually got dealt with in the Port. "I'm Flint's partner, and I've come to move you to a more comfortable location."

The Rev were squeezed so tightly in the small room that she wasn't sure she could get inside.

The interpreter cleared his throat and managed to say something. Whether it was what she had said or not, she had no idea.

Then a Rev came forward, his upper arms displayed, something she had never seen before. She knew that Rev had arms and four strange legs that sort of absorbed into their squishy skin when they weren't using them, but she had never actually seen them. The Rev spoke in a weird, high-pitched growl, and the interpreter stammered out the words in English:

"The Rev aren't leaving until they have Maakestad."

DeRicci had learned only one thing about the Rev in all her years working in Armstrong: lying to them was the worst thing anyone could do. But the truth wasn't pretty at this moment either.

"Tell him I'm just trying to make him more comfortable," she said to the interpreter.

The interpreter spoke. The Rev growled at DeRicci,

and its eyes bulged more. The entire room seemed to vibrate with the force of its words.

"The Rev, um, don't want to be comfortable. The only way they'll be comfortable is if you get them off this—these next words are untranslatable. I suppose if they were English, it would be something like Goddamn, but in Rev it's more like Stupid Yellow Gloves, which makes no sense but then, when do curse words make sense? Anyway, they'd be more comfortable if you get them off this . . . rock and on their way so that they can complete their duty. If you can't do that, then tell them why. They demand to know."

The interpreter spoke rapidly. DeRicci hated his asides, and wondered if that was part of his usual method.

"Spare me the commentary," she said softly, making sure she looked at him this time, "and just give me the most accurate translation you can."

The interpreter bobbed his balding head and huddled even closer to the wall.

Then DeRicci said to the Rev, "Look, as you can tell, diplomacy isn't my forte. We've had a delay in bringing the woman to you and I'm not sure what it is. Let me go find out and I promise I'll be back within the hour."

The interpreter was speaking as she did. The Rev's emotion collar had grown even darker.

"There is too much stalling. What is wrong?"

"My partner has been handling this," DeRicci said, trying to stick to the truth as much as she could. "He told me that he was taking care of everything and that he would be back at the station soon. All I can do is wait, just like you. If you like, we can take you somewhere bigger and cooler—"

"No," the Rev said. "We will stay here. You will be back within the hour with the woman."

"I'll be back with news," DeRicci said. "I can't promise the woman."

"Why not?" the Rev said. "What has happened to her?"

"I'm not sure," DeRicci said, and that was the truth. "As I said, I'll find out for you."

"Quickly." The Rev actually growled the word in English.

"Quickly," DeRicci said, and stepped back into the cool hallway, pulling the door closed behind her, before she sneezed. Then she sent another message to Flint—*Rev becoming a problem. Would you get back here?*—annoyed that he hadn't answered her first one.

She wasn't equipped to handle these creatures, and she doubted Flint was either. She turned around and headed for the main Division. She'd make the duty clerk request diplomatic help.

Maybe real bureaucrats would know how to stall the Rev. She certainly didn't.

Flint drew his laser pistol and trained it on Ekaterina Maakestad. "Set down your purse," he said.

Her eyes widened. She looked very innocent. She had to know that such a deception wouldn't work anymore; her actions had shown her to be very cunning. He wasn't going to make the same mistake DeRicci had.

That purse was a marvel, though. It looked too small to hold a weapon. Even when Maakestad slipped her hand inside, a subtle move that he wouldn't have noticed if he hadn't been watching for it, it didn't look as though there was anything threatening inside.

But he knew the damage to the aircar had occurred because a laser pistol had been fired into the secondary systems and that laser pistol was missing. Which meant that she had it.

And she was trapped with him in this small room. She would go for it. Any smart person would.

"Set down the purse," he repeated, "and don't even think about using the weapon."

"Better do what he says." Paloma sounded regretful. "If there's any weapons fire in here, my security system will kill the shooter."

Maakestad clutched the purse to her side for a long moment, obviously taking in the yellowing walls and the low-tech feel of the office. Then, after a moment, she let go of the purse and it fell to the floor.

Flint had her. The search for the fugitive was over.

Paloma watched him from her desk as if she hadn't seen him before. He hadn't moved. He still had his pistol out, his thumb still on the trigger.

If he took Maakestad back to the Division now, the Rev would seize her. She would disappear into that prison ship, and no one would see her again.

She wouldn't be broken like an adult taken to the Wygnin, nor would she be eviscerated in the way that the Disty did. Instead, she would do years of hard labor—labor so difficult that some humans died while performing it—because she had done her job well.

Maakestad stared at him, her gaze defiant. There was no hope on her face at all, and no resignation either. She would go with him, but she would fight him all the way.

And wasn't that what he would do in her position? After all, what had she really done wrong? She had taken a risk, probably a calculated one, trying to save her client from Rev prison on a charge that he may or may not have been guilty of. If anyone failed, it was that nameless client, who had betrayed her by committing a similar crime. If the client had remained straight, nothing would have happened to Maakestad.

Flint had taken a lot of risks, most of them in the past few days. He weighed the odds and calculated the gamble, betting the letter of the law against what he could get away with, all because he was trying something he believed in.

If he had been a lawyer on Revnata, he might have done the same things Maakestad had tried.

Flint had no idea how long he stood there, holding the pistol on her. She didn't move. Neither did Paloma. If he fired now, it would be his choice. The security system would take him out after he had taken out Maakestad.

He was informed, and he still had a choice, just as she had. Only he knew it wasn't worth the risk. He wouldn't sacrifice his life to take this woman's. She wasn't that kind of criminal, and he wasn't that kind of man.

"Give me the purse," he said, and his throat felt rusty, as if he hadn't spoken for a long time. He wondered if his thought processes had shown on his face, and if they had, what the two women had made of them. "Kick it to me."

She did. It slid across the uneven floor, snagging on a crack. She had to push it one more time to get it close to him. He used his own foot, like a soccer player corraling a ball, to pull the purse beside him.

Then, keeping his gaze and his pistol trained on Maakestad, he bent down, picked up the purse, and handed it to Paloma. She raised her eyebrows at him, and for a moment he thought she was going to smile.

He was glad that she didn't.

"How much do I owe you?" he asked her.

She blinked, as if she had forgotten what they had been discussing. But she recovered quickly. "Twenty credits."

"That's cheap, Paloma. Charge me what you'd charge your usual customers."

"You're not my usual customer, Miles. Twenty credits. That's all."

Maakestad continued to watch him. There was a wariness in her face. She thought that Paloma had somehow known she was coming and had turned her over to him.

Let her think that.

"Give me your account and I'll transfer the credits," he said.

Paloma handed him a paper business card. He had never seen one before. "The number's on there," she said. "Transfer the funds when you leave the office."

He nodded. Then he turned toward Maakestad. Slowly, deliberately, he lowered the pistol.

A slight frown creased her forehead, but other than that, she didn't move.

"We can keep the Rev busy for the next few hours, maybe. After that, they'll search for you themselves. Of course, if any of the street patrols find you, they'll bring you in. If you're not out of Armstrong by the end of the day, you're on your own." Flint put the pistol back on his hip. "You got that?"

Maakestad nodded, looking stunned.

"Good," he said. "I hope I never see you again." And he let himself out the door.

It seemed very bright outside, illuminating all the dirt clinging to the buildings and the dome. He had never really seen how filthy Armstrong was before.

Paloma was probably watching him through her system, wondering what he was doing. DeRicci had wondered what he was doing when he had left her at the hospital. And Maakestad probably wondered what he was doing when he left her inside.

He knew what he was doing. He was making a choice.

But he had a few things to finish before he could think about himself and his own future.

Flint sighed and headed toward the City Complex. He needed to speak to an attorney.

27

Ekaterina was shaking. Her legs felt as if they were going to buckle beneath her. She stared at the closed door for a long time.

He would be back. She knew it. He had done this as a bluff, and he would be back with a bevy of officers, restraints, and some kind of armored vehicle she couldn't tamper with to transport her to the Rev.

But he didn't come back. The door remained closed, and she was alone with the old woman. The Retrieval Artist named Paloma.

Finally Ekaterina looked at her, unable to contain her astonishment. "I thought he was a cop."

The old woman smiled fondly and looked at the door. "Oh," she said softly, "he's so much better than that."

Chief of the First Detective Unit Andrea Gumiela sat on top of her desk like a woman who couldn't be contained. Her office was larger than any other on the fifth floor, and once upon a time DeRicci had coveted it.

Now DeRicci didn't even come all the way inside the door. She hovered in the frame, feeling awkward for even making a request.

"I'm not up to this," DeRicci said. "I'm afraid I'll only make the situation worse. I don't know how to handle the Rev. The Wygnin, maybe. But the Rev are out of my realm of experience. I'm relying on rumor and half-remembered lessons from the Academy, and that's not enough. We need someone with real diplomatic skills to take care of this."

Gumiela crossed her arms. "This is a mess of your own making, DeRicci. If you had managed to hold on to the woman—"

"I'm not denying that, ma'am," DeRicci said. "I'm just trying to keep this from getting worse."

"Where's your partner? The chief told me that you both were supposed to take care of the Rev until the fugitive was found."

"He handled them earlier while I finished up one of our other cases. Now he has some business on yet another case, and I'm supposed to watch them. Only he knows some Rev and I don't, and frankly that interpreter the chief brought in is next to worthless. He's cowering down there right now. He practically gibbered at me while I was trying to talk with the Rev the last time."

"The chief already made up her mind," Gumiela said. "This is up to the two of you."

DeRicci shook her head. "The Rev aren't cooperating. Their emotion collars were turning colors before I even came to see them."

"I can't override the chief," Gumiela said.

"Look," DeRicci said. "I already know that I'm persona non grata around here. I screwed up with this Maakestad woman and that's just one screw-up in a series of them. But I'm telling you that handling the Rev is beyond me. There are a bunch of Rev in that interrogation room, and they seem to be goading each other on. I can continue trying to handle them, but I don't know what the hell I'm doing. You need a diplomat."

"DeRicci, I've told you—"

"Demote me, fine me, fire me, I don't care. But *do* something. These Rev aren't going to listen to me or Miles anymore, and so far as I know, no one has found Maakestad. That creates a problem that could become some kind of weird interstellar incident. You can blame me for anything that goes wrong, but please, please stop this from getting worse."

Gumiela tilted her head slightly, as if she were surprised by DeRicci's outburst. Didn't she realize that sometimes DeRicci actually cared about her job? Of course not. They all thought DeRicci screwed up because she didn't care.

Maybe if she didn't care, she would do a lot better.

"All right," Gumiela said after a moment. "I'll see who we can get, and I'll send them down. Are you going back to talk to them?"

"I promised them I'd be back in an hour with news. We have"— DeRicci checked her link—"about forty-five minutes now. I don't think they'll be real happy to see me again, but if I don't show up, they'll be even angrier. So if you can get your diplomat here before then, we might all be better off."

"I'll do my best," Gumiela said, getting down off her desk. "In the meantime, find that woman. If we have her in custody, all of our problems are solved."

It took three different messages and some actual discussion across links for Flint to find City Attorney Reese. He was at the Port, finishing negotiations with the Wygnin on the Wilder case.

Flint stopped there first. He didn't want to see the

Wygnin, but he needed to speak to Reese before he put everything in motion.

Flint arrived at the meeting room just outside customs. This area was the nicest part of the Port. The walls were a shiny black material that could change color and texture at a whim. The carpeted floor could also change, according to the preferences of the groups holding the meeting.

Only the conference table remained the same. It had been made on Earth several hundred years ago and had been used in a famous library. It was a rich wood, with clawed feet and brass buttons as trim.

The matching chairs were pushed out in haphazard positions, as if people had just left them and forgotten to slide them back into place.

Another door, at the opposite end of the room, still stood open. It led to the restricted areas of the Port.

Flint peered through the door. Reese was in there, and so was Carryth, the attorney Reese had gotten for the Wilders. Jonathon Wilder, his arm around his son, stood close to Reese and they appeared to be talking.

The boy had his face buried in his father's shirt. His entire body was shaking, and after a moment, Flint realized that Jasper was crying.

It wasn't hard to figure out what had just happened. The Wygnin had agreed to Justine Wilder's terms. She had gone with them, leaving her family behind.

Flint entered the smaller room and cleared his throat. "Excuse me," he said, "but I'm here to see Reese."

Jonathon Wilder looked over at Flint. Wilder's face was ravaged. He had aged decades in the last day. His eyes were filled with a devastation that Flint recognized, the kind that came with an unimaginable loss.

"It'll only take a moment," Flint said.

Reese nodded, then spoke softly and touched Wilder's arm. Wilder pulled his boy closer and looked at the door leading to the terminals. His wife must have just gone through there to a place that Flint wasn't sure he could imagine.

How awful it must have been to let her go, not realizing what she had done until just a few hours ago, and then knowing that even if she did come back— even if the Wygnin let her go or Wilder finally won some kind of court case—her personality would be destroyed forever.

Reese came over, Carryth at his side. They left Wilder staring at the terminal doors, his hand moving soothingly across Jasper's shoulders.

Flint couldn't even look at the boy. He'd tried to reassure him that everything would be all right, that his sisters and, by implication, his family would be fine.

But for all his good intentions, Flint had lied. Maybe the Rev were right. Maybe, in some circumstances, deception was criminal.

"Be succinct," Reese said as he approached. "This hasn't been the best day of my life."

Carryth shot him an annoyed glance, one that he couldn't see. Carryth understood that the hurt party here wasn't Reese. It was the Wilder family. They would never be the same.

"Did all of the Wygnin go with Mrs. Wilder?" Flint asked, hoping that he'd gain even more time.

"If only it were that easy," Reese said.

"Of course not," Carryth said. "Three Wygnin left with Mrs. Wilder. The other two remain, waiting for young Ennis."

"Well," Flint said, sounding businesslike, as if he were concerned rather than trying to manipulate the system. "I'm afraid we have a problem there."

"Don't tell me they've taken the baby," Reese said. "We haven't finished the negotiations. Did they just go to that hotel and take the kid?"

"No," Flint said, wishing he were dealing with Carryth. Carryth, at least, seemed reasonable. "I just wanted to remind you that we have no legal right to hold on to Ennis."

"What?" Reese said so loudly that Wilder flinched. He looked over his shoulder, then seemed to realize that the discussion didn't concern him. His shoulders rode up and down in an obvious sigh, and he turned back toward the door where he had last seen his wife.

"We can only keep people for twenty-four hours without cause," Flint said.

Carryth stroked his jaw as if Flint had made him think.

"What about the Wygnin warrant?" Reese said.

"So far, they haven't proven that the child they want is the one they had." Flint made sure he sounded confident about this. He was buying time again, but didn't want to be too obvious about it.

"Much as I don't want to admit it," Reese said, "if the Wygnin were right about Mrs. Wilder, then they're right about Ennis."

"But they can't prove they're right," Flint said, "and that's all that matters to us."

"Plus there's no guarantee that they are," Carryth said softly. "They may have jiggled the warrant with Jasper Wilder just so that we would make this assumption about Ennis Kanawa."

Reese shot him a panicked look. "They're not that cunning."

"We don't know," Carryth said. "We try not to deal with them anymore because we don't always understand what they're thinking."

Reese swore. "If we let that kid go, and then they prove that he's theirs, we could be in a lot of trouble."

"We're supposed to respect the Wygnin's laws on their soil," Flint said, making his voice stay calm. His heart was beating wildly. "They can respect ours here. We can't hold this family any longer than we already have. In fact, we've had that boy longer than we should have."

"He's right," Carryth said. "You have to let them go."

Reese's panic seemed to grow. He glanced at the door that held Wilder's attention, probably still seeing Wygnin in front of it. "So if the Wygnin bring the right warrant, who is going to deal with them?"

"You are," Flint said.

"Probably in court," Carryth added.

"Why did this land on us?" Reese asked. "Why couldn't Earth have picked them up or Mars? How come we got this case?"

Carryth met Flint's gaze, but neither man spoke. Flint wondered how Reese would react if he knew that a lot more cases would be coming their way unless someone stopped Disappearance Inc.

Reese ran a hand through his hair. "Am I supposed to notify the Wygnin of this?"

"No," Flint said. "When they bring the proper documentation, you let them know we followed our laws."

"What if I notify them anyway?" Reese asked Carryth, deliberately turning away from Flint.

"Then you wouldn't be acting in the best interests of the city." Carryth gave Flint a sideways glance. Carryth obviously knew Flint was playing at something, and was going to help. "If someone could prove you failed to follow our laws strictly out of self-interest, it could be enough to get you fired, maybe even disbarred."

Reese swore. He glared at Flint. "Let them go. But make sure they know they have to come back here the minute we summon them."

"I will," Flint said.

"You'd better." Reese pushed past him and headed into the conference room.

Carryth started to follow, but stopped just before he got to the door. "I hope you know what you're doing."

"I do," Flint said, and hoped he wasn't deceiving anyone—especially himself.

<u>28</u>

A knock on the door made Jamal start. His gaze met Dylani's. She looked terrified. Ennis burst into tears.

He was cuddled against Dylani's shoulder. She had been walking him around the room, trying to soothe him. He'd been fussy all morning, but this was the first time he'd broken into complete sobs.

The knock sounded again. Jamal was shaking. They were finally coming to take Ennis from him. He knew it. These last few hours, while precious, had just been the beginning of his personal hell. He would remember them always as the last time he'd failed his child.

"They know we're here," Dylani said as she patted Ennis on the back. Her head tilted toward Ennis, whose cries could probably be heard in the street.

Jamal knew she was right. There was nothing more he could do. Somehow he had thought they would give him more time. He would be able to find a solution and feel that he'd done more than beg.

But he was out of time.

Ennis was out of time.

Jamal pulled the door open. Flint, the detective who had taken them to Ennis in the first place, stood outside.

"So soon?" Jamal asked.

Flint didn't answer that. Instead, he said, "May I come in?"

Jamal wanted to say no. He wanted to close the door and hide his child, but he did neither. He stepped aside, and let the man who was going to take his baby into his hotel room.

"I have to record this conversation," Flint said. "I hope you don't mind."

Jamal shrugged. Ennis was still crying. His wails would be the dominant sound on any playback, not that it mattered. The officials probably just wanted this recorded in case anything went wrong.

"Go ahead." Dylani sounded resigned. But she gripped Ennis so tightly that the boy was beginning to squirm.

"I have a few questions to ask you about another investigation that I'm doing," Flint said.

Jamal shook his head slightly. For a moment, he wasn't sure he had heard correctly. "What?"

"I'm doing some related work on another investigation. I'd like to ask you some questions."

"What's going on?" Dylani asked. "How come you people think we're involved in crimes that have nothing to do with us?"

"It's just information that I'm after, ma'am." Flint sounded calm, unlike the man who had warned them that seeing their child again might not be a good idea.

Jamal had an odd sense that something wasn't right here. He slowly backed toward the window. He wanted to look out to see if Wygnin were below.

"The case I'm working on," Flint said, "involves Disappearance Inc. It seems they were sold a few months back, and the new owners have decided to reveal Disappeareds' whereabouts, for a price. We've had a lot of trouble because of it in just the last few days."

Jamal froze. So that was what happened. His gaze met Flint's, and Flint quickly looked away. In fact, Flint moved so that Dylani couldn't see Jamal's face.

"So?" Dylani asked, oblivious to her husband's reaction.

"There are a lot of untrustworthy companies out there," Flint said. "It makes my job both easier and harder. I'm worried that this could happen again. You don't understand the difficulties we've been through these last few days, and if there are other unethical Disappearance services, well, then we're in for a long year."

Jamal was holding his breath.

"What are you trying to ask us?" Dylani's voice had an edge to it that Jamal had never heard before. The harshness made Ennis stop crying and look at her as if her words were directed at him.

"Have you heard of Data Services? They're a Disappearance service, and so far as I can tell, they're the only ethical one left. Some of the other services have been contacting people in trouble with various alien groups, but Data Services waits for people to come to them. They seem to be the only one these days."

Flint was telling them where to go to get help. Or was he? Jamal felt very confused.

"I haven't heard of any Disappearance service," Dylani said. "Have you, Jamal?"

She finally turned to him, and something in his face made her pause. She looked from him to Flint, and then back again.

"What in the—?" She started, but Jamal stepped

toward her and put a finger over her mouth, effectively stopping her.

"I haven't heard of any service either," he said. "I'm surprised that there are any ethical ones left."

"Just Data Services, from all I can tell," Flint said. "You sure you haven't heard from them?"

"No, we haven't," Jamal said.

Flint nodded. "Well then, if that's all you know, that's all you know. Thanks for your time."

"You're welcome," Jamal said, keeping his hand over Dylani's mouth. Ennis played with his fingers, the tears forgotten.

Flint grabbed the doorknob as if he were about to turn it, and then he stopped. "One more thing. I'm not sure if you're aware that under Armstrong law, we can only hold Ennis for twenty-four hours. Since the Wygnin haven't yet provided us with a proper warrant, you people are free to go."

Dylani dipped her head away from Jamal's finger. "We're done then? They can't come after us anymore?"

"They can come after you anytime they want," Flint said. "But they can't take Ennis again until they have a proper warrant. Knowing the Wygnin, they're trying to get one."

"This isn't done?" Dylani asked. "Is that what you're telling us? We can leave but we'll never be free?"

"That's what happens in cases like this. As long as they can find you, they will." Flint said that last directly to Jamal.

The message seemed clear. Jamal went over each piece in his mind. The conversation had to be recorded by law, so Flint was not able to talk freely. He made up some story about a case involving Disappearance services so that he could tell them about a reputable one. And now he was giving them a chance to escape.

Somehow Jamal would find a way to afford it. Even if he could only pay for Ennis's escape, he would. He would do whatever he could to keep his son away from the Wygnin.

"Good luck," Flint said.

"Thank you," Jamal said.

Flint smiled at him. It was a real smile, warm and sincere. He reached out, put his hand on Ennis's head, and closed his eyes for a moment, almost as if Ennis were a child he loved.

Then he opened his eyes, nodded, and slid his hand down Ennis's neck to his back, patting it before letting go.

Ennis gave him a bewildered stare. It made Flint's smile grow even wider. He nodded at all three of them, and left.

Jamal leaned against the door.

"Did I hear—?" Dylani started, but Jamal put a finger to his lips.

He said, "Why do you think he had to record that conversation? So they know he did his job?"

Dylani mouthed a small "oh" and cradled her son. "Well, if his job is letting us know we can get out of this horrible hotel room, he did just fine. I don't understand the rest of it, though."

"Neither do I," Jamal lied. "It doesn't concern us."

But it did. It gave him hope. And, it seemed, Flint had bought them time.

DeRicci had nearly reached the interrogation room when something crashed. She knew where the sound had to be coming from. The Rev.

She wasn't late. She knew that. She'd been very careful to watch the time.

But apparently their patience was at an end.

She ran the last few yards and found the door to the interrogation room open, the window smashed, and the chair the interpreter had been sitting on sticking out of the wall.

The Rev were in the hallway, smashing holes in the permaplastic with their lower limbs, their emotion collars flared and deep maroon.

DeRicci screamed down her public link for backup. She needed some kind of help here before this spilled into other areas of the Division.

The interpreter was huddled inside the room, his hands over his head. He didn't appear to be hurt, but she couldn't tell from this distance. He wasn't alone. One Rev remained in there, pounding a spot in the wall between interrogation chambers.

DeRicci had read about things like this. When negotiations broke down, the Rev resorted to violence. Most cultures were afraid of them because they were so big and they could destroy so much so quickly.

The hallway smelled of ginger and rotting melons. DeRicci resisted the urge to put her hand over her face. She tried to flag down a Rev, but they didn't seem to see her. Instead they continued slamming their lower limbs against the walls.

At first, she thought the reaction was random, and then she realized they were following a prescribed plan, destroying one area before moving on to the next.

She had no idea what to do. In all her years in Armstrong, she had never encountered anything like this before.

She couldn't even tell which of the Rev had spoken

to her before. God help her, her eyes were not trained enough to tell the differences between them, even though she knew there had to be some.

One of the Rev swiveled its head, and its eyes, bulging all the way out of its tiny face, seemed to focus on her.

Then the entire group surged forward, trapping her against a wall.

29

On his way back to the Port, Flint sent a message requesting an interpreter and a room where he could meet with the Wygnin. DeRicci should have been the one to meet with them—she, at least, had studied their culture as her alien-training at the Academy—but he didn't dare involve her with this.

If it failed, he wanted it to be on him, and him only.

The Port had given him a small conference room not far from interstellar holding. The Wygnin and the interpreter were already inside. Two space cops stood outside, just to make certain everything remained in order.

They nodded at him as he passed them. He didn't recognize either of them, but he nodded in return. They knew who he was, just as he had always known who the success stories were. Most space cops dreamed of moving up to detective, and few ever got the chance.

Flint had thought it would be such a relief holding this job. He had been so wrong.

He opened the door to the conference room and immediately felt a wave of emotion. Fury, mostly, mixed with confusion and anger.

DeRicci had warned him that Wygnin emotions

could be overwhelming, that an unprepared detective could mistake what the Wygnin were feeling for his own emotions. She had been trained to deal with this, to block those emotions. He had not.

He resisted the urge to close the door and try again. Instead, he tried to gather himself as he went inside.

Only two Wygnin remained. They were not sitting. They stood side by side at the head of the table, staring at the door. Flint got the sense that they had planned that emotional assault to throw whoever came to visit them off balance. Anger rippled through him and he struggled to set it aside, reminding himself that it wasn't his anger. It was theirs.

An interpreter sat at the table. She was human, but just barely. Her expensive enhancements had left her looking like a Wygnin wannabe. Her hair, skin, and eyes were a matching gold. She was whip-thin, and she held her long fingers against her stomach, the way the Wygnin were doing.

After nodding to her, Flint looked away. She was clearly not an ally of his.

Fortunately, the room was big. If it were small, the emotions would have overwhelmed him. As it was, he was going to have to fight to get through this.

He kept his eyes downcast as DeRicci had instructed. "Thank you for coming."

The interpreter began speaking, and he felt oddly disoriented. It took her longer to translate his words than it took him to speak them.

Then one of the Wygnin spoke, its voice melodious. "We thought you were going to bring the child."

"You still don't have a valid warrant," Flint said. "We couldn't confirm the boy's identity."

"But you confirmed the identity of the other child."

"Yes," Flint said. The fury was growing. He wanted

to clench his fists, shout, do anything he could to get rid of the feeling building inside him. "But the cases are not related, at least so far as we can see. So it doesn't matter if one warrant was right. The other isn't."

"We already know about the problem with the warrant. We are resolving it," the Wygnin said. "Do we need our attorney again?"

Flint had forgotten that they met with DeRicci and a battery of attorneys. Of course, she hadn't told him much about that meeting. She never told him much. That was what made their partnership so awful—

This time, he did clench a fist so that he could stop his errant thoughts. They had nothing to do with this. It was just his mind casting about for a reason for the chaotic emotions he felt.

"No," Flint said. "I've just come to inform you that we had to follow our laws."

He sounded calm, at least to his own ears. He hoped he seemed calm to theirs.

It felt odd to speak with his head down so that he wouldn't make eye contact. That was contrary to his way of doing things.

"What do you mean?"

He thought he heard menace in the Wygnin's voice, but he couldn't be certain. He couldn't trust his reactions to these creatures.

"Under our laws," Flint said, "we can only hold someone without cause for twenty-four hours."

"You had cause," the Wygnin said.

"No," Flint said. "We couldn't prove that Ennis Kanawa was the child you wanted. I set him free just an hour ago. I suspect the family is on their way home to Gagarin Dome right now."

The fury became so overwhelming that Flint felt dizzy.

"You should have notified us of this," one Wygnin said. As the interpreter spoke, the other Wygnin did too.

It said, "This is a trick."

"No trick," Flint lied and hoped that the Wygnin couldn't detect lies as easily as the Rev sometimes could. "I made a recording of the conversation I had with the Kanawa family. You may listen to it if you like."

"We would like to," said one Wygnin.

"And we would like the original to make certain you have not tampered with this," said the second.

"You'll have to check on getting the original with the city attorney," Flint said. "But I have a hunch the hotel where the Kanawa family was staying also keeps records. It's not the most upscale place, so it probably monitors its guests."

In fact, he knew it did. That was why the police often recommended that place to people who stayed there. It was a calculated risk telling the Wygnin about that; he had no idea whether Jamal and Dylani Kanawa had discussed the reasons for Ennis's kidnapping.

But even if they had, it would take a lot of time before the hotel turned over the records to the Wygnin. The family would be among the ranks of the Disappeared by then.

Flint leaned against the table. He could no longer sort out his emotions. They churned inside of him. The dizziness had grown worse, and he was having trouble concentrating on his own thoughts.

"While the recording plays," he said, "I'm going to

step outside the room for some air. I've been up all night, and it's beginning to catch up with me."

He plucked the chip off his sleeve. The chip was so small, he was afraid he would lose it between his fingers. He squeezed it and set it down as his own voice filled the room.

May I come in?

He stepped into the hallway and closed the door, leaning on it. The emotions vanished as if they had never been, leaving his heart racing and his breathing erratic.

No wonder it took so much training to deal with the Wygnin. He hadn't been in there more than ten minutes, and he could barely separate himself from them.

He wondered how much training people who were sent to Korsve had. If they had no preparation in dealing with the Wygnin, how could they even know that their actions had been their own? Had anyone studied Wygnin manipulation, done over time? And what about the confessions humans made in Wygnin courts to things the Wygnin believed were crimes? Why did the multicultural tribunals accept such confessions? Wouldn't they have been given under duress, something humans stopped accepting centuries ago?

Flint shuddered. These last few days had destroyed any belief he may have had in the rightness of his job. He couldn't continue forward, enforcing laws that he didn't like and solving crimes that he didn't believe were wrong.

Disappearance Inc had been wrong in selling out its customers, but the law said such a thing was fine. The company was destroying hundreds, maybe thousands, of lives, lives that were already in tatters because of a justice system that seemed to accept all cultural standards as normal except the one Flint thought best.

Was it the best? He didn't know. But he knew that giving up an infant to pay for his father's crimes, no matter how heinous, was wrong. He knew that forcing an eight-year-old to lose his mother because she hadn't realized she built a house in a forbidden place was also wrong, and he knew that demanding that a woman spend the rest of her life doing backbreaking work because she successfully defended a criminal was wrong too.

Someone pulled the odor open. Flint turned. The interpreter stood there. She seemed to sway, just like the Wygnin. Flint wondered if she knew that of all the beings in that conference room, she was the most alien to him.

"We've finished listening," she said.

He felt a momentary flash of worry that was all his own, not sure how the Wygnin would react to the words he had spoken in that hotel room. He had tried to be circumspect, but anyone familiar with human discourse might understand the message he had given to Jamal Kanawa.

Then again, maybe not. He had asked the questions first and told them they were free to go second. The two things did not seem to be related.

He nodded to the interpreter and stood up straight, no longer leaning against the wall. Already he could feel the threads of emotion, but they seemed weaker. Or perhaps he had learned how to manage them.

He stepped inside. He hadn't realized that this room was done in light browns or that the air smelled faintly of the interpreter's lilac perfume. All of those details had gotten lost in the stress the Wygnin emotions had put him under.

The interpreter sat down. Flint went to his place at the opposite end of the table. The Wygnin hadn't moved, and the chip lay where he had put it.

"Your mention of Disappearance services is intriguing," one of the Wygnin said. "You realize such things are illegal."

Flint's mouth went dry. "Of course I do, which is why we've been so busy this week. In addition to your two cases, we've had a Disty vengeance killing and some problems with the Rev. It was while I was dealing with the Rev that I realized Disappearance Inc had been selling out its clients. I needed to know if anyone else was, so that our department can plan for more weeks like this, and I wouldn't be able to find out that information on my own. People like the Kanawas attract the worst elements. It didn't hurt to ask."

He looked up and met the Wygnin's golden gaze, feeling the brush of emotions more complicated than he could express. He forced his gaze away and wondered if he had said too much. Sometimes no explanation was better than too much explanation.

The interpreter was watching Flint. Had she understood and said something to them? Or was she so lost in Wygnin fantasy that she had forgotten her own humanity?

"It seems," the Wygnin said, "that you are being honest with us and you have done what you can. Next time, we will know about this arbitrary twenty-four-hour law and plan for it. In the meantime, we shall document the trail we have taken to find the Kanawa family and we shall take it to the authorities in their home city of Gagarin Dome."

Both Wygnin bowed slightly. "We appreciate the time you have taken to inform us of the changes."

"You're welcome," Flint said, feeling awkward. He looked at the interpreter, silently asking if he should do anything else.

"I think that's all, detective," she said to him. "The Wygnin now have other things that they'll have to attend to because of the inadequacies of Armstrong law."

So she had missed it. He tried to contain his feeling of relief. He didn't know if the emotional bleed-through went both ways.

"Thanks," he said, and left the room.

Outside, he took a deep breath, as if clearing his lungs of the emotions he'd been feeling. He'd done all he could. Now it was up to Jamal Kanawa to protect his son.

And Flint had to focus on his own future. He hadn't been lying to the Wygnin. With Disappearance Inc selling out its files, the job of detective had just become hideous. Rather than facing these dilemmas every once in while, he would face them daily.

And he wasn't willing to.

Before he went back to the detective unit, he needed to see the chief—and resign.

30

The Rev seemed huge as they came toward DeRicci. The nearest took his upper arm and slammed it into the wall beside her. She could feel the vibration in her back, and plastic shattered around her, slicing her skin.

They were making a weird keening noise, and the maroon of their emotion collars was working its way throughout their pale skin.

Officer in trouble, she sent through her personal link, using the nonverbal section she usually kept shut off. *Hurry.*

Another arm went through the wall above her, but she didn't cringe. She wasn't sure how to react to a Rev attack, but cringing hadn't done the interpreter any good.

"Hey!" she shouted. "Hey! I'm early, here. There's no reason for this."

The Rev had crowded so close to her that she was choking on their rotted-melon stench. One of their arms brushed against her, and she gagged at the cold, clammy feel of their skin.

"Back off!" she shouted again. "You're in my Division, on my soil, and subject to my rules. This is a riot, and we will punish to the fullest extent of the law!"

She had no clue if they would do that or not. She

knew nothing about the agreements Armstrong had with the Rev, but she was willing to bluff.

The Rev did not move. They had stopped punching the walls and they had stopped advancing on her, but they hadn't backed away either.

"Can you understand me?" she said, able to lower her voice now. "Because if you can't, we need to get that interpreter guy out here."

And that was probably the stupidest sentence she'd ever uttered. Because how could she direct the Rev to move so that she could fetch the interpreter when they didn't understand her?

One of the Rev peeled away from the back of the group and vanished from her sight. A moment later, it reappeared, carrying the interpreter. The Rev's hand was clamped to the back of the interpreter's neck and the poor man was swinging, his feet off the ground and his face so pale that he as though like he was about to be sick.

Apparently they had understood her well enough to get the interpreter, but not well enough to do without him. And she was on her own. No one had come down the hallway, no one had even tried to save her, not yet.

She wanted the damn diplomat, but she doubted he would get here on time.

"All right," she said to the Rev. "I'm going to tell you what's going on."

She might as well. It was her mistake, and they were already tearing up the station. The situation couldn't get worse—she hoped.

"We have the entire police force combing the streets of Armstrong, looking for the woman you want," she said.

The Rev emotion collars vibrated as if they were

making a sound that she couldn't hear. The interpreter, still being held up by his neck, moaned.

"Translate it," DeRicci said to him, even though she knew at least some of the Rev had understood her.

He did, which was pretty amazing since he barely seemed able to draw a breath.

"You did not keep her in custody?" the Rev closest to DeRicci asked. She wondered if that was the same one who'd spoken for them all before.

"We tried," DeRicci said, deciding not to lie at all. "She escaped."

A high-pitched whistle went through the group. They shuffled slightly, and DeRicci had to fight to keep herself from cringing. She couldn't see through the doughy Rev bodies to know if help had arrived.

"Your partner, this Flint," the Rev said. "Did he know this when he spoke to us?"

As the interpreter put that sentence into English, his face got red and sweat dripped off his chin. He thought Flint had lied to the Rev and that terrified him.

That was all the warning DeRicci needed.

"I don't know," she said, figuring her statement was somewhat true, since she didn't know when Flint had first spoken to the Rev. "I haven't been able to talk with him much the last day or two."

Again, truth, but probably not the kind the Rev appreciated.

"If he lied to us," the Rev said, "you will all pay."

"I don't think that's the issue here," DeRicci said.

"I will not translate that," the interpreter said, wheezing slightly. "Truth is always the issue with them."

"Translate it," DeRicci said. "I said it, not you, and besides, half of them understand anyway."

His red face got even darker, but he translated for her. The Rev did not seem to react to her statement. They all stared at her in silence.

"The issue," DeRicci said into that silence, "is that we can't find this woman. Maybe you should help."

"You're going to send angry Rev onto the streets of Armstrong?" the interpreter's voice squeaked.

The Rev holding him shook him and then dropped him. He landed with a thud, crying out in pain.

"What are you doing?" a human voice cried out from behind the Rev. DeRicci couldn't tell if the voice was directed at her or at the Rev.

The Rev scuttled backwards, opening a path between DeRicci and an unenhanced man with long gray hair and a pot belly.

"What are you doing?" he said again, and apparently he was speaking to her. "There was a request for a diplomat. And I just got here. You're not licensed to negotiate with the Rev."

"I requested you," DeRicci snapped, "and you're late. The problems I anticipated have already started. The chief wanted me to handle this, and I am, so butt out."

"She just told them truth doesn't matter," the interpreter said from the floor. He had a hand on the side of his leg. His knee was twisted at an odd angle.

"Did you?"

"I said it wasn't the issue," DeRicci said.

One of the Rev spoke. Its high-pitched growl went on for several minutes, during which the diplomat kept glancing at DeRicci. Then he answered in Rev, his hands clamped at his side.

When the interchange was done, he said, "Apparently they think this matter is already resolved. You have told them the truth. They say they can tell. They believe you're the only one who has understood them here, and they're grateful for all you've done."

He sounded as if he disapproved of all that he was telling her.

DeRicci let out a breath she hadn't even known she was holding. She had stopped them. She couldn't believe it.

The diplomat said, "In deference to your wishes, they'll return to their ship and await word of the fugitive. And if we need their help searching for her, they will assist in any way they can. They learned when she commandeered the yacht that she was a treacherous person, and they believe it might take some time to capture her."

DeRicci leaned her head against the wall. Some of the plastic crumbled, and she stood up suddenly.

"They want to thank you again for all you've done, and for being the only human in this Division to take their desire for honesty seriously."

DeRicci felt as if she had walked into someone else's life. "Thank them for me."

He spoke Rev for a moment. The Rev all looked at her and, in unison, their emotion collars faded. One by one, the collars absorbed back into the skin. They waddled their way down the hall, apparently going back the way they had come.

DeRicci called down her link for a medic. The interpreter moaned and lay back on the floor.

The diplomat glared at her. "So you've learned something about the Rev, have you?" he said when the Rev were out of sight.

She shook her head. "I thought they were going to kill me."

"They might have. Someone should have told them about the missing girl earlier."

"I wasn't here earlier."

"Well, you lucked into the only way of appeasing them. I'd say good job, but I see you neglected to tell them who lost the girl in the first place."

He glared at her one final time, apparently for emphasis, and then he walked away. DeRicci let out another long breath. What an awful hour. It was amazing. When she did the right thing, she got a reprimand and when she did the wrong thing, she saved the day—and got a reprimand.

She wondered if she would ever be in anyone's good graces again.

"Don't worry about him," the interpreter said, surprising her. She had thought he disliked her, and now he was comforting her. Maybe he was relieved the Rev were gone. "He's just mad that you did something he wouldn't have even considered."

DeRicci went over to him. "I sent for medics."

"So did I," the interpreter said. "They'll wait until the Rev are back in the Port before they come. I'm sure word of angry Rev has been all over Armstrong by now."

"You're sure he wouldn't have told the Rev the truth?" She couldn't believe it, not if the truth was the best way of dealing with the Rev.

The interpreter nodded. "He's a politician. A human politician. We're not the most honest species anyway, and diplomats have secrets to protect. Most of the ones assigned to the Rev know that the job could be their death warrant. That's probably why he was late."

"Why do you translate, then?" DeRicci asked.

The interpreter grimaced and shifted, obviously in pain. "Usually I deal with written Rev and tapes of meetings conducted in Rev. I don't remember the last time I did a real-time translation."

That explained a lot, DeRicci thought, but said nothing. "Will they get angry like that again?"

"No," the interpreter said. "Not unless they believe they're being lied to again. They can sense it, and it makes them crazy. You did a courageous thing back there."

DeRicci studied him for a moment. He'd been a loyal translator even though he had thought the situation was mishandled. She could respect that.

"You did a courageous thing too," she said, and then she sat down beside him, so that he wouldn't have to wait for the medics alone.

31

Flint was no longer a detective.

The chief hadn't been in, so he tendered his verbal resignation to one of her assistants, who really didn't seem to care. She had handed him a special hand-held with a standard resignation form on it. He had filled out the proper dates and times and then signed it. A note on the top of the form said that it would be sent to everyone who needed the file.

In other words, it would go everywhere within the city—and maybe beyond. Since he had asked to be terminated immediately, he needed a special pass to get into the detective unit so that he could clean out his desk and take his personal files off his computer.

He sat in his office now, his hands shaking slightly. This was his last chance to get information from the department's system and he planned to use it.

Disappearance Inc's new file system was as easy to hack as he had thought it would be. It was clear the files had been transferred from a more complicated system. There were thousands of names, dating back decades.

All of that would have overwhelmed him if he had remained a detective. But he wasn't one anymore.

He was downloading to his personal hand-held. It

was going to take some time to complete the transfer because the department's system was old, and because there was a lot of information. He left the hand-held on the desk and kept the desk screen dark so no one passing by could see what he was doing.

Then he picked up a box he had been given downstairs and started placing his personal items in it. He stared at his crystal graduation certificate from the academy. It had meant so much to him once. He was amazed that it didn't any longer.

The assistant chief had asked, as a matter of form, what he planned to do next, and he had told her he didn't know. But he had a hunch. He toyed with working for a Disappearance service, but what if the company was sold and they did the same thing Disapparance Inc did? He would never be able to live with that.

So he had to figure out how to take care of himself and stop Disappearance Inc. He'd gotten an idea as he left the chief's office. Now all he had to do was see if he could make it work.

The rumor reached DeRicci as the medics carted off the interpreter. Flint had quit. The reasons varied according to which rumor she heard: He'd been fired for letting the Rev tear up the station; he'd fallen in love with the fugitive; he'd run away himself.

DeRicci didn't believe that last, and the middle reason seemed preposterous. But she wouldn't put it past the powers that be to fire him for doing the job they had wanted him to do.

She hurried to his office and found him behind the desk, a box beside his chair and a ratty stuffed dog on his lap.

"What's that?" she asked.

"It belonged to my daughter," he said.

She stepped inside the office and closed the door. She had forgotten about his daughter. He'd had a family once, but he never spoke of them. She thought of him as a single man who lived alone, whose driving ambition had been to be a detective. Nothing more.

And there seemed to be a lot more.

"They're saying downstairs that you're leaving."

He nodded.

"Why?" she asked.

"This is not for me, Noelle."

"Yes, it is. I haven't seen any one more suited to the job." She wasn't sure why she pushed so hard. She knew that she would have to struggle to keep hers, even though she had subdued the Rev uprising that afternoon. But she did love it here, even during weeks like this, even when she said she wanted to quit.

He leaned back in his chair. There was already something different about him, something less restrained. "Have you thought this through, Noelle? Disappearance Inc is selling out its files. We'll have more weeks like this, more cases just as tough coming through the Port. In fact, that'll be the bulk of what we do."

She hadn't wanted to think about that. She leaned against the door. "We can ask for other assignments. After the way I handled Maakestad, they'll probably give them to us."

He shook his head. "I'm not willing to do that. Disappearance Inc should be stopped."

"They're not breaking the law," DeRicci said tiredly.

"I know," he said. "But what they're doing should be against the law."

DeRicci crossed her arms. If she knew one thing

about Flint, it was that he usually figured out what his next action was going to be before he took it. "You have some kind of plan, don't you?"

He didn't meet her gaze.

There were only a few things he could do that would use all of his skills. And it was clear that Disappearance Inc's actions disturbed him.

"You're not going to try to find all those Disappeared, are you?" DeRicci asked. "You're not going to warn them."

He didn't move.

"Look, Miles, it would take you years to find all the Disappeared in Disappearance Inc's files. By then, they'd probably be dead or in an alien prison."

"I know." His hand-held beeped. He picked it up and slipped it into his pocket.

From his tone, she could tell that he didn't care how difficult it would be. He was probably still idealistic enough to believe that saving one person from their past would be enough.

But it wasn't.

"You can't do anything about this," DeRicci said. "You just have to accept it."

Flint stood, shut down the screen on his desk, and double-checked the desk drawers. Then he picked up the box and came to the door.

She blocked his exit.

"You can't change my mind, Noelle."

"Leaving isn't right, Miles. Stay here. We'll figure something out." Her voice rose in frustration. He was the best partner she'd ever had. She didn't want him to go.

He shook his head.

She looked into his blue eyes. They were long-lashed and clear. She had never noticed that before either.

"You'll regret this," she said as she opened the door.

"Somehow, I think you're wrong," he said, and left.

32

Data Systems' offices reminded Flint of Paloma's. They were in the same section of town, and their façade was just as filthy and tumbledown. Their security wasn't as well hidden as Paloma's was, probably because they knew their desperate, panicked clients would look for security first.

It had taken Flint nearly an hour, but he had managed to talk his way past the receptionist and two mid-level managers. He was now deep in the warehouse where Data Systems' staff did most of their work.

He could tell, just from the layout, that their records storage—if they even had any—was off-premises. He suspected that building would be even harder to find than this one.

He sat in a large office with no windows. The walls were decorated with street scenes from various cities, all of them on Earth. He recognized New York and Paris, but some of the other cities, where the land seemed flatter, the sun seemed brighter, and the old buildings looked as if they had been made of mud, were unfamiliar to him.

The scenes made him realize that in all of his years, he had never been off the Moon. A simple commuter trip to Earth for a week, and he might have seen wonders he only read about. He hadn't even tried.

There were domes on the Moon he hadn't been to either. He'd been too consumed with his life—first, raising a family and then, when he lost that, becoming a detective.

How narrow his existence had been.

A woman came into the office and closed the door. She was slender to the point of gauntness, and despite her considerable enhancements, she still had shadows under her eyes.

"My staff tells me you have a proposition for me, Detective," she said as she sat on the rocking chair near the Paris wall. So this was Colette Bannerman, head of Data Systems. Flint wouldn't have expected someone so brittle.

"I'm no longer a detective, Ms. Bannerman." He took the seat across from her, an angular chair that turned out to be more comfortable than it looked.

"I know," she said. "We checked."

Which was probably why they had let him get this far into their building.

"Are you here to apply for a job?" she asked.

"No." He took a deep breath. It was time to see if his idea would work. "Disappearance Inc is selling out its clients. Every file, from the beginning, is available for purchase."

She raised her eyebrows, and her hands gripped the arms of the chair. "Really? How does that concern us?"

He folded his hands across his stomach so that she couldn't see them shake. His future—and thousands of others—depended on her response to his proposal.

"I have their files," he said. "You should know that I did not pay for them."

She frowned.

"And I will turn them over to you if you contact everyone in these files and help them Disappear all over again. Most of them will pay your normal fee."

"Most?" she said. "Disappearance Inc predates Data Systems by decades, and we have nearly a million clients, Mr. Flint."

The "mister" sounded odd to him. No one had called him that in a very long time.

"I hate to sound like a businesswoman, but I am. I can't afford to help clients who can't pay me."

"Really?" He willed himself to sound calm. "I'm going to give you more clients than you've ever had, and most—probably seventy-five percent or more—will pay you. You'll make more money than you know what to do with. You're already a rich woman. Do something for your community. Consider the remaining twenty-five percent charity."

She shook her head slightly. "You don't understand business, Mr. Flint. In order to help that twenty-five percent and to process all these new customers so quickly, I'd have to put out quite a capital outlay."

His fingers tightened, digging into the flesh on the backs of his hands. "I checked your financials, Ms. Bannerman. Data Systems can afford this. And your credit is good. Even if the company can't afford the upfront money, you can."

She smiled slowly. "You're thorough."

"I want to make sure these people are taken care of. All of them." He paused. "Including Jamal Kanawa and his family."

Her gaze flickered just once, and that was enough to confirm that the Kanawas had been there to see her. But of course, she wouldn't verbally confirm or deny whether they had or not.

She was that good.

"What do you get out of all of this, Mr. Flint?"

"A one-time fee of ten million credits, payable up front." He had debated that for a long time, and then decided he needed the money. He needed to choose when he was going to work again.

"That's a lot of money for an ex-cop."

He shrugged. "I'm a young man, and I'd like to retire."

She leaned back in the chair. Its rockers creaked as she went back and forth. The movement didn't suit her, but she didn't seem to care. She was studying him, probably looking for an angle.

After a few minutes, she seemed to have found it. "You could just give me the information. If you want me to do this out of the goodness of my heart, you should do the same."

He had expected this argument sooner. "I need an incentive to give you this information."

"I would think that concern for others would be incentive enough."

"Concern for others made me get the information. Now I want to make sure the information is in hands that will value it."

To his surprise, she smiled. "You're good, detective."

This time he didn't correct her. "I'm also right."

She nodded. "Ten million credits."

He handed her his account numbers on a card, just as Paloma had done for him. Only his had been handwritten because he hadn't had much time. "Up front."

Bannerman didn't hestiate. She set the card down on her nearby desk, scanned the numbers, and then smiled at him. "Done."

He checked through his link. She had done it, just

as she said. He cursed silently. She had played him better than he had played her. She didn't balk at the fee, which meant that he should have asked for more.

He took his account numbers back and slipped them into his pocket. Then he gave her the hand-held. He'd never had anything important on it because he'd always used the station's systems. The only information on it now was Disappearance Inc's files.

"A pleasure doing business with you," he said.

"And you."

They stood; then she extended her hand. He took it. For the first time, she seemed to soften just slightly.

"I promise," she said. "I'll make sure these people are safe."

"That's why I came to you," he said. "Because you're one of the only companies in the business to keep the promises you make."

33

Three days later, after he'd had time to sleep and reflect, Flint went to Paloma's office. He'd actually gone to the trouble of making an appointment with her and, as he approached the door, he found that he was nervous.

Flint thought that odd. He knew he was making the right decision. If he had had any doubts about that, they had faded when Data Systems accepted his proposition.

He had helped more people and changed more lives for the good by not following the law than he had in all the years he worked as a police officer.

He let himself inside the office. Paloma was sitting behind her desk, smiling at him. "So, what's so important that you have to make an appointment like a real client?"

Something in her voice caught him, some concern, some worry. Did she actually think that he would use her to find a Disappeared? He didn't have anyone to search for. He had thought she'd known that.

"I don't suppose you know what I did the other day," he said.

"Besides quit?" she asked.

"Yeah."

"And let a woman Disappear when she should have gone into police custody with you?"

"Yeah."

"No," Paloma siad. "I don't know what you did."

So he told her about Data Systems and the way he'd sold them all of Disappearance Inc's files.

To his surprise, she didn't laugh or compliment him. Instead she looked at him gravely. "How do you know you can trust these people?"

"You told me I could."

"And you trusted me?"

Ah. She was testing him. She had always tested him. So he told her something he had planned to leave out. "I double-checked your information. I did some digging on my own as well."

She threw her head back and laughed. It was a rich, warm sound. "Good boy. You'd make a good Retrieval Artist."

And that was his opening. "I know," he said. "I want to buy your business."

Her smile faded. "There's no business to buy. I haven't had clients for years."

"But you have expertise," he said. "I want you to train me."

She looked more serious than he had ever seen her. "I'm not like those other Retrieval Artists. I have standards."

"I know," he said, sitting on her desk and taking her hand. He was finally stepping into his future, and it pleased him like nothing had in years. "I want to learn from the best."

The Disty had turned a sickly shade of green. Its eyes were lined with blue and its lips were yellow. Its hands shook.

It stood alone on the narrow street, a light rain falling on it, making its skin shiny. Disty looked so tiny when they were standing near human structures. Even the aircar parked across the street looked bigger than the alien standing on the stoop.

Ekaterina Maakestad had to look down to see the Disty. She stood near the door of the Vancouver Addiction Center and smiled.

"Come on in," she said to the Disty. It was shivering. The rain was cool, which wasn't unusual in this part of Canada, and the creature didn't have a coat. "We help everyone here."

The Disty stepped inside, its movements dainty. Ekaterina smiled at it, hoping to put it at ease.

"My name is Emily," she said. "I'm going to do a preliminary interview and get you to a counselor."

As she walked him toward the interview room, where they'd have some privacy, she marveled that she would be working with the Disty after all. Every kind of addict came to this center except Rev. The Rev didn't believe in letting other races see their weaknesses.

The only thing she didn't like about her move to Vancouver was her proximity to San Francisco and Simon. But she had learned in the last month the importance of self-control.

She was lucky to be here. Staying here, as the people at Data Systems told her, was up to her. Most people got discovered because they tried to return to their old lives.

She wouldn't, no matter how much she missed Simon. She valued this new life too much.

The outer-edge colony was new, so new that the buildings were made of modern permaplastic. The dome was half constructed and shook in the planet's bitter winds. This place, which didn't have an English name yet, was inside the Rev's home system. The Rev had given the colonists a small continent toward the Arctic Circle, where it would always be cold and somewhat dark.

But Jamal didn't care. His new house was so small that his old house in Gagarin Dome now seemed like a mansion. There wasn't even a separate bedroom for Ennis—not yet, anyway.

He pulled the blanket up to Ennis's shoulders. Just that morning, his son had informed him in broken English that he was too big to sleep in his baby bed. He wanted a real bed, like Mommy and Daddy's, and he'd get one soon.

Ennis sighed, his eyelashes twitching as he dreamed. Both Jamal and Dylani had agreed that they would stop watching him sleep, but so far they hadn't. By unspoken consent, they took turns staying up all night, making sure that nothing came through a window to steal their son away.

They knew that they would have to stop this over-protection soon. And they would.

But not yet.

Jamal kissed his son on the forehead, then settled into the chair. He loved these long nights, watching Ennis sleep. These moments were precious; he was lucky to have them.

And this time, he knew it.

ABOUT THE AUTHOR

Kristine Kathryn Rusch is an award-winning writer in several genres. Winner of the 2001 Hugo Award for the novelette "Millennium Babies," she has also won the *Ellery Queen* Readers' Choice Award for best mystery short story. She is also a winner of the *Asimov's* Readers Choice Award, the *Lucas* Award, the World Fantasy Award, and the John W. Campbell Award.

She has published more than fifty novels in almost a dozen languages, and she has hit bestseller lists in the *Wall Street Journal, USA Today,* and *Publishers Weekly.* Her science fiction and mystery short stories have been in many year's best collections.

The Retrieval Artist novels are based on the Hugo-nominated novella "The Retrieval Artist," which was first published in *Analog.*